BLACKGAMMON

BLACKGAMMON

HEATHER NEFF

ONE WORLD
BALLANTINE BOOKS · NEW YORK

A One World Book
Published by The Ballantine Publishing Group

www.randomhouse.com/BB/

Library of Congress Catalog Card Number: 00-107069

ISBN: 0-345-43611-3

Text design by Mary A. Wirth

Manufactured in the United States of America

First Edition: October 2000

10 9 8 7 6 5 4 3 2 1

To Tanisha Makeba and Aviva Helena

Sisters, daughters, friends.

Acknowledgments

Many loving and supportive voices have encouraged me in my quest to complete *Blackgammon*. My deepest thanks must go to many people, but especially to my brother Michael Mayson, whose hardworking dedication to his dream has been a model for my own; to my agent James Wolf, who responded calmly and humorously whenever I was close to panic; to my daughter, Aviva, whose patience, faith, and unselfish encouragement allowed me to make this endeavor a joyful part of our family life, and to my husband, Marcel, who always found the floppy, printer driver, or missing cord at the eleventh hour. I also want to thank Eastern Michigan University, which awarded me a sabbatical leave to complete the manuscript, and my many colleagues and students, who showered me with encouragement at every step along the way.

It was Associate Publisher Cheryl Woodruff, my editor at One World, whose cogent vision and fierce perceptiveness were instrumental in the difficult process of molding two separate novels into one book. Cheryl stood by this project during its long evolution and provided me with both ready encouragement and incisive commentary. I thank her deeply for offering me this great opportunity.

Most of all I'd like to thank Tanisha Makeba Bailey, who read it, listened to it, talked with me about it, and always believed in it. And in me.

BLACKGAMMON

FLIGHT

Understand this, Michael: There's no such thing as sanctuary.

When I finally fled, bolting up the house on the dawn of that icy New Year and just hours after you boarded the plane, I wasn't sure where I was going. I took a taxi down from the hills with only one bag of the barest essentials. Stood at the airport counter for what seemed a century, while an attendant studied the lists and finally said, "I'm sorry, Miss Emmanuel. The only available flight leaves for Paris in forty minutes."

Paris, I thought. Well, of course.

I told myself that once I got there I'd go to the next counter and find a flight away from my past. But that wasn't going to happen. We were late leaving Nice. And everything out of the capital was booked. It was the end of the holiday, you see. I'd have only one choice—to go from gate to gate, like a beggar, and take my chances as a standby from despair.

So I gave up. Flew to Paris. Took the *métro* into the city. Emerged at the Gare de l'Est and walked (the direction completely beyond my control) the single block to the Canal Saint-Martin. Across the foot-bridge rose the steel-framed masterpiece of Anya's newly renovated factory. And there, to the north, lay the tomb of my past, waiting to be excavated. Waiting to be revealed.

It took me exactly four hours to find out that the building was still standing, and now belongs to the city. It took me exactly forty-two minutes to walk into a clerk's gray office and sign an open-ended lease. And it took me even less time to bang my one bag of barest essentials up the circular staircase, turn the bony key in the rusting lock, and walk inside.

The name Chloe Emmanuel opens doors, you see.

It was amazingly unchanged after twenty-four years. Still damp and cold and still badly in need of paint. Not that the walls weren't Pollocked with droplets from a thousand vanished masterpieces, the earnest attempts of supplicants to the high altar of Art. Like me, they prayed that they could pierce the chrysalis of their doubt and emerge as artists. *Artist:* as if Art and Exist could become consummate in something as densely inept as a human being!

Behold the shadowy studio lit by a skylight; the small kitchen and black-veined bath. Behold the tight bedroom with its stained mattress. Behold the cracked mirror, broken easel, and the red-brown smear on the wall. I listened for echoes of voices raised in rage. I looked for traces of my tears on the splattered floor. But no, there had been joy in that room as well, even though sometimes the joy was hard to remember.

That's one of the trickier aspects of being Chloe Emmanuel.

Another is living up to my reputation as the "Preeminent Black Artist in Europe." For many years I've woven a cat's cradle through Paris, Berlin, Madrid, Vienna. I've lived in Florence and Belgrade, Stockholm and Amsterdam. I've been critiqued in books; I've taught at academies. I have works in six national museums and countless galleries. Rich girls learn about me when they take Introduction to Art History.

Sometimes it's hard to live up to my public persona. It's become even more difficult now that I can't paint anymore.

Oh, it began quietly. First, a gnawing sense of dissatisfaction that made me work for months on a single portrait. Then, a complete inability to discern subtle differences in shading. Finally, I felt a smothering certainty that all the work I'd ever done amounted to little more than painful scratchings. The grace that infused my brushes for so many years left them barren. My house grew silent with the solitude of untouched canvases.

And although the evidence was there for everyone to see, no one—not even you, Michael—realized that Chloe Emmanuel was finished.

So it was somehow fitting that twenty-five years after I abandoned the States, New York came calling. The prestigious Humes Gallery would virtually be mine, with an apartment, interviews, even a post at my old alma mater. The prodigal daughter of African descent would return from a quarter century of European exile to be welcomed by her great, loving motherland. I could imagine the hype: Black Artist Conquers the Old World, Then Returns to Master the New! I could even see Malik showing up at the airport with a dozen long-stemmed roses, hoping to get some positive spin out of our doomed marriage.

How could I tell them that I was no longer a child of those dizzying urban streets? No longer molded from the pop rhythms and political slogans and social movements of their culture. Long ago I had climbed off that train, smashing myself through the sieve of Paris, then vanishing into the strange incubation of a house in the hills of Nice with a view of the sea.

I couldn't tell them that after so much success, the scaffolds on which I constructed my art had collapsed. I could no longer sculpt. I could no longer paint. The artist they were ready to honor no longer existed!

So despair brought me back to Paris. Back to the very room where my artist's life began. For weeks I rarely left my empty cell. I crouched beneath the skylight watching winter flay the world. Food meant nothing; drink even less. I cut off my hair so I wouldn't have to comb it. My clothes grew bitter and stiff with my silent tears.

It took me many weeks to find the courage to try again. Furtively, I brought a handful of tubes into the chamber. Days later I managed a few brushes. Then came the frames. And at last, the canvas.

Finally I stood naked beneath the skylight. I studied my scarecrow body in the dull, blackened mirror. With gently trembling hands I placed a canvas on the easel, and, ignoring the mocking laughter that raced through my head, I lifted a brush to the taut, young fabric. Maybe, I prayed, it hasn't left. If I can face the woman in the mirror, maybe I'll be able to—

And then I caught my reflection in the pane of hard light. How could I dare touch that canvas? I'm hollow. Brittle. Ridiculous.

"Chloe? *Tu es la?*"

The words leapt cruelly from an unswept corner of my past.

"Chloe. It's me. Open the door."

No! Impossible. How could he have found me? And here, of all places! I didn't move, hoping (as I'd hoped so many years before) that he'd think the room was empty.

"Chloe, I want to talk to you."

I didn't want to see him. I couldn't bear for him to see me. And yet, the very sound of his voice reminded me that there was nothing left but Lucien.

Soon he was standing beneath the Vermeer light, his hair a rough white halo. He was vested in cashmere over gray wool, and his eyes retained their ironic wariness, the teasing tension that so attracted his prey. Yes, that once snared even me.

"How in the hell did you find me?"

"Hunter's luck, I guess." He scoured the room—the haunted stage of our great tragedy—with the same precision as on that first night, a quarter century before. His vulpine gaze took in the mosaic of my empty cavern; shabby clothes; and scissor-sheared, rough, graying hair.

"You look very well, Chloe." (He lied so easily!) "You haven't worn your hair this short since Aix."

"That's right. I buried that version of myself a long time ago."

He raised an eyebrow, preparing to charm, but I thought I'd keep it tight.

"Why are you in Paris, Lucien?"

"A sales contract. A holding company out of Brussels wants to import Tunisian olive oil through a warehouse in Marseilles. Of course"—his golden eyes held mine—"it's suicide to represent three nations that speak different versions of the same language."

He paused, perhaps to let me appreciate his enduring beauty. "Why are *you* in Paris, Chloe?"

"Isn't it obvious that I'm in hiding?"

"You don't have to hide from me."

I stared at him in silence. Lucien and I had not spoken to each other for months. We hadn't met for over a year. And many lifetimes had passed since the hundred days that we were lovers.

But now his manner shifted and his voice softened. "I'm selling my business," he explained. "I've bought a farmhouse in Villefranche, near the sea. I think we should try to finish what we started so many years ago. After all, Chloe, I've never really loved anyone but you."

Slowly I began to smile, feeling the smile bloom into a grin and then explode into laughter. I dropped my head into my hands and laughed even longer. He watched me guardedly.

"Excuse me, Lucien," I said, wiping my eyes. "It's just that I've never heard anything quite so sad."

His expression sharpened; he always enjoyed the game. "Would it be so difficult for you to trust me, even after all this time?"

"It wouldn't be difficult," I replied. "It would be masochism."

He exhaled slowly. "I'm staying at the Meurice. Give it some thought, and we'll talk before I leave."

"Lucien," I said as he reached the door, "don't tell anyone you found me."

He paused, satisfaction flooding his face. "I'll keep your secret. You've always kept mine."

After he left I walked slowly to the virgin canvas and stared into the deepest whiteness of my life.

I didn't really think Emil would want to see me, but instinct replaces reason in desperate times. And I certainly was desperate.

So I let the shower strip me. I smoothed my rebellious kinks into a semblance of civility, and unearthed something clean to wear. To my astonishment, winter had vanished and the world outside was reeling in a patchouli of warm asphalt and hyacinth. Bubbling with ecstatic children, the Parc des Buttes-Chaumont led me down to the Avenue Jean

Jaures, where I turned west toward the boulevard Rochechouart. Soon I was absorbed into the throng of black Paris, a roaring market of saltfish and plantains, cowrie shells, and Ghana plaids. Up ahead, beneath the raised *métro* tracks, stood the Théâtre des Xenos, the mecca of French immigrant culture.

And, of course, he was everywhere. Posters on the kiosks; flyers stuck on every streetlight and phone booth. A head shot mounted on the marquee. Even his words ruled the quarter: *The Importance of Telling the Truth: A Series of Lies by Emil Mathurin.*

The dreadlocked woman at the ticket booth seemed strangely familiar. Perhaps a memory from my earlier life. "Miss Emmanuel! What a pleasure!" she cried in Creole. "Don't you remember me? I'm Celestine, Emil's cousin! Have you come all the way from Nice? *Mon dieu,* he'll be so delighted to see you!"

I considered telling her that Miss Emmanuel was no longer with us, but she was already pulling me into the building. The lobby swirled in an unguent of popcorn and clove cigarettes, a resonant collage of press photos and publicity posters. Above the doors leading into the theater hung my immense painting of Les Xenos's original players. Emil dominated the forefront, and in the rear of the canvas stood a young woman with untamed hair and deep, searching eyes—

But Celestine was tugging me through the leather-padded doors with the joyful impatience of youth. To my horror I realized that the houselights were up and the theater held a fair number of people: I had stumbled into a press conference for Emil's newest production.

A single spotlight embraced a man sitting alone on the lip of the stage. His long legs balanced on the back of a chair in the orchestra pit as he verbally jousted with a phalanx of photojournalists. A royal blue sweatshirt, embroidered with the name of his theater, warmed the chestnut in his skin, and the single diamond he wore in his left ear sent fractals of piercing light into the darkened theater. As we descended the aisle, my heart fluttering like a fractured wing, I could see the angled hollows of his cheeks and the tilt of his dark, slanted eyes.

I hadn't expected to find him gray. His strong active hands, clasped loosely over his knees, had grown heavier. Yet his body still resisted repose, and he twisted energetically as he spoke, his head raised high to abate the glare of the footlights.

"So why wouldn't I run for President of the République?" he repeated, his light, roving voice unchanged. "Because then, my friends, I'd have nothing left to criticize!"

There was laughter (as always), and he raised his hand to invite the next question. Celestine was pulling me steadily closer, her palm cool and dry over mine.

"Why did I give up my television program?"

We reached the front row of journalists as Emil broke into his startling grin. "With television you're always selling someone else's product, and—"

Celestine picked her way through a collection of tripods and carefully placed microphones.

"—my motive has always been to sell nothing but—"

Celestine reached the edge of the orchestra pit. She pulled me forward, and suddenly I was shoved into the sphere of light, only inches away from Emil Mathurin. The one man I have ever truly loved. The one man I intentionally drove away.

His eyes bounced down to my face, and his smile shattered. His sudden wordlessness was so surprising that someone in the back asked loudly if his battery had run out. He glanced up, collected himself, and announced to the assembly: "Actually, I thought I'd seen a phantom. But here, ladies and gentlemen, stands, in the flesh, a dear friend, the acclaimed artist Chloe Emmanuel."

He leapt lightly down from the stage and embraced me to a sparkle of flashes. He then posed, with Celestine on my other side, while the photographers surrounded us and took more shots.

"Miss Emmanuel," someone asked, "you've been based in the South of France for a number of years. Has a special event brought you to Paris?"

Emil glanced at me, and our eyes met. "Yes," I said.

"You were associated with Les Xenos in their early days," another journalist called out. "Are you planning to work with them again?"

"If they'll have me."

"Have you?" Emil said dramatically. "I don't know how we've survived without you!"

Always the actor, he kept his arm around my back while fielding a few more questions. And always the gentleman, he refrained from addressing me directly until we were alone in his dressing room.

Lowering myself onto a stool, I barely recognized the stick figure that looked back at me from the mirror above his makeup table. Photographs and programs were pinned haphazardly over the cork walls, and a rack of assorted costumes listed toward a corner. The only trace of my presence in his life was a rough sketch I'd done of him in the beginning, even before we were lovers.

He leaned against the door and folded his arms across his chest. "Why have you come, Chloe?" he asked with a directness that snatched my last ounce of courage away.

"I—I just wanted to see you," I began.

He shifted impatiently. "That's not entirely true, is it? You've come because after all these years you need me again and you hope my door is still open."

There was a hush. Then his expression softened and his hands came up, palms raised. "The vessel is empty," he said quietly. "I've got nothing left to give."

Mute, I stared helplessly at the tall, dignified man who stood before me. How could I hope to explain in words what I'd always been helpless to express without my brushes?

He stepped aside, still a study in grace, and I felt the cool breeze of the corridor. When I found my breath I was back outside, a stranger in a mass of thousands.

This is where our present tenses collide, Michael. This is the moment you enter the story, Little Sister. I tracked you down, which wasn't easy, because Drew—your once-beloved husband—has all but abandoned your home in mourning. I learned that you were in Paris with your lover. I came to your hotel room and found you there with him. And I brought you to this broken place, so that at last you could see this broken woman.

What I'm about to do isn't fair, Michael. You see, the only way I can survive is to finally tell the truth. I'm going to destroy every illusion you've ever had about Chloe Emmanuel. I'm going to introduce you to a woman you've never known, despite our twenty-five years of trust.

I've got only one night, Michael, to right a lifetime of wrongs. To tell you what you deserve to know. What you must know in order to save yourself. And, perhaps, to save me.

We've got some dark hours ahead of us, Little Sister. I can only hope that there'll be some light when we reach the dawn. So. How should I begin?

"Hello. My name is Chloe. My life was destroyed when I was five years old."

ONE

1970

You know, Michael, I remember exactly when I told you that first lie. It was the very day we met—Midsummer's Eve in Washington, D.C., nineteen hundred and seventy.

I remember that the day was sweltering. Five thousand percent humidity. Every tourist in the capital was desperately trying to avoid heatstroke, so the National Gallery was overrun with noisy, shoving Midwesterners.

I had withdrawn into an inner gallery to study one of my favorite pieces, a Degas pastel of a woman drying herself after her bath. Drawn into the sensual curves and richly muted colors, I completely missed the blind advance of the six-inch platform shoe that hammered down on my toes. Crying out in pain, I swallowed back an expletive and began bouncing on my other foot.

"Oh, man— Are you okay? I'm so *very* sorry!" You could barely choke back the laughter that welled up behind your feigned distress.

"Fortunately," I muttered, "I've got another foot just like it."

"There's a bench over there," you suggested. "Sit down and I'll get some help."

"You didn't quite manage to cripple me," I answered, finally looking into your face. I discovered the rascally grin of a precocious child beneath a young woman's astute gaze. We observed each other for one long moment while you struggled to hold back your laughter.

"Girl," I said, with an unwilling smile, "where're you going in those Frankenstein shoes?"

You sighed, genuinely apologetic. "I was supposed to meet someone, but he didn't show."

"So you took out your revenge on me!" Gingerly I tested the floor. "You're risking somebody's life in those things!"

"My grandmother says that, too." You paused. "Are you a tourist?"

"Oh god!" I gulped. "Do I look like one?"

I allowed you to survey my robe of tiny batiked flowers. My head wrap picked up the floral pattern in a slightly darker tone. Loose wisps of hair formed a soft mane around my face because, frankly, I hated combs.

"I guess," you ventured, "that you look like . . . an *artist*?"

I laughed. "I'm on my way to Paris to work that out." I tipped my head toward the Degas. "Understanding these portraits helps me express myself when I paint. I hope that one day I'll make a living with my brushes."

"Books do that for me. I'm going to be a writer—" You hesitated, shocked at your own confession.

I looked over at your glowing face. Reaching across the difference in our ages, I offered you my hand. "Hello. My name is Chloe."

"And my name," you answered, *"is Michael."* You waited for me to react to your unusual name, but I thought it suited you. Strong and purposeful.

We continued to chat as we walked down to the museum café. I remember noting that we were the same height (while you described the boy you were supposed to meet), and about the same weight (you admitted that it bothered you to sneak around behind your grandmother). And I remember thinking that even your hot pants and outrageous shoes couldn't hide your "nice girl" perm and teacher's-daughter diction. We could easily have been mistaken for sisters.

"Where do you shop?" you politely inquired while curiously eyeing my Nigerian cotton.

"New York, mostly. I used to live with a fashion designer, so I know where to go for imported fabrics."

"New York?" you exclaimed. "I'm going to live there one day! I'm going to have a penthouse apartment and boyfriends from all over the world!"

It was my turn to laugh, but I held myself back when I saw your hurt expression.

"That sounds like a pretty good plan. Just make sure all those boyfriends don't get in the way of your writing."

"They won't," you replied with amazing self-assurance. "I believe that the First Commandment in a relationship is 'Respect Thy Freedom'!"

"Oh, really?" I cocked my head as you continued, looking me straight in the eye.

"Sure. It's okay to mess around, as long as you know who you really love."

"First you have to believe in love," I replied, unable to swallow the sadness in my voice.

"You just haven't found it yet," you answered with the ageless wisdom of youth. We fell silent, and I watched you as you watched the tourists, one stalky leg bouncing restlessly over the other.

We met many times during the following weeks, talking about anything and everything and all the things I would have shared with a sister. You began to dress like me, replacing your Lolita getups with colorful scarves and African prints. One day you arrived with a head of wild, unstraightened hair, and giggled as you described your grandmother's horror. I bought you a silk-covered book from China and encouraged you to write while I "studied" my favorite artists—Bacon, Degas, Cézanne, Kahlo.

"Why don't painters ever show the world the way it really is?" you complained while staring at an Impressionist sunrise.

"Some paintings are metaphors for reality. The artists use just a glimpse of life to tell us something about the universe."

"But nothing in this entire museum looks like *my* universe. The only black people in those paintings are slaves!"

"I know, Michael. I intend to do something about that."

"Then you won't spend your time in Paris painting pictures of the Eiffel Tower?"

"Not a chance, baby. My work is going to tell some kind of truth about who we are."

"And so will my books," you said confidently. "Hey—I've got an idea: Let's take a vow!"

You raised your hand, and, trying to keep a straight face, I pressed my palm against yours. Staring straight into my eyes, you spoke like the professor you were destined to become.

"Repeat after me, Chloe: *On my honor, I vow to be a strong black woman, to become a success, and never to let a man turn me away from my dreams.*"

I'll never forget that image of you—that vibrant, honey-skinned young woman who glared so fiercely into my face, challenging me to be my best so that you could follow.

"Chloe, will you stay in France until I get there?"

"I don't know—I'll only have enough funds to last a year."

"I know there's no *black* men in France." You giggled. "But promise me you'll have an affair with at least *one* monsieur!"

I sucked my teeth. "Girl, I'm going to be so busy painting I won't even remember what a man looks like."

You grunted in disgust, and I burst into laughter: "Okay, Little Sister: If I find an acceptable *black* Frenchman—one who'll agree to have a passionate affair—I'll think about staying in France until you show up."

We laughed, and I grasped your fingers. "You don't have to follow me to Paris, Michael. There's a big world to explore." I pulled off my earrings, the full-fleshed Kore figures that represent fertility, and pushed them into your hand.

"The world is yours, Michael." I put my arm around your shoulders, holding you close for the first time. "You've got to be you, whoever that is."

I left for Paris a few days later, my suitcases filled with my dreams. You promised to write and I promised to call, but neither one of us knew how deeply our friendship would flow over the following years. What was the lie I told you that first day? Well, you know the answer already. I lied when I said that I didn't believe in love. For although I was a casualty in the marriage game and pretended that no man would ever come between me and my art, my heart lay open and ready for the taking.

The plane tore through the clouds, revealing the blue-gray city below. Impossible! We were still much too high up to make out anything but abstractions. I squeezed my knees together and strained to understand the stewardess. Oh, Jesus yes—she was speaking French!

French. I had a sudden instant of raw terror. What if I couldn't cut it? What if the bedroom French I learned during my seven years with Reginald Roman wasn't good enough? What if I ended up a hopeless hinkney who couldn't tell the Left Bank from the Right? And what if my paintings were hardly better than paint-by-number kits, fit only to be hung in somebody's shag-carpeted, fake-wood-paneled rec room?

"Whatever happens," I whispered as the fasten-seat-belt sign began flashing to the beat of my heart, "at least your real journey has begun."

I had to remind myself to breathe as I stepped out of the plane and floated down those glass escalators into the terminal at Charles de Gaulle. Anya was posed at the foot of the escalator. Anya, in onyx silk with a wheat-toned wrap draped over one shoulder. My Anya, with cropped frosted hair and sea blue eyes.

"Pardon me," she said in lilting French. "You must be the famous painter from New York—"

"And you are that brilliant fashion designer from Paris."

"Anya Beauchamps," she announced with a little bow.

"Chloe," I said. "Just Chloe."

I was in her arms for about five minutes. We really lost ourselves for a little while. We were trying to drown in the well of absolute trust we'd built in New York, twelve years before. Back then we'd been inseparable. In fact, Anya was the first person who ever told me that I could paint.

Finally she stood back and pondered me, and I believed her like nobody else when she said, "Chloe, *tu es magnifique*."

Her car was tiny, Italian, and a convertible.

"The weather's almost never good enough to put the top down," she explained as she slid a pair of dark glasses over her eyes. I smiled across at her, and she chuckled a bit with an uncharacteristic shyness. "I'm sorry, Chloe," she shouted as she jerked the car into gear. "I don't get to speak much English anymore."

I devoured the stop signs, billboards, and flat fields of grazing cows, not really believing that I was in France, heading toward Paris.

"It's three of my girls—my models," she was saying. "They got fed up with the city and hired this villa for the summer. You'll love it. *C'est vachement chouette*."

She glanced across at me and patted my hand. "Tomorrow I take you into the city to your *atelier*. It's perfect. Good size, excellent location . . ."

I looked past her at the brown fields and occasional small buildings dotting the landscape. In the distance I could make out the blue jewel: Paris.

"Your studio is on a hill next to the Buttes-Chaumont, the most beautiful park in the city," she continued. "It's a good quarter, not far from Montmartre and the Marché Saint-Pierre. But it's quiet. You won't run into other Americans each time you step outside your door. And best of all, you'll only be a few minutes from FAB, my factory."

A studio of my own? In the heart of Paris? How could I tell her I'd be satisfied to live in a shed and paint on a street corner? I wanted only to be here. Nothing else mattered.

"How're you feeling?" she was asking me.

"Like a fuse."

"Well, we mustn't burn you out before everything gets started."

"Everything what?"

"*La fête,* of course. Come now, Chloe," she said, throwing me a crafty smile. "Did you really think I would let my best friend in the world arrive in Paris without arranging for her to meet *tout le monde*?"

The villa *was* a villa. We passed through towering gates and mounted a circular drive to a miniature Versailles built in pink stone with a small bubbling fountain in the courtyard. Inside the echoing foyer a winding staircase looked gracefully over the marble entry. Great windows projected dancing rainbows along the walls through the crystal chandelier. The house belonged to someone who'd inherited it but preferred his other properties in warmer, sunnier places (it was the start of high season in Monaco, I'd learn later that evening). The house was, so to speak, abandoned property.

"I could never live in New York," the model Hélène complained as she led me up the winding staircase to my room. "I spend all my money in the boutique in Soho. Then I go out to the club and six girls have on the same dress—only they buy it for nothing at the flea market!"

"That's a heavy problem," I sympathized. She moved like oiled popsicle sticks beneath her sheer cotton tunic.

My room was done up in period, with marble-topped chests and gilt-edged walls. I dozed uneasily on the canopied bed and awoke to the sound of Hélène and her two housemates noisily creating their faces in a suite down the hall. Bright snatches of their conversation floated by as they dashed between rooms, borrowing lipsticks and earrings. With their sun-browned skin and eyes bordered with turquoise, they might have been treasures carted off from some Oriental expedition.

"They wouldn't hire Silke because she can't walk!"

"She doesn't care; she got a cover in Milan last month."

"Yes, but she's almost twenty-five—she won't get many more!"

Anya was in the echoing stone kitchen quietly savoring a plate of escargots. She looked over and squinted.

"You haven't stopped loving your aquas, have you, Chloe? Whose is this?" Reaching up, she smoothed the bodice around my shoulders.

"You know I don't have designer money."

"Oh," she grunted. "It's a nice piece, anyway. But you should lower this a little. Show off *ta belle poitrine*."

"My 'pretty chest' is not public property. And anyway—your guests will be seeing plenty." My hem halted at midthigh.

"You've always been too modest."

"I'm not on display here."

"Of course you are."

"I don't pose. I paint."

"And this is Paris, not Washington." Our eyes met, and there was a brief, silent struggle. "Anyway, you could easily model," she conceded with a compliment that was more like a condemnation.

It was late when the Italian sports coupes and British sedans began purring up the circular drive. Michael, I wondered what you would have made of the trays of smoked oysters floating on the shoulders of uniformed waiters, or the Eiffel Tower of champagne bottles rising gracefully in the grand foyer. At seventeen, you weren't much younger than Annick, Sylvie, and Hélène, who made a staged descent of the circular staircase in transparent nylon tunics that ended just below their hips. The guests roared and someone remarked that Arcadian Greece had been the theme of Anya's last show.

In the sunken drawing room a pianist tiptoed through some bossa nova and I wanted to go in and listen, but Anya had other plans. Holding me securely around the waist, she planted us in the villa's marble entrance and methodically presented me to every person who came through the door.

"Here she is!" she'd announce while kissing the guest twice on each cheek. "The woman who is most responsible for my success!"

"Enchanté," I'd stammer in embarrassment.

"You must see her work, Jean-Pierre," she'd interrupt, her hand shackling my wrist. "Soon we'll all want to own a Chloe."

The guest would turn to me with a curious, slightly mocking smile. "Thanks to Anya, you are already well known in Paris," he or she would say, eyes flickering over my unadorned dress and loosely bound hair. "How delightful to finally meet you . . ."

As the champagne tower diminished, the bacchanal intensified. A haze softened the sharper edges of the evening, and I settled back into the fine mist of jet lag and expensive drink.

"You've known Anya for many years," a handsome older woman addressed me in unaccented English. "What was she like when you lived in New York?"

"She was a masterpiece. She always dyed her hair to match the colors of her designs."

Across the room I could see my friend in her elegant black shift, the nucleus of a group of admirers. I caught her eye and she waved.

"Well," the woman responded, "it never hurts to defy expectation." She peered at me more closely. "Tell me: Were you lovers?"

"You mean, lovers with each other?"

"That is generally what the term suggests."

"Not in my dictionary."

"But I understand that Anya frequently—"

Seeming to appear from nowhere, my friend took my arm and steered me firmly across the room. "Don't look back," she hissed through clenched teeth.

"Who the hell was that?"

"Someone you don't need to know."

"She asked if you and I were lovers. Do you sleep—"

"She's a gossip columnist, and of course not," Anya answered with a ventriloquist's smile. "Or at least, not officially." Slipping an arm around my waist, she pressed her cheek against mine. "Sometimes you invite people you don't particularly like because of the good things they can do for you," she said in a rough whisper, her face still plastered into a grin. "You must, however, be very careful that they don't try to do just the opposite. Now let me introduce you to my very best photographer, Jules Monseaux."

The moment Anya was called away I escaped to the muted echoes of the cavernous kitchen. Racks of gleaming pots hung from the ceiling, and my splintered reflection was thrown back from a row of polished knives. I studied my face for a moment, wondering if the tense, cautious woman with full lips and deeply shadowed eyes really was me. "Hey, girl—" the steely face whispered. "Are you sure you can handle this?"

Two young women in identical black bodysuits and short, blond-streaked hair sauntered in. One was British. They nodded politely in my direction, then continued their discussion.

"Let's go. La Cirque has got to be more interesting!"

The blonder of the two, who spoke with a whining French accent, shook her head. "I really want to see him tonight."

"No, you just want to screw him tonight."

The young woman twisted away and stared restlessly out of the window. Her companion laughed. "You can't be serious about Lucien. He'll never be serious about you."

"I always take my emotions seriously," the Frenchwoman declared.

"Darling," her friend retorted, "with Lucien it has nothing to do with emotion. And anyway," she chastised, "you're too old to be confusing lust and love."

Anya strode into the kitchen, obviously looking for me. She once again walked me slowly down the long corridor toward the music and the guests. Her face was outwardly calm, but I could feel the effort it required for her to hide her irritation at my disappearance.

"When I couldn't find you I thought that perhaps you weren't well."

"I'm tired, but feeling fine."

She paused, searching for the right words. "I know that all the introductions annoyed you, but they are important for your future. Many of these people have both disposable income and are great collectors of art."

"But this is a party."

"Don't be naive. A lot of important business is conducted in settings like this."

"I just got off the plane."

"Things happen fast here. And whether you like it or not, you're not a successful artist unless money changes hands."

"I don't look at my work that way," I protested, but she raised a manicured finger.

"Then paint, Chloe. I'll take care of the rest."

When she saw my face, she leaned forward and hugged me hard. "I've dreamed about this for a long time. It always seemed right that you should be here with me in Paris."

Coolly we appraised one another, and I remembered her as she looked many years earlier, in New York. She had been a Renoir then—desirably full-bodied and given to dressing in pastels—a genuine work of Impressionism, except for the hunger in her eyes. Now she was lean and blond and angled, a study in Cubism—and the hunger in her eyes had deepened.

"Dreams can come true," she was saying. "If you let me help, we can make some very big things happen, you and I."

I blinked, trying to free myself from the steel in her gaze. Keeping my voice light and natural, I smiled. "Let's speak French from now on. If I'm going to live here, I might as well dive in."

Her eyes lit up. *"Oui, c'est cool, ça."*

Much of the party went by in a skirt's swirl. A very tall and very graceful black woman in a raw silk sheath put some R & B on the turntable and began to work the floor in that velvety, understated sway that Africans do.

"*Eh, vas-y,* Aziza!" someone said, and she raised her proud head, closing her marvelous doe's eyes. It was nice to watch her high hips and upturned breasts moving beneath the fabric, and soon others began to dance, too.

Someone shrieked, and I glanced over my shoulder to witness the blonde from the kitchen leaping into a man's arms. The rough linen of his sleeve brushed her bare back as he turned her around smoothly and elegantly in time to the music. Anya appeared from nowhere and stood silently beside me, her gaze fixed on the couple with an unexpected intensity.

"That would be Lucien," I said loudly, above the pounding bass.

"How do you know?"

I shrugged, my gaze drawn back to the fluid movements of the dancers. The black model had a white man circling her with a quiet desperation. She swayed sensuously but never let him close enough to touch her. Many of the couples were sewn together, their locked hips moving in unison. As the heat increased, the rhythm of the music captured my pulse and I ached to join them. Then a low, sandy voice began speaking clearly and slowly enough in French for me to understand every word.

"So you are Chloe, Anya's famous American friend."

I turned, curious. And what I found surprised me: deep-set gray eyes flecked with gold. A full mouth and slightly flattened nose. Expensively dressed, Lucien emanated an air of casual elegance, perfect self-assurance. But something wasn't quite right.

"I'm Anya's friend, but I'm certainly not famous."

"Give it a day or two."

"I'm in no rush."

"And Anya approves?"

"She has for twelve years."

"Twelve years?" he snorted. "That alone makes you famous."

"Is it so hard to be her friend?"

He brought a cigarette to his heavy lips, clasping it loosely in the cusp of his middle and ring fingers. "Perhaps I lack your patience."

"Real friendship," I replied, "is about loyalty."

"Neither loyalty nor patience are embraced by the ambitious. And Anya is nothing if not ambitious."

There was an unmistakable confidence in his excellent command of my language, and in the way his granite eyes probed mine. "So tell me, Chloe: Are you ambitious, too?"

"Not for this," I asserted, letting my gaze sweep the room. Bodies undulated; music pulsed.

"Then for what?"

"Freedom," I said very gently, as if the word were so delicate it might break up under the touch of my tongue.

He was again within my gaze, his eyes dancing. "What exactly is freedom?"

"It's stopping the past from murdering the future," I explained, repeating my secret litany.

For a long moment the party swirled around us. "My name is Lucien Laurent," he announced, his face revealing a deep and cynical certainty that whenever he was ready, like the others, I'd be ready, too.

"Another of Anya's famous friends?"

"Oh, I am everyone's friend," he declared with a generous smile. "How did you learn to speak such good French?"

"Trying to please someone, of course."

"Well, I hope he appreciated it."

"I didn't say it was a man."

"You didn't have to." He threw back his head and for the first time genuinely laughed.

"We women do try very hard to please," I commented.

"Don't worry." He drew hard on his cigarette and sent out a jet of smoke. "I'm easy to please."

He turned to look at the dancers. His profile was fauvist: the chin was prominent, and I mused that beneath his thatch of curls his ears were probably pointed, like a faun's. Under the jacket, he was gracefully and powerfully built.

But there was something else in Lucien's manner, something tense and secretive beneath that practiced calm. When his eyes met mine, I understood that it wasn't really the deception that bothered me. It was the fact that I wasn't supposed to realize I was being deceived. His secret was intended to compel, to attract, to seduce. And Lucien Laurent needed to seduce.

"Would you like to dance?" he asked.

"Oh, yes," I answered, vaguely amused that out of all of the beautiful women in the room, he had found his way to me.

"But," I added, deciding to tell him the impolite, undiplomatic truth, "I don't want to dance with you."

And I swept past him down the stairs and into the sea of dancers. The music took me. It felt good. The black woman was swaying nearby; she smiled and called out, *"Ça va, ma soeur?"*

"Oui," I responded, truly at ease for the first time that evening.

"I'm Aziza," she said, her high hips weaving arabesques into the music. "Welcome to Paris!"

After a long while I went out to the terrace for cooler air. Couples lounged beside the pool or spoke in low tones by the carefully tended flower beds. I followed a slate path past rose gardens and ornamental basins with grinning cherubs. The party faded, and soon I approached an old greenhouse, its vaulted arches rising into the night sky. A soft light glowed inside, as if candles were flickering between the shadows of gigantic palms.

Someone laughed; another voice answered with a deep, vibrant murmur. I was turning to go, thinking that I had stumbled upon a midnight tryst, when someone took my arm. It was one of the photographers, a short man in tinted glasses who spoke English with a strong German accent.

"Are you finding the party enjoyable?"

"I always enjoy parties," I said, noticing that he did not let go of my arm.

"Then let me show you the rest of the party," he said, leading me with a gentle but firm step toward the greenhouse. He opened the door and stood back so that I could precede him.

The hot air was saturated with the thick odor of wet earth and geraniums. A tiny oil lamp cast weird shadows through palm leaves, distorting the limbs of several women who were sprawled out in attitudes of lazy intoxication, skirts hiked above their thighs. The men leaned back, laughing in wandering voices at unheard jokes while cigarettes sent winding ribbons into the darkness. A single bottle of champagne stood uncorked in the center of the circle.

The German moved forward, leaned over one of the women, and called her name softly. She looked up and they kissed. Someone spoke to me, and after a moment's uncertainty I stepped carefully forward, trying to avoid the disembodied tangle of arms and legs.

It was probably because of the darkness that I didn't see the needle until I was practically standing on the woman. Folded over, she was applying the syringe calmly and deliberately to a vein near her ankle. Her head of rusted copper fell back to reveal eye sockets as empty as stone. The others watched, their casual banter masking an invisible razor-sharp tension.

I began moving backward like a character in a Cocteau film, like Orpheus returning through a mirror from death to life. My running steps echoed on the flagstones as I sought the shelter of the music, the voices, the night.

Anya was perched near the top of the stairs with her photographer, a foaming tulip glass rolling back and forth between her palms. She excused herself and walked down the hall with me.

"You won't get much sleep with all this noise."

"In exactly sixty seconds," I said, "the next French revolution couldn't wake me."

She sat on the bed, watching as I undressed. "You know," she remarked in a feline voice, "you're more beautiful now than ever before."

I shrugged. "It matters a lot less to me now than it did then."

"Come on, Chloe: Getting a divorce from Regi wasn't a divorce from all humankind."

"My libido doesn't run my life."

"Does painting stop you from eating? From talking? Or breathing?"

"I don't need sex to live."

"You're too young to say that."

"I'm too old not to realize that."

"Good lord—you *did* need to get out of America!"

Once again we looked at each other, both of our expressions openly measuring. She lit a cigarette.

"You've always been too careful, Chloe. There are times when you absolutely have to take chances."

"Every chance isn't worth taking."

"*Eh, merde.* It's time you broke out of that reclusive, introverted shell that you pretend is your artistic detachment!"

I studied her handsome face, flushed with excitement and drink. "Thanks again for the party," I replied dryly.

In the long hall she crossed paths with Lucien and his blonde, who were entering a bedroom. He turned and saw me standing at my door. Our eyes met. He smiled warmly and wished me a good night.

And that, Michael, was the start of my life in Paris.

"And did you see that gold lamé sack? Would you believe that Vauthrin tried to do a whole line—yes, nightshirts and panties and even men's ties in it?"

Anya's voice crowded the circular stairwell as we bumped my suitcases up to my new home. Gray light sifted through pigeon smears on the cracked skylight, and the wooden steps groaned under the weight of our ascent.

On the second landing Anya halted and began searching her sealskin sack. "I hope you appreciate how difficult it is to find anything in Paris," she remarked as she fitted a bony key into the door. "We're extremely lucky that this friend of mine decided to try his luck in Milan and didn't want to sublet to a stranger."

The wooden door rattled open to reveal a deep, high-ceilinged room that was badly in need of paint. A gas stove squatted near the entrance beside a rumbling refrigerator the size of a safe, and the only other furniture was a scarred table and a pair of rickety wooden chairs. An open arch led to a small chamber dominated by a mattress, a battered armoire, and a yellowing bath. The morning light sifted through the skylight to cast the studio in the subtle indigo of a garage.

"We can fix it up a bit," Anya remarked as she jerked open a set of French doors that offered a view of the winding street below. "We'll go to the Marché Saint-Pierre this afternoon and look at curtain fabric. Then we can jump down to the Île de la Cité for some plants. The Marché aux Puces might have an antique mirror for that corner by the door—"

"There's a mirror in the doorway."

"You also need a rug. I know a little place where the Arabs sell beautiful—"

"Paint stains rugs."

"But it's so raw—"

"This is a studio."

"But you'll be entertaining—"

"I'll be *working*."

"Naturally!" she said smoothly. "You'll decorate it *à la Chloe*." She faked a smile while slipping out of her suede blazer. "Let's get you unpacked. I need to get to the factory."

Soon we were walking down the sloping street to her car. "So how did you find this grant?" she was asking.

"Pure chance. One day I noticed an announcement on the bulletin board at work: 'Corporate funding available for a full year abroad. Applicant must show promise in the visual/plastic arts.' I sent them some photographs of my stuff and went in for an interview. They've got obscene money and they have to unload it for tax purposes."

"You see," she said as we reached the glistening Alfa Romeo, "there are advantages to living in America."

"America's great if you don't get shot by a Klansman or fried in a riot or beaten to pulp by some overzealous law enforcement officer."

"No one forced you to live in New York or Washington."

"I had to eat, Anya."

"They don't serve food in other places?"

"Not always when you're black."

"Really, Chloe," she snapped as she shoved the car into gear, "it wasn't so bad when I lived there!"

"Black people were still *colored* when you lived there."

Her answer vanished beneath the roar of the Alfa, so I turned my attention to Paris. The boulevards unfolded before us, a montage of Art Nouveau apartments, street vendors selling everything from rubber bands to Bibles, finely arched Doré subway entrances, and people in robes and jeans and silk and leather. It was Truffaut. It was Degas. It was just like I pictured it.

The Fabrique Anya Beauchamps, or FAB, was located on the Canal Saint-Martin, a block from the Gare de l'Est. Anya roared into a parking space bearing the panel "A.B.," and we entered the bright foyer of an enormous brick building, a renovated warehouse of towering windows that looked out over the water.

"Everything in order?"

The receptionist leapt to her feet and handed a wad of messages to her employer. Anya's eyes measured the girl's tight, honey-toned dress and matching flats, coming to rest on her carefully clipped hair. The receptionist lowered her eyes.

"That color likes you," Anya remarked with professional informality. "Come up to my office during your break. We'll find some lipstick that works."

The street level of Anya's factory was used primarily as a storage area for fabrics, supplies, and the finished pieces from her previous collections. The upper story of the building was partitioned into a bright, spacious studio, a number of fitting rooms, and a small auditorium with a stage and runway.

Anya stopped to greet everyone we met, taking care to introduce me to each of her employees. Looking far more ordinary in broad daylight, some of the models I'd seen at the party were being pinned into yet unstructured pieces of material. One or two other women whom I recognized were sketching or painting at drafting tables near the windows. Jacques Brel chanted softly beneath the feminine voices; the air was ribboned with the blue smoke of unfiltered Gauloises.

"So, this is FAB," Anya said with a wave of her hand. "I bought this old factory and had it renovated with the money I made from my first collection. That is, after taking care of my debts." She glanced around critically. "I've been lucky. We manage to do enough business from this little space to make everyone happy and without losing our . . . friendliness."

"It's overwhelming," I said, with genuine admiration.

"Well, it hasn't been easy. The best collection in the world still has to get the right press, with the right guests, or it gets ignored. I need wealthy people, important people sitting in the front row, wearing my pieces." Slowly she led me through the tables. "I need to be different enough to garner attention, but similar enough to the others that no one will feel absurd in my designs." She stopped to finger a fragile, oyster-toned silk. "It's quite a complicated game."

We paused at one of the great windows, and she looked out at the flickering lights on the canal.

"Chloe, I'll be counting on you to give us a hand when we're under pressure. And you know I'll pay you well."

We both laughed, and it almost sounded natural. We entered her vast office and settled into leather chairs. Rough sketches and swatches of fabric were pinned to the walls. Many of the dresses I had seen on the women at the party were Anya originals, and I realized with a start that they looked great—even on real women.

"So tell me, Chloe. What are the stipulations of this famous grant from the corporate rich?"

"None, really. I can live and work as I please. They've given me enough cash not to starve, but I won't be wearing Anya originals. There's only one thing," I added. "I'm required to exhibit my work by the end of the year. Anywhere. Even on a street corner. I've got to prove that I didn't spend the time drinking pastis in Saint-Tropez."

"No street corners!" Anya's eyes narrowed as her thoughts turned inward. "When you have something to show, I'll make a few phone calls. All right?"

I found it hard to believe that Anya would do so much for me. Things like this didn't happen in New York. She looked into my eyes and read my thoughts.

"Oh, come on, Chloe. I wouldn't be sitting in this chair if not for you!"

I was sad for a moment; sad that I had put all my hopes on Reginald Roman and stayed in New York when she'd caught the plane for Paris ten years before with that six hundred dollars—all of my savings—after a big fashion house offered her an apprenticeship. I had wanted to go with her, and she'd urged me to come, too: "You can paint, Chloe! You don't need that *espèce de cul*!" But I had placed my bets on the gorgeous black Canadian who spoke French and said he wanted to marry me. . . .

"You're thinking backward again," she remarked, lifting her legs casually to the top of her desk. "You still don't understand why it fell apart, do you?" She drew deeply on a cigarette, a thick shaft of smoke decorating her words.

"I loved Regi," I said defensively.

Her voice became low and humorless. "And Regi loved getting that green card."

A wash of light from the window illuminated the room and caught the bronze buckles on her suede pumps. She leaned forward. "All right. You met an untalented jerk from Quebec who sleeping-beautied you to the altar. Fortunately, you woke up and got out."

I closed my eyes against the piercing light. "It's not quite that simple."

"You're right," she agreed. "The truth is that you've always been attracted to men who mistreat you. Well, I'm only glad you didn't have any children."

I bit my lip hard, remembering that Anya feasted on the raw energy of an argument. She leaned back, baiting me. "You've got to stop looking for ways to keep yourself from succeeding, Chloe. You have one year to do what you should have been doing for the last ten. If you work hard, I think you can get your career rolling so fast that it won't stop if you return to the States."

"*If* I return?"

"If you're willing to fight, and let me clean you up a bit, we might be able to make something great out of you. After all," she added ironically, "you're thirty-three years old, Chloe. You have nothing left to lose."

Anya was right, of course.

Back in D.C. there was nothing and nobody to go home to. Most of my classmates had become registered members of supermarket savings clubs long ago. My mother was dead, my brother was locked up, and my father had written me off when I refused to become a nurse or a teacher.

So I found myself looking at Paris through your eyes, Michael.

I really missed you. It was as if you were some lost part of me—self-possessed, passionate, the things that I might have been if my life had been different. Now, faced with this one last chance to make something of myself, I quietly decided that I would succeed, if only to show you the way. I know that it sounds crazy, but I really thought that if you fulfilled the promise of your womanhood, then everything I'd been through wouldn't much matter. Somehow both of us would be saved.

So I created a living portrait of Paris for you, Michael, sending off drawings of things both quaint and beautiful. Like eating couscous by candlelight in sandalwood-scented restaurants. Standing in a silent, sun-drenched gallery of the Louvre. Crawling through the skeleton-stacked catacombs beneath Denfert-Rochereau. Or watching the Africans select broiled goat heads for their Sunday dinners.

I couldn't really translate the truth about Anya's world. A seventeen-year-old didn't need to know about the models' nights in basement *boîtes* with sweat-drenched walls and acrid, Gitanes-soaked air. Their faceless affairs with lovers who were shared and compared in the quest for the elusive "Big O." I didn't want to darken your fantasies with stories of the girls who vanished from the runways after making the sojourn from *l'herbe* to *la drogue*, their beauty disintegrating along the way.

I wasn't ready to explain why I didn't meet a handsome prince. My letters reminded you that I didn't believe in love; I had come to Paris to paint. But secretly I didn't understand why neither the graceful blue-black Africans in their turquoise robes, nor the thatch-curled Arabs with their ruddy complexions ever so much as let their eyes linger on me as I roamed through their quarters of the city.

"Oh, you sweet child!" Anya exclaimed when I mentioned it to her one day. "France is much more sophisticated in its racism than

America!" She laughed, delighted by her superior grasp of the nuances of discrimination.

"You see, in the States, if you're not white, you're black. Here, we have an entire hierarchy of social privilege based on skin color." She tossed her hair from her eyes and spat a bit of cigarette paper from the tip of her tongue.

"For example, blacks from the French Caribbean are well tolerated. After all, the Antilles are still French possessions, and we reward their cooperation by giving them French passports."

"But I never see any blacks in the stores or businesses—"

"Well, having a French passport and living like *real* French people are entirely different things."

"That's not so different for blacks in America."

"Wait until you've heard the rest," she said wryly. "Black Africans are only allowed to do the most menial labor. The French don't particularly bother to hate them; it would be a waste of time. After all, it's the North Africans—the Arabs—whom we truly despise."

"But why? They're French-speaking and—"

"Chloe—it's only been eight years since they kicked us out of Algeria! Most French citizens are still fuming about our humiliating retreat from a colony we'd held for more than a century."

"But what does that have to do with me?"

"When you're walking through Paris, you're perceived as a French national. A woman from Martinique or Guadeloupe. *Une Antillaise.* In the eyes of the Africans and Arabs, you'd never have anything to do with a man who is lower than you on the social ladder!"

Anya tilted her head coyly and waited for my reaction. "You see," she concluded, pleased by my confused silence, "all those years of American racism didn't teach you anything about the rest of the world!"

I decided to steer clear of the intrigues of Anya and her entourage at FAB. I found a part-time waitress job at Le Kansas, a bistro in Les Halles. Practically hidden up a winding cobblestone passage, the restaurant offered a New York deli menu that was tremendously overpriced and very popular with the expatriates. Guests drank frosted mugs of watered Milwaukee beer and feasted on greasy pastrami and rye. Pallid cheesecake and syrupy banana splits were also available, along with breakfasts of pancakes and cheddar cheese omelets. I worked evenings, which left me the daylight to explore Paris and the midnights to paint her.

After my shift at Le Kansas one evening, one of the other waitresses found me in the staff dressing room and announced that I had a visitor.

I was surprised: It was a Monday, and nearly eleven. Zipping up my jeans, I grabbed my shoulder bag and walked out into the nearly empty restaurant. Two or three tables were eating cheesecake and sipping steaming espressos with Drambuie. I recognized no one. Turning to leave, I only then noticed the figure at the bar.

"Lucien?" I asked, stopping at the familiar face and sliding onto the next stool.

"At your service," he answered pleasantly. His eyes remained unchanged, but he raised his brows a fraction and his smile deepened. "May I buy you a drink?"

I signaled the bartender, who poured me a tonic water. We were silent for a few moments, and he met my curiosity with a casual, plenty-of-time expression. Lucien Laurent was well over thirty; his eyes were shadowed and his hands, manicured and sporting one heavy gold ring, lay flat on the counter. His impeccable appearance was matched by an air of indifferent conquest, as if he were walking away from a high-stakes game in which he had won something that he wanted—but didn't particularly need.

"How did you find me?" I asked politely.

"I'll tell you over supper."

I heard a murmur of low voices and realized that the other waitresses were watching us from the kitchen. Lucien looked over at them and nodded, and they disappeared in a hail of giggles.

"You turned them into schoolgirls!"

He shrugged. "There's a girl inside every woman."

I set my glass firmly on the counter. "Thanks. But it's late and this woman's heading home."

"*S'il te plais,* Chloe," he said softly. "I've wanted to see you again, but I haven't had any free time."

"Too many schoolgirls?"

"Not a chance. I've been in London producing television ads for a line of French shoes."

"That's interesting."

"Au contraire," he countered. "Television is a celebration of stupidity." Taking a silver case from his pocket, he offered me an English cigarette. "Let's have a glass of wine, and I'll give you ten stunning examples."

"I'm sorry. I paint at night."

He studied me for a moment. "Then let me drive you home."

Lucien's car was an apple red MG with a caramel leather interior. He punched a tape into the eight-track and the Temptations spilled out. I wondered if he'd chosen the music especially for me. He put the car into gear and without a word roared into the night.

"I hope Paris is treating you well," he commented as we passed the Sébastopol Arch.

"We're madly in love," I answered.

He snorted. "I'm glad that Paris loves *someone*." The MG raced across the shining, empty streets.

"Come now, Chloe. Won't you give me an hour of your time this evening? I only want some company."

That's not what you want, I thought, steadfast in my resolve that I hadn't come all the way to France to end up being some slick gigolo's Monday Night Conquest.

We roared up the hill and lurched to a stop in front of my door. Lucien turned the engine off and leaned toward me. I retreated, my hand groping for the door handle.

"What is it?" he asked, amused.

"I'm not right for you," I declared with uncustomary frankness.

There was a pause. Both of us knew that the film was out of sync and the voices were no longer matching the lips of the characters. The dialogue was about to become embarrassing.

"Why do you dislike me so much, Chloe?"

"I don't know you well enough to dislike you."

His smile faded, and his voice gained a soft earnestness. "I'm trying to change that."

"Why? There are plenty of other women who'd be glad to like you."

Lucien's eyes soaked up the aqua light of the dashboard. He wasn't wearing any cologne. How strange that such a perfectly constructed, immaculate man was scentless. After he's gone, I thought, nothing will remain.

"I really do hope to see you again, Chloe."

"There are more important things to hope for," I replied rudely.

He lowered his window and quietly called to me as I mounted the stairs. I turned.

"À bientôt," he promised.

In September you made me your sister, Michael. I still have that letter, and I've read it often over the years. You managed to put into words something that I'd always wanted to express on canvas. In some ways that letter, written by a young woman not yet eighteen, changed my life. It was your letter, I believe, that became the genesis of my so-called masterwork, *Seraphina*.

September 2, 1970

Dear Chloe,

Comment allez-vous?

Thanks for the wonderful sketches! They're hanging all over my bedroom! I really like the one of that gypsy woman sitting by the fountain. Did you let her read your palm? That crystal ball stuff seems too crazy to me, because you never really *know what you're going to do until you're faced with a decision, right?*

Like a few years ago, when my mother decided she wanted me to live with her again. I'd been with my grandma since grade school, when suddenly she thought that if I came back to Chicago my father might come home, too. My grandmother gave me the choice—I could either stay with her, here in D.C., or go back "home" and have a "real" family.

You know, all those years I'd been in Washington I longed for a mother and father. I dreamed of living in a "normal" family, like my friends at school. And then, when I was faced with making the decision, I suddenly realized that my "family" is here in D.C. and my true *parent—the source of my strength and support—is my grandmother. She would do anything to protect me. She'd give me the world if she could. And she always makes me feel like I can reach the sky.*

You're part of my real family, too. You're patient and generous and incredibly brave. If I have just a few ounces of her strength and your courage, I'll make my dreams come true, just like you! Please think of me of me as your little sister, Chloe! I hope that one day I'll be as cool as you!!

Love,

Me

P.S. I haven't forgotten to live by our vow! Strength, success, and dreams!

P.S.S. Please send me some drawings of foxy French men!

By the time I got that letter, I'd completely dropped out of Anya's world. More from a sense of curiosity than any real interest, I'd accompanied her to a number of parties in handsome, elegant apartments with handsome, elegant people. Usually I spent the evenings in an awkward corner, my clothes and hair violently at odds with the designer décor. Lately I'd managed to dodge her invitations, preferring to spend my free evenings at my easel in the dying summer light.

One Saturday the phone rang. Anya's impatient voice shattered my quiet day. "This is special, Chloe—it's being given by one of the biggest music producers in France. Everyone will be there."

"Everyone but me."

"You need to meet people."

"I need to paint."

"Yes, but you must also cultivate business relationships."

"Did I hire you to manage my life?"

The phone went silent. Then it sighed. "All right, Chloe van Gogh. Mail your ear to me in care of my factory."

I truly was struggling with a painting. It was large—one of the largest canvases I had ever tried. I had begun it weeks before, first drawing the design of an African woman dressed in colorful kinte cloth as she crossed a rushing avenue with her baby bound to her back. In her hands she bore not the woven baskets of her homeland, but the plastic shopping bags of Paris. Her hair was braided, and a slight rain was falling, so she had one hand raised to cover her eyes.

As I progressed with the portrait, beginning with the shades and prints of her garments, moving on to the muted grays of the urban landscape, I began to lose myself in her. Every detail, from the shadows of the fingers that clutched her bags, to the shape of the baby in his warm cocoon, filled me with an inner stillness. I touched her diffidently with my brushes, then sat across the room, both fearing and admiring her. Slowly her body emerged from the empty plains of the canvas. She began to live, telling me in a soft secret voice about the sun and spices of her home, and politely requesting that I work on her brows, her round shoulders, or the full warm flesh beneath her chin.

Finally I knew that I'd have to complete her face. I went back to my pencil sketches and found that although I had drawn many African women, none quite captured the blend of perseverance and sadness she required. So I studied my own face for long hours, staring and scowling into a mirror, trying to find the eyes and the lips of this woman driven by hunger from the heat and kinship of her world to a life of cold isolation in Europe.

And that Saturday I awakened to find her face on the edge of my mind, suspended between brush and dream. I leapt on the painting before even putting the tea into the kettle of boiling water, before opening a window to bring in the dawn.

I worked all day, although I had little sense of the time. I could tell by the changing light that the minutes were becoming hours, but I studied her eyes, then the shadows on her nose and the swell formed by her lips, with a passion that bordered on love. She was, for me, the essence of womanly strength—of surviving in order to *make life possible for the next generation.*

At dusk I washed out my brushes and took a long shower. Then, crouching on one of the old wooden chairs, I ate an apple and chewed some bread, my eyes never leaving her. In the semidarkness she indulged me with a fleeting smile. "Seraphina," she whispered. I wished with all my heart that you, Michael, could see her.

Cleansed, refreshed, and unburdened in a way that I had never before known, I glanced around my small room and felt my spirit soar. This was an evening to celebrate, to be with other people. I pulled on some jeans and shook my hair loose and bounded down the hill, the city twinkling like a million jewels below.

The Fountain Saint-Merri in the center of Les Halles was surrounded by a thick rabble of tattered people and the mood was even more festive than usual. Passing the spitting sphinxes at the Châtelet, I traversed the Île de la Cité and gained the Latin Quarter. The tavern Polly Magoo roared with the beer-steeped shouts of sidewalk politicians, and the burgeoning restaurants along the cobblestone alleys were crushed with milling tourists. Roaming Frenchmen stared keenly at me, but I kept my eyes averted and continued my solitary pilgrimage through the night.

At the boulevard Saint-Germain I stopped to gaze at the wild cats lying like sacrifices on the ruin of Cluny, the Roman bath. The streets toward Saint-Michel were a tangle of Asian restaurants, and all was dark toward Jussieu, so I mounted the rue Saint-Jacques, passed the Sorbonne, and strolled slowly toward the glowing dome of the Pantheon. Looking back, I could see the towers of Notre Dame rising like bleached bone in the crisp autumn darkness.

At the top of the rue Saint-Jacques a narrow door revealed a minuscule bar, filled with yellowing film posters hung like the stations of the cross on dingy, smoke-grayed walls. It was nearly eleven, and the customers formed a shouting, sweating mass, so I squeezed into a space at the zinc counter and signaled the barman, who poured me a glass of wine. My eyes swept the crowd, coming to rest on a cracked mirror that threw back the distorted reflection of a man sitting hunched over a little table, his face shrouded in shadow.

Lucien Laurent.

I waited, slowly sipping the wine, to see the woman who would surely join him. As time passed he remained alone. He sat before a row of empty glasses, his stillness a pillar amid the vortex of music and laughter.

For almost twenty minutes I studied the composition his body created. He was all angles of uncaring solitude in that room full of worn-out people. He ran one slow hand through his thick matted hair and then dropped it heavily to a smoking ashtray.

Finally I found the courage to work my way through the squirming, sweaty crowd, pushing gently, excusing myself repeatedly, but always keeping Lucien in my gaze. The crowd parted fluidly, as drinking people will do, and at last I was by his side.

"*Salut,* Lucien."

He looked up, startled. Quickly he arranged his features. "Chloe? What in the world are you doing here?"

"I couldn't resist the elegant atmosphere. And you?"

He lifted his cigarette with shaking fingers, pressed it to his lips, and without inhaling, lowered it again.

Realizing that something was wrong, I started to turn away.

"Let me buy you a drink before you run off, Chloe," he said, his voice level and ironic. "And don't worry: I won't try to drive you home tonight."

The waiter brought me a *rosé* and Lucien another double scotch. Watching me, he raised his glass and calmly drained the amber liquor. The empty glass took its place beside its brothers. He smiled.

"I'm glad you're here. Perhaps you can guide me in my quest."

"Quest?" I repeated politely.

"For freedom, of course. You remember: To keep the past from murdering the future," he recited in a slow, taunting chant.

"Lucien Laurent is ready for that?" I asked, ignoring his sarcasm.

"God, no! But of course, Chloe is. She's fled her past and come to France, where she's free to be an artist. Here in Paris she can paint. She's a new Eve in her own private Eden."

My pulse quickened in anger, and his smile deepened.

"You think," he continued slowly, "that you'll have a show in a big gallery and rich buyers will line up and critics will shout praise and you'll be a success, a happy and whole woman, and you'll paint and travel and live the way you please."

He gestured like a priest granting a blessing, then shook his head slowly as the dull lamp shattered his face into a series of shifting fragments.

"I wish with all my heart that it could happen that way, Chloe. But I'll tell you a secret: This world, whether you like it or not, is not much different from the world you're running from."

"I don't believe that."

"Good. Try not to believe it as long as you can."

Pulling a few notes from a leather wallet, he slipped them under a glass. Unsteadily he regained his feet. Turning, he bowed gallantly and offered me his hand. I hesitated, then let him lead me through the packed bar and out into the night.

The midnight was laced with a cool, sobering wind and the vision of Notre Dame looming up from her island below. We began walking slowly down the Mount Saint-Genevieve toward the cathedral. I was already calculating the distance to the next *métro* station when he chuckled at some private joke.

"Let me guess what you've heard about me, Chloe." He narrowed his eyes in a show of thoughtfulness. "I'm good in bed. Consistently unfaithful. And difficult, if not impossible to resist? Well," he said, lowering his head conspiratorially toward mine, "it's all true."

Lucien's accent had roughened, taking on the guttural intonation of the French working class. "The place I came from was almost empty of French people, although it was only four kilometers from the Eiffel Tower. You've never seen the suburbs of Paris, Chloe. Flat, gray, endless, and endlessly miserable.

"My father hated living among foreigners because it reminded him of who he wasn't and never would be. My mother made the mistake of being a foreigner—" he smiled at me, his expression bitter "—and my father never forgave her for it. He used to tell me every day, 'I don't care what your mother says! You are French, *French,* and you must be proud of it!' "

Lucien paused. "I didn't really understand that he was a drunk until

I was eleven years old. And that alcohol was the reason why we couldn't make it back into the city to live with the people he loved so much and feared so deeply."

He stopped by a darkened doorway, his eyes fixed on the pavement. "But you are here to paint, Chloe. Here, in the City of Light." His arms came up in a sweeping gesture. "You see the monuments, the museums, the great boulevards. You see the sunlight on the statues in the parks and the cafés and restaurants and stores.

"You don't see the dirty children at Barbès who have never been inside a school. Or the women with needle marks on their thighs and necks, waiting for tricks at Pigalle. Or the men with faces flushed by wine at dawn, starting off for another day of work in the factories at Clichy. Have you seen any of this in Paris, the City of Light?"

He emitted a guttural snort that ended with his coughing hard into his fist.

"Do you know how the police treated the students when they tried to open the universities to people like me? Do you know what the good French citizens did to their Algerian neighbors just a few years ago? Have you walked through the streets and read the plaques in memory of the schoolchildren we deported to Auschwitz and Dachau? Have you ever heard of Drancy? No, of course not. You're here in Paris, the City of Light. You've come to paint. And everything here is full of beauty."

An old man stumbled out of an alley, tugging at his pants, while a slow thread of dark liquid filtered along the sidewalk and into the street. Lucien's eyes were riveted to my silent face.

"Tell me, honestly: Do you see enough true beauty around you to fill up a single canvas?"

We came to the Seine, and the lights of a tourist boat on the river sent dizzying patterns across his face. The wind rippled his hair and whipped at my own dark curls. Lucien stopped, wheeling around and coming so close that I smelled the bitter perfume of cigarette and alcohol on his breath.

"Well, I'm sorry to bleed all over you," he whispered, smiling at the startled expression in my eyes. "I've been dreaming of my escape to a little village in the south of France."

He seemed to soften all over, and drew closer to me. His full lips grazed my forehead, and I reached up, grasping his forearms before his mouth could find mine. I felt him encircling my waist, pulling me so close that I thought I could feel his beating heart. He looked down, his eyes mirrors of the undulating river.

"Why," he asked in a rough voice, "are you alone?"

The scarlet flashes of a police van wheeled past, smattering the water like drops of blood. I felt him pulling away, leaning back and drawing in a scotch-filtered breath. "Tell me the truth, Chloe. This is a night for truth."

"I've always been alone," I began haltingly, searching for the words. "Even as a kid. I hated dolls and skates and lacy dresses. I wouldn't join the clubs or sing in the choirs. I didn't even want friends."

Lucien moved a fraction closer, nodding for me to continue.

"And then one day I picked up a brush, and it all made sense. My mother died and there was some money and I convinced my father to send me to art school in New York."

"And you met Anya."

"We roomed together for two years. When she left, she begged me to come to Paris with her. But instead I got married." Unexpected tears leapt into my eyes, and Lucien reached up to brush them away, but I turned my head.

"I went to work so he could paint. Pretty soon he realized that selling his paintings was a lot more about charm than talent, which meant that a wife was dead weight."

I said it all in one hurried breath and wiped my eyes while that ugly, familiar pain radiated up in my chest.

"Now you live on painting alone?" Lucien asked softly.

"I always have."

He laughed dryly. "You know, I'll be thirty-eight in a few months, and I've never loved anyone. Most of the women I've been with never wanted anything more than a good fucking. Which," he added, "brings me to you, madame. What is your excuse for not wanting a good—"

"I know what I'm here to do."

He looked down at me, gloating with the certainty that I was lying.

For a moment I wavered, unsure whether or nor he was right. Then I took the bait.

"She looks like you."

"I used my face as the model."

I was sitting at the table with my knees folded beneath me while a shrewd and gently sobering Lucien examined *Seraphina*.

"No, Chloe. It's in her spirit. Like her creator, she adapts. She even appears to assimilate. But her real quest is for survival." He broke off, slowly scanning the brown and black faces that lined the walls of my studio. "Do you really see yourself in these lost people?"

"I guess I'm one of them."

"No. Your demons come from within, not the outside world."

"Really, Dr. Freud?"

He sat down beside me, enjoying my resistance. "You know, this is the first time I've ever seen you in normal light."

"Ah. Inspection time."

He gently grasped my chin and pretended to study the aggressive black coils exploding over my shoulders. Grunting softly, he then appraised the darker upper lip and the full lower lip suspended over my strong jaw. Clearly the face sculpted out of slave and master's blood, that nexus of hatred and bittersweet desire, pleased him.

"You don't need to be in Paris," he asserted, still holding my face. "You don't need Anya Beauchamps. And you don't need that money from America. Because you, Chloe, have a gift."

Lucien's words were both compliment and criticism, and I pulled away. I felt him gazing lazily and expertly at my body, deciding where to rank me in his *Catalogue des Femmes*. The chair creaked as he settled back, pushing out his legs so that the heavy thigh muscles stretched long and taut. He reached forward and fingered one of my kinky curls.

"Why do you keep such a distance between us?" he asked, sable smooth. His hand moved down my cheek, coming to rest on my collarbone.

"Instinct, I suppose." Again I moved away from his touch.

"No. You're afraid of your beauty."

"You said there's no beauty in Paris."

Lucien's eyes traveled over the portraits I'd painted of the streets' people. When he spoke, his voice was low and thoughtful.

"Have you ever seen the watercolors by Jules Pascin? Fifty years ago he painted child prostitutes. He captured a beauty that's both extraordinarily fragile and saturated with suffering. He painted those little girls, and then he killed himself."

Lucien looked up, his face cloaked with a sudden melancholy. "I need you, Chloe. And I promise I won't hurt you," he murmured, holding out his hand.

Very slowly I moved toward him and again he took my fingers, pulling me gently down to his lap. I felt stiff and unyielding as he breathed me in and closed his eyes. I could smell his skin and see the smooth flesh where his shirt had come open. Against my hips his pelvis was hard, and I closed my eyes, drowning in the almost-forgotten sweetness of being held by someone. Could he feel my fading resistance?

I raised my head carefully and looked long at the purple lids of his eyes, the heavy, relaxed lips. Lucien's head dipped down to touch my shoulder, and his nostrils flared silently with each breath. Watching him, I was filled with a naive and cynical wonder. Then I did something I never believed I would do: I shook him gently, took his fingers in mine, and led him to my bed.

It was obvious that Lucien Laurent was used to waking up in unfamiliar places—he rolled over as I emerged from the bathroom the next morning, stretched, and said, without the slightest sense of embarrassment, "Let's make love."

It was a simple suggestion, and as direct as any man had ever been. And yes, there was that fleshy part of my consciousness that screamed to find his secret scent, that wanted to consume him in the way that men mount and satisfy themselves on women. But there was also a terrible banality in the promise (or threat) of his seduction and I couldn't bear to listen to the patented phrases and feel the commercial caresses that he shared with nameless and numerous other women, on the toss of a coin, the explosion of a champagne bottle, or the smoke of a summer night.

"No, thanks," I said, finding it strangely hard to breathe.

He swiftly tore back the covers and the room was filled with the warm odor of his flesh. I knew this script: The kisses, at first tender, then probing and insistent; the lips on my nipples and thighs, the cool sheets beneath the thrusting, painful pleasure, then the nothingness of love without love.

But he stopped in front of me and stared for a brief instant into my deeply angry, deeply aroused eyes.

"What's your game, Chloe? You bring me to your room, invite me into your bed, then treat me like a criminal because I think you want to make love."

"Weren't you waiting for a woman in that bar last night?"

"A woman? No. I used to go there often when I was young. I thought it was the perfect place to celebrate the fact that I buried my father yesterday."

My heart fluttered. "You should have told me, Lucien."

"Why? He and I hated each other." He shrugged and turned away, reaching for his clothes. "I want to show you something, Chloe. Will you come with me?"

I hesitated, and he glanced back at me. "Come. There's nothing to be afraid of."

An hour later we emerged from the underground *métro* station in a shimmering September light. I was completely unprepared for the strange vision that commanded the view in both directions. A dark wall, some three stories tall and stretching as far as I could see, rose up out of the shadows, blocking the strained traces of autumn sun. "What is this?" I gasped.

"It's the Château de Vincennes."

The massive fortress, crouched behind a deep grassy moat, bore the traces of nearly half a millennium of French history. Leading me down the long boulevard, Lucien talked softly about the enormous sandstone facade and the castle within. "It's only a ruin, now," he said, "but it's been my refuge since I was a child."

"You come here often?" I asked.

"This is where I live."

We entered a crumbling house at the end of the street, facing the château. The facade had grayed, and many of the windows were hidden behind yellowing shades and dusty, rotted plants. The twilight house looked like a lifeless dwelling smothered by its stony neighbor. Inside the narrow, dank foyer, a minuscule wrought-iron elevator took us slowly and noisily to the roof.

When we reached the top floor, Lucien preceded me through a passage to a raw wooden staircase leading to what was obviously the attic. He pressed a button, and the hall was illuminated by tarnished lamps that revealed four identical doors. Silently he turned the key in one of the locks.

"Please come in."

I entered a deep, narrow room that commanded the front of the house. One corner ended in a compact white kitchen—a gas burner, a sink, and a brace of wooden cabinets. Two wide mansard windows broke the curve of the sloping ceiling. A desk faced out from one of them, and the other sheltered a single ficus plant. Lucien strolled past packed bookcases that ran the length of the chamber. Throwing open a door at the rear, he disclosed a small chamber with naked white walls, a simple wooden armoire, and a bed hidden beneath a white duvet. Even the wooden floor was bare.

Either a monk's cell, I thought, or solitary confinement.

He led me toward the glass-topped table in the center of the main room, then went to the stove, turned on the gas, and began filling a coffeepot. The austere flat was bathed in reticence, the only bit of color a bouquet of bloodred anemones in the center of the table. I looked up, my eyes searching the severely plain furnishings and coming to rest on a single framed sketch that I recognized as one of Anya's designs.

"What do you think?" he asked, his back turned to me.

"It's—it's not at all what I expected."

He chuckled, the sound absorbed by the low, curved ceiling.

"I have a confession to make, Chloe. I have never brought a lover here."

"Never?" I said, not bothering to hide my disbelief.

"Most women don't like trains and taxis and rusty elevators and narrow staircases and small beds. They don't tolerate attic apartments in run-down buildings on the outskirts of the city. They don't want to lower their heads beneath sloping ceilings. They don't like wooden floors without carpets. They prefer to deny all evidence of their lover's humble beginnings."

A flame of frustrated anger ignited inside of me. "I'm not one of your plaster-brained models. And I'm not your lover."

He laughed again. "That's right. There's no place in your life for sex," he taunted. "You've got more important things to do in Paris. But tell me, Chloe— Did you want me this morning?"

I wavered. Lucien's eyes darkened. "Say it. And be honest."

Flushing with embarrassment, I capitulated. "I wanted you this morning."

"And you still want me. This moment. Now."

"Yes." I dropped my gaze.

"But you'd never let me touch you because I'm a white man." He raised his brows sardonically. "You've never had sex with a white man."

"No," I answered defiantly.

"Why not? You're not attracted to white men? We're lousy lovers? Or perhaps we simply haven't suffered enough for you."

I raised my furious, humiliated eyes. He was standing at the stove, a white towel thrown over his shoulder, his face wrapped in a sneer. Snatching up my jacket, I moved to the door.

"Wait, Chloe. I'll drive you home."

"No, thanks. I enjoy trains and elevators and other inconveniences."

"I enjoy you pretending not to want me."

"I don't have to pretend."

He reflected a moment. "We'll see," he said.

I didn't write to you about any of this, Michael. And how could I? I didn't want you to think that Lucien, who was little more than a calculating, self-serving womanizer, was making me break our vow. I was determined to be strong, successful, and never to let any man—not even Lucien Laurent—turn me away from my dreams! I had come to Paris to be an artist, and no one was going to stop me.

So the next morning I set out for Saint-Germain-des-Prés, portfolio under my arm, intent on finding a gallery to exhibit my work. On the rue de Seine I took a right up into a tiny alley and found myself in front of a window filled with ritual masks from Africa and the South Pacific. Summoning up the courage you believed I possessed, I lifted my head and walked inside.

It took a moment for my eyes to adjust to the dim lighting. The sunken room ran narrow and deep beneath a beamed roof, with recessed lamps transforming the masks into strange gods. The floor was matted with a heavily woven reed rug, and everything smelled of dried eucalyptus and clove cigarettes.

"Elles vous plaisant?"

Startled, I discovered a slender black man in the darkened rear of the gallery. His legs were casually crossed as he leaned in the doorway, his arms folded across his chest. He came forward at my *"Bonjour,"* revealing flawless mahogany skin and fine, curly hair. His eyes rested appreciatively on my face, then leapt downward to my portfolio.

"I hope I can be of service to you," he said in a French brightened by the music of the Caribbean.

"Who's the artist? These masks are wonderful."

"His name is Jean Lampocinado. He's a friend of mine from Martinique." He paused. "You're an artist, too."

"Yes: Acrylics and oil."

"And you're American. You know, we get plenty of dancers and singers from your side of the Atlantic. But I very rarely meet a woman who paints." His hand came out. "Jacques Colombe."

"Chloe." He nodded, waiting for my surname. "Just *Chloe*," I added.

"This is your portfolio?"

Nodding, I swung the folder up to a showcase, and he grimaced. "Not enough light in here. Let's go across the way."

Leaving a *"Fermé"* placard on the door, we descended the rue de Seine to La Palette, an elegant old café that was still practically empty. Choosing a table bathed in soft light, he carefully examined the photographs of my work. "These are quite compelling. You're influenced by Bacon."

"I only wish I could infuse as much emotional power into my portraits."

"You do, but the power is different," Jacques said thoughtfully. "Bacon's work seems to capture the energy that struggles outward from within his subjects. Your paintings are focused on the external forces that oppress them, and—" he glanced up at me "—the internal struggles that they undergo to survive."

I blinked hard and he laughed. "Sounds like a sales pitch, eh? Well, that's my role in the process."

"Process?"

He laughed. "You're looking for a gallery, of course. I'm always looking for artists. My role is to escort you down the road to fame, and your role is to improve my fortunes along the way."

The waiter appeared, greeted him warmly, and Jacques ordered coffee for us both. Then he glanced over at me from beneath lowered lids, his gaze warm enough to melt chocolate. "Excuse me for my directness," he apologized. "It's sometimes difficult being alone in the gallery all day." He ran his thumb along the edge of his jaw. "You've been here . . ."

"Three months."

"Yet you've already dispensed with the tourism. There's not one picture of a bridge, statue, or monument in your portfolio. I applaud you for that. But what makes you think that anyone will want to buy these paintings of African women and homeless Arabs?"

"Profit doesn't tell me what to paint," I said.

"There's no art without buyers," he said in a cool, mocking voice, reminiscent of Anya's. "You, Chloe dear, need to come to terms with that."

His last words left the frost crackling between us. He lit a Canadian cigarette, taking his time. When I didn't respond, he smiled.

"Now that that's out of the way," he stated, "let's begin again."

I felt a dull thickness in my throat, and I opened my mouth, struggling against the urge to insult him. He waited a polite moment. "Let me be specific: What can you do here in Paris that you couldn't do at home?"

"Breathe," I muttered, hearing the absurdity of the answer as soon as it cleared my lips. Strangely, he didn't rebuff me. Instead, he leaned back in his chair and, finishing his coffee, asked quietly: "Why no surname on your work, Chloe? No family? Husband? Ancestors?"

"Chloe is name enough."

There was another long pause while Jacques peered into my face, openly measuring.

"If you'd like, there's a free space in the spring. I'll show you, provided you have enough work to fill the gallery."

"Thank you," I whispered, clasping my trembling hands together beneath the table.

"Don't thank *me*," he answered tartly. "I plan to make a lot of money on you."

Anya pretended to be shocked when she swept open the door to her apartment. "My god, she's not chained to her easel! What brings you to the realm of the living, Chloe?"

She was wearing one of her signature pieces, a flowered silk caftan, and her hair had been feathered to a frosted shag. Automatically she assessed my appearance, kissed me lightly on both cheeks, then swirled away in a cloud of dark rose.

"Wow, you smell good!"

"It's my next project," she answered without slowing her pace. "I'm creating my own perfume. Can you imagine it? My scent will accent the lives of millions of women. Men will grow old remembering their lovers by Anya. And, of course, it will be an excellent aphrodisiac."

"What about the population boom?"

"Great sex has nothing to do with procreation,"she asserted, "but great sex *can* make me more money. All the advertisements for Anya will feature models wearing my designs. I predict that designer perfumes will be the gold mine of the seventies."

I followed her down a long passage broken by half-moon tables bearing great arrangements of dried wildflowers. Signed copies of her early sketches were matted and framed to match the lavender in the vases, and a thick Oriental runner muted the creaking inlaid floor.

"How about a coffee?" she asked as we entered the spacious, tiled chamber. "Some buyers were in from Geneva, and we ended up at La Tour de l'Argent last night. Would you believe I'm just getting out of bed?"

She poured two coffees and joined me at the table, leaning swiftly forward to fix her attention.

"Something's happened. I can see it in your eyes."

"I found a gallery this morning!"

My words caught her off guard and she sat back as if stunned by an invisible slap. For the breadth of a second there was silence, then she regrouped and put words to her emotions. "That's unbelievable, Chloe! How'd you do it?"

"Luck, I guess." Watching the subtle changes in my friend's expression, I briefly described Jacques and his promise of an exhibition in the spring.

"Well, I'm just overjoyed for you! It certainly sounds ideal." She swept herself up and, taking her coffee cup to the sideboard, pulled a cigarette from a blue box and lit it pensively.

"He'll only charge a reasonable commission, of course," she said without looking at me.

"We haven't discussed the details yet."

"Well, perhaps I'd better come along when the time is right. Or I could send my attorney."

"First I've got to have enough work to fill the gallery."

"And you need to meet some people. Otherwise there'll be no one to buy those paintings!"

"I'll let Jacques worry about that."

"Does this mean that you and he are—?"

"No, Anya. I need a gallery, not a lover."

Returning to the table, she became sisterly. "Honestly, Chloe. Underneath your great artistic devotion, there must be some tiny little desire to—"

"*Merde!* You sound exactly like Lucien."

An electric tension reverberated through the kitchen as she took in my words.

"Lucien? Are you seeing Lucien Laurent?"

"We met by chance in a bar."

"By chance in a bar? Men aren't stray dogs. Or—" cold pools formed in her eyes "—are you in heat?"

My breath caught in my throat. Then, with exaggerated enunciation, I told Anya to fuck herself.

"*Vas te faire foutre,* Anya!" she mocked. "I don't care if Lucien uses me and throws me in the toilet!" She shoved back her chair and stomped to the sink, jerking on the hot water. "I can't believe he'd try it," she muttered as a cloud of steam separated us. "I can't believe he'd go after you!"

"He's not *after* me."

"Let me guess: He told you about his alcoholic father and pathetic, immigrant mother. He told you that he needs you. Then he—"

"Nothing happened between us!"

"After surviving that bastard Reginald, I can't believe you'd let Lucien exploit your talent!"

"*You* wouldn't hesitate to exploit it!"

Our eyes met, and she lifted her chin imperiously. "Working in my factory would bring you into contact with some of the wealthiest and most powerful people in Paris. Which, I think, is better than carting around other people's dirty dishes."

"Well, god bless you, Anya!"

"Chloe," she managed in a voice a shade more controlled, "you're too old to wander around this city pretending that you're not a part of the real world. I know you're an artist. I know you're a foreigner. I know you believe in your self-righteous celibacy. But I also know that if you don't stop living in fiction, the cold facts are going to fly you back to Washington in steerage."

"Neither you nor Lucien will have anything to do with that."

"You'd be surprised!" she spat, rising to her full height, her skin stretched taut over her cheekbones. "Lucien Laurent and your former husband are cut from the same pattern, but Regi was an amateur in comparison. Lucien will consume you. He will take over your life and affect your work and—"

"I don't need you as my bodyguard, Anya."

"You, Chloe, don't know what you need."

Instantly I found myself clattering down the stairs outside her apartment, groping the wrought-iron elevator cage for balance against the roar in my head. Shaking with rage, I stormed blindly onto the narrow rue des Archives and wove my way through the crowded square in front of the Hôtel de Ville. Blindly I crossed the Pont Louis-Philippe to the Île Saint-Louis, where I took refuge on the willow-curtained bank of the Quai de Orléans.

Anya's words had transformed my joy at finding a gallery into the misery of my failed marriage. She'd always been an expert in pointing out my inadequacies, and much too often she'd been right. Yes, Lucien Laurent was a high-risk flirtation. But I wasn't falling under his spell—I would *never* allow that to happen!

Despondently I crossed the Latin Quarter, finally gaining the rue des Écoles. Saint-Germain-des-Prés was draped in a shroud of blue car exhaust, so I mounted the rue du Bac, finally gaining the frenetic intersection of Montparnasse, where the steel skeleton of the new skyscraper rose into the twilight. Dark-suited Frenchmen peered into my face, and some spoke to me with familiarity, as if the color of my skin gave them automatic access to my body.

Restless and distracted, I wandered past the entrance to a café-theater called La Cité des Rêves. The evening's performance was a play called *L'enfer Blanc*, or *White Hell*. Publicity posters hanging outside the ticket booth depicted a troupe of black actors who looked young, vibrant, alive. And the troupe's name, Les Xenos—perhaps an abbreviation of xenophobia?—called out to me. Impulsively I bought a ticket and went inside.

La Cités de Rêves was once the medieval site of fire-eaters, street actors, fortune-tellers, and jugglers. The ancient buildings had been destroyed, and now a vast, simple room that served as both café and theater dominated the courtyard. Eight or nine of the forty-odd tables were filled with Parisians who chatted pleasantly over a glass of wine. I took a small table near the front and ordered *une brune*.

Soon the houselights went down and spotlights illuminated the empty stage. A mournful saxophone lolled and sighed as two young men strolled from the back of the café through the tables to the low stage. They were wearing fedoras and zoot suits and were engaged in a heated conversation.

"It doesn't make sense," the taller of the two was saying. "And if I get to do it again, I want to know."

"Again?" cried his companion, amazed. "You already got your ass killed one time, and you want to let them do it to you again?"

"Hey, brother: It wasn't the dying that was hard—it was living without knowing what I think I know now that I'm not living anymore." The audience tittered.

"Oh—so you're willing to go through all that again?"

"Sure, brother. As long as this time they let me be *white*!"

The tables exploded into laughter.

I listened, entranced. The two men, in a sort of limbo between death and life, were waiting to get their reincarnation orders from the archangel. After thoroughly discussing the issue of whether it was better to be black or white, they decided to ask the angel to allow them to be white, just for a short time, on earth. They accordingly arrived in Paris (in whiteface), where they found themselves having relationships with two "typical" Parisian women, who were also blacks "on leave" from limbo to try out white life.

The comedy escalated when the four realized that they preferred their old color—because living white was simply too painfully empty. They couldn't dance, sing properly, live on sunny islands, or eat hot, spicy foods! Even worse, they were burdened with the responsibility of hating every nonwhite they saw! What followed were failed suicide pacts, attempts to murder one another, and finally the committing of a capital crime—the assassination (or mercy killing) of a white politician whom they also believed was a renegade black—in order to get the guillotine and meet once more in limbo. As the play ended, several "white" sociologists sat before a television camera, debating a recent, unexplainable rise in white-on-white crime.

When the curtain closed for the fourth time on the crowd's continuing ovation, the lights went up and I realized that the house was packed. Excited chatter sprang up all around me, and I sat alone, staring at my empty glass.

"You must be the critic from the *Journal of Superior Taste*."

I looked up. Beside the table a tall figure was throwing off the kind of heat that hushed the conversations around him. His full dancer's thighs supported strong square shoulders that tapered to a narrow waist, but it was his pirate's smile that momentarily robbed me of any response.

"I'm Emil Mathurin," he announced as he sat down, instantly and completely at ease. "What can I get you?"

Caught in the warmth of his vibrant gaze, I felt a sudden, adolescent self-consciousness. "Well, um, dark beer," I stammered.

"Ahhh," he replied, lowering his voice sensuously. "A woman who prefers earth-scented oils and exotic fruits."

"I've always liked mangoes."

"Then you'll *love* what's on my menu," he declared without blinking.

Much taller than he seemed onstage, the actor was amazingly comfortable with his body. During the performance he'd moved in subtle, compact ways while enthralling the audience with a startling range of facial expressions. His great gift, however, was his lilting, velvet voice, which mimicked and mocked, seduced and persuaded.

He ordered beer for us both from a waitress who licked him with candy-store eyes. He pretended not to notice.

"What do you call yourself?"

"Chloe."

"Yes," he said, his eyes roaming over my face, "it suits you."

He'd hidden his hair under a variety of hats during the performance, and now I could see that his wiry locks were woven into a thick, shoulder-length braid. His chestnut skin was smooth and matte beneath the low lights, and I longed to trace the strong nose and full brown lips with my sculptress fingers. But there was something compelling about his eyes—something I couldn't quite capture.

Stretching, he smoothed the loose coils back from his face in a gesture of fatigue. "It's fun, you know, but it really drains me."

"The play was incredible," I said shyly. "Who writes for Les Xenos?"

"This was my piece, but all of us contribute to the repertoire." He glanced at the other tables. "We've played here for three months, and the house gets bigger every night. Believe me, no one ever expected a bunch of colonials to succeed in a café-theater as important as this."

"Then you're new to Paris?"

"Hell, no. Everybody who comes from a colony has had Paris crammed down their throats their whole life. I could have walked around this city blindfolded the first time I got off the train."

I laughed, and he appreciated it. "You're American," he observed.

"I'll never get rid of this accent!"

"Why should you? It's *yours*! Besides," he added conspiratorially, "it pisses the French off so badly when they hear those bastardized forms of their hallowed language. That's why we prefer to speak Creole. It raises the national blood pressure!"

We laughed again, an instant complicity springing up between us.

"You're from . . . ?"

"Guadeloupe. The darker of the French Caribbean sisters."

Suddenly ashamed of my ignorance of West Indian geography, I didn't ask him what he meant. But he didn't seem to care. He pressed his elbows into the table and took a deep swill of his beer, bringing the heat of his gaze to me.

"What are you doing in Paris, Chloe?"

He listened attentively to my short narrative, and when I finished, he said, "And of course there's no time for a man."

I laughed to hide my embarrassment. "I've got more important things to do than chase men."

He paused, his eyes twinkling. "There'd be something wrong if you didn't."

It was a strange exchange, made stranger still by the fact that he wasn't just looking *at* me. He was looking *into* me. I shifted, strangely moved. A French couple approached the table to ask for his autograph, and the woman blurted out, "M. Mathurin, I'm sure you're going to be a star one day!"

"Shhhh, don't tell anyone!" he whispered, pretending to look around nervously. "You're going to give the government a good reason to deport me!"

Turning back to me, the actor's facade vanished, and I was looking into the face of a different man, his expression focused and calm. "Please excuse the interruption," he said gently. "I'd like to know what you paint."

For a moment I was abashed, unsure how to describe my work. He waited patiently.

"I paint—I paint my people," I said. "But I paint them as they really are. I'm not just looking for beauty or perfection."

He grunted softly. "Sometimes the greatest beauty is found in imperfection. And often," he paused, his voice dropping to a private register, "knowing our imperfection helps us to see our own beauty."

There was a lull, and the noisy room faded, leaving us absolutely alone together. I swallowed, and the sound seemed to explode in my throat. When I inhaled, my breath roared through my body like a great rush of water and I felt exposed, vulnerable. And intrigued.

The waitress called him, and reluctantly excusing himself, he strode to the bar. I couldn't stop myself from staring at the face set on high cheekbones, with slanted, almond-shaped eyes. A bergamot of Africa and Asia, he radiated an intensity that made him far more compelling than men who were nothing but beauty. Throughout his brief phone conversation he never released me from his gaze. When he returned to the table, something about him, too, had changed.

"Will you paint me sometime?" he asked, his dark eyes glittering.

"Absolutely."

"Can we start tonight?" He leaned forward, his face a few inches from mine.

"No," I managed over my banging heart. "I'm—I'm working on other things right now."

"Then come and have dinner with us. We always go out after the show and plot our invasion of France."

"Invasion?" I echoed.

"Certainly," he replied with a quiet gravity. "You see, Les Xenos has a purpose, Chloe. It's our mission to make the French acknowledge their responsibilities to the peoples they've exploited throughout the world. It's time that we had something to say about life in the colonies.

And we insist that our voices become part of the national political discourse."

He glanced around at the packed room.

"Les Xenos have chosen a nonviolent way of fighting because we believe that the greatest change is won by persuasion, not fear. We truly believe in the teachings of Gandhi and Mandela. We saw the advances brought about for your people by Dr. King."

I smiled sadly. "King and Gandhi were murdered, Emil. And the South Africans certainly have no intention of freeing Mandela."

"All men die," he answered, "but their ideas live on. Les Xenos may never be rich or famous, but all the French people who leave this theater tonight have learned something about black people. And about themselves."

Breathlessly I reached across the table and touched his arm. He covered my hand with strong, warm fingers, flooding me with an emotion that was both sensuous and fraternal.

"You understand, don't you, Chloe?"

I nodded, my breath trapped in my throat.

"Come out with me tonight," he murmured. "Let me show you *my* Paris."

Emil's dark eyes held my face, and his lips softened into a coaxing smile.

My rage toward Anya was suddenly gone. Jacques and his gallery had no meaning. Even my fluttering attraction to the gigolo prince seemed a wine-induced madness. Here was someone who might truly understand the nature of my painting. Handsome, politically engaged, creative, and intelligent—even *you*, Michael, would have approved of Emil Mathurin.

"I'm not free tonight," I lied, struggling to bring my deep fascination under control. "I work most evenings at Le Kansas in Les Halles. Come by the restaurant when you're not onstage, and we'll have more time to talk."

His fingers lingered on mine. "I'll come to you," he promised, "and when you least expect it."

I walked out into the autumn night and paused, as if entranced. Emil's voice stayed with me as I made the long trek across Paris. As I reached the door to my studio, I was struck by the fact that for the first time since my arrival in France I didn't feel alone.

I called you late that same night, Michael. I'd been working hard on a portrait of a little boy who fed bread crumbs to the pigeons on the street outside my studio, his long burnoose dusty and frayed. His mother, holding a new baby at her breast, called out to him in Arabic, and he ignored her until she slapped him hard across the forehead. Day after day I watched this strange ritual, amazed that the child never learned to respond to her voice. Then it occurred to me that he was probably deaf.

"I can't believe you're calling all the way from France!"

"And I can't believe you're home on a Friday."

"Here I am, a senior in high school, and Grandma won't let me go out till I finish my homework! What time is it in Paris?"

We talked about your classes; then, with your characteristic directness, you asked the one question I didn't know how to answer.

"Well, Chloe, who is he? I know you're calling 'cause you met somebody! And don't give me that stuff about not believing in love!"

"I've met a million people, but I'm working much too hard to get involved with anybody. And speaking of which, I've found a gallery to exhibit my paintings!"

"That's great!" you affirmed. "But don't try to change the subject."

"There's no subject to change."

The phone went silent. Then, as if my conscience were speaking, you said: "Chloe—is he white?"

"No, Michael! The *only* man I've met who could even remotely interest me is most definitely black."

I heard an exaggerated sigh of relief. "So there *are* black men in Paris?"

"Every color, shape, age, and faith. The streets are full of them!"

You were quiet for a few moments. "Well, then," you said, "now I know you're never coming back."

"I'll be back next July when my grant money runs out."

"Chloe—" your voice expressed a longing that I recognized from the depths of my heart "—please, please, stay in Paris."

"Why, Michael?"

"I need you to be my destination."

I laughed quietly. "No, Michael. The only destination you've got to reach is *you*."

Within days my painting found its own destination, and it changed the course of my life. One afternoon I stumbled upon a café near the Trinité, and sitting with an open pad on my knees, I began sketching a pair of young lovers sitting a few feet away on the terrace.

Their clasped hands crossed the round tabletop and their legs were entwined, their knees touching. A dark forehead met a lighter one, but their faces were so close that they resembled an inkblot—two halves of an identical silhouette on a folded piece of life. I could hear the low murmur of their voices, though their lips hardly moved. Alone in the world, they were mythical creatures; the intensity of their emotions made them seem the pure essence of love.

My attention was drawn to the opposite side of the street, where six police officers in full riot gear suddenly appeared on the sidewalk, tramping in unison. Quickly they surrounded two or three brown men who had been selling trinkets from wooden crates posed along the curb. From my safe table I could see only dark boots and shining helmets, but suddenly there was a muffled cry that sent the pigeons screeching up into the trees. One of the crates flew into the street and the cheap watches and gilded plastic bracelets bounced and skidded into traffic.

The policemen split into pairs, like a single cell dividing into new versions of terror, and each pair clutched one of the vendors by his arms. Bent double under the pressure of his captors, one man tripped on his burnoose and fell face-first onto the pavement. A boot launched forward while the other officer jerked him up by the arms. Ignoring his bloody face, they threw him into the back of a waiting police van.

The light changed, and cars flooded the street. A moment later the van and crates and policemen were gone. The pigeons were gone. The lovers were gone. Only a few pieces of gold-colored plastic, smashed under the weight of reality, lay like tinsel in the center of the asphalt.

My impotent fury began to subside only after I'd stood for a time beside the fountain in the church garden, my eyes coming to rest on the small children using twigs to guide yellow leaves through the brackish water in the basin. The sky had darkened with herds of silvery purple clouds, and I struggled against a soul-deep urge to walk the short distance to a store—preferably an expensive store—and to break something irreplaceable.

That night at work I spilled a glass of red wine on a college student from Rhode Island who was loudly bragging to her girlfriends about a gorgeous Arab she'd found on the boulevard Saint-Michel and bedded in a cheap hotel. As I mopped the bloodred liquid from her cashmere sweater our eyes met, and she looked away, unable to hide her distaste.

I left the restaurant late. First I tried the boulevard Saint-Michel, really looking at the dark men who roamed the streets in the search of white flesh. Usually those same men ignored me, calling out at the white women as rudely as the hecklers on the streets of New York. I observed them carefully as I walked, seeing for the first time that each of those men, from the reed-thin Tunisians to the swarthy Moroccans, had a different face, a different body, a different story—even if they shared the same rage.

For I was beginning to know that rage. I had come to understand it that very afternoon. And much as I had wanted to expend my fury by enacting a crime, they sought their retribution on the soft bodies of their conquerors, filling the hallowed alabaster flesh with their brown seed. Unlike me, they had no special talents to broker, no money from wealthy Americans to support them, no ambitious French friends to help them find work or apartments or to introduce them to the upper echelons of society. They had no way to create a record, even of their own suffering, except to leave it inside the wombs of their enemy.

My heart slamming in my chest, I stood against a wall in the center of the Latin Quarter, ignoring the cold and watching a young man with shiny black curls and finely chiseled features leaning over an overweight Frenchwoman and gently biting her ear. She reached inside his jacket, her hands traveling to his swollen pants as his lips slid down to her mouth.

I heard a voice close to my ear. *"Ça va, ma belle?"*

We shared the same skin color, but his hair was long and smooth, and his mocking eyes were an improbable green. His face danced before mine, and I blinked back tears as he reached up and boldly stroked my cheek.

"No—" I whispered, drawing in my breath as he leaned full against me.

"You're enjoying my brother so much," he said in a low voice, nodding his head toward the other couple. "There's no reason for you to be alone." He moved in front of me, bracing his arms against the wall.

"Don't do this," I managed through trembling lips.

"I'll only do what you want," he promised in a perfume of alcohol and cheap aftershave. "Don't be afraid," he urged, his voice a velvety stream. "I can give you great pleasure—"

Roughly I shoved him away, retreating from the sharp laughter of several other men standing in a group nearby. Staggering into a tiny North African pastry shop, I stood at the counter and shakily sipped at a glass of steaming spearmint tea beneath a blinding fluorescent light. My face was greasy with the sweat—despite the cold night air—of my secret, shameful lust. And that night I sat before an empty canvas for a long time, realizing that just because there was nothing left for me in the States didn't mean there was anything for me in Paris.

One afternoon a knock on my door revealed the model, Aziza. She came in shyly and stood in the center of the studio. The diffused sunlight created a hazy halo in the soft fringes of her hair, and her eyes reflected the earthy browns of her mud-cloth tunic.

"How did you find me?"

"Anya, of course." She chuckled, glancing around the room in an exhilaration of discovery. "She's been talking about you for years, you know. You're the legendary black American who made all her dreams possible."

"If only I could do that with mine!" I said dryly.

She gave a hummingbird laugh. "From that first night I could tell that you really *are* different. You observe everything. You prefer listening to speaking. And you value your privacy."

She was suddenly so still that the cowrie shell on her dangling earring came to rest against her cheek. "It's very rare, this ability to live both without and within. To let the world see what you want them to see. And to have someone else inside. It's been a long time since I've met anyone so much like me."

She began strolling through my haphazard gallery, making cooing sounds and singing softly under her breath. Silence fell while she stood in front of *Seraphina*. Finally she turned to my most recent portrait, a darkly lit study of a man whose face, half cast in shadow, bore an unwilling resemblance to—

"Have you fallen in love yet?" she asked, her eyes trained on the painting. "And don't worry: I won't tell Lucien!"

"Lucien's not even a candidate." I laughed. "I need a utopian man—someone who's strong, wise, independent, respectful of my work—"

"And an expert lover!" she concluded, her face bright with merriment. "Ah, if only such a man existed! My boyfriend is called Christian-Noël Antoine Marie de la Salle. He's as rich and useless as his name is long." She paused. "You have to be careful with these men, you know!"

"I prefer my men black," I said.

"Color doesn't matter! My father and brothers have a whole stable of potential husbands waiting for me in Senegal. If I go home to visit, I may never get away again."

She glanced across the room at me, and the faint sunlight carved out soft hollows beneath her high cheeks, forming sensuous shadows around her doe eyes. My fingers ached for a brush.

"What about you, Chloe? Are you friends with the black Americans who live in Paris?"

"I didn't come here to speak English and complain about life at home. There's so much more to learn about the world."

"You know, I have a penthouse with a view from Boulogne to Vincennes. I travel the world, and my boyfriend's parents live in a castle. But," she paused guiltily, "I don't see many other Africans. There's always a price for success."

Suddenly she dug in her bag, producing a photography magazine. "What do you think?"

Eyes blackened like a jaguar, a nearly naked Aziza graced the cover.

"It's hideous, isn't it? Look what they've done to my face! My god, they see an African and think *beast*! Chloe—I want you to paint me one day. But I want a real painting, something that shows who I am inside."

"Oh, Aziza," I said, savoring the thought, "I could paint you a hundred times and never capture the same woman twice."

For once she didn't smile. "I'm paid a great deal to give people that impression."

When she spoke again, her voice had fallen to a somber whisper. "I must do something this afternoon, and I don't want to be alone. Will you come with me?"

A taxi took us from my studio to the southeastern end of the city, halting before a domed white building. We passed through arched gates and entered a tiled courtyard ringed with silver granite and well-tended rosebushes. Through another passage I found myself in a low-ceilinged, elaborately ornate tearoom with brass tables and deep, comfortable cushions, perfumed by the lingering scents of sandal, peppermint, and lemon.

Aziza gave me her gentle smile, then guided me past a seated man wearing a fez to a hidden doorway. We proceeded down a delicately lit hall around a heavy curtain and into a dark, aromatic room, where beyond swelling wooden arches I could see the forms of women's bodies stretched out on mats along the marble floor. Aziza took two white robes from a woman with a pale blue tattoo on her forehead, and we entered a long gallery echoing with the musical tones of Arabic and lilting laughter.

She led me to a corner, where she began to undress. I hesitated, glancing around self-consciously.

"It's all right," she said with dancing eyes. "In the *hammam*, we're all the same."

We undressed in silence and put on the white robes, hanging up our clothes on pegs forced into the wall, then walked slowly into the adjoining hall.

Shell-shaped stone basins lined the tiled walls, and through the wet, white air I could barely discern the pastel-drawn apparitions of women from alabaster to onyx, maiden to grandmother. Some were languidly pouring water over their waist-length hair, while others relaxed against the white marble, working a burgundy paste through their ringed fingers, talking and laughing or gazing vacantly into space.

"What's that?" I asked Aziza as a young woman spread the gritty paste on an older woman's scalp.

"That's henna, of course. Women in my world would never put chemical dyes or bleaches on their hair."

My white robe was unbearable in the heat; I took it off. Aziza did the same, saying, "Thank you, Chloe. We must enter this place unclothed, for this is where we women of Islam cleanse both our bodies and spirits."

We continued walking slowly down the long hall. There was a flat, raised area in the center upon which women lay, a shimmering tangle of faces and limbs. At the far end of the hall was the basin from which billows of scalding steam poured out to meet us.

"I come here to renew the part of me that Paris destroys," Aziza explained, her words muted by the heavy air. "Sometimes I think it's the only way I'll survive that woman on the magazine cover."

We seemed to wade into a bright amphitheater where the floor descended in narrow ledges toward a round, open basin filled with frothing water. Heat was pumped in through brass screens from some unseen source, and the temperature rose as we climbed slowly to an upper ledge.

Carefully, almost in slow motion, we came to the highest level of marble and slipped into a corner. My limbs seemed unbearably dense, but the stone was smooth and cool to the skin of my back and thighs. It was too hot to speak. I was already bathed in the water pouring from every pore of my body. Aziza stretched her long legs out beside me, and slipped into a kind of waking sleep, her eyes closed and hands open at her sides.

Some of the other women stroked their arms and legs with sponges and pumice stones; several were rubbing oils gently into their skin. All of us, nude, were as indifferent to each other as sisters—an exquisite, unsettling, intimate tableau.

My mind wandered. I was a child, drawing silent pictures at the kitchen table as my mother screamed at my older brother. Then I was in New York, weeping as my husband packed his belongings. Finally I was here, in the safety of the heat, with a man beside me whose face slowly took on the sculpted features of the actor Emil. . . .

Infused with a soul-deep sense of peace, I felt the loneliness pour from my body in the rivers of salty sweat. I let myself drift into an exquisite calm of nothingness where there was no pain, fear, or confusion. I was calm and whole. I was Chloe.

After a long while I wandered out into the hall and stood beneath an ornate spigot, splashing water over my body. Aziza followed. She went over to one of the basins, her lean body moving with a gazelle's grace, and filled a flask with cool water. Slowly she poured the water in a flowing arc over her shoulders, then over mine. We sat together on a cool marble platform, and she began to massage her scalp, her perfect breasts rising and falling as she worked her long fingers through her thick black hair.

"Chloe, I'm pregnant." Our eyes met. To my unasked questions she answered, "Five or six weeks. And yes, by my Frenchman."

"Does he know?"

She paused. "Not yet. He often says he wants to marry me. But they babble this way, the French, and it would be dangerous to believe him. And," she added, "I don't really care what he thinks. I want to be a mother."

"Then," I responded, "I'm happy for you."

We both listened to the flat echo of voices filtered through the blanket of heat.

"No one will understand," she whispered as we lay down on the pale stones, "but you." She reached for my hand. "I do know why you paint, Chloe. Your paintings will never cause you pain."

September 30, 1970

Help, Chloe!

I started a mini-revolt in my homeroom today by saying that black women shouldn't put perms on their hair. I haven't straightened my hair since I met you last summer, and everybody from my minister to my teachers thinks I'm a "fallen woman"! I tried to explain that black women can be beautiful without trying to look like they're white, but nobody will listen to me. I wish you were here so that they could see how beautiful natural hair can be!

Another thing—the other girls refuse to understand the meaning of the earrings you gave me last summer. I tried to explain that they represent fertility, but those idiots said they were just fat, ugly women! You know what? I don't care what they think! When I wear those earrings, I feel closer to you!

I'll bet the French really respect black culture. I'm sure that in Paris the beauty of our people is recognized and respected. I can't wait to get to Europe! Write me soon, okay?

I love you and miss you.

Me

Your letter made me smile, Michael. I could picture that revolt in your homeroom—all the girls waving their nail files in outrage while you stood over them, my Kore earrings dancing provocatively beneath your springing mane. You were already embracing the teacher that lived in your blood, already discovering the truths that would guide your life.

But your letter also made me sad because I knew that Paris didn't see the beauty of our people. The faces I captured in my paintings were never meant to be seen. Your letter reminded me why I had to keep my eyes focused on their silent suffering, and never, ever look away.

Each Sunday morning a flea market seemed to spring up out of the concrete at the Porte de Pantin, the rim of the North African quarter of Paris. Scarecrows in ill-fitting suit coats and white skullcaps filled torn plastic bags with clothing fished from heaps of garments strewn across the raw pavement. The wind scattered rags and cans in a mocking waltz around their poverty while the vendors, who slouched on folding chairs, sucked cigarettes and murmured discordant, rambling songs.

I perched myself high on a stairway overlooking the market and began sketching the lonely figures. Some foraged patiently through the piles, searching for a jacket or an overcoat to wear against the autumn rains. Others lifted out a tiny soiled sweater, a woman's lace-edged slip, or even an orphaned shoe to send to their distant kin. No one spoke, and the men barely lifted their eyes. Despite the dank cold of the early morning, my fingers flew over the paper, guided by the heat of their solitude.

Suddenly an unfamiliar sound came boiling up from below. Standing, I quickly scanned the scene. A dense crowd had gathered around a figure that was gesticulating wildly and speaking with exaggerated diction. The sound that I had failed to recognize was their laughter.

I descended the steps and drew closer to the swelling group. I could hear the voice of the speaker, who was mimicking in turn a French police officer and an illiterate immigrant. As the two characters enacted a ritual of fear and abuse, the listeners heartily roared out their amusement.

Then the crowd shifted and I could see the speaker—a tall black man in worker's overalls and a black beret. His angular face was screwed shut against an imaginary policeman's baton; his slanted eyes seemed to light up the gray morning. Twisting his lithe body in mock defiance, he hurled a series of expletives in Arabic at the *gendarme*'s retreating back. He pretended to kick the policeman in the pants, and ended his performance with a sweeping bow that was met by howls of approval.

For nearly an hour I remained in the crowd, watching the actor as he enacted a series of scenes from immigrant life, each one bolder and more provocative than the last. A newly arrived African went into a high-class department store and attempted to buy his first pair of boots. A devout Muslim tried to pray in a public garden. A young family went to the movies, not realizing that the film was a "porno."

The cheers grew so loud that two or three *gendarmes* appeared, peering darkly through the bodies to get a look at the performer. Ignoring them, the actor moved smoothly into a farcical imitation of some tourists who unwittingly stumble into an all-black quarter. He closed his performance with a mocking, heavily accented rendition of *La Marseillaise* and a deep, acrobatic bow.

I pushed my way through the applauding crowd, hoping to catch him before he could vanish into the sea of restless men.

"Emil!"

He whipped around, searching the unfamiliar faces. His grin exploded as he recognized me. "It's Chloe! *L'artiste!* What are you doing here?"

"And you?" I wondered. "What's happened to Les Xenos?"

He strode forward and embraced me, kissing me twice on each cheek. "The company is fine, the play is a success, and I'm doing what I enjoy most in the world!" He glanced around quickly at the shabby, lonely men. "These people will never be able to afford the theater. So I bring the theater to them."

Wrapping an arm around my shoulder, he and I began walking slowly through the piles of soiled, scattered clothes.

"How did you find this sad place, Chloe?"

"I come here often," I explained, indicating my sketchbook. "I've never seen such loneliness. It's as if searching through these rags is a way of finding the families they left behind."

He peered down at me perceptively. "You identify with them," he said gently.

"I—I don't know," I stammered, naked to his gaze.

"They're invisible to the French. No one ever asks who cleans the sewers and takes away the garbage. No one cares whether they live or die." He paused. "I'm glad you paint them, Chloe."

Michael, I stood there beside him, not trusting myself to speak. Because Emil Mathurin was the first person I'd met in Paris who understood the purpose of my art. Suddenly he grinned, his lips parting to reveal perfect teeth. His arm tightened around my shoulder, drawing me closer to his radiance. My head barely reached his chin, and I could see the soft fringes of his braid disappearing beneath his beret.

For a time we stood together, wrapped in a silent embrace. Then he spoke very softly, his voice very deep.

"Destiny's brought you to me twice, Chloe. I know I'd better act quickly, before someone else steals you away. Look—" He reached for my sketchbook. "Here's my number at the theater. Call me, *s'il te plais*." He closed his hand over mine and held my fingers gently. "Now, remember: Our future lies here, with your art."

I nodded, smiling, and he turned again to the drifting men. *"Mes amis,"* he called loudly, "have you heard the amusing tale of the Moroccan who tried to marry a Frenchwoman?"

I rose early the morning of Anya's show, washed my hair, and even did my nails (with polish, Michael, not splattered paint!). Finally, I slipped into a dress of scarlet mohair—designed especially for me by Anya—and loosened my damp, heavy braids. Folds of furry fabric cascaded over my shoulders and breasts, softening and romanticizing my frame. The savagery of the fabric and the freedom of my own unkempt locks transformed me into an Amazon goddess—a full-bodied, deep-hued stranger.

A convoy of trucks and trailers from the television networks screeched white noise while a crowd of guests and onlookers chattered excitedly outside of FAB. My special pass got me past the uniforms and into bedlam.

Models who were all stockings and elbows tittered shrilly, trying to displace the stress caused by the lenses and eyes that would soon decipher every detail of their bodies. I found Anya grilling the stage manager, who scuttled off clutching a list of lighting instructions. She appraised me tersely and gestured toward her crisp white suit with matching spats and a cream silk tie.

"You're splendid, Chloe. Please help with the zipping. When the show starts, go out and sit in the front. I want you to watch carefully and tell me how it *really* looked. *Entendu?*"

She didn't want me to argue.

When the music began, I slipped out to my seat next to Jules, Anya's personal photographer. The house darkened, and the runway illuminated. A hush fell over the packed auditorium and then, in a flourish of synthesized trumpets, the show began.

It was strangely exciting to see the first of Anya's designs plunge into the spotlights—my heart was pounding and my mouth was dry.

Two tall redheads in matching auburn suits, tailored with a totally unexpected and terribly precocious flounce over their *derrières*, strolled with nonchalant vigor along the causeway into a fireworks of exploding flashes. One of the women was attired in a breathtakingly narrow cigarette skirt while the other sported wide-legged trousers. The clothes I had sketched three months before, pinned onto the models' lithe bodies, and had seen paraded up and down the factory floors acquired a different life in this moment of truth.

As quickly as they came, the redheads were gone, replaced by another pair, this time blond, who wore similar variations of the jacket, but with shorts. They were greeted by another rain of camera flashes, and then they, too, disappeared behind the backdrop while the next models followed with a breathlessly coordinated accuracy.

Aziza appeared alone. There was an appreciative ripple through the audience as she gazed coolly from left to right, slowly lifting her long arm to place a hand on her hip. It was hard for me to see her clothing, for she dominated all color and pattern with her being—she was both wild and elusive, and I realized that if I painted her a thousand times I would never catch the *essence* that took possession of that crowd.

The show went on, changing as the music changed, from day wear to evening wear, to the miscellaneous wear that included everything from bathing suits to lingerie. The minutes sped by and the cameras flared and the crowd tittered and sometimes a wave of laughter spread through the room when a model wore some appropriately ironic expression, or used a gesture, to suggest pleasure or disdain.

When I saw the last design—Aziza in a sheer organdy sheath with embroidered seed pearls over her pelvis and breasts—the wedding dress!—floating down the runway, I knew that Anya had succeeded in every sense of the word. My old school friend really was a star!

At that moment all the models filed out onto the runway, and, to a mighty round of applause, Anya walked out in her white suit and bowed simply, and with intense pleasure, to the roaring audience. I could see the iron in her glowing with the heat of her triumph. My heart stirred and I wondered again what might have happened if I'd come to Paris with her a decade before. Here, before my eyes, was evidence of what willpower and courage and talent could achieve.

The applause lasted for many minutes. Jules reached over and hugged me. I opened my eyes. I looked over his shoulder. I saw the smiling, clapping crowd. And I saw Lucien Laurent, one row behind us, less than six feet away.

It was one of those moments that happen only in a movie. Jules released me from his embrace and turned back to the stage. As if in slow motion I found myself facing the man in the elegant dark suit, his face cool and expressionless. At the same moment his eyes flickered down from the runway to me.

We looked at each other, neither of us smiling. There must have been surprise in my eyes because there was surprise in his. Slowly, almost as if he had never seen me in his life, his eyes traveled the length of my body, measuring, exploring, discovering. I had forgotten how I was dressed. I had forgotten my flowing hair and the lipstick and shadow and the brilliant scarlet fabric molded sensuously over my body. All I could see was the flashing gold ring as his hands continued clapping, mechanically clapping, and his face, which did not change expression, as though I were a perfect stranger.

And I saw his eyes again come to mine, and in a prolonged second of understanding, I knew that he was willing himself not to respond. He was holding his face in its symphony of calm with all the strength he had. Only his eyes—his infamous, fabulous eyes—surrendered the depth of his feeling as I stood so very close and yet so far away.

Beside him someone stirred. A woman! I should have thought *first* of her: Lucien would *never*, I realized with shattering certainty, have come to something like this alone. She leaned forward and gazed around him, intent on knowing who could rob her of his attention.

We looked into each other's eyes.

Ash blond and fine featured. A simple dark dress of Italian design with a rich border of lace at her neck and wrists. As she looked at me she raised her chin and slipped one of her arms through his. Her expression asserted that she owned him.

And his eyes, still trained on my face, still denied me any sign of recognition. Before I could move or even speak she was pulling him through the applauding crowds. I watched helplessly as he disappeared without resistance into the noise of his other life, his true life.

Within minutes Jules had pulled me through the crowds as well, and we found ourselves blending into the brilliant host of models, assistants, agents, and photographers. In the white lights the dressing rooms became a surreal theater. Bottles exploded into thick foam; men's roars and women's peals burst from every angle and arms reached around hips and shoulders to pull bodies together in abandoned delight.

Jules and I fought our way to Anya, who threw herself into his arms and rocked back and forth. Then she came into my arms with a strength that squeezed me into a broken doll in a shop of overwound toys.

Stumbling away, I accepted a glass of champagne. Behind a row of mirrors Aziza leaned coolly against the edge of a dressing table, Christian-Noël standing in front of her with his hands on her hips and his head close to hers.

I found the bathroom and closed the door on the noise. For many minutes I pressed my forehead against a mirror, listening to the party. I took a deep breath, stood up straight, and finally looked into the glass. The shadows of the room gave an eerie depth to my features. The floating hair, even wilder now from the humidity, formed a rough mane around my expressionless face. I examined the large dark eyes and my lipstick-smeared mouth, bloated by the tears beginning to wander silently down my face.

The door flew open and the mirror tossed up the glint of shiny white shoes. Anya came up behind me, grasped my shoulders, and waited.

"Too much champagne," I said to our reflection.

"*Tu te foutres de ma guele?* Do you think I'm stupid?" She circled me and leaned on the neighboring sink. "What is it?"

"The show was superb," I said hoarsely, averting my eyes.

She tilted her head. "Thank you, and don't lie."

Flushing with shame, I blurted out the truth: "I saw Lucien out there. With a woman."

Instead of triumphant disdain, my confession was met with such a long silence that I ventured an uncertain glance at her.

"Oh, Chloe," she said quietly. "This isn't really your fault. I should have swallowed my pride and told you this long ago." She took a deep breath. "I have a very good reason for trying to keep him away from you. Lucien and I used to live together. It didn't last long, and it ended very badly."

Instantly it snapped into focus: Her strange silence when he appeared at the villa that first night. Her fury when she discovered I'd spent time with him. Her endless, repeated warnings . . .

"You lived with him at Vincennes?"

"God, no," she sneered. "No woman has ever defiled that monastery." She stood tall, pushing her hands along the crease of her ivory trousers. "It's a pattern: He moves in. Stays while it's expedient. And then, when he's tired, or bored, or drawn to someone else, he just vanishes." Her voice hardened. "At first it was intense. Passionate. Almost overwhelming. But after a few weeks everything seemed to slip out of control. And when he loses control—" She stopped speaking, her fingers plucking at a loose thread. "I'm telling you, Chloe. Lucien can become a very different man when he's drinking."

Silenced, I lowered my head.

"Let's clean you up," she said softly. "He's just not worth this."

We emerged hand in hand some twenty minutes later, my face washed, my troubled heart lightened. Looking taller than usual and dressed in suspendered black tuxedo trousers and a white turtleneck, the gallery owner, Jacques Colombe, pushed his way through the crowd to me. We embraced, and he took my hands in his.

"You've been in France only a few weeks and you turn up at the private party of one of the newest and best designers in Paris!"

"Anya and I have been friends for years."

"Why didn't you say so, Chloe?"

"I didn't think it mattered."

"Things like that always matter," he said with a look of amused curiosity.

"Then I suppose you'd like to meet her."

He nodded eagerly.

Anya was swallowed by a small pack of glittery fashion critics, but she reached for me as I approached, holding me close while rearranging the flaming fabric on my shoulders in a possessive, sensual manner.

I didn't listen as Jacques went into a tirade of compliments. Across the room I caught a glimpse of a staggering model clutching a champagne bottle by the neck, but there was no sign of Lucien.

I felt Jacques slip his arm around me. "You should have been on that walkway, Chloe."

Aziza strolled past, her eyes cool and victorious as Christian-Noël followed in her wake. She winked at me, a smile playing around her lips.

"Another friend of yours?" Jacques asked quickly. "That man she's with comes from a very old noble family."

"How do you know all this?"

"These are my clients, Chloe."

Jacques greeted people, introducing me as if we had come to the show together. He kept one arm looped loosely around my waist in a perfectly ambiguous gesture: even I couldn't tell if we appeared to be friends or lovers.

Late in the party the gallery owner turned to me. "I've never spent a proper evening with you."

I laughed, amused. "You never thought I was important enough."

He shook his head. "An American feminist," he pouted, "who hates to let a man flirt even a little bit! Let's go have dinner somewhere, and I'll make up for it."

After a lobster and white wine supper composed carefully from an eleven-page menu, we arrived by taxi at my studio. Somewhere along the way Jacques had picked up the newest Beaujolais. I searched the kitchen for glasses worthy of the wine while Jacques, I suppose, silently calculated the monetary potential of every painting in the room. Then I in turn sat at the table, measuring the width of his shoulders, the weight of his thighs, the firmness of his tight, muscular rear. When he turned around, he caught my careful appraisal of his body, and he raised his brows.

"The artist at work."

"I learn by studying."

"That explains pieces like this," he said, standing before *Seraphina*. "She is truly magnificent." He came over to me, leaning down to speak in a rough whisper. "In fact, she's almost as beautiful as you."

His strong hands lifted me easily into his arms. He caught my lower lip between his teeth and sucked my tongue hard into his mouth. I was submerged in his scent of salty bay rum as his fingers steadied my head.

"Very nice," he murmured, kissing me again.

Then his lips were on my face, my neck, and my mouth again, and he leaned hard against me, some imagined dance beat driving his pelvis forward in a slow, sure rhythm.

No, I thought, as his electric hips shot a crackling jolt against my celibacy. No, no, no. This was too fast. I wanted the chance to decide, to choose, to *desire* before giving myself to a man. I tensed up, and Jacques reached down, pushing my hand against the mound at the front of his trousers.

"Let's play sculptor," he suggested, a taunting triumph in his eyes. Without another word he began unzipping my scarlet dress. His hands slid the fabric away from my shoulders, then gathered up my breasts, his fingers tugging at my nipples. My own flesh came angrily to life. The edges of the room softened. And my resolve to remain manless began to waver.

"Slow down, baby. This is too fast," I gasped, the words lost in the insolent probing of his mouth. I thought he laughed as he began pulling me firmly toward the bed. His tuxedo pants fell, the suspenders cracking sharply on the wooden floor. He sent one of his shoes rolling toward the table.

"In France," he murmured as the mattress welcomed his weight, "it's considered bad luck to make plans before making love." Planting his hands on my hips, he pulled me down hard to straddle him. For an instant I teetered on a pivot between the indescribable sweetness of being one with a man, and the hideous truth that sleeping with Jacques was little more than sex in exchange for his gallery.

Holding myself back against the pleasure that was already flooding my body, I told myself that this must be a painless price to pay for the certainty of my future as an artist.

Then my future changed.

"Chloe!"

The voice was so ravaged, so ferocious, so *close*, that Jacques and I both froze.

"Chloe! Open the door!" The command reverberated weirdly

down the echoing tunnel of the stairwell. Then there was a violent pounding. Someone was kicking the door so hard that its hinges groaned.

"What the fuck is this?" Jacques cursed. We leapt to our feet, snatching our clothes together. The banging increased. Jacques looked at me strangely, his eyes suspicious. Drugs? The police? Boyfriend or husband? Before I could say anything, the kicking started again, and I crossed the room quickly.

"Who is it?"

"You know who it is! Chloe, let me in!"

I paused, a molten anger hardening the spaces in my heart that only moments before were open to surrender. "Go away," I said in a low voice, my head close to the wood.

"I'm not going anywhere!" He slammed at the door with his fist, and I snatched it open in a reflex of outrage.

Lucien Laurent. He stood before me in the same clothes he had worn that morning, but his tie was gone and his hair was matted as if he had driven through the city at high speed. Chest heaving, he stared at me with savage eyes.

Lucien Laurent. The "stranger" from only hours before. I looked down, noticing that his hands were clenched into fists.

"No, Lucien," I said in the calmest voice possible.

"Yes, Chloe," he rasped.

It took all of my courage not to move, not to allow him into the room. "Go away," I repeated, forcing exactly the same pitch, the same tone into the words as before.

He lifted his head, his eyes fierce. Then, with terrifying intuition, he said, "Have I interrupted a private showing?"

I began to close the door. He caught the edge with one white-knuckled hand. "Chloe," he said ominously. "Now."

Again I attempted to close the door, and once again he caught it. I stepped back in surprise at his boldness, and he shoved past me to find himself face-to-face with Jacques.

Jacques was at least a full head taller than Lucien, but he was of a leaner, finer build. The gracefulness of the black man was underscored by his calm posture, while Lucien stood, a glowering study in compacted violence. I retreated to the door while the men regarded each other, two wild stags with raised antlers.

"Are you insane?" Jacques asked darkly.

Lucien took in the other man's clothing, the open bottle, and the tension in the room. His eyes leapt to my loosened dress. "So, Chloe. A different set of rules?"

"This is no game, Lucien."

Upon hearing Lucien's name, Jacques began to smile. He nodded his head in an imperceptible gesture of recognition, then looked coolly at me.

"Chloe, shall I see this gentleman out?"

"You're not seeing me anywhere," Lucien growled, taking a step toward Jacques.

"You don't own me, Lucien!"

His eyes shot to me. "And he does?"

I glanced at Jacques, who raised his eyebrows. "It seems that we're both quite taken with you. So tell us, Chloe: what do *you* want?"

The room went airtight. I stood rooted to my silence, unable to choose. Because Lucien was right, Michael. Paris was no sanctuary, and I had seen it, breathed it, tasted it every day since my arrival. I had come to the City of Light to find freedom, and instead I had discovered poverty, racism, and loneliness.

But I had known other miseries, too—my inability to paint in America, my wretched marriage, my dark, dark childhood. I had to ensure myself a future—a chance to become what I had come to Paris to be.

Lucien Laurent meant nothing to me. It was my art that mattered. I needed a gallery. A place for *Seraphina*. A gallery was the key to my future.

"Lucien," I stated, loathing myself with every cell of my being, "I want you to go."

"I can't leave," he said with terrifying perception, "because giving yourself to him would mean you've become one of *them*."

I felt tears leap into my eyes.

Jacques saw the tears. "Decide," he said.

"I can't," I stammered, my voice faltering.

"Then I'll decide for you," Jacques said. In a swift movement, he snatched his jacket from the back of the chair and walked up close to me. There was a menacing shadow in his defeated eyes. He smiled mockingly and lifted my face with his fingers. Then he kissed me, slowly, first on the left cheek and then on the right, and without a word pushed past Lucien.

I wiped my tears on the scarlet fabric as the door slammed. Lucien stood without moving, without even looking at me. When he spoke, there was no triumph in his voice.

"Today you looked so different—such a part of their world. But, Chloe—" he reached down and touched the flaming fabric "—I don't need you this way."

"Don't talk to me about *need*, Lucien." I lowered my head to hide my tears.

There was another second of stillness, then he said, "I didn't admit to myself until this morning how terribly I do need you."

"You fucking white bastard," I whispered in English.

"I need you so much. Please believe me." He brushed the hair away from my face, gathering me into his arms. "I'm sorry I hurt you. But I was so afraid. So afraid . . ."

I don't remember hearing any sound, except our breathing, after that. Because we were making love in a kind of frenzy, our clothes cast away and eyes clenched tight against the light. There was the somber room and the bed and the silence of a forbidden act. I was a girl again, filled with bittersweet hunger and unspeakable guilt. Lucien's hair trapped my fingers and his legs held me fast, his male scent saturating the chamber with the desire I'd sensed in every woman who had said his name. There was darkness in the pleasure—darkness in the way his body consumed mine, taking me whole and deep with an instinctual skill that swallowed up my resistance.

And then came that last, fleeting moment when I knew that there was no way of protecting myself. Drawn by the flecks in his eyes, the insistence of his touch, and even the sweet acidity of his sweat, I opened the passages and let him enter the fortress of my flesh, and the untried tower of my heart.

I stopped speaking, trying to quell the tears that always came with my memories of Lucien. You watched me, deeply moved, then pulled me into a hug. I understood that you wanted to protect me from my sadness. But, Michael, I hadn't even come to the difficult parts of my story.

"I've always wondered how it happened," you said quietly. "You left D.C. so determined to stay free. And that just seemed to vanish."

"I couldn't describe my attraction to Lucien, because I didn't understand it, myself."

You smiled wryly and nodded in understanding. "I saw Drew a whole year before I ever mentioned him to you. And that was when I called to tell you that we were getting married."

We laughed, and I wiped my tears as you stared at the blank canvases.

"It's funny: as much as we love and trust each other, neither one of us could admit that we were giving away our hearts. Does that make us weak, or strong, or what?"

"It depends, I guess, on who we gave them to," I answered.

"Well, Chloe, since this is a night for confessions, maybe it's time I told you the whole truth about how Drew won my heart. And how Jonathan Bennett took it away."

TWO

Well, Chloe, I guess my story really begins in 1981, on the afternoon I came to say good-bye to Andrew Dalton Northcross.

I'm sure that you can picture it: late summer in southern coastal England. Wildflowers leaping out of gardens and the gray sea frothing with holiday-makers. The campus is almost deserted, but the sleepy university town of Levant Hill is bustling with tourists from London and Birmingham and Manchester. They find the town quaintly beautiful, as I had when I arrived the year before. But now, at the end of my appointment as a guest lecturer, I've decided to put my life in England behind me. I've got exciting plans for the future, Chloe. Nothing, and no one, is going to stand in my way.

I can still remember even the most minute details of that day: the bitter nutmeg and cinnamon scent of coffee squeezed through pipe smoke; porcelain clicking and glass striking wood while accenting laughter or disagreement; sun filtered through noontide rain, warming the sills of leaded windows stacked with textbooks, and Keith Jarrett playing in the background.

I remember: My fingers type out invisible poetry on a book cover beside a ring of coffee from the saucer. There are rings on three of my fingers. We don't hear the easy rambling of the tourists' voices; we can't think of anyone else. Our concentration floats on the sea of sound, the waves of smoke and steam and the late summer sun.

As usual, our talk is both nonsensical and filled with great meaning. He speaks in a solemn voice, and I respond in turn. This conversation is the lifeline that ties me to the man I love. The man I am prepared never to see again.

His assertion: "And that's why this text is ultimately Eurocentric in its undercurrents. Ericson knows nothing of the Sub-Saharan African cultural tradition."

My answer: "He'd probably argue that the values intrinsic to African life were subsumed by European traditions."

"Personally speaking, I despise tradition."

"You can afford to. You're an Englishman who specializes in African literature. You've built your career on rejecting tradition."

He laughs softly, sucks on his pipe, and looks at me; but my attention is drawn over his shoulder to some Impressionist abstract of summer leaves. He slips his hand next to mine, comparing our fingers. He is silent. He takes this moment to consider me.

Finally: "Three days, then?"

"Then what?" My thoughts return to the table, and I glance over at him.

"You're really returning to America in three days?"

"I don't have a job in England. And your immigration service stamped 'One Year' in bloodred letters in my passport."

He puffs, and the smoke separates us. He shifts his legs, settles into his chair.

"Who will discuss books with me when you're gone?"

"You'll have no trouble finding my replacement."

"But no one will ever argue with me like you do."

"That's likely."

"Am I so intimidating?"

"What's intimidating is how much you enjoy arguing."

Now Drew's smile broadens, and I'm smiling, too. There seems to be a hush in the coffeehouse while he concentrates on his next words.

"Is there someone special waiting for you at home?"

"Actually—" I grasp a handful of braids, letting them drift through my fingers "—there are several someones."

"Tell them that one of the professors doesn't want you to leave."

I shrug. "That won't matter. I always do what I want."

"Then I guess he'd better convince *you*."

"That won't be easy. I have no reason to stay."

"What if one of the professors was in love with you?"

"You're talking in the third person, Professor Northcross. What does the first person want to say?"

He takes a deep breath. "Stay."

"Because you want me to?"

"Because *you* want to."

We stare at each other, both surprised at how soft and strident our voices have become.

"I'd have a whole lot to teach you."

"I've dedicated my life to learning."

"We haven't even . . ."

Our heads are close together, and I can smell the pipe tobacco and coffee, along with his scent of lavender.

"Teach me *that*, too."

For just a moment, I pause. "I'm already packed."

"I'll unpack you."

"I have nowhere to live."

"Live with me."

"The immigration police—"

"Can be dealt with."

"Not unless I'm married."

The room holds its breath. "Then I'm asking you to marry me."

"I don't believe in marriage."

"Before I met you, neither did I."

The roar of the coffeehouse rushes around us, drowning out the sound of our breathing.

"Professor," I ask, "is this just the Good-bye Sweepstakes?"

"The prize?"

"Predeparture sex."

"No, beloved adversary. I want you to live with me and be my wife."

We sit together, looking at each other as if the afternoon would never end.

"There is one thing—" Drew says, suddenly piercing the wonder "—what have you done with that white dress?"

It was the white dress, Chloe, that began it all.

Levant Hill was a small liberal arts university located an hour from London and highly respected for its international faculty and gifted students. Housed in a cluster of restored seventeenth-century buildings, the institution prided itself on its success as a tightly knit academic community enriched by the contributions of many visiting scholars.

Andrew Dalton Northcross's lectures had always been a focal point for some of the liveliest political discourse on campus. Many brilliant students attended because he was a recognized expert on African literature. Others came because of his legendary personality or his controversial views. But at least the first two rows of the auditorium were always filled with women who wanted nothing more than to listen to his voice, watch him move, and simply dream.

Gracefully tall and possessing a deep, emotive voice, Drew had a face that was carved from a schoolgirl's fantasies. He sometimes joked about the discomfort caused by a beauty that made perfect strangers turn and stare. But he didn't hesitate to use his green eyes, pouting lips, and cleft chin, when he saw a woman he desired.

For years his position as the Faculty Bachelor had given rise to vigorous debate and vicarious pleasure around the campus. He fastidiously avoided all contact with his colleagues' wives and daughters, and he never dated a woman who was not at least in the final stages of her dissertation (because he appreciated the intellectual rapport) and at least twenty-five years old (to avoid gossip and the charges of cradle robbing).

He had once embarked on a particularly passionate affair with an extremely gifted Brazilian linguist. She loved becoming enraged over trifles and was fanatically possessive, which did not sit well with a man of Drew's character. Their public arguments entertained the university for an entire term, and he was very relieved when she boarded the return flight to São Paolo.

The term before my arrival he had dated an East German who'd been allowed three precious months outside the Wall. She returned willingly to her homeland, and he hadn't tried to stop her, because although she was dark and brooding with hints of the Slav in her golden eyes, Drew never confused desire with devotion.

So when yet another term began, the thirty-seven-year-old Andrew Northcross, already a full professor, strode into the lecture hall with his head held high, assured that somewhere in the crowd of admiring faces waited the woman who would intrigue, or at least amuse him for the weeks to come.

And indeed, destiny complied. He glanced around the room, his green eyes coming to rest on the splendidly simple white dress near the top of the amphitheater. His face revealed that he liked what he saw. The dress brought out the muted gold in my tawny skin. Two or three of my intricate braids slipped teasingly across my piercing gaze as I waited, fists pressed into high cheekbones, to judge him.

Looking out into the sea of faces, Drew took a deep breath and a hush blanketed the room. He began to speak, and the other hundred or so students began taking notes. I listened without moving, a column of cool in a room of gently swaying wrists. As the hour progressed I watched him watching me. At the end of the lecture a number of students rushed up to greet him, and I vanished while he was surrounded by admirers.

Fresh out of graduate school, I'd accepted a one-year position in Levant Hill to find out how the Brits felt about people of color. I came to Drew's lecture only because I was curious about a white man teaching African literature. Curious to see if, indeed, he had overcome the prejudices of growing up in a white, colonial nation. I didn't expect much—this was England, after all.

I went to the next lecture in the handwoven skirt you brought back from Morocco, Chloe, and it took him a while to find me in my corner, just four rows from the front. I saw him examine the pattern in the fabric, trying to guess its origin. And I boldly met his gaze as he talked about African women on Caribbean plantations. Once again, at the end of the hour, I vanished while he fended off a rush of groupies.

Then I was assigned a tutorial at the same time as the lecture. I resigned myself to never learning the answers to my unasked questions about the famous Drew Northcross. Until destiny again intervened.

I attended the new faculty party with a group of lecturers from the Department of Romance Languages. I was wearing my white dress, of course (it was the only nice dress I owned). And suddenly he was standing beside me, eclipsing the others as if they were made of mist.

He was taller than I'd imagined, and I'm a tall woman. His eyes took in my restless dissatisfaction, the low-burning anger he'd often felt as a younger man.

"Michael Davies." I extended my hand.

"Drew Northcross."

"I know. I've attended your lectures."

Only two, said his light green eyes.

"Your views on the devaluation of black women in slavery are compelling, but I think you're completely mistaken." I laughed lightly, offering him a challenge.

"Really, Miss Davies?"

"I believe that the shared labor practices of agronomic West African society were not drastically altered in the fields of the plantations. Black women really lost their social status with the imposition of an Anglo-European family structure that denigrated working women—"

"This sounds like the beginning of a long conversation."

"That depends on whether you'll listen to a different point of view."

Drew really looked at me then—at my mouth and braids, my shoulders and the tilt of my head—as I stared straight at him. "And by the way," I added, "I am *Doctor* Davies."

"Thank you for informing me. I wouldn't want to miss a chance to address you by your title."

We went on looking at each other a moment too long. A pulsing at his temple quickened. Then we both realized that the room was watching us.

He moved away to the next group of people and the next conversation. But secretly he observed the white dress, making note of my voice, my laugh, my inclination to stand on one straight hip while throwing out the other leg, my pelvis tilted forward. He read the athlete's grace and the scholar's power, and he knew that I was willing. Yes, he saw it in the way I lifted my head from time to time to meet his eyes across the room. We were already engaged in the game; it was now a question of how long both of us would want to play it.

Eleven months, Chloe. It was eleven months from the night of that party until the day I came to the coffeehouse to say good-bye.

We arrived at Drew's flat that afternoon, breathless from four flights of stairs and a painful desire that stopped us from speaking for the first time in almost a year. I had just agreed to become his wife, though I had never so much as eaten a meal with him. We had never been on a date. Never seen a film together. Never held hands and never kissed. I had never been to his apartment. He had never seen me in less clothing than the white dress I had worn to the party eleven months before.

During those eleven months Drew and I had met every Friday afternoon in that run-down coffeehouse on the edge of campus. I had wandered in the first time by chance, craving an espresso after weeks of drinking flaccid English tea. Drew strolled in a few moments later; he was a regular patron. He greeted me and politely asked how I'd been doing since the party, and our conversations began. In the ensuing weeks we arrived at the same hour, and sat at the same corner table, and talked for two hours, sometimes three. Then he always glanced at his watch, excused himself, and disappeared. I never saw him during the week. I never told anyone about it. And I never knew whether he would actually appear the following Friday.

Why did I do it? Boredom, at first. He was the most interesting man I'd met in England. With time, however, things grew so intense that I couldn't imagine my life without those secret Friday meetings.

Over the months Drew scrutinized my muscular thighs, high

breasts, and flawless skin—while we discussed everything from politics in Sub-Sahara Africa to Neo-Realism in Italian cinema. Having grown up during Vietnam, Selma, and Watergate, I offered him novel insights on race and class and culture. It was one such idea, I explained, that had brought me to England.

"Jane Eyre."

"Jane Eyre?"

"Yes. I read it and my life was never the same."

"But your doctorate is in black literature."

"There's a very important black woman in that novel."

"It seems you'd have to go to the Caribbean, not to England, to understand Bertha Mason."

"Oh no, my dear Dr. Northcross. It was England that drove her mad, not Jamaica."

"But it wasn't Rochester's fault. Her own mother and grandmother were mad before her."

"Come now, Professor. You and I both know that it was that classic divide called 'the color line' that destroyed both Bertha and her mother. That line was created by slavery. After all, Creoles are the spawn of a racially polarized world that enacts its sexual fantasies on women who can claim membership in neither racial group, and are thus without social protection."

"Great lord, Dr. Davies!" he exclaimed ironically. "I thought *Jane Eyre* was about a poor man torn between the safety of a civilized British relationship and the threat of complete moral corruption in the primitive, pagan colonies."

"Don't be simplistic, Dr. Northcross."

"You identify with this Bertha Mason?"

"I wanted to understand something of the culture that created her."

"And what have you learned about us?"

I paused, looking directly into his eyes. "Far more than you want me to know."

He managed a laugh when I said that, sitting across from him at our usual Friday table. And his sensuous eyes told me for the hundredth time that he wanted to hold me late into the night, telling me tales of his past life in Africa.

Finally, that chance had come. At the door to his flat Drew searched his pockets for his key, a terrifically banal act that seemed to acquire metaphorical significance as we carried our relationship over the threshold and into its next life.

He led me into his apartment and then turned shyly away. I found myself in the center of a pool of dusty sunlight, glancing at the bookcases lining the walls, the potted plants and trinkets that were the flotsam of his previous love affairs. My hands were thrust casually into my pockets, and I let my backpack slide down my arm until it hit the floor. Then I stood up, stretching to my full height, and shrugged.

"Why did you keep this a secret for so long? It's nice here."

"Do you think so?"

"Don't you?" I sauntered toward him, lowering my voice. "Or was it too risky, Professor?" Reaching up, I touched his heart. "You don't know whether this is sex, or love, or neither, or both."

Drew covered my hand. "Do you?"

Again I shrugged. "I don't think either one of us knows the truth, yet."

With this, I moved his hands to my breasts. He looked down, feeling my nipples harden under his touch. This was too easy; this wasn't what he'd imagined.

"Dr. Davies—"

"Don't complicate anything, Professor. We've talked long enough."

Standing on my toes, I brushed my lips along his pulsing throat. His hands moved to my hips. Again he hesitated.

"Michael?" His eyes were so dark that they were little more than shadows.

"Drew?" I tested his name softly.

Something happened in him, then: We were no longer strangers who talked ourselves into intimacy. The closeness was breathlessly real, and far more than physical desire. He leaned forward but paused just as his mouth met mine. There was a moment's hesitation, time enough for me to wonder what his lips would feel like. His breath was warm and sweet, and he made a low sound, a kind of reedy sigh that brought his mouth gently, probingly to mine.

He moved closer, perhaps driven by a desire to love my body as he'd loved my mind. We had splintered ourselves away from our sexual selves for too long. Now it was time to be whole.

And so we lay together, stroking and kissing until there were tears in our eyes, and we both laughed soundlessly at the way our bodies responded to each other's touch. Then I held his hips and pulled him slowly and deeply into me. We looked into each other's eyes and together found our rhythm. The union seemed to last a long time—longer than I would have believed possible, except that fused together, we were transported to a place where all was sensation, and our skin and hair and breath were electric beneath an undulating current that was deeper than our heartbeats. Never had I been as close to a man; never had I surrendered so much to a stranger. Never had I found myself staring into my lover's eyes with such complete trust. I heard his urgent voice, telling me what it felt like for him and asking softly what would please me. His hoarse whisper said that he loved me, and we got there together, filled and surrounded with each other.

Confessions made during sex usually evaporate after the passion. Drew left the curtains open and the lights off as night fell, and we shared a cup of ginger tea, looking out over the campus. I lay on my back with my braids splayed across the bed. He covered me with his robe while he padded into the kitchen, and returned to find me warm and naked, a landscape of hills and valleys and forests and his robe tossed disdainfully to the floor. He sat beside me and we both waited for the sense of irritation that always comes after sex—the need to be alone, whole and at peace, before some careless remark breaks the spell woven by physical pleasure.

But that feeling didn't arrive. I looked at his body, marveling that only minutes before it had been part of my own. The room was filled with my fleshy scent of jasmine mixed with sandalwood. I reached up to stroke his square shoulder.

"You're beautiful, Professor Northcross. I can't see you as a white woman sees you. But I'll admit that you are quite some man."

He was surprised; he tilted his head. "Do you think that race has something to do with this?"

"Have you ever had sex with a black woman before?"

"Every woman is different, Michael. You're an individual."

"Of course—I forgot you lived in Africa."

"Africa has nothing to do with us."

"You didn't have sex with African women?"

"If I did, I wouldn't dishonor them now."

"And you're sure you're not playing out some ritual from your background? You know, those fantasies about master and slave?"

"Drink some tea, Michael."

I rolled over. "Tea after sex. It seems so Commonwealth."

"It will help you collect your thoughts."

"My thoughts aren't scattered."

"Your brains are," he said coldly. There was a moment of tense silence. Then he spoke. "You didn't imagine it, woman. When I said I love you, I meant it. Not because my ancestors enslaved and oppressed your ancestors. Not because I'm tempted by your 'dusky' skin. Not even because of some latent desire to 'civilize' you. I simply love you, even if you'd like it to be more perverse."

"And tomorrow?"

"And always. I've loved very few people in my life. When I say it, I mean it."

I looked out into the night. Drew leaned forward and kissed the crown of my head. Then he sighed. "I'm about to lose you, and I've hardly begun to know you."

"Then hold me, Professor."

He held me throughout the night, touching and kissing me until our passion rose again and again. And then he told me stories about his childhood years in a boarding school, and his young adulthood in Africa, and kept me spellbound until dawn.

We slept until noon, then went to my room to collect my bags. And then the second evening fell, and I strolled nude through the flat.

"Do you need a shirt or something?" He was standing at the kitchen counter, cutting onions.

"I'm perfectly comfortable," I replied.

"Perhaps I'm not," he said.

My hands went to my hips. "Can't stand to see it if you're not fucking it?"

Putting the knife down carefully, he regarded me with judging eyes. "Do you want to have sex all the time?"

"I thought you'd offered me a home."

"Then treat it with some respect."

"There's nothing 'disrespectful' about my body."

"But there's a time and place for everything."

"I don't have to share your values about nudity."

"This has nothing to do with values."

"Both class *and* culture, Professor."

"Then I'm just another middle-class prig?"

"You're just another white man who likes it with black women—in secret."

"Don't reduce me to a racial stereotype!"

"Then what offends you? The same body that gives you so much pleasure?" Now I was truly angry.

"Michael, is this some kind of test?"

"If it is, you've already failed."

"Because I asked you to dress?"

"Because I'm not on this earth to please you."

This was obviously a revelation to him. He watched me turn and walk to the bedroom, where I lay down, naked. After a while he came in.

"I guess I'm not used to sharing my flat."

"I've still got a plane ticket."

"I don't want you to leave."

"You're not ready for me to stay."

"But I can't lose you."

"I'm not *yours* to lose."

"That's true," he said, his voice trembling. "Whether you use that ticket must ultimately be your decision."

He left the room. A few moments later I rose and began packing. Drew stood wordlessly behind the kitchen counter and watched me pass the door as I collected the few personal items I'd taken out of my bags. Finally I dressed myself. When at last I emerged from the bedroom, suitcases in hand, I found him standing there, still holding an unsliced onion.

"Why are you doing this?" he asked, his voice rising. "You said—you said you love me." Drew was aware that a note of pleading had crept into his voice. I stood with one leg out, my weight balanced on the other, holding my bags.

"I haven't agreed to live with you, Drew."

"I asked you to *marry* me."

I pushed out a long breath. Sinking down on one of the suitcases, I leaned forward, bringing my hands together and resting my arms on my knees.

"I'll be honest with you, Drew. A long time ago I made a vow not to let anybody get in the way of my dreams. Spending the rest of my days at this quaint seaside university with its stone buildings and classrooms with beamed ceilings just isn't in my cards. Look, man—after this job, my next destination was Cuba!

"And frankly," I added with a shrug, "I'm not ready for a permanent relationship. I like men and I intend to enjoy them. I'm told that you aren't exactly programmed for fidelity, either."

He started to speak, but I held up my hands.

"I'll admit that I wanted to have sex with you from the first moment I saw you. And it's been a great adventure, secretly meeting in our little coffeehouse all these months, keeping things purely platonic. But marriage? That's a whole different thing."

"I could make you happy, Michael."

"Here? Without a mirror I'd forget what my people look like."

"This campus has students from all over—"

"Brown and yellow people don't exactly qualify as substitutes, Drew. And what about kids? It's hard enough to raise biracial children without doing it in this isolation."

"Then we'll leave England."

"And go—?"

"Back to Africa. It's something I've always intended to do."

I raised my brows. "Whew. It's pretty hard for me to trump that card."

Drew stirred. "Do you see this as a game?"

"Come on, Professor. We both know it's a game. And you don't want to live without it." I stood up restlessly. "Perhaps no other woman has ever played so well. Perhaps you've grown a little bored with having to find a new opponent each and every term."

"Do you honestly believe I only see you as an 'opponent'?"

"Lots of women would be delighted to have sex with you! But how many women can talk and think and challenge you? I'll bet you've been searching for a long time. And when I came along, you decided to wait with the sex and see just how far the 'intellectual mating' could go."

"You've wanted it, too."

"Of course, Drew. But not for the rest of my life."

"People change and relationships change. We've already moved into a new phase."

"You can't even look at my body!"

"Did you never think that it's just too much for me?"

"What, a woman's body?"

"No," he said. "*Your* body. The body of the woman with your mind and your spirit, your strength and your wisdom. I've never known anyone like you."

I lowered my head. "Listen: I don't need a man who has turned me into some kind of icon. I'm a woman. I have fears and weaknesses and needs." I raised my head. "I know that I play some games too well. I've had to in order to succeed in your world."

Walking around the counter, Drew knelt down and took my hands. "Michael, I'm nearly forty. Until I met you I thought that a permanent relationship was merely a foxhole, a hiding-out place that people crawl into because they can't face life alone. And then I saw you and everything changed." He lifted my chin and looked into my eyes.

"I thought that if I pursued you like an ordinary woman, inviting you to dinner and movies and weekend excursions, you'd think it was just for sex. But I believed that if I treated you differently—that if I showed you how much I value your ideas and your feelings—perhaps there was a chance."

"But you're still a stranger."

"I will always love you, Michael. I'll always be honest with you." He paused. "There'll be other planes. For now, say you'll stay."

We remained in that pose, with Drew kneeling before me in perfect vulnerability. I stared into his green eyes. *On my honor,* I thought, *I vowed to be a strong black woman, to become a success, and never to let a man turn me away from my dreams*. Well, wasn't it a sign of strength to choose love over countless flittering relationships? Couldn't our willingness to commit ourselves to each other be considered a kind of success? And why shouldn't a man share my dreams?

"Professor, I'm willing to give it a try. But first you've got to pass inspection."

His brows went up. "By your father?"

"Hell no. By somebody who *really* loves me."

Of course, Chloe, that was you.

So we flew down from London to Nice. You met us at the airport that broiling September afternoon, walking out onto the shimmering tarmac with the bearing of a queen. Drew watched as you held me close, and blinked self-consciously when you looked into his eyes.

You chauffeured us up the steep, winding hills that formed the base of the Alps, your little Deux Chevaux sputtering and complaining. Rounding a sharp ridge where the road licked the cliff, we gasped at the sight of Nice, its houses like sugar cubes tumbling down to the turquoise coast below.

Finally we caught a glimpse of the restored villa cresting a copse of resinous pines. "Oh my," Drew said appreciatively as we ascended the long, poplar-lined drive and came to a grinding halt beside the house. The rows of French doors were thrown open, and we could hear voices conversing in the pauses between Piaf ballads. Yanking up the hand brake, you threw a wry smile over your shoulder.

"My artists are planning a little reception to welcome you, so act like you're extremely pleased!"

You gave us a small room at the rear of the house, the room once inhabited by your former husband, and as soon as we were alone Drew asked whether you were married.

"No," I answered ironically, "although Chloe has a way of finding and discarding men at a moment's notice."

"Then you're two of a kind," he replied, taking me into his arms.

"I'm not talking about lovers," I explained. "Chloe has a long history of living with people she doesn't love and never quite getting it right with the ones she does."

"I won't let you make that mistake," he promised as his lips found mine.

As soon as I got back into my clothes, I dashed up the stairs to find you in the studio with one of the artists. You motioned for me to enter, and I went out to the balcony, where I listened to you explaining the benefits of using a harder brush when blending pigments.

After a while you joined me, and we stood together, staring at the gray-blue sea. Strands of your hair, hennaed to a burnished mahogany, peeped out from your loosely tied scarf, and I could see the outlines of your breasts through your India-cotton blouse. You didn't look much different from the woman I'd met in Washington eleven years before. That is, except for the lingering sadness in your eyes.

"So you've burned your ticket, Little Sis?" You slipped an arm around my waist.

"Actually, I stashed it in my journal, just in case. It's good for a year."

"Smart thinking. Things can look pretty different after you've been here a while."

"Look who's talking! I wouldn't even be here if not for you."

"That's crazy. The day we met you were already planning your escape!"

"Come on, Chloe. You paid for me to come to Aix those three summers. And I only finished grad school because you took care of my tuition after Grandma died—"

"My money didn't earn those grades, Michael. You're here because you had the discipline and the willpower."

"I was only living up to your image!" I laughed, but you shrugged in response.

"You left me no choice, Michael. I wouldn't want to let my smart and sassy little sister down."

"Well, since I'm staying in England, we'll see a lot more of each other."

"That could be too much of a good thing," you replied. "I won't be able to make up any pretty stories about my life anymore."

"You don't have to make anything up. You've got a wonderful house, a fabulous career, and the chance to travel the world—"

You looked at me as if daring me to say what we both knew to be true: That you were living your life without the man you loved.

Instead we hugged and stared at the distant, patient sea.

"Remember the dress I wore at your wedding?" I asked, and you nodded, the orange sky illuminating your face.

"I had it on when I met Drew."

"Well, then, something good did come of my marriage," you remarked dryly.

Later that evening we drove down into Old Nice and dined at a sidewalk bistro on the beach.

"Michael says you lived for a time in Africa," you remarked to Drew as I savored a bowl of fresh sea mussels.

"Yes, I spent ten years in Rhodesia. I was a student first, then a teacher in a small village on the eastern border. It was very difficult to leave." He looked across the table to me. "I hope to go back one day."

"What's stopping you?"

"When I returned to England, I wrote a book that criticized white rule. I came to be considered somewhat of a spokesman for the black resistance. At present I'm *persona non grata* throughout southern Africa."

I looked up in surprise. "You never told me that, Drew! Are there any other big surprises in store for me?"

"A lifetime full," he replied, fixing me with his after-midnight eyes.

The next few days passed in a kind of bliss. Drew loved everything about you, Chloe—your house, the rocky hills that he could wander for hours, and the extraordinary paintings that seemed to fill every corner of every room. You talked together easily, leading me to the realization that actually he was closer to you in age than to me. He shared your passion for travel, and had visited many of the places about which you'd written to me over the years. And he loved the art of conversation; he loved talking with the artist-tenants who shared your home and were willing to discuss any subject that flew in through the window. He spent many hours challenging both you and your artists to endless games of backgammon on the board Emil brought you from Africa.

That week in Nice also gave us time to settle something that kept nagging at me.

"You're thirty-seven and you've never wanted to get married?" I asked him one afternoon as we sat on a ridge overlooking the sea.

"Once, perhaps, but it didn't work out." He looked at me perceptively and shook his head. "You don't think I'm capable of giving up other women, do you?"

"I'm not sure I'm ready to be with just one man," I answered, meeting his gaze. "I've always believed in open relationships—you know, where both partners could be free, as long as they were completely honest about their feelings."

He looked away, tracking a lone seagull as it plunged toward the water.

"Is that what you really want, Michael?"

I hesitated, wondering if one day I'd regret my words. "Yes, Drew."

On our last morning in Nice, when the other artists had abandoned the atelier for an excursion into the windy hills, you leaned forward at the great oak table and said, "Friends, it's time we got to work."

Drew looked up from his newspaper, and I put down my bowl of coffee.

"Can we help you do something?"

"Absolutely," you answered enigmatically. "But we'd better move fast if we want the best light."

The authority in your voice precluded further discussion, so we both rose immediately and followed you up the stairs to the bright studio. A large canvas was already prepped, its fine gray-white coat of paint nearly dry. Wordlessly Drew and I complied when you told us to undress. You posed us quickly, as if you knew exactly what you wanted.

For the rest of the morning the room was silent except for the rich planing of brushes and the melodious chanting of wind chimes in the fragrant garden below.

Later that day Drew and I ventured down to a beach and spent the afternoon among the last of the vacationers basking in the Riviera sun. When we returned, I was hungry and tired, and once alone in our little chamber, I stripped off my damp bikini and turned to face him.

"You spent the entire day staring at other women."

"Other women?" He reached up and stroked the concentric curves of my breasts formed by the red-brown aureoles and even darker nipples.

Troubled, I pulled on a dress and moved out of his reach. "I'm talking about those white women with whistling caverns beneath the peroxide and enough tanning oil to self-ignite in the sun. What is it, Drew? Ultimately a white man has to have a white woman?"

He leaned in the doorway, more amused than serious. "Race has nothing to do with my feelings for you."

"Of course it does. Race defines who I am."

"As does your intellect, your womanhood, your education, your economic class, and your personal experience."

"Yet all those things are still affected by my race!" I responded hotly.

He took a very deep breath, as if his next words were darkly inevitable. "A black man automatically understands you better?"

"It's instinctive, Drew. There are things that I don't even have to explain to a black man."

"What you share is an *American* racial experience. You might see the world very differently from an African."

"But race plays a decisive role in the way I live."

"While I agree that race may unite two people, there are other reasons to be together."

"I don't like white people, Drew."

He laughed ironically. "To be honest, Michael—neither do I. But that really isn't the issue, is it?"

"You're white—"

"I am Andrew Dalton Northcross. Don't hide behind your color just because something frightens you."

"You think your whiteness frightens me?"

"No. It's loving me that you're afraid of."

I stared into his eyes. "I was raised with a certain set of values. I only started dating white men because there were so few black men at school. And sex with white men was just a kind of exploration. Part of my studies—you know, the liberal arts and humanities. But getting *married* to one? That's like denying everything that happened over the last four hundred years. Giving myself to the oppressor. Exiling myself to a plantation."

"Don't let your background become a prison, Michael. Make this journey with me. If we let our love guide us, maybe we can find a way."

He reached for me, but I brushed past him and rushed up the steps to the quiet studio.

"Chloe," I blurted, "am I crazy? I hardly know him. He's ten years older than I am. And—" the words seemed to back up in my throat "—and he's *white*!"

You laid down your brush, wiping your hands on a paint-stained cloth. "Look at this, Michael."

You stepped back. A cool gray simmered behind a nexus of warmth: Drew's corded forearms were wrapped tenderly over my breasts, the tip of one hickory nipple visible beneath his olive skin. My expression was boldly direct, my eyes fierce as I stared out from the canvas. Drew, however, was pensive and calm, his dark head pressed lovingly and protectively against mine.

"This is my gift to you. It will see you through your lives together."

"Do you think I'm crazy?" I repeated, my eyes still fixed on the image of Drew.

You looked at me a long, silent moment. "Only if it's crazy to marry the man you love. And only if it's crazy to be loved as much as that man loves you."

It was all in the portrait, Chloe. Somehow you'd figured it out, while I was still struggling with the conundrums of melanin. You understood that Drew loved me, not because we were different, but because we were alike in so many ways. He loved my restless anger and thirst for independence. He shared my passion to travel the world. He embraced the unknown and hated the mundane. Drew loved the very things in me that had driven other men away.

And so we were married, very privately, near his home in Exmoor, then we honeymooned in a fishing village in windswept Cornwall. Walking for long hours along the rocky coast, we tried to map our way through the minefields that lay ahead.

"No one's going to accept me," I said, referring to our colleagues at the university. "I'm a black American woman in a very white, very male, very British world."

"You're a scholar and an intellectual," Drew replied, pulling my hand into the pocket of his jacket. "On top of that, you're smarter and more articulate than all of them put together."

"None of that's ever made a difference before," I argued, and he laughed.

"It will this time, Michael. I won't have it any other way."

"So what are you going to do about it?"

"I'm going to make it clear that if there's any nonsense, the university will lose not one, but *two* of the finest professors in the field," he said calmly.

"You'd leave Levant Hill for me?" I asked, astounded.

He stopped walking and looked deep into my eyes. "Don't you understand, Michael? There's nothing I wouldn't do for you."

I was offered a permanent position at the university, and found myself teaching just a classroom away from my husband—with the entire department speculating on how long our marriage would last. I tried to ignore the poorly concealed mockery in their sardonic smiles, but one day I burst into Drew's office, overcome with frustration.

"They treat me like I'm the Plaything of the Month!" I exclaimed.

"They're just disappointed," he softly replied, aware that a lecturer was lingering just outside the door. "For ten years they lived vicariously through my relationships. They can't forgive you for convincing the Faculty Bachelor to get out of the game."

"So now they're placing bets on when you'll go back to the table!"

"Their opinions meant nothing to me when I was single. They mean even less to me now."

He raised my chin and looked into my eyes.

"We have to create our own world, Michael. Our world has to be both bigger than this campus and yet so small that no one else can fit inside. We have to protect each other and fight for each other and guide each other through all the madness. It's the only way our love will survive."

We had to learn how to live together, which wasn't always easy for a thirty-seven-year-old bridegroom and his headstrong, decade-younger wife. We'd argue over trifles, become ridiculously angry, then reconcile in ways that made us want to argue some more.

The tiny community of Levant Hill had never seen anything like the Handsome Professor and his Queen of Sheba. When people on the streets turned and stared Drew stopped walking and stared right back, sending me into gales of laughter. The occasional rude comment in a market or pub elicited something even ruder from my husband. I was often surprised at how quickly and effectively he silenced the ignorant locals.

Even more stunning was the manner in which he handled our university colleagues. When someone remarked at a party that "Michael must know some kind of voodoo to have tamed 'Randy Andy,' " he answered without a beat: "If you had sex more than once a year, you'd certainly find it much easier to understand. . . ."

But how could they understand a bond that grew deeper with each passing day?

"Just ignore them," Drew muttered when a group of female graduate students snickered as we passed.

"I'll make those bubbleheaded bitches kiss my black ass—" I began, but he pulled me close, lowering his voice to a calming murmur.

"They just can't bear the thought that no one will ever love them the way that I love you."

"How do you know that?" I rasped, hoarse with anger.

"Because it's so obvious," he replied. "No one ever could."

"That's just romantic bull—"

"Not one of them has your beauty, your strength, or your wonderful mind, Michael. Won't you ever really believe that you deserve to be loved?"

Chloe, I looked into his face and saw that he meant it. Tears filled my eyes because whether I admitted it or not, some Made-in-America part of me refused to comprehend that any man could ever truly love me.

We haunted Brixton's Caribbean restaurants and the theaters of London's West End. I took up running and stopped eating meat, and Drew soon regretted teaching me to play squash. I came to love the cool gray mornings scented by the salty sea breeze and mild winters that rarely saw snow. Together we rambled across the British countryside visiting the ruins of ancient castles and abbeys.

My professional life developed, too. Even the most dismissive of our colleagues eventually admitted that I was their superior in the classroom—especially when term after term my classes were so packed that I had to turn countless students away. I was elected the department's official student adviser, and given special seminars and honors courses to teach.

During the university holidays Drew and I explored the rest of the world. I remember rambling through Barcelona's seaport, eating paella with sailors and their painted women. Fields of black tulips bowed before us under Holland's periwinkle skies. During the autumn we hiked the Welsh hills of Snowdonia, and the summer solstice saw desire beneath the druid moon near Stonehenge. I came to love Florence, Lisbon, and Cairo. And, of course, we celebrated each and every New Year's and Bastille Day with you in Nice.

We bought a rambling old house in Levant Hill and filled it with the spoils of our travels. Turkish kilims warmed the wide-planked floors, and teakwood screens made arabesques of the windows. Luminous folk art from Mexico and Haiti hung alongside your painting of the Moroccan city of Essouira. And we began a collection of Kore figurines from cultures the world over.

As the days turned into years, our passion never cooled. The sound of his voice continued to make my heart leap, and the tips of his fingers on my wrist were a promise of sweet, wicked pleasures to come. Drew could make me an offer with his eyes, and we'd end up wrestling like teenagers in the back of the car!

But our period of deepest happiness came when we took a leave from Levant Hill to teach in the emerging nation of Zimbabwe. We both came alive in this new world, Chloe, which was glowing with the fires of its liberation. With England and America far behind us, we, too, were freed to create our own kind of love.

Our home? A tiny house in Harare where we slept beneath a net and illuminated the rooms with fragrant oil lamps. Drew wore simple shirts and loose-fitting pants, and I shaved my head, wrapping myself in flowing robes that rustled gently with my steps. During the hottest months we'd bathe in cool water, then feast on fleshy mangoes and plantains. Many nights we lay awake, talking in whispers or making love to the timpani of monsoon rains.

At the college my lectures were animated, passionate, full of humor. For the first time in my life I felt my teaching had real meaning, for I was contributing to true social transformation. I cared deeply about my students, and they responded to me in like fashion. I discovered a whole continent of authors who'd been left out of my American education—and spent hours listening to *mbira* musicians as they gave voice to the struggles of their people. Inspired by the great cultures of southern Africa, I soon completed my first book, *The Griot's Song*.

Drew worked hard to establish links between black writers and British publishers, and our home was filled with animated discussion. He was often called upon to mediate some dispute between older white academics and their young black peers, and he became a leading adviser in the creation of the university's first African studies program.

Zimbabwe strengthened us, Chloe. I remember Drew's face as he watched me sway through the room to the sun-slatted light of the jalousies. I felt him taking measure of my contentment. I sensed his deepening dependence on my love. And sometimes, when he looked across at me during a vibrant discussion with our African friends, the desire in his eyes took my breath away.

Yes, it frightened me to be loved like that. Never in my life had I felt so valued. But there, in Zimbabwe, I was one with the world, and it seemed that anything was possible—yes, I could even lower my emotional armor and let the world come inside.

"Do you ever regret marrying me?" he asked one night as we lay together beneath the gently billowing mosquito net.

"You keep me too happy for that," I murmured, sighing as he lazily caressed the smooth skin of my inner thigh.

"Then you don't feel the need for other men?"

"Not *now*." I laughed.

The night was weighted with drilling insects and fluttering birdsong, and our lovemaking was so slow and easy that his next words almost drifted by.

"No other woman will ever be you, Michael." Soft lips grazed my breast.

"Are you still interviewing?" I whispered vaguely.

His forehead was pressed against mine, and his voice grew reedy and low. "Only to remind myself why I keep coming home to you."

From somewhere deep inside I struggled against the realization that this man I loved—the man with whom I was making love—was telling me that he still wanted other women. But he pulled me closer, saying, "No one else matters, Michael. No one. I will always, always love you."

And strangely, that thought quelled the secret part of me that watched the liquid haunches and subtle muscles of the black men of Zimbabwe. Like me, Drew still sometimes longed to taste the unknown. There was still some part of him to be conquered. To be desired. To be *won*.

"Just love me," I said to the night. "Love me and I'll always love you."

Our pact of love-trust was sealed with those words, and I truly believed that no one and nothing would ever tear us apart. There was no reason to think that anything, even our return to Levant Hill, would ever change our love.

And for twelve years, nothing did.

Year thirteen.

You remember, don't you, Chloe? Everything began to crumble during our thirteenth year. It was just after Drew's fiftieth birthday. We took the train up to York to attend the opening of your exhibition at the Minster Gallery, and we were having dinner in a quiet pub in the Shambles.

"Where's your next conference?" you asked him casually, and we were both surprised by his reply.

"It doesn't matter, Chloe, because they're all so bloody boring. I go to them only when they're stupid enough to pay me to speak."

"I thought you enjoyed the intellectual *intercourse* with your peers," I replied, referring to the rumors of his private "sessions" with female participants.

"Are you working on a manuscript, Drew?" That was you, Chloe, politely changing the subject.

"Seven books and a million articles after arriving in Levant Hill," he answered, "I hope I'll never write another word again."

"What are you talking about?" I cried, truly exasperated.

"The fact that I have nothing more to say."

"But everything you say changes your students' lives."

"Perhaps," he answered. "But how many times do I have to say it?"

Later that night we were closeted in your room, Chloe, while Drew slept restlessly down the hall.

"Did I hear some reference to Drew and other women?" you asked gently.

"He denies it, but our colleagues have brought back some interesting tales from their conferences." I paced to the window and stared blindly at the spires of York's towering gothic cathedral. "I guess it's really my fault."

"Your fault?"

"You remember my philosophy of free sex and true love, don't you? Well, when we first got married I insisted that we should have an open relationship. That we should be able to sleep with other people, as long as we were completely honest about it. And, of course, as long as we always came back to each other."

"So," you said quietly, "Drew's practicing what you preached?"

"I don't know," I answered with tears in my eyes. "I don't think he's lying, but sometimes I don't even recognize him anymore."

"Have you tried talking to him?"

"My mother taught me never to talk to strangers."

There was a long silence.

"Michael, do you remember when you first brought Drew to Nice? I took a good, careful look at this older man, this white man, who'd asked you to marry him. And one afternoon when you were playing with the cats I saw him gazing at you. In his eyes I saw his willingness to brave the ignorance of the world to be with you. I saw his vulnerability to your acceptance or rejection. I saw his desire, and his awe, and his confusion over his own emotions. Only once before have I seen a man so deeply in love."

Standing, you crossed the room and took my shoulders.

"Try to understand him," you said, seeing the helpless anger in my gaze. "He may just need some time."

"Time for what?" I cried in frustration, and you smiled patiently.

"Drew had been teaching for years before you even met, Little Sister. He may be tired of the sameness of his life."

"Or the sameness of his wife," I replied bitterly.

I no longer knew who he was, Chloe. Drew would vanish for hours into the study and come to bed late, too exhausted to make love. The mournful music of Miriam Makeba and Hugh Masekela—exiled African artists—became his closest companion. My concern was refused, my complaints ignored. Calmly, with a voice of stone, the man repeated time and time again that nothing was wrong. And you, Chloe, counseled me to wait.

I never dreamed that two years later I'd *still* be waiting.

Or that in the space of one evening everything would begin to change.

That night I came out of our bath in a black dress cut low and close, with a woven scarf from a market in Dakar draped loosely over my shoulder. Drew was moving back and forth between his suit bag, laid open on the bed, and the laundry basket. He was talking about the conference in New York that he'd returned from earlier that day. I neither listened nor responded. Finally he looked up.

"Where are you going?"

"The cocktail party for Jonathan Bennett."

"Christ! I'd forgotten about him."

"I called your hotel to remind you."

"I didn't get a message."

"You weren't in your room at five in the morning, so I didn't leave one."

"I went to the theater, got in late, and turned off the ringer."

"Of course you did," I said, picking up my wallet and keys. We'd had this argument so many times in the past two years that it seemed pointless to repeat it.

"Let's go out for a very quiet dinner, then stop by the party on the way home."

"Then I'd have to listen to your stories about the conference."

Once again he examined me, his eyes settling on my long legs. "Well, perhaps I'd better come with you. I want to be there when our guest professor gets a look at you in that dress."

This party was like every other faculty party since the distant days of the white dress. Too many people were crowded into the flat. Mozart poured from hidden speakers while cheese melted and biscuits moldered near an untouched fruit tray. The women, bearing the names of the educated elite—Daphne, Elizabeth, Emily, Ann, and Jane—all sported wool skirts and cashmere sweaters, strings of pearls and plain wedding bands, and brushed shoulder-length hair from wan faces.

Enter the black dress, cut low over bronzed skin, and the flash of the gold-threaded kinte scarf. I stepped into the room and struck a subtle pose, enjoying the piranha stares. Coming in behind me, Drew lowered his head to avoid hitting the door frame. Women's smiles deepened at his arrival, a casual hunger flittering in their eyes. He made his way toward a bottle-laden table, grasping the shoulders of friends and holding, for a moment, the hands of their wives.

"Good lord, Drew, " someone cried, "has keeping up with Michael put that white in your hair?"

"Naturally," he answered without a trace of irony. "It's hard work pleasing such a beautiful wife."

In a darkened corner a small circle congregated around a black man in a sports jacket: Dr. Jonathan Bennett, our guest professor from America. Someone made a joke, and Bennett laughed, shifting his muscular frame easily. From time to time his eyes foraged the crowd as if searching for a familiar face.

"How did you and Drew spend the holiday?" Ann Davison asked me.

"We were with my friend Chloe in Nice."

"Well, we never got farther than the Scottish Highlands. Eric's 'ancestry' kick." Ann raised her glass toward her husband, who stood talking with another professor. "It rained every bloody day. Eric played endless games of chess with the innkeeper, so I buried myself in a mountain of steamy romance novels."

"Did I hear something about chess?" Darren Sargent stopped on his way to the bar. "Have you been playing, Ann dear?"

"I'm not good enough for Eric."

"And it bores me, so don't even ask," I added.

"Bores you, Michael?" Darren rolled his eyes in astonishment. "Chess is the ultimate intellectual challenge!"

"Oh, no. Every possible move has been defined by rules."

"Human culture couldn't exist without rules."

"Yet all cultures are still subordinate to the one true rule," I insisted. "*Chance*. An earthquake, a plane accident, a stray bullet."

"That has nothing to do with chess," Darren countered.

"Of course it does. The true challenge of any game is to overcome the unforeseeable. That's why backgammon—a game of skill *and* chance—is so much more entertaining."

"Chess is as complex as the minds that meet over the board."

"That's certainly true, but a pawn will always be a pawn. And anyway, you men only *pretend* to play by the rules."

The guest professor, Jonathan Bennett, was still penned in a corner, surrounded by faces that desperately needed some sun. I saw his surprise as I sauntered forward, all sculpted legs, honeyed cleavage, and short, natural hair. His startled eyes appraised my youthful face, framed by gold earrings in the shape of little fertility goddesses. My full, dark lips played beneath eyes that stopped him short—he instantly understood that I was perfectly indifferent to the opinions of others.

"Welcome, Dr. Bennett. I'm Michael Davies."

He needed only seconds to set down his drink, stand up to his full height, and take my hand into his own. "Michael Dav— You can't be the author of *The Griot's Song*?"

I nodded.

"I've loved your book for years. I always assumed Michael Davies was a man."

"Disappointed?" I raised my chin and lowered my lashes while he savored his discovery.

"I'd say—" he paused "—it's the worst news I've had in years."

"I'm very pleased to meet you, Jonathan. And unlike my colleagues, I really *have* read your work."

"Then we already have something in common."

The tip of his tongue traced the smooth edge of his perfect teeth as his smile deepened. Something began to shimmer in the depths of my belly.

"Long trip?" I asked, holding my voice steady.

"I almost bailed out somewhere over the Atlantic."

"Waste of time. We were determined to have you."

"So you'd have sent out the Royal Navy?"

"We'd have let the sharks chase you to shore. You know . . . budgetary concerns."

"Haven't you heard that black men can't swim?"

"Certainly, but all professors can walk on water."

We laughed to hide the tension that seemed to crackle each time our eyes met.

Bennett watched my earrings dancing in the low light. "What do you do here, Michael?"

"I'm the department's African-Americanist. Your counterpart."

"Then I'm even happier I stayed on the plane."

"Hopefully you'll still feel that way by the end of the year. Things can get dicey at times."

"Oh, I'm a survivor. Almost nothing surprises me these days."

"Isn't life boring without surprises?"

"No," he replied, gently cocking his head. "I just spend my time surprising other people."

"Now, that will keep you busy."

"Speaking of busy, were you responsible for that lovely apartment I've been given?"

"No. But I did buy a few things to brighten it up."

"Then you and I should have a housewarming party."

We both looked up as Drew approached, one hand in his pocket, the other cupping his sherry.

"Jonathan Bennett, Andrew Northcross," I said. The men shook hands.

"Your trip went smoothly?" Drew asked.

"Everything was copacetic."

"I'm glad. Michael has had some interesting encounters with overzealous customs agents," he said, possessively stroking my back.

Bennett glanced at Drew's hand, then looked back into his eyes. "We met once before, Dr. Northcross. Atlanta, at a Soyinka conference."

"Atlanta? Let's see—that was before Wole got the prize. Did you deliver a paper?"

"No," Bennett replied warmly, "but I'll never forget yours."

"I'm impressed. After all, it's been at least eleven or twelve years."

"Fourteen. You compared Soyinka with several black American dramatists."

"It was the first draft of what later became my third book."

"I admire your work," Bennett said with a smile, "although I don't often agree with you."

Drew threw back his head and gave a hearty laugh. "Now that sounds terribly familiar," he said, looking down at me. "Perhaps the two of you should trade notes."

"Perhaps," Bennett replied, "we'll trade far more than that."

For a moment there was silence all around. Then Drew turned his head and said softly, but firmly, "I can hardly stand up. I, too, survived a transatlantic crossing today. Dr. Bennett, you must come to dinner as soon as you're settled."

Drew's sudden formality was ominous. Glancing at Jonathan Bennett, I smiled as graciously as possible. "Rest well. Drew's assistant will get you home."

As we walked away I heard Jonathan Bennett asking the graduate assistant whether Drew and I were somehow related.

"Oh goodness, yes. They're married, of course. Have been for ages."

"I see." Bennett smothered his surprise with a groan. "I'm dead, man! Please get me home, before I fall out."

Lying on the bed after the faculty party, a book in one hand, an uneaten apple in the other, I watched my husband as he emerged from the shower. His hair was still dripping, and he had wrapped himself in a loose terry robe that fell nearly to his ankles.

"You know, it's been six months, Drew. Sometimes I feel like Maggie the Cat."

He looked across at me, drying his hair with a hand towel. "Don't start with me tonight, please. I'm truly exhausted."

"That's right, you're lagged from your fascinating conference in America."

"And that wonderful evening with our brilliant colleagues."

"You must hate it when their wives drool over you."

"You weren't exactly running from Jonathan Bennett."

"Could the infamous Drew Northcross be jealous?"

"Mickey—" he walked over and sat on the bed. "I know that this has been a difficult period for you."

"Difficult?" I evaluated the word. "Read: We don't fight about anything, but we don't agree about anything, either. You insist on traveling alone to your many intriguing conferences. We need an archaeologist to explain our sex life—"

Drew dropped his robe, and the sight of his firm, muscular body made me angrier. "Perhaps I've got it all wrong," I said. "Maybe what we really need is to stop pretending this is a marriage."

"It's not that I don't want you," he said. "Maybe it's my age. Or maybe I've been in Levant Hill too long. I don't know: It's as if nothing makes sense anymore."

He leaned forward, intending to brush my lips with his own, but instead found himself kissing me deeply, my mouth hot and full. His body responded immediately, and he slid his hand to my breast.

"No, Drew!" I pushed him away. "You can't use me like a tool and put me away."

Helplessly he paused, finally letting his fingers gently trace my shoulder. I steeled myself against his touch.

"I love you," he said softly. "And everything will work out as long as I know that you really love me."

"That's right. Love means never asking who you're really sleeping with."

Soon the light went out and we lay like stones in the darkness while the bed shook with my tears.

I had inherited the most beautiful of the faculty offices, a deep, warm room brightened by a bay window and thatched with the shadows of tall oak trees. In the summer, green leaves filled the room with their shimmering shadows; in the autumn, students' voices filtered up through their dry whispering. As our marriage crumbled, I spent more and more time in this retreat, trying to avoid the bickering that had somehow replaced real communication.

That crisp autumn morning, just a few days before the start of classes, someone knocked on my office door, startling me out of my reverie. "I'm here," I replied, "as long as you're not looking for Professor Davies."

"Then I'll just take Michael," a man answered. The door bounced open, and a large crate entered, supported by long legs in jeans and expensive running shoes.

"What's this?"

"Your new officemate."

"What's happened to—?" Before I could finish, I recognized Jonathan Bennett. He staggered to the empty desk opposite mine, dropping the crate heavily onto the floor.

"Guest professors have their own offices!" I exclaimed. "Hang on. I'll call the secretary."

"No—stop! This really is my fault," he said sheepishly. "I asked Ursula whether I could have an office near yours. She said everything was full, but there's an extra desk in here."

I examined him carefully. An engaging warmth very nearly masked his astute, secretive eyes. I knew instinctively that he had gained many lovers with those eyes, even more than with his full mouth or muscular build. Jonathan Bennett was a study in tensed grace, a cat poised to spring. But like the feline, he concealed the true extent of his strength and speed.

"Jonathan, I'm the department adviser. I use that desk for student conferences."

"All I need is a little space," he replied. Leaning against the desk, he raised his right hand. "I promise to be a quiet, cheerful, and invisible officemate."

Slightly annoyed, I turned to my work. Bennett opened his box and began removing books.

"Why isn't your photo on your book jackets?" he asked, breaking the silence. "You could be very famous at home."

I laughed. "After fifteen years England's my home, now."

"You don't miss the States?"

"Not particularly."

"And black people?"

"I've got students from all over the world. More, in fact, than in all my years of study in America."

"And I'll bet you've been to Africa."

"Drew and I lived in Zimbabwe shortly after the independence."

Bennett returned to his unpacking. "I've always admired academic pairs like you two. You share your interests, your careers, your love life—it's really impressive."

"I guess we've been lucky," I said quietly.

"I married a fellow student back in grad school. We lasted seven years, then finally gave up when we couldn't find jobs in the same area."

"That's too bad."

"It was hard," he agreed. "But being divorced has given me the freedom to really pursue my career. Got any kids?"

"Never slowed down long enough."

Bennett dropped several more books on his desk. "I've got a nine-year-old son who lives with his mother. Malcolm. We considered many names, but it was always Malcolm. There are some things in life that you simply know." He glanced over at me. "I know you'd make an excellent mother."

"Really? And what are my qualifications?"

"You're intelligent, well traveled, and greatly accomplished. And of course," he paused, "you're a very beautiful woman."

Again, something stirred in me, and I glanced over at him. Bennett smiled with warm, sincere eyes. Then he ducked his head and glanced away, suddenly ill at ease.

"Hey," he began awkwardly. "I want to apologize for the way I came on to you the other night. I had no idea you were married to Andrew Northcross. I certainly wouldn't want to begin my stay here on the wrong—"

"It's cool," I answered. I returned to my work, feeling slightly bemused. I didn't want to share my office with anyone, but realized that ironically, I hadn't thought about Drew for a full seven minutes. Strange revelation. And perhaps reason enough to put up with my new officemate.

I know that you're a very private woman, Chloe, but personally, I love to entertain. Over the years Drew and I opened our home to students and professors, neighbors and friends, and I thought that this evening—a sort of welcome for Jonathan Bennett—would be pretty much the same as all the other dinner parties I'd given. Of course, I was mistaken.

I laid the table with heavy ceramic plates bearing an Ibo motif, and decided to serve the Médoc in the hand-thrown clay goblets you yourself made for us. I'd baked a dark bread and the house was rich with the scent of simmering rosemary and basil. I even selected a series of rare jazz albums and stacked them on the console, lest Drew should decide the evening called for nothing but his beloved Masekela.

Amanda and Robert Herrington had already arrived. Clothed in her inevitable Shetland ensemble, Amanda was perched on the edge of the sofa, sipping sherry and gazing self-consciously at the heavy-breasted Kore figurines gracing the end tables. Robert immediately engaged Drew in a conversation about department budgets and future hiring—the kind of talk that sent me scurrying to the kitchen to check on the food. Amanda offered to help, but I swiftly declined her assistance. Being trapped in the kitchen with the likes of Amanda Herrington was worse than listening to her husband's rambling monologues.

Jonathan Bennett was late, and I wondered if Drew shouldn't have offered to pick him up. It was a common joke that Americans were always late. I'd always felt defensive about the suggestion that my fellow countrymen didn't have the courtesy or the intelligence to arrive for dinner on time. So back in the kitchen I checked the rice once more, slamming the lid down on the pot with a bit of vigor, and sipped a glass of wine while tapping my foot on the flagstone floor.

At last the doorbell rang, and I heard Drew's welcome. I smoothed my hair and, opening the kitchen door, strolled down the short hall to the drawing room, feeling the cool lapis silk billow against my skin.

In the center of the room stood Jonathan Bennett in a tweed jacket, shaking hands with Amanda. To his right was a small woman with flowing light brown hair, wearing painfully tight jeans. Drew was carrying out the introductions in his low, resonant voice. When he looked at me there was amusement in his eyes.

"Here's Michael," he said lightly.

Bennett presented me with a small box of chocolates, carefully wrapped with tissue paper and a complicated bow. "Hey, office partner," he said smartly, and I remembered with a start that I'd forgotten to tell Drew that Jonathan Bennett planned to spend a year at the desk only a few feet away.

"We were afraid you got lost."

"I did. But actually—"

"It was my fault," the young woman interrupted. "It took me hours to get dressed, which is really crackers because all I've got to wear is jeans."

All eyes in the room were upon her. None of us failed to perceive every inch of her lower body, perfectly outlined by pants that were at least two sizes too small. The long-sleeved sweater she wore was short enough that her midriff, complete with a navel ring, appeared when she shrugged her shoulders. As she spoke, she extended her hands and pulled her fingers stiffly through her hair, tossing it out of her eyes.

"This is Kristin. I've just hired her as my assistant," Bennett explained.

"Kristin's a former student of mine," Drew said. "How have you been getting along, Miss Proctor?"

Kristin smiled and shrugged a second time. "I was away in Perth after I completed my B.A. But I'm back, and I hope to finish my master's in the spring, Professor Northcross. Jonathan has agreed to direct my thesis."

"And what's the subject?" I asked, hoping my voice didn't reveal my irritation.

"Well . . ." Kristin looked unwittingly into my eyes, and for a moment was struck dumb.

"Kristin is very bright," Bennett put in coolly. "I'm certain that we'll find something fascinating to do together."

Drew glanced toward Robert, whose eyes had not left the young woman's jeans. Amanda's gaze had leveled into a squint of distaste that matched the firm set of her mouth. Well, I thought as I turned back toward the kitchen, at least Amanda would have something other than me to gossip about.

The table had to be set for another guest, an extra chair had to be found, but at last we were all seated and served, and glasses of wine were emptied while we ate our meal.

"You're vegetarian?" Bennett asked me.

"Not entirely," I answered, "but I don't eat meat."

"Michael will eat fish if it costs enough," Drew teased.

"That's a shame." Bennett sighed. "I was counting on you for a bit of down-home cooking."

"Like those concoctions they serve in your American delicatessens?" Robert interjected. "Corned beef with Swiss cheese, sauerkraut, tomatoes, pickles, and cole slaw—"

"On an onion roll!" Bennett laughed, shaking his head wistfully.

"You Americans will eat anything," Amanda commented with a dour smile.

"Not true," Bennett replied, matching her expression. "You won't get me anywhere near a blood pudding!"

"But a blood pudding is delicious!" Robert protested, slightly piqued.

"So are our insane sandwiches," Bennett answered graciously, patting his lips with his napkin. "You'll have to come to lunch and let me make one for you."

"What, an American male who cooks?" Amanda exclaimed.

"With the divorce rates so high, American men have to."

"That's entirely the reason why Englishmen don't get divorced: They're afraid they'd starve," Drew offered quietly.

There was general laughter. "Don't tell me Robert can't cook at all," I said to Amanda.

"I'd never let him try. I already have him telling me how almost everything needs to be done. At least I don't have to argue with him in the kitchen."

The whole table laughed again, and Drew reached over and took my hand.

"Arguments brought Michael to me," Drew said softly. "I guess they keep her by my side." They were all looking at me, now, as I met Drew's eyes. He was trying to tell me something, but it irritated me that he used a dinner party as his forum.

"How long have you been together?" Bennett asked, pouring himself another glass of wine.

"Fifteen short years," Drew answered, his eyes never leaving my face.

"And such passion!" Amanda declared in a voice laced with irony.

"I think it's amazing," Kristin offered. "I was only nine years old when you met."

"Commitment isn't as rare as people pretend," I stated, raising my glass to my lips.

"But some people do put up with a lot just to stay together," Robert remarked.

"Or hide behind excuses such as their reputations or their duty to their children," Bennett said.

"You don't think such duties are important?" Drew asked him.

"It's all relative to the situation. But I think that often it takes more courage to leave than to stay," Bennett responded lightly.

"You speak as if courage is the most important virtue," Drew said. "But I think love must conquer all, no matter how facile that seems."

"And what about men who sleep around while claiming they love their wives?" Amanda asked, watching Drew carefully.

"Some couples have an understanding about such things," he answered, avoiding my eyes. "The point is that we have to be honest about what we really feel—"

"Then cheating is okay," Bennett interrupted, "as long as the lovers confess to their spouses?"

"Love will survive, as long as there's truth in the relationship," Drew insisted.

"But a good lover can really mess that 'truth' thing up," Bennett countered, glancing across the table at me.

"Only if we confuse the boundaries between sex and love," Drew answered, intercepting that glance.

"Of course, *you've* never had that problem," Robert laughed.

"One is physical and the other spiritual," Drew explained. "It's our emotions that cause most of the problems."

"Now I see why you're such a masterful professor," Bennett said as he raised his glass to Drew. "You'd never be *enslaved* by your emotions!"

The two men stared at each other, Drew's eyes glittering above his inscrutable smile, Bennett's face fixed in an easy grin above his glass of red wine.

"Don't we have two heavyweights in the ring tonight?" Amanda commented.

"There's no match," I said with irritation, "because there's nothing to win." Rising, I lifted a stack of dirty dishes.

"Do you need any help?" Amanda began.

"No, thanks. I'd have more fun yelling at Drew," I called over my shoulder.

In the kitchen I snatched a carton of ice cream from the refrigerator and slammed the door shut with my elbow. Drew took bowls down from an overhead cupboard and opened the utensil drawer, avoiding my eyes. With our backs turned to each other, we each dug for the necessary scoops and spoons, the room silent except for clanging silver. Then we turned simultaneously and stood face-to-face.

"I'm sorry, Mickey," he said.

"He's our guest, Drew."

"But he's such a . . ." He searched for an apt description of Jonathan Bennett.

I began to smile despite my anger. Suddenly we were transported to a scene from our past: we were standing on a hill, high above a village in Greece, gazing at a blue-black sea in the dawning sun. My braids were blowing in the *mtelmi*. A gull wound its way over the red rocks, and in my hands I grasped a twig of the sweet wild thyme that perfumed the hillsides. The air was heavy with jasmine, and my face was full of love as he turned and gave me the smile that always sent my heart crashing against my chest.

"Shall we give them something to talk about?" he asked me now.

"Right," I said sarcastically. "That's what our marriage has come to." I turned to walk past him, and he caught my arm.

"Wait a minute, woman," he said. "Jonathan Bennett and the Herringtons are not important." He slipped his arms around me and pulled me to his body. Leaning forward, he pressed his face into my hair and inhaled deeply.

"Wherever you go, the air is full of you," he whispered.

I carefully extracted myself from his arms and looked up into his eyes. "They're waiting, Drew."

He looked down at me, and his face melted into a cunning smile. "All right. If you don't want to be serious, let's have a little fun." Raising his voice, he almost shouted: "No! I won't let you!"

"What?" I whispered, caught by surprise.

"I won't allow it in our home!" Drew's eyes glittered with delight. My face exploded into a grin of complicity.

"You, Andrew Northcross, have absolutely nothing to say about it!"

Drew increased the volume slightly. "I most certainly do! What the hell do you think you're doing?"

"Whatever I want! I'm not some toy you brought back from your travels in exotic lands!"

Tears of laughter formed in Drew's eyes, and I had to ball up a fist and press it against my mouth to keep from exploding.

Soon I led the way out of the kitchen and back into the dining room. Robert and Amanda sat with scarlet faces, studying a book of Degas sketches. Jonathan was standing at the window, looking out into the night, and Kristin was inspecting the plants. Drew and I exchanged glances; then in a sweet voice I invited my guests back to the table.

Robert and Amanda were the first to leave. After a careful inspection of Drew's jazz collection, Jonathan Bennett reluctantly admitted that he should probably get Kristin home.

"But you two have me baffled," he said as he helped her into her coat. "One minute you're making war, and the next minute you're making love. I can't tell whether you're just teasing us or whether you're teasing each other or whether it's a mixture of both."

I glanced at my husband and was surprised to find an expression in his eyes that I had never before seen. "Perhaps," Drew responded coolly, "you're simply not capable of understanding."

"I never realized that professors behaved like real people," Kristin said, looking from one man to the other in mock bewilderment.

The tension broke, and we pretended to laugh.

"Well, thank you for a most interesting evening," Bennett said. "I enjoyed the food, the conversation, and," he paused, "the drama."

Kristin nodded in agreement. "I couldn't have imagined what you were really like when I was in your class, Professor Northcross."

"You still don't have a clue, Miss Proctor," I said, slipping an arm around his waist.

When the door closed Drew looked down at me.

"Great party, Dr. Davies."

It had been my habit for fifteen years to go for a daily run along the seaside cliffs that bordered the edge of the campus. I took great pleasure in running faster and longer than students who were half my age, and although I appeared to run for pleasure, I took my sport *very* seriously. No one of sound mind, Chloe, ever interfered with my running.

One afternoon as I was warming up, someone called my name. Jonathan Bennett emerged from the gymnasium wearing training pants, a T-shirt, and a grin. He scanned my body, his eyes resting a microsecond too long on the vee of my tights.

"Hey, Dr. D!" was his jovial greeting. "How about a little fun?"

"Hello and no." I knew instantly that there was no coincidence to the timing of Bennett's arrival. "I'm here to work."

"Then let me work you."

"I prefer it alone."

"You just haven't met the right partner."

Bennett stood beside me with a radiant face, his hands on his hips as if he were ready to go. Without another word I took off, tossing one quick look in his direction. He immediately fell in beside me.

For some ten minutes we ran without speaking. I kept a slow but steady pace, gradually building in intensity until I reached a comfortable speed. Bennett was in good shape; his breathing remained regular, and he matched me step for step.

Soon we cleared the university buildings and were approaching a series of earthen footpaths that led toward the cliffs.

"How far do you run?" he asked.

"Twelve kilometers a day."

"In miles?"

"Seven to eight."

"Not bad."

I felt him increase the pace, but I said nothing. I didn't want to race him, but I didn't want to fall behind, either. I knew that he was trying me out, attempting to see how much I could, or was willing to take. So I increased my stride, lifting my head to regulate my breathing.

"Do you race?"

"No. My self-esteem is fine."

"Typical female response."

"Typical male attitude."

"So men who compete suffer from a lack of self-worth?"

"Either that or undersized dicks."

That shut him up. We ran through an open gate and found ourselves high above the sea on a rough, hilly path that wound along the coast. Savoring the clean salty air, I eased back the speed and recovered my normal pace. I looked out at the calm water, deliberately ignoring my uninvited partner.

We ran for another ten minutes, then fifteen. The path cut through banks of thick clover, patchworked with thistles. Seventy feet below us the sea foamed up lazily against cement breakers, and a steady wind blew into our faces. Jonathan was beginning to breathe heavily, but I was just getting warmed up. Subtly I ran faster, increasing the pace so casually that it appeared to be a part of my normal routine. I kept my arms relaxed, swinging lightly at my sides. My breath came in short puffs, my footfalls light and even.

Soon Bennett was running more heavily. His feet struck the ground hard, and his breath was ragged spurts. Great rings of sweat darkened his shirt, and he spat out a bitter liquid as we crested a hill. Edging the speed up just a bit more, I shortened and increased my pace until I was running with utmost efficiency.

Now we were engaged in a true contest. I used my light frame to fly along the path, my body a finely tuned machine and my spirit joyful and free. Head held high, I focused my thoughts and kept my shoulders loose and relaxed. Bennett's strides became less regular, and he began to swing his torso in a useless effort to increase his power. There was frustration in his panting and discomfort in his increasingly heavy footfalls.

We had only passed six kilometers, less than half of my normal route. As we approached a fork I called, "I think I'll run a bit longer today. We've already passed five K's; if you're tired, this would be a good point to turn back."

I felt Bennett waver between determination and defeated rage. He ran a few more steps, then turned away just as we reached the split. Without a word he changed direction. Then, softly he muttered "Bitch!" as I surged ahead.

I returned to the office with a private glow. Bennett stood over his desk, glowering at his calendar. He didn't speak. It was some time before I heard him clear his throat. He had placed himself on the edge of his desk.

"You weren't very friendly out there."

"Running is private time for me, Jonathan."

He slid off the desk, his face breaking into a cool smile. "It's pretty clear that you're compensating for so many years of isolation."

"Oh! A free, ten-second analysis from the world-famous Sigmund Bennett."

"I understand you better than you think," he asserted. "Let's see: Ballet lessons at five; piano at six. Catholic schools with uniforms, then the debutante ball at the AME church full of fake virgins in altered wedding gowns when you hit sweet sixteen—"

"Let's try again," I snapped. "Teacher's daughter. Abandoned by father who never contributed a dime. Volleyed between mother and grandmother, Chicago and Washington, and nothing but inner-city public schools. No ballet. A little bit of piano, and certainly never a debutante."

"Never a debutante?" he said in mock astonishment.

"I grew up in the same America as you, Jonathan. Lived in both the North and the South through the Kennedys, Malcolm, and King. Spent my life in schools like checkerboards, where the white and black never once overlapped. Watched Civil Rights become Black Power and finally grow into Affirmative Action. Now, what part of the 'American experience' has escaped me?"

"Mine."

He sat down suddenly and stared at the floor.

"My sharecropper parents broke their backs over the same couple of acres where our ancestors slaved. When their first son was born, they named him LeRoy J. Bennett, after an uncle who had escaped to Harlem and never came back." His anger seemed to vanish as he spoke. Instead, his voice went low and thoughtful as he continued his story.

"They left Mississippi before L.J. could walk, because some civil rights worker promised them a better life in the North. So instead they sweated out their lives in the factories of Gary, Indiana, trying to feed six kids, keep up the payments on the used Dodge, make the rent on our three-room tenement, and send money to the folks down home."

I sighed. "Bennett, I—"

He looked up quickly, and I stopped at the pain in his eyes.

"When little L.J. said he wanted to go to college, they told him to get his black ass over to the factory. So when he went and got himself a scholarship instead, his father kicked his ass, told him to get out and never come back.

"Of course, life at the U. wasn't exactly heaven. L.J. heard his roommate tell somebody that all of us are named either LeRoy or Duane. Then he went on to explain that L.J.'s 'peculiar odor' came from a diet of squirrel meat and chitlins. And he said that he'd never bring his girlfriend to the dorm if L.J. was around. Who knew, after all, what a nigger might do?"

"I understand," I interrupted. "You changed your name from LeRoy J. to Jonathan. You studied harder and graduated sooner and never let anyone or anything stand in your—"

"That's right. I fought my way to becoming Professor Jonathan Bennett, doctor of philosophy. But to them," he added in a voice like gravel, "I'll always be little black LeRoy."

A brittle wire ripped loose from its socket, sending a vibrant current of energy snapping between us. Then something strange happened: Bennett's eyes cleared, and for an instant someone indescribably young and vulnerable looked back at me.

"Michael," he whispered, "I never dreamed that this could happen."

"What?" I asked, confused.

"I never dreamed that after so many years, so many meaningless relationships, I could fall so hard for someone."

"Who?" I whispered.

His eyes leapt directly to mine. *"You."*

For a moment I sat in a silence so complete that I heard the squirrels scurrying along the branches outside.

"Me? But I'm married, Jonathan."

He stood up and crossed the room, speaking in a low, clear voice. "Not happily, Michael. I've seen the way you look at him. And I've seen the way he looks at you."

"Where do you—"

"It's obvious. Andrew Northcross used to know what he wanted: His career. His books. His conference adventures. And his stunning wife with the perfect body that matches her excellent mind. He's had it far better than most men, and yet those things don't seem so important to him anymore."

"You don't know anything about Drew."

"I'm a *man*, Michael."

The subtle force behind his words silenced me, and I watched as Bennett reached out and gently grasped my fingers.

"Back home, you could be a major academic voice, especially with your years of travel and living abroad."

"You're suggesting that I abandon my husband and job and go back to America with you?"

"No," he said carefully. "But I could arrange for you to do a semester, or even a year abroad on my campus in California. It would give you, well, *both* of you time to figure out what you really want."

His hands closed over mine, and he moved close. Suddenly I saw myself sitting stupidly, eagerly, waiting for his next move, and I flushed with anger. I stood up. Bennett stepped back, finally releasing my hands.

"There are many kinds of happiness in this world," he concluded. "I could help you find yours, Michael."

You know, Chloe, only a few months earlier I would have told Jonathan Bennett to go lie down in front of a bulldozer. But something in his words resonated deep down in a place that I thought I'd hidden from the world. He sensed—no, he *knew* something that no one else had realized—that my life was falling apart.

Standing in front of the mirror in our dressing room, my thoughts flickered back to the vow you and I had taken so many years before: I'd be strong and successful, and never let any man turn me away from my dreams! What was happening to me, Chloe? Who the hell was Jonathan Bennett? And where in hell was my Drew?

As if by instinct, Drew came in that evening with a bundle of heather. He closed the door and, drawn by wailing strains of Miles, walked softly up the stairs and peered into the bedroom. He found me wrapped in a ball on the woven rug, my arms wound tightly around my legs.

He dropped to one knee and the blossoms fell close to my face. Slowly, I raised my head, biting so hard on my lips that I tasted blood. Carefully, he settled himself on the floor and pulled me into his arms.

"I'm sorry about the way things have been lately."

"Lately?" I pushed myself up, shaking my head in disgust. "I'm tired of lately, Drew."

"Then let's talk about the future."

I snorted and pulled away. "I honestly don't know if we have a future."

My pronouncement was met with silence. Drew was staring into my eyes as if it were the first time he had really looked at me in months. His brows came together, and he leaned forward, pressing his lips slowly against my forehead.

"Forgive me, Mickey."

Now I gave in to my bottomless fatigue, and I softened, as I had softened for fifteen years. He held me until my breathing slowed to the measure of his heartbeat, then slowly lifted me up to our bed. His arms laced around my waist, he very gently pressed me down beneath him.

I looked up and was astonished to see the face of a younger Drew Northcross. He gazed back at me with arousal in his eyes, and I felt my body quicken with desire.

"There was a time when it made sense," he murmured as he deftly opened my sweater, "to never risk falling in love. So I didn't take that chance."

He slid the wool away from my shoulders and paused, his warm fingers brushing the tips of my breasts. The world hushed, leaning close to hear.

"Then I met you," he throttled, "and you changed my life."

In a fluid movement his lips found my nipples as his hand traced a whispering path across my belly to the hair below.

"I've never understood how I searched the world for someone, only to look up in my lecture and find you staring back at me one day." One finger tested the springy tangle through the sheer fabric.

"But I thank God you came—" he brought his lips to mine "—and stayed."

I felt myself float upward as we kissed. I saw him undressing me as if I were a child. My sadness drifted around us, receding into the darkness as his deep flesh met mine.

"I'm sorry, Michael," he whispered. "I've never intended to hurt you."

Wordless, I lay outside of myself and watched as he commandeered every muscle, every hair, every pore of my body. He began telling me that he loved me, and he said it again and again as he found his way into my body. It had been so long since he had made love with me that soon my hips were rolling with his and I was consumed by a throbbing, womb-deep pleasure.

I'd found him. He had come back to me.

It was nearly sunrise when Drew rose silently, stealthily, his hips and shoulders dismembered by the darkness. I climbed out of bed and soundlessly followed him as he made his way through the labyrinth of our life. I watched wordlessly as he hardly reacted to the burn of rough upholstery against his knee, or his bare feet moving from icy tiles to the wooden floor. Finally he came to our study where, among the weirdly grinning African masks, he stood sentinel at the window, impervious to the cold.

He remained there as the sun began to rise, watching the blazing ball burn the darkness into day. Then suddenly he raised his arms and began to sway, his limbs bloodred in the livid light. He turned and dipped, his eyes squeezed shut, while repeating a strangely garbled chant. Heart beating with an unfamiliar fear, I saw a man dancing his desperation while intoning his loneliness to the relentless dawn. In a sudden gesture of surrender he dropped to his knees, pressing his long frame into an awkward ball. Strangely broken, Drew stared toward the new day and wept deeply, in long, tearing sobs, as if he were ripping the wounded soul out of his body and setting it, after many months of agony, free.

It was only then, as I remained frozen just outside the door with my heart slamming in an inexpressible terror, that I began to see that my love alone would never be enough.

I closed my eyes, trying to block out the memory of that desperate, self-hating man.

"I don't think I've ever felt more helpless in my entire life, Chloe. I was watching Drew self-destruct, and there was nothing I could do about it."

"You continued to love him, Michael."

"But it didn't help. And the worse things got, the more I blamed myself for breaking the vow that you and I took back in D.C. Had I managed to become a strong black woman? The strength that I showed the outside world was just a mask to hide my growing fear and confusion. Was I a success? My career was completely bound to my life in Levant Hill. And what about all my dreams? Well, I'd given them up when I married Drew."

"But loving Drew didn't break our vow, Michael. It just tested it in a different way."

Your expression turned inward, and you, too, were looking back. "Let me tell you about the real test of our vow—how to rediscover your strength when the man in your life attempts to destroy you."

You looked into my eyes and placed my hand and my heart inside of your own.

"Michael, I'm going to tell you how I survived. And I'm going to tell you something else: how I finally learned to love."

THREE

And then, in the late autumn of 1970, came the one hundred days.

I couldn't tell you, Michael, because I didn't know how to explain it. I never intended for it to happen. I didn't even know him. Yet in a matter of hours Lucien Laurent proved that the fortress around my heart was made of glass.

In the beginning, phantoms of other women crept into bed with us, and I heard their murmurs, smelled their hair, and tasted their bittersweet perfumes. As if he could feel the pulse of my fears, Lucien's eyes would open and he'd whisper, "Don't be afraid, Chloe," and he'd hold me until my body flowed into his. Drawn to his warmth and lulled by his heartbeat, I plunged headlong into his ocean.

Lucien was like a narcotic, Michael, filling me with an insatiable need. We lived in the realm of the senses, hidden away from the world in his flat at Vincennes. There were late, saxophone-scored suppers (a fine Bordeaux, a rich paté, and Brie on crisp baguettes) that stretched into slow, lovemaking dawns (his golden eyes half-closed in ecstasy and the scent of his glistening flesh). He overcame my resistance with sweet, small gifts—bouquets of scarlet anemones, tiny bags of Belgian truffles, a beveled flask of dark jasmine oil. In many ways, my life with Lucien was like a dream.

"C'est quoi?" he asked one evening as I smiled up at him from my sketchbook.

"It's hard to imagine the sexy Lucien Laurent standing over a stove," I teased.

"It's only natural," he responded. "Food is, after all, life's second greatest pleasure."

"And its first?"

"Seeing what my beautiful artist has on her easel."

Paris was in love with us, too, Michael. I still remember the sunlight on his face at a sidewalk café, and kissing him in the autumn-ripe woods of Vincennes. Most of all, I can sometimes feel the sweet, hard rise of his powerful hips arched under mine in the darkness.

The intensity of our passion made the weekdays hard to bear. When we parted in the mornings, Lucien heading for his office while I returned to my studio, I couldn't wait until the evening, when he'd appear at Le Kansas, or find me hard at work, paint-flecked and famished. I discovered that he loved to laugh, to listen to African music, and to tell biting stories about his reckless, troubled youth.

"The first time?" He lay with his hands behind his head, listening to the rain skittering along the metal roof overhead. "I don't know, twelve or so."

"Twelve?" Disbelieving, I leaned up on an elbow. "You could already—?"

"Certainly. The girl was much older—maybe sixteen—and was quite an expert. I was scared I'd mess it up, knock her up, or get caught. But," he added ironically, "I was even more scared she'd say I preferred boys."

"So you were already irresistible?" I asked, imagining him as a curly-haired, golden-eyed teen.

"Irresistible?" He snorted. "I was a thug who specialized in beating people with bricks."

"Didn't your parents know?"

"My mother didn't have much schooling, and her French was very poor, so she avoided my teachers. And Antoine Laurent was either in the factory or drunk. When I got into trouble he'd beat me half to death. Which, of course, meant that he didn't beat my mother." Lucien rolled over and lit a cigarette, then concentrated on the stream of smoke struggling toward the ceiling.

"One night I went to a party with a woman I'd met in the Luxembourg Gardens. I had on my best clothes—a shiny suit from the street market at Barbès—and this friend of her family appeared. He took a good look at me and said to her: 'Be sure to leave some for me when you've had enough.' I had never been so humiliated in my life.

"So I crawled into a corner and watched those people. I was amazed that there was so much filth in power—that so much was exchanged in borrowed beds and darkened rooms. I decided that if all it took was sex and the willingness to play their game, I didn't have to be poor."

"What about Anya?" I asked in a small voice.

"Anya's world is made of people who'll do anything to succeed. Anything. The rich come there, to those parties and those fashion shows, to pick and choose what they want. And when they're through with us—"

"But did you love her?"

"Anya's idea of love is a leash." The wind sent a spray of cold rain against the window. "We were too much alike. No love can survive so much hunger."

"Do you love me?"

He pulled me close, his face softening as he looked into my eyes. "I've never known anyone like you," he replied gently. "You're giving me a whole new life."

My last ounce of resistance scattered like dust with those words. I began wearing my hair loose because he enjoyed tangling his fingers in the rough curls when we made love. I found myself in hip-length skirts and thigh-high boots, my face drawn on with lipstick and eyeliner. He liked me in nylons and tight-fitting sweaters, so I even purchased an underwire bra. When women eyed him on the streets I'd savor the thought: *"Forget it, baby: this man is mine. . . ."*

Beneath our passion, however, lurked the disquieting fact that I was still required to exhibit my paintings. So one morning I put on my bravest face and went to Jacques's gallery. I found him sitting in the office, and he leaned back in silence, his face settling into a sardonic mask after taking in my new look.

"Tiens," he sneered softly. "When I didn't read about any unsolved murders, I assumed you survived."

"I want to apologize for what happened that evening."

Scratching the back of his neck, he looked me over as though I were soliciting donations. "Chloe, Chloe, Chloe," he chanted softly, shaking his head with paternal disapproval, "I hope you realize what you're doing."

"My private life is private, Jacques."

"Not when it comes to my gallery."

"Your gallery?" I repeated stupidly.

"I'll make this exceedingly simple," he said in a slow, mocking voice. "Galleries sell art. So they need buyers who are willing to buy that art."

"I'm not a businesswoman, Jacques."

"Oh, *merde*!" He stood up and folded his arms over his chest. "Let me explain something to you, Madame Picasso. Black women can sing and dance. Sometimes, when they're extremely lucky, they can walk the runway. But they do not get into this scene. They do not paint."

"But—"

He raised a hand to silence me, then let it drift slowly downward. "I figured that since you're returning to the States I could offer my clients a first look at a potential star. I was willing to take the risk, the time, and to put up the money to create you. But I needed your cooperation."

"You mean my cooperation between the sh—"

"Now you've taken up with this hustler. You're going to lose that lovely, mysterious anonymity, and I'm going to lose a lot of my clientele."

Holding my voice steady, I asked, "You won't show me because of Lucien?"

He sighed again. "Some of your work is truly good. But," he added viciously, "I don't support pimps."

"There are plenty of other galleries in Paris," I shot back.

"True. But if you think that the color of your skin makes no difference," he stated with chilling calm, "then I was wrong. You really *are* a tourist."

Why didn't I tell Lucien?

Why *did* I tell Anya?

She let me cry for a few minutes while she sat on the edge of her desk, one foot tapping the floor in irritation.

"Well, I expected things to fall apart from the inside, not the outside."

"You're wrong about Lucien," I said, wiping my eyes. "We're really happy. I've never felt this way."

She looked me over, her shrewd gaze coming to rest on my stylish, high-heeled boots. "Well, I'll say one thing: being with him has been very good for your closet."

"He's not the man you think he is!"

"Your great love affair is worth losing this gallery?" she challenged.

"No gallery owner's going to control my private life."

"Successful people don't have private lives."

"Are you saying that Jacques is right?"

"You need a gallery."

"There are other galleries."

When she didn't respond, I looked up in frustration. "You're the one who wanted me to get involved with someone!"

She took a deep breath and the abrasiveness left her voice. "Just be careful, Chloe. Devotion and exploitation may look different at the start. But they end the same way."

"My ability to paint has nothing to do with our relationship!"

"Your ability to paint," she replied, "has *everything* to do with it."

"Lucien is not interested in my career."

Anya stood up slowly and walked to the window. "I do know him, Chloe. I know how it feels when he's making love to you. And I know that soon enough things will change."

"He will never get involved with my art!" I insisted.

She wheeled around, her face dark with rage. "Tell me, Chloe: Are you deliberately naive or just plain stupid?"

Was I stupid? My life with Lucien seemed perfect, yet I struggled against a secret, mocking voice that chortled hysterically whenever I tried to envision a future with him. Somewhere deep inside lurked the phantoms of my unhappy past, chanting like a bullying child: *"Strength, success, and dreams!"* And in those brief, blinding instants of self-honesty, I wondered what in the hell I was doing with an admitted opportunist. An unrepentant womanizer. A *white* man.

But, Michael, Lucien made me ache when he stroked my knee. His sandy-voiced tales made me long to roam the world by his side. And he never probed the secrets in my eyes, but simply kissed those eyelids tenderly after making me scream.

"Have you seen that gallery owner since the night of Anya's show?" he casually inquired one night as we lay sated in the darkness.

"I'm giving him some time to cool down."

"Should I have a talk with him?"

"Sure." I laughed softly. "Why not splash some acid into the wound?"

Lucien paused. "I could scout some other galleries for you." Anya's mocking smile pirouetted between us.

"No, thanks," I murmured, my heart fluttering ominously. "I'll be all right."

Soon afterward I accompanied him to a photo session to shoot the advertisements for a new perfume called *Divine*, one of his largest accounts. He asked if I'd like to watch, and I'd gone along out of curiosity.

We entered an imposing house near the Pont de l'Alma, not far from Paris's most prestigious designer boutiques. An entire floor of the building had been hollowed out and rebuilt as a photographer's studio, its huge spaces draped in flowing sheets and hung with racks of spotlights.

Lucien embraced the photographer, a lean, heavily mustached Italian named Alessandro, and they began talking rapidly. My introduction was measured by the photographer's swift and critical gaze, but before we could speak three women in oversized coats and baseball caps bounded in, howling with laughter. A man with a long ponytail sauntered up behind them.

"You're late, Giovanni!" Alessandro said.

Giovanni's onyx eyes leapt to Lucien, and his face split into a brilliant grin. "How've you been, Luc?"

"Very busy, Vanni." He gestured toward me. "This is Chloe—"

"You're American?" the young man cried. "Are you an agent?"

"Sorry."

"I'm cursed!" he wailed in mock disappointment.

The women exited the dressing room wearing nothing but flesh-toned panties. Their small, upturned breasts formed oval arcs as they began to arrange themselves expertly in front of a white backdrop.

"Where do you want me?" Giovanni asked, casually stripping off his shirt and pants to reveal hours of careful, deliberate weight training.

"In the middle," the photographer answered as he began adjusting the lens of a very large camera.

"Can I put some music on?"

"Morning music, please. No screeching guitars or dying saxophones."

I watched as the scene arranged itself before my eyes. A stylist moved like a flittering butterfly from one model to the other, patting hair into place and powdering alabaster skin. Then the women settled into various positions, their arms placed on one another's shoulders or backs, or across one another's chests in protective, sisterly embraces. Giovanni stood tall and bold in the center of the group, like a bronzed, naked Dionysus, a contemptuous sneer splayed across his features. The camera whirred and snapped.

I watched, a sense of distaste growing in my belly. Lucien glanced at me. "What's the matter?"

"It's so primitive."

"American women aren't as evolved as you think," he replied with irritation.

"Even if most of us aren't burning our bras, you don't have to put us back in caves."

Alessandro looked over at us. "What's the problem?"

"Sorry to disturb you," Lucien said politely. He took my arm and guided me to the rear of the room.

"You see," he whispered, "women want a perfume that attracts men."

"But not necessarily men like *that.*" I pointed to Giovanni, whose bulging arms were now wrapped across his chest like a cinematic Samson.

"All right," he said ironically. "Since you're the only *real* artist here, I'll tell Sandro we need to make some changes. You set it up."

Lucien walked away. I knew that such shoots were very expensive; in fact, he was literally paying for this studio by the minute. Yet even more than the question of cost, Lucien was challenging me to prove my artistic ability when put under pressure. This was no oil portrait that could be painted and repainted according to my mood. Feeling a sense of helpless anger swell up in my heart, I scrambled through my mental catalogue of images, artists, even scenes from old films, desperately seeking something I could use.

At that moment one of the models leaned forward and was draped in the long veil of her hair. She pushed it back over her shoulder, but one fine tress flitted forward, a strand of early summer wheat in a loving breeze.

"Bingo," I whispered. Nervously I crossed the studio. Alessandro looked over at me politely.

"I'd like—" I paused. Both men waited. The models were waiting. "I'd like for you to soften the lights."

The photographer straightened up and sighed. "You're certain? I'll need a little time."

"Yes," I said boldly.

"All right. Take a break!" he called to the quartet, who instantly burst into squirrelly chatter. The stylist materialized to begin her ritual brushing and powdering. While the photographer adjusted the equipment, I kicked off my shoes and walked out onto the white sheet.

"Do you have any metallic eye shadow—something that shimmers? And a strong hair spray?" The stylist nodded, her eyebrows raised.

I arranged the women in a loose triangle, the tallest kneeling on the floor, with Giovanni behind her. The other two women stood on either side. I directed the stylist to smear the glittering shadow over their lids and, as if they were storybook fairies, up across their brows to their temples. We then outlined their chins and collarbones with the makeup, so that their bones seemed illuminated with shimmering, powdery stardust.

Carefully I created the pose, asking Giovanni gently to lower his face against the crown of the tallest model's head. The other two models brought their own heads together, forming a sensual grouping of bodies. The stylist arranged their flowing hair so that their nipples were no longer exposed, and then I suggested that they clear their faces of any expression: they were to appear guiltless, guileless, innocent.

I heard a grunt from the rear of the room, and Alessandro came forward to scrutinize the scene. Without a word he nodded, then went to adjust the lights further. He softened the spots, opened two or three umbrellas and screwed them onto tripods. In a moment the camera was whirring again. I stood in the front and watched, forgetting the passage of time. I had created a living work of art.

Finally the photographer clapped his hands. "That's enough for today. Go and get cleaned up." The models immediately broke out of their pose, twisting their necks and working their jaws and fingers.

Slowly I walked over to the camera, waiting for Lucien to join us. The photographer carefully removed the film, writing something on the can and picking up a little brush and air pump to dust off his lenses.

Lucien stood by, also waiting for the verdict. Alessandro turned to me.

"You're an artist, aren't you?"

I nodded.

"Pre-Raphaelite, of course. The idea of sensual innocence." He shook his head slowly. "Not too many people appreciate that anymore."

"Will they sell?" Lucien asked.

"Who knows?" Alessandro replied with a shrug. Turning back to me, he dropped his professional facade for the first time. "Trying to educate the industry, huh? I wish you luck, darling."

Once outside, I stopped Lucien in the middle of the sidewalk. "What did that little challenge prove?"

"That you can do more than spend your life chasing galleries."

"With your loving guidance, I suppose."

"You'll never succeed by yourself."

"I'm not here to make money for you."

"Then make some for yourself!"

"Not doing commercial crap like this."

"You think it's better to hide in your miserable studio?"

Stung, I heard my voice go shrill. "I didn't come to Paris to work for white people!"

For a moment he didn't speak. "What is this, Chloe? Yet another form of your black pride?"

"If I fail," I answered, enunciating every word, "at least I'll fail with my black thighs closed!"

Lucien's eyes went opaque with fury, and he lunged toward me. The world pitched into a soundless vacuum as his open hand flew forward. I flinched and staggered backward, preparing myself for the blow. But at the last instant he somehow restrained himself, instead gathering up a mouthful of saliva that he spat at my feet.

A sudden onslaught of traffic roared up the avenue as I began running up the street, the Arc de Triomphe looming crazily in the distance. I'd gone only a few paces when he caught me from behind and snatched me up into his arms.

"I'm sorry, Chloe," he cried, smothering my face in kisses. "Forgive me!"

"Forgive you?" I pulled away from him roughly. "I should thank you for your honesty."

He took my hands and stared pleadingly into my eyes. "You don't understand. If I could be like you . . . if I had your strength and your talent and your pride I would—"

A bus growling up the busy avenue drowned the rest out. But looking at his troubled face and staring into the eyes I could never quite capture on canvas, it simply didn't matter. Michael, Lucien had become my life.

November 18, 1970

Dear Chloe,

Next week is Thanksgiving and I'll bet you forgot all about it! You must be busy because I haven't heard from you for a while. I'm really busy, too. I took my SAT exam last week, and I think it went pretty well. I'm planning to write my college applications over the Xmas break. I finally told Grandma that I want to go to New York, but she won't even consider turning me loose in "Sin City"!!! She wants me to stay at home and study at Howard, but I desperately want to get away from here. One of my teachers said he'd help me get a scholarship to Boston U. What do you think?

I'm dating a guy from Trinidad named Norris. He's the captain of our track team, and he's teaching me how to run. And yes, we've gone "all the way" (don't worry, it's rubbers or nothing!). To be honest with you, I'm not nearly as attracted to him as I was to Gordon (my first), but Norris is really tall and fine and he has an incredible accent. Guess I need to go on a Caribbean vacation!!

So, Chloe, have you fallen in love with that black guy, yet? Write me soon and tell me all about him. And tell me about the paintings you're working on right now!

Miss you! Love,

Me

P.S. I think about you all the time, especially when all the brainless beauties get together to plan their fascinating futures as housewives! *Remember: We're strong black women who break all the rules and succeed. And we never, ever let a man turn us away from our dreams!*

Something fell out of the envelope, and I bent down to retrieve the photograph of a slender young woman with intensely bright eyes. A patterned scarf encircled her handsome face, and little Kore figures danced in her ears. Smiling through the sudden tears that leapt into my eyes, I read the dedication*: To Chloe, my big sister and best friend. I love you! Michael, Class of '71.*

Surrounded by my canvases, I wondered whether I'd ever be the artist you expected me to become. And I asked myself why it was impossible for me to tell you about Lucien.

The document from the immigration police seemed innocent enough; I was invited to go to the nearest immigration office and present my passport and visa for "verification," so that they could check my employment status and update their records.

The morning was dark, with shreds of leaves dancing in a cold rain as I ascended the steps from the *métro*. Crossing a steep pedestrian bridge that arched over a six-lane highway, I found myself facing row upon row of identical cement skyscrapers stretching off to the north as far as I could see. Suburban Paris. Lucien's home.

I had to ask several people for directions. No one seemed to understand my French. When I chanced upon the right street, I was shocked to find a line of people extending at least a block from a low, cinder-block building. Most were brown-skinned or black, and many were clad in long robes and sandals, despite the rain. All of the women wore the veil.

I took my place at the rear of the line. A tall young man in jeans and a blazer immediately turned to me. "You don't have to wait here."

"Why not?"

"French nationals can go over to the next building."

"I'm not French," I said, and he raised his eyebrows in surprise.

"Where do you come from?" he asked, his eyes wandering over my hair and skin.

"North America. The United States."

"An American who comes to work in France?" He whistled through his teeth. Several other people turned to stare at me.

I looked down the line of expressionless faces. Several of the women had babies tied on their backs. Unlike my *Seraphina*, however, their eyes were drained of passion, of any visible determination to survive.

"If you're American, why are you in France?"

"To learn more about my craft. I'm an artist."

He translated my words to the people standing beside him, then turned again to me. "I happen to be a student, too," he said. "One day I will be a doctor."

The woman beside him spoke as she hoisted her baby to her hip and covered him against the cold rain.

"She is wondering why you can't learn about art in America," the young man said.

"I can," I explained, "but I also want to see other parts of the world."

His eyes narrowed. "In my country we say that Americans are like gods. You have everything. You want for nothing."

"Where do you come from?"

"Upper Volta. Do you know it?"

I shook my head, embarrassed.

"You see? Like a god, you decide who exists and who does not."

"Either a god or a very ignorant person," I said. "I'm afraid that I come from the second group."

He looked deeply into my face. Then his eyes softened. "A truly ignorant person is one who either doesn't know his ignorance, or can't admit it," he said.

At the door a uniformed security guard looked at my letter, then signaled me through a packed hall to an inner office. I tapped politely on the door, then opened it and came upon a graying bureaucrat in a dandruff-flecked, blue polyester suit.

"Sit down," he commanded without looking up from the stack of files on his desk. The cubicle was painted a painful orange-red, and the rectangle of window looked out over a tangle of electric transmitters at a buzzing power station.

I sat on a shaky wooden armchair with my knees touching the scarred desk.

"Your papers," he said. An ashtray filled with butts sent a violet, noxious snarl of smoke into the mottled air. I placed the government's letter on the top of the stack of files.

"I asked for your papers!" he shouted, enunciating his words as if I were either an imbecile or deaf. His eyes shot up from the documents centered on his desk. Stunned by the hatred in his gaze, I remained frozen, my eyes locked on his withered face.

"You have thirty seconds to show proof of your identity," he snarled, "before I call security and have you remanded to the police."

Silently I placed my passport on his desk. He picked it up, his fingers trembling very slightly.

"You are not a student?"

"No."

"You may continue to work at the restaurant until your visa expires."

"I have no intention of working there a day longer."

We again stared at each other, our faces only a few inches apart, and his hatred of my color, my gender, my very *being* bounded between us like a maddened pinball.

"You cannot extend this visa," he stated softly. "You must leave France in seven months."

Snapping my passport closed, he tossed it to the soiled floor. Stunned, I struggled not to react.

"Hurry up!" he ordered me. "Others are waiting!"

I picked up my passport like a whipped dog and placed it carefully inside my bag. The man again turned to his files, and I moved silently to the door.

Crushed, I managed to hold back my tears until I got outside. A cold drizzle was falling from the exhausted sky, and a low fog had descended over the cement buildings. Retreating toward the *métro* station, I fixed my swimming eyes on the pockmarked asphalt and silently counted my footsteps.

"Hey. Hey!"

I looked up to see a tall figure wrapped in a trench coat that tugged restlessly with the wind. His left arm vanished around a dark woman whose hair blew almost to her waist. Sweeping off his beret, he threw me his winning smile. Emil Mathurin.

"You never called, Chloe!" he exclaimed in English, grasping my hand and bringing it to his lips. He presented me to his companion, whose murmured greeting did little to hide the resentment in her exquisite hazel eyes.

"I hope you're not coming from over there." He jabbed his thumb toward the line of waiting immigrants. "That's a special inferno the French use to punish foreigners for daring to live in Paris."

I wiped at my mascara-stained cheeks and he hoisted out a great sigh.

"I'll buy you a coffee, and you can tell me about it. Perhaps," he added craftily, "I can use it in my next play."

He spoke to the woman in Creole, and she obediently kissed his cheeks and continued on her way. Taking my arm, he followed me into the smoky café and shouted at the barman, who waved a greeting.

We slipped into a padded booth, and he pumped the tabletop jukebox full of money. A fast-paced calypso began, the steel drums spilling out like jelly beans. Absently fingering the wiry coils along his forehead, he nodded in time to the music.

Emil's body emanated a restless energy, yet his gaze was focused and astute. His eyes had swept over my short skirt and smeared eyes when we entered the café. Now he produced a bandanna from the pocket of his trench coat and watched as I tried to clean my face.

"Still painting, Chloe?" he asked kindly.

I nodded, unsure of my voice.

"And I'll bet there's a boyfriend by now."

I nodded again but found it strangely difficult to meet his gaze.

"Oh, well," he grumbled good-naturedly. "I'll see those paintings sooner or later."

He glanced away to order two *cafés au lait* from the North African waiter. They chatted for a few moments, Emil throwing a few Arabic expressions into their palaver, and when he turned back to me he reached across the table and lifted my chin.

"Pitite an mwen!" he said softly. He flicked his head toward the government office. "Looks like they almost made a zombie out of you."

I wiped my eyes. "I don't know why I'm putting myself through this."

"Only an American would say that," he replied. "Most immigrants are so happy to live in a relatively safe, stable country that they're willing to ignore the meaningless abuse of those pitiful bureaucrats. That won't be the last time that someone treats you badly in this country. But you must live *sans illusions et sans regrets*. Do you understand? No illusions. No regrets."

"But that place was insane."

"Pardonnez-moi," he said sarcastically. "Nothing's insane in America."

"America isn't paradise, like everyone seems to think."

"And France isn't paradise, like some Americans seem to think."

I was silenced. He was still looking at me, but his tone softened. "Living here isn't quite as easy as you expected?"

"I don't know," I stammered, my eyes burning with tears. "I thought I could leave all that hatred—the war, the riots, the racism—behind."

"Paris was supposed to be your private sanctuary?"

"I'm *painting*, Emil," I said urgently. "For the first time in my life I'm doing what I was born to do!"

He raised his hands in a calming gesture. "No matter *where* we live, we'll still be black. There's a price we have to pay for that. Those things you were running away from—the hatred and anger—those things are here, too. Even if they wear different costumes and speak a different language."

The waiter brought the coffee, and Emil leaned closer, his voice somber.

"Listen to me, Chloe." Hesitantly I looked into his handsome, expressive face. "I'm from an island of black people. When those white folks come down from France and try to tell us how to live, we smile and then go right on doing things our way.

"I remember sitting in a classroom when I was a little boy, and this teacher was telling us all about Oedipus, the guy who killed his father and married his mother. The prof was in love with this story. He had tears in his eyes, and he was acting out all the parts, and my cousin Lillia cleared her throat and suddenly my neighbor Peepee started to giggle and then the whole class was hysterical. We were falling out of our chairs, rolling on the floor, and the teacher was screaming and waving his arms, and Lillia kept saying, *'But where is the tragedy? Oedipus made an honest mistake!'* "

"I don't understand, Emil."

"You can't," he said in a low voice. "You've spent your life in the white man's world where life is a tragedy and death is a tragedy and love is a tragedy and being alone is a tragedy. The white man is drowning in his *existence tragique*, while he's strangling and starving and killing everyone who won't join the spiritual suicide."

He paused. "But you don't have to drink the hemlock, Chloe. You must reach inside to the core of your creativity. And then," he added, "you must live your life joyfully."

I started to respond but faltered. Emil sucked his teeth softly.

"You really are scared, *pitite mwen*!" He touched the tear caught in my lashes. "Don't worry, Chloe. You can't step into the same river twice. When I look at you, I see a survivor."

He stared at me for a long, naked moment and something happened that wasn't supposed to. My sense of helplessness faded, as if replenished by the promise of his strength. I felt the tips of his warm fingers find my face. Beneath the table his legs grazed mine. And his probing gaze filled me with an indescribable blood trust—as if he, too, had known the isolation of being unloved. The terrible need to create. The soul-deep weariness of being alone.

Jesus—the realization ripped through my mind—I've *never* felt this way about Lucien!

The jukebox stopped playing and the coffee cooled as we continued to stare at each other, his hands cradling my face. Then he leaned forward, his full lips brushing mine in a caress that was much warmer and gentler than a kiss. I gasped as his mouth again met mine, his skin cool and sweet and filled with longing.

"Oh, Chloe," he said breathlessly, and shoving the image of Lucien out of the way, I moved toward him. Our lips met and our mouths opened and the touch of his tongue sent my heart slamming against my breasts. Forgetting that we were in a public café, I reached for his shoulders, intending to pull him even closer to me.

Instead he drew back, blinked, and grunted sharply. Troubled eyes met mine for a vanishing second, then he groped about for his trench coat and began to rise. I reached for his arm.

"I'm already late to rehearsal," he said, avoiding my eyes. He stared into the distance as he buttoned his coat, then exhaled slowly and looked down once more.

"There's someone else in your life, Chloe." He held up his hand to stop me from speaking. "Please try to understand: I'll have to leave until it's right for me to stay."

Helplessly I watched him lope off into the early winter, his lean silhouette hunched up against the cold.

What the hell was I doing?

I made my way to Lucien's flat at Vincennes, completely forgetting my misadventure with the immigration police, my lips still tingling with Emil's gentle kiss. My mind was so saturated with his beckoning gaze that I ignored the strong smell of alcohol that entered the flat with Lucien. He declined to eat the food I'd prepared, withdrawing into a silence broken only by the dull click of a bottle of scotch against an ever-emptying glass.

After a while I joined him at the table, opening a new pack of unfiltered cigarettes.

"When my mother died of cancer I told myself I would never, ever smoke. I guess this proves the road to hell is paved with Gauloises."

He ignored my bad joke. I put the last match into the ashtray and, taking care not to upset the vase of anemones at the center of the table, nervously raised the stubby cigarette to my lips.

Lucien had selected the music, and now a low sax was murmuring its way through the night, the brush of cymbals shushing a dirgelike bass. A faint police siren bleated repeatedly on the street below. Lucien lifted his head, his face etched with shadow from the hanging lamp as his hands found their way into his matted curls. The scotch bottle stood half emptied at his elbow.

"You've been too quiet this evening, Lucien."

"Sometimes one simply feels like listening."

"And drinking," I observed sarcastically.

"So fucking what?" he barked. Something menacing in his voice, not in the words themselves, made my heart leap. He was looking at me with a measuring, vigilant gaze—a predator baiting his prey.

"Well," I said lightly, "what do you want to talk about?"

"Let's talk about your childhood," he remarked casually. "You've heard all about mine."

I drew hard on the cigarette, feeling his waiting eyes. "My childhood? Why?"

"Because childhood is something we all have in common," he retorted, again raising his glass.

"There was nothing special about it," I said in a level voice. "I went to school, to church, then home—"

His brow furrowed and his voice grew tight beneath its softness. "Your father?"

"Worked in a tire factory."

"And your mother—"

"Died ages ago."

"Brothers and sisters?"

"A brother who went to 'Nam, came home in a straitjacket, and inhabits a psycho ward."

"You never mention him."

My voice sped up, and I heard a shrillness beneath my words. "I was a kid when he left, and I only saw him once after they shipped him back."

"Then who *do* you have in America?"

"There's Michael, of course. She's like a little sister—"

"That's it?"

"It's the past," I insisted, stubbing the cigarette into the ashtray. "Like you, I've left all that behind."

"Well, now," he said very softly, "let's review our notes. First we're in Ohio, where Chloe is born. Chloe's mother dies. So Chloe moves to New York. Chloe gets married and divorced. So Chloe moves to Washington. And Chloe's life goes on hold until the plane lands in Paris." He paused. "All of that amounts to a little less than nothing."

"So what?"

"So I stopped by Anya's this afternoon." His hands grew still. His next words reverberated like a tightrope. "She assumed I knew about that bastard and his fucking gallery."

The room seemed to darken. Thoughts spinning, I mumbled the

only words that were moving slowly enough to be spoken. "It really doesn't make any difference."

"He's refusing to show your work because of me."

"He's refusing to show my work because I didn't sleep with him."

"But you would have slept with him if not for me."

"I could have slept with him anyway."

We stared at each other. Could he see that I was trembling?

"You're becoming ambitious, Chloe. Taking lessons from Anya?"

"She has nothing to say about my life."

"Then why did *she* know if I didn't?" He paused. "That's right: She's your *friend*."

I swallowed hard. "I wasn't trying to hide anything."

"You simply *forgot* to tell me?"

"I was trying to work things out."

"You were trying," he spat, "to *keep* me out."

"Why would I do that?" I stammered.

"Because your friend Anya wouldn't have it any other way."

Restlessly I stood up, buying time to think. Pulling another cigarette from the pack on the table, I wandered around the small kitchen, looking for matches.

"Sit down, Chloe. We're not finished."

I ignored him, glancing around at the bookshelves.

"Sit down," he repeated, an undertone of menace lacing the command.

Suddenly I remembered having seen him empty the loose change and matchbooks from his pockets into a small wooden box placed unobtrusively on a low shelf near the wall. I crossed the room and opened it even as Lucien loudly called out my name.

Reaching into the box, my fingers closed on a cool metal object—a lighter?—and I pulled it out. His chair shrieked weirdly, and his bottle of scotch smashed to the floor amid the scarlet blossoms.

"Lucien— What's this?"

He was standing crookedly beside the table, his entire form now a darkened silhouette. Against the hollow, drifting music, I heard his condemning, "Let there be Truth."

In my hands lay a small silver frame encircling the yellowing photograph of a hulking man with dark hair. He loomed over a fine-boned, very black woman. A curly-headed boy of perhaps seven or eight leaned shyly into her skirt. The family was posed against a wall of stone, their faces squinted up against the white sunlight.

"That photograph," he intoned emotionlessly, "was taken across the street at the castle. It's one of the few happy days I can remember from my childhood. By the end of that evening he had fractured two of her ribs."

Lucien's jaw. His flattened nose. His deep, hooded eyes. On the woman's face. The black face.

"Your mother?" I whispered.

"Grew up in the Côte d'Ivoire, came to France as a servant, then married a first-class brute."

"But, your mother—"

Lucien snorted softly. "Didn't have much of a chance, I'm afraid."

"Then your mother, " I repeated hoarsely.

"Yes, Chloe. My mother was African."

Everything fluttered for an instant with my thumping pulse and sweating hands. And then the world went hurtling down an icy chute of realization. "That means you—"

He looked at me with eyes of stone. "What, Chloe?"

"You're *black*."

"Am I?" His face had become a shadow without tone or depth. But his voice, that sandy voice that lured every woman from her reticence into his embrace, had gone rough and low.

My voice, however, was exploding with rage.

"You're a fucking lie," I hissed. "*Nothing* about you is true! Not even your goddamned skin!"

"Would you have slept with me sooner if you'd known?"

"You hypocrite! You've got everyone thinking—"

He burst into mocking laughter. "Sweet, pretty Chloe. You were so very proud you'd never had sex with a white man."

"I'm still proud of that," I said, "but you make me sick."

"But why?" he answered as he moved away from the table, sauntering slowly toward me. "I simply choose to keep my past private. Just like you."

I backed away from him, coming up flush against the bookshelves. He moved in close, his smile now weighted with contempt. "Now that I'm black, let's *really* make love."

I tried to move away, but he threw his arms up on either side of me, pressing his body hard against mine. "You don't have to be ashamed," he added as he forced his thigh between my legs. "I'm far more African than you."

Afterward, I ran.

It felt good to run in the December night.

It felt good to run through the wind-whipped tears that seeped into my mouth and down my chin to my heaving chest below. It felt good to let the splintering pain of my heels on the icy sidewalk work its way up my calves and into the tender joints of my knees and hips. After all, the frozen pain was collateral against the bruises already forming on my upper arms and jaw.

He had hit me twice. Once, because I tried to slap him. And then, after he was finished, because I called him a motherfucker. He smacked me hard and stumbled away, his pants loose around his ankles, and threw up violently in the toilet. While he was still retching, I scrambled into my clothes and fled.

I spent that night wrenched up tight on my yawning bed, trying to call sleep down upon the raw wound of Lucien. I pushed away the images of his face: the eyes that had blackened out to yawning pits as he pulled me, struggling, to the floor. The arms that pinned my shoulders back while he leaned over me, slamming his body into mine. The disinterested wail of a distant police car as he lurched from me, disgusted by my soiled flesh.

At dawn I knelt in my shower, an acolyte in the temple of despair, and scrubbed and scrubbed and scrubbed. Then I kept a silent vigil as the shadows fell early across my studio, staring at the portrait I now knew I would never complete.

How could he do this? I wondered, broken and numb. Doesn't he see how much I love him? I watched clouds of dust floating in the cold rays of sunlight to form reliefs on the rough plaster walls. Somehow, I knew the answer to both questions, though it was impossible for me to admit it: *The liar in Lucien had recognized the liar in me.* And the hatred we felt for ourselves bound us together in a sad and pathetic dance toward our inevitable destruction.

When the door opened at dusk on the third day, I could barely make out the outline of his figure in the darkness. He found the switch, and only then did I see what I had never dreamed of seeing—that he was broken, too. He came and sat beside me at the table, keeping his face turned away. Three words:

"I need you."

And once again I led him to my bed. When he touched me, my skin seemed to ignite. His unchecked growth of beard scoured the sweet flesh of my inner thighs, but I knew that my nails left blood on his back. Neither one of us could live in truth, but when he wept, the sound of his tears helped me pretend that healing him was a way of healing myself.

You see, Michael, I needed Lucien as much as he needed me.

The sky was whirling snow a few days later when I crossed the Bir-Hakeim Bridge, and I was lost in the labyrinth of high-rises dominating the western tip of the city. After wandering for a time I found a white tower that pierced the falling evening like an icy needle. A uniformed doorman interviewed me politely, then rang the apartment while I waited in a hall of mirrors lined with artificial Christmas trees. Finally I was directed to an elevator serving floors twenty to forty.

Standing ankle deep in plush carpet, I knocked gently on a carved wooden door and waited for a time. I knocked again, and then a third time, but there was no answer. I had turned to go when I heard a soft movement behind me. A figure wavered in the shadows, a ringing silence wafting out behind her. She motioned for me to enter.

As we kissed in greeting, Aziza seemed like twigs in my embrace. Wasted and ashen, she vanished into the folds of a somber gown, her hair hidden beneath a wrap. She preceded me into an echoing, low room with a wall of glass. Beneath us lay the Tinker Toy Tour Eiffel, the wandering brown Seine, and the blizzard-softened towers of Notre Dame.

There was little furniture in the vast chamber. Sheepskin rugs strewn with woven pillows, a carved teak table, and a brass samovar met my gaze. Another door led to a gleaming, empty kitchen, and yet another down a curving hall to the bedrooms. Aziza stood silently beside me, her eyes fixed on the panorama of swirling white veiling the city below.

"How're you doing?" I asked lightly, ignoring the obvious.

"Did you think I swallowed a bottle of pills or something?"

"No, Aziza. But I hadn't seen you in so long. We're all worried about you."

"Oh, Anya cares only about her collection." She gestured for me to sit beside her on the rug, then searched for the energy to speak. A shadowy smile flitted over her wan face. "But I know when you're thinking about me, Chloe. Often I can feel it, especially late at night."

We were mute for a few moments, engulfed by the snow.

"You've got a real palace here," I said with forced cheerfulness.

"It's my golden prison," she murmured. "No one can get in without permission. And I have nowhere else to go."

"Maybe you need a roommate."

"I had one, until he learned about our baby." She laughed darkly. "He says a black child would 'sully' his family's line. I'm good enough for his bed, but not to be his wife."

"He's an animal," I replied.

"I know," she said tonelessly. "But it doesn't change the fact that we were together for a long time." She paused. "He claimed he didn't care what they thought. He followed me everywhere. Called, sent roses, came to the shows, the parties, even my fittings. Never—" she paused, her words hanging suspended in the air "—never have I known a man to pursue a woman the way he pursued me."

There was a long silence. She closed her eyes.

"I told my brother. He said that if I bear this white man's child, I will no longer be a member of our family—"

"Christian-Noël is not important," I said. "Your brother is not important. Anya is not important, and neither are any of the others. The only two people who matter in this world are you and your child, because without you, she'll have no one."

"But how will I survive? No one measures your art by your appearance, Chloe. But my appearance is my art. And *look* at me! I may never model again."

"Aziza," I said, "you must stop seeing yourself through their eyes. You have *never* been more beautiful. You are more perfect, more whole, more complete, than ever before. Because, Aziza, you are not the woman on those magazine covers. You're real."

I touched her face gently, and she came into my arms and began to weep with great, low sobs that echoed weirdly in the spreading darkness. I stroked her back and sang to her, and as the sky blackened her face softened and her belly slowly ceased to heave. A great calm invaded the room. Gathering herself into the very essence of stillness, she placed her hands protectively on her stomach and turned her sculpted face toward the snow. The wintry night brought her exquisite profile into a perfect silhouette.

"Aziza, let me paint you. No makeup. No lights. Exactly as you are now. You'll show this painting to your baby one day, and she'll see herself, too, waiting to be born."

Her hands stroked the slopes of her gown. "Do you think she'd want to see me like this?"

"This face," I said, as I traced her naked features with my loving fingers, "without the lights, the paint—this is the true face of her mother."

The baby moved, and Aziza brought my hand to her stomach. The feeling was like water rippling beneath my fingers. She covered my hand and held it there as if I were giving her my blessing.

"I do love her, you know. Otherwise I would have . . ." She glanced up at me, and I knew that somehow a light had pierced through the pain. "Thank you, Chloe," she murmured. "When can we begin?"

I sent you a book of French poetry for Christmas, Michael. Folded between the pages were little watercolors of my studio, Aziza, and Emil Mathurin. I told myself that I'd write you about Lucien over the holidays when the restaurant was closed and I'd have time to explain things properly. I didn't include any sketches of him because I found it impossible to get his eyes right. I didn't want to send you anything less than my best work (I told myself), so the story of my Great Love Affair (as Anya continued to describe it) would just have to wait.

Of course, I hadn't mentioned anything to her about the photograph in Lucien's box, or what happened the night I discovered it. She was too busy talking about her next collection to notice the seismic changes in me. And I was an expert at hiding my feelings. After all, I'd been doing it practically my whole life. So whenever anyone did happen to ask about my relationship with Lucien, I'd tell them that he made me the happiest woman alive. I was so good at lying that I almost believed it myself.

Lucien had been invited to a Christmas party in Passy. An important client would attend. This was the first time we'd appeared in public as a couple, so I was especially careful with my makeup and hair. When I presented myself for inspection, he nodded in tight-lipped approval.

The room was shivering with sequins, black polyester, and gold lamé. Warmth was forbidden on these carefully constructed faces, and our entrance was met by a gauntlet of mocking stares.

"Another cheerful evening in fashion paradise," I remarked under my breath.

"Sometimes one needs to breathe air without turpentine."

"That's right. You feel at home with the Designer Inquisition."

"There are times when you should think about someone other than yourself."

"Don't worry. I'll spend the whole evening thinking of you."

The apartment was backlit with moody, dramatic splashes of light that played well on high cheekbones and painted eyes. I drifted, picking up a glass and a cigarette and speaking to the few people I knew.

Someone asked me to dance, and I let myself be led into another room. A *chanteuse* in a snakeskin gown was vying to be Motown *à la Parisienne*, rocking back and forth with a harlequin grin. I glanced at my partner, an older man with thinning gray hair whose eyes said he was feeling a bit sorry for me.

"Didn't we meet at Nikki's party?"

I shook my head, retreating from his bourbon breath.

"Of course, you don't go to La Cirque?" he asked, his voice a locust's scratch above the childlike wail of the singer.

"Of course not," I replied as I caught a glimpse of myself in a smoky mirror. Even with my best dress and stylish shoes, I resembled Cinderella before the ball.

In a noisy arrival I saw a man who seemed familiar beneath a heavy growth of beard. Too late I recognized Christian-Noël Antoine Marie de la Salle with an olive-skinned beauty. Unfortunately his eyes met mine and he lurched across the room, his arm locked around his companion.

"I know you," he said thickly.

"Yes. I'm Aziza's friend, Chloe."

His face slammed shut, and his insinuating smile was instantly replaced by a sneer. "Tell her hello," he managed, his eyes moving to the other woman. "And tell her that I know what she's trying to do." He reached up and squeezed his partner's cheek between his forefinger and thumb. "You know better than to do anything like that, don't you?"

Lucien appeared, as gracious and relaxed as a zombie.

"Ah, Christian-Noël. How are you?"

"Look at this," the other man answered, gesturing toward the woman. "As you see, I'm just fine."

Her eyes met Lucien's and something passed between them. I stiffened, and Christian-Noël laughed delightedly. "You'd like some, would you? Not a chance, friend. This one's after more than a pretty face in a nice suit. This one believes herself to the manor born."

He let out a howl and, placing a hand on Lucien's shoulder, bent almost double. Then calming himself, Christian-Noël whispered to his date: "What's your name again, darling?"

"Pathetic bastard," Lucien commented, leading me back to the bar for another drink.

"Are you enjoying this?" I inquired, as a staggering woman in dark glasses left a scarlet smear on someone's white mink wrap.

Lucien's eyes unwillingly found mine. "Part of my business is being seen, Chloe."

"You don't really want them to see you."

"It depends on who's looking," he replied, meeting the gaze of a towering Viking with full lips and sculpted short hair.

"I must be ruining your image," I remarked, struggling to keep the defeat out of my voice.

"You," he responded with the meanness of his third double scotch, "are proof that I have no more image."

"Don't worry: I'll keep your secret."

"Yes," he said darkly, "you will."

I snatched my arm free and crossed the room. From a corner I watched his dark curls bent in confidence over a white-haired woman in pearls. Coolly she placed a heavily ringed hand on his shoulder, rolling back her head to peer at him from deep blue eyes.

Two young men standing nearby turned to take me in more closely. The taller of the two, slender and caramel-colored, leaned over with a cool smile. "And what do you do?" he asked in perfect American English.

"I paint," I answered dully, and he took a step closer.

"Lucrative vocation."

"I don't paint for profit."

He laughed. "Of course not. That's the great calling of our people. We do the things for spiritual reasons that white people do for money."

"Such as?"

"They sing in operas while we sing in churches. They dance in ballets and we dance on street corners. They write books and we have our lovely folktales."

"You think that black culture is inferior?"

"Oh god, no!" he said impatiently. "Just impractical."

"So what do you do?"

"I'm one of those fools who dances," he said with a dismissive wave of his hand. "I couldn't stand the smell of all that oil and paint thinner, and I'd hate being closed up all day with some brushes and a piece of cloth!"

"My feelings exactly," said a voice beside me, and I discovered Jacques, cigarette and wineglass in hand, smirking at me with his deeply shadowed eyes.

"So tell me, Chloe: Where are you exhibiting?"

The tears that filled my eyes left me afraid to speak, and, emboldened by my silence, he reached down and traced my collarbone with a mocking finger.

"Your friend wrecked your chances in Paris."

"He stopped me from getting involved with you."

"Correction: He stopped me from showing you." His finger moved with outrageous boldness toward my lips.

I knocked his hand away, seeing his pleasure deepen at my anger. Slowly and deliberately, he inspected my clothes and hair. "I really wonder what he's trying to prove."

Before I could speak, Lucien was upon us. "Let's go, Chloe," he announced flatly, propelling me away from the gallery owner. The sea of closed faces opened as he guided me through his business associates and former lovers. In the strange kind of nonsilence that surrounds the unwanted, I thought I could hear every whisper, every laugh, every sneer.

The December night closed in with a smothering cold. Christmas lights swayed dizzily in a low wet wind, and shreds of paper skittered through the empty street. We climbed into the car, but Lucien's blanched knuckles remained frozen on the key. Wet smoke and stale alcohol perfumed us both, and snatches of conversation and endless, colorless music floated down from the open windows overhead.

Suddenly he shoved the car into gear, and jerking across the cobblestone square, he ripped into traffic with a relentless disrespect for the law. Just once, as he took a corner at full speed, I said his name in a low voice.

"Yes, Chloe?" he answered, his eyes moving to mine from the slick pavement.

"Take it easy."

"Of course." The car accelerated.

We took a nauseating course through narrow passages and residential streets over the back of Montmartre, coming out at Pigalle and wheeling into Barbès.

Soon we jerked to a stop in front of my studio. Within minutes we were upstairs and I saw that he had a bottle of scotch. I watched in silence as he fumbled through my cabinets and, finding no clean glasses, lifted the bottle to his lips.

He had pulled his tie free, and his rough curls wound like tendrils along the base of his throat, choking the pale flesh. The hand clasping the bottle was bone white at the knuckles, and his legs were braced awkwardly against a chair.

I slipped out of my coat, trying hard to avoid my reflection in the bedroom mirror. Moving casually through the studio, I scanned my paintings, making note of which were dry and varnished, and thus less vulnerable to damage. Quietly I placed *Seraphina* and the still-evolving portrait of Aziza behind a stack of blank canvases. Then I moved to the opposite side of the room, trying to prepare myself for whatever might come.

Lucien drew a smooth, deep breath and set down the empty bottle.

"So, Chloe," he sneered. "Ready for some more truth?"

"You don't know anything about the truth." I kept the table between us.

"I know that it's over between us," he said, swinging the sledgehammer hard. My world exploded like a block of ice.

"So that's it?" I cried over my pumping heart. "Dump the excess and drive away?"

"Of course," he said emotionlessly.

A despairing fury surged up in my chest, and I forgot my fear. "You parasite! You were only here to take what you wanted—"

"What could I want in this trash heap?"

"Your blackness," I spat. "That's what it's always been, from the very first night. All that talk about being poor in Paris. All that crap about honesty and survival. You came to me to find that lost part of yourself, that hole which all the money and sex in Paris can't fill—"

He lurched forward, and I stumbled back against the arched opening to the bedroom.

"You think that living as a black would save me?" he cried. "Black men clean the sewers in Paris, and I won't be anyone's slave!"

"You can't spend your life impersonating your enemies!"

"And you can't spend your life alone in a studio, making love to your paintings."

"My paintings are more real than you are!"

"And more real than *you*, too," he mocked, coming up so close that I could see the flecks in his glowering eyes. "What are you hiding, Chloe? Why do all your doors slam shut whenever I ask about your childhood?"

I tried to move past him, and he grasped my upper arms, shoving me back against the arch. "Look at me," he snarled, forcefully grabbing my jaw. "Do you see your reflection in my eyes?"

"I hate you!" I screamed, wrenching my arms free and pushing him away.

"Then you hate yourself," he replied with brutal perception.

Once again I tried to escape, but he was faster. Pressing me hard against the rough plaster wall, he spoke with terrible precision: "You knew where I came from before you brought me here. And," he added very softly, "I never told you I loved you."

"You are Antoine Laurent's son," I rasped, praying my words would rip his soul apart. "There's nothing left in you that your mother could love."

The blow came so fast that I didn't see it. He struck me with his closed fist, and the room ignited as my head slammed back against the wall. I went down hard to my knees and elbows. The tips of his shoes, wavering slightly as he stepped aside, came into sudden sharp focus. Then he bent low and grunted as he hoisted me up and began dragging me across the floor toward the bed.

I never told you—

I thought that I was screaming, but all sound was sucked into the kaleidoscope of pain roaring up from my knees to my face to the back of my skull

never told you never loved you

as the rough floorboards tore my stockings and splinters ripped at my thighs, my twisted arms vised behind my throbbing head so I couldn't

loved you I loved you

break free from his alcohol-driven fury or the black holes in his face or the strange empty silence around my

I love

sweet boiling lips and blood-tattered cheek and the hot-swelling skull

you!

And his shoes slammed into my ribs as he heaved my hips up to the edge of the mattress. I tried to pull away, and he struck me again and again, the blows knocking me on my back and cracking my jaw against the bedframe.

He tore away the shreds of my stockings. He leaned over me. He opened his pants in one smooth motion and held down my arms with his weight. And I would have resigned myself to letting Lucien finish the job started by someone I trusted so many years ago, except that I was no longer a child. He had already taken away my chance for a gallery. He had broken my dignity and defiled my body. There was only one thing left for me to save: *my art.*

So dredging up a shred of strength from deep inside my battered soul, I wrenched my arms free just as he pushed himself between my thighs. Ignoring the vortex of pain engulfing my battered flesh, I kicked at him as hard as I could. My heel glanced off his upper thigh, missing its swollen mark. But I had nailed the flat plane of his pelvis, and he screamed and bent double. I crawled away, leaving a bloody smear on the wall when I lost my balance. He came right behind me, moving in deadly silence. Facing my terror, I rose on unsteady feet, snatched up a mat knife, and turned the raw razor on my lover.

It must have been two, or perhaps three hours later that I pulled myself up from the floor. The room was dark, which was certainly no surprise because I had fallen against the light switch during our struggle. Banging into my broken easel, I groped my way through the mess of tubes and brushes to the canvases scattered violently throughout the studio. One by one I picked them up, blowing off the dirt and dust, leaning them lovingly against the wall.

Aziza was there, radiant in her patterned cloak, a kinte wrap folded elegantly above her maternal gaze. The wandering men were there, including the group that gathered around a street actor at a flea market one day. The deaf child from the park was there, and Emil grinned out from an unfinished sketch I'd begun from memory. And then I found *Seraphina*, mercifully untouched, her face still filled with dignity. Only one large painting had been destroyed: the strange, eyeless portrait of Lucien.

At last I made my way to my crumpled bed. Ignoring my bloated face, blistered hands, and ragged black dress, I shrouded myself tightly with the sheets. Distant horns from a police wagon blared up from the streets below.

Merry Christmas, Chloe.

I lay there, looking through the skylight at the cold night sky. Each second seemed like an eternity passing through my swollen, bloody breaths. Yet even worse than the pain was the wrenching despair that was so familiar, so true, that it felt like my oldest, closest friend. "What did you expect?" I whispered through a child's splintered lips. "There's a price to pay for breaking your vow. . . ."

There were at least three more hours before daylight would cast its shadows on how, after one hundred days of the madness called Lucien, I'd begin the re-creation of Chloe.

I was marked for a long time, Michael.

The holidays came, and I spent them alone, whispering, "Strong and successful . . . strong and successful . . ." like a mantra. I had nearly let a man destroy my dreams. Unable to hold a brush properly, I spent Christmas Day staring into blank canvas. Both of my eyes were black, and my lips were split and swollen. There were bruises along my arms and thighs, and my knees were ripped raw from their waltz with the floorboards.

I feigned sickness and managed to avoid Anya, Aziza, and Le Kansas. The only card I got was from you.

But it didn't matter. The shards of my heart were sharp enough to slit my veins, so I numbed myself to any feeling. At night, however, I wept my soul loose from my flesh, the sound echoing weirdly through the studio's dense shadows. Whirling in the memory of Lucien's voice and his touch, I hated my desperate, shame-filled longing for him.

You called me on Christmas, Michael. Fortunately my mouth had healed enough for me to speak with reasonable clarity. Fortunately your grandmother made you limit the call to three minutes, so I didn't fall prey to your amazing perception.

"Emil is *gorgeous*!" you shouted, your voice crackling over the wire. "When's the wedding?"

"Emil?" I repeated stupidly. "Oh, you mean the sketch I sent you?"

"There are *no* men like him in America! Nowhere! Chloe, you'd better—"

"Get some more painting done," I reminded her. "Emil is just a friend."

"It's okay to fall in love with your friends," you retorted.

"And how is Norris, your friend from Trinidad?"

"Now it's Henry. Basketball player. Tall, dark, and *really fine* . . ."

Your grandmother intervened, reminding you that our time was almost up.

"Chloe, if I earn enough money next summer, can I come to see you at Christmas?"

"I may be living across the street from you by then."

"No way!" You laughed. "Happy New Year, Big Sister. I love you!"

"And I love you, too," I whispered, my face running with tears.

When I was presentable, I returned to Le Kansas to find the regulars indulging in gluey eggnog and pheasant in drag as turkey. They were too busy drinking to pay any attention to their despondent waitress, and left huge tips when they staggered out, their rum-heavy breath lacerating the rain-soaked air.

A few days after the New Year the manager came into the restaurant kitchen and told me that a man at the bar wanted to see me. *Déjà vu.* I was so sure it was Lucien that I danced with some spilled pineapple juice and almost broke my ankle—but when I limped to the front I discovered Emil, puffing an American cigarette and sipping a Dutch beer.

"So you really do work here," he remarked, raising one eyebrow at my strange gait. I eased myself gingerly onto the stool beside him, wondering whether he would notice the lingering shadows below my eyes as we kissed in greeting, twice on each cheek.

"Why would I lie?" I asked with a trace of hostility.

"Who knows?" he responded. "After all, I'm both amusing and harmless." He took a good swig of his beer, ignoring the frosted mug and little dish of American peanuts on the counter beside him.

"Dark house tonight?" I asked, reluctantly admiring the high ridges of his cheekbones and his deep-set, slanted eyes.

"Our day off. The show's been held over and we're making lots of money," he explained, gesturing toward his expensive brew. "Is your boyfriend around?"

I shook my head, looking away.

"Then let's go to your place. I've finally got time to see your paintings."

Stomach tensing, I managed to respond civilly. "Tell me, Emil: Why should I take you home with me tonight?"

"I've already told you: I'm both amusing and harmless!"

"But it's late and I'm tired."

"Then I have an even better idea." He leaned toward me so that his shoulder rubbed mine. "Let's go to a dingy, impersonal café and have a trite and meaningless conversation."

A grudging smile tugged at the edges of my face, and he began shaking his head.

"No, Chloe. I absolutely refuse to go anywhere near your studio, no matter how much you beg. There's our completely platonic relationship to protect."

Now I *really* laughed—for the first time in weeks. "Emil, I don't know who's talking—you or that expensive beer."

"Hey, I'm just a mindless, uncivilized black man from the colonies. Expensive Dutch beers refuse to inebriate me."

I soon found myself moving painfully fast to keep up with his pace along the boulevard de Sébastopol.

"You get taller each time we meet," I remarked, noting that my head barely reached his shoulders.

"Well, my height depends wholly on the character I'm playing, as does my weight, my shoe size, and the condition of my teeth."

"So who are you tonight?"

"Any man you need me to be."

"That," I muttered, "might be a mistake."

"On the contrary," he said, placing his arm loosely around my shoulders, "I love difficult roles."

Leading me into an Egyptian coffee shop, he paid for two pastries consisting of honey poured over a mound of pistachios. We sat on orange plastic seats under fluorescent lights that hummed in a warm contralto, and Emil ordered coffee from a sweating, heavyset man in a soiled apron.

"Oh, la la," Emil said under his breath. "Do you think he's the pastry chef?"

"Probably not. He'd eat more than they'd ever sell."

I took a quick glance at the actor's beret and worn overalls. His braid was now long enough to tuck into his collar.

"It's nothing to worry about," he remarked without raising his eyes.

"What?" I stammered, embarrassed.

"My disguise. I learned a long time ago that it's safer on the streets when a black man remains virtually inconspicuous."

"That's what you are?"

"In Paris there is nothing more conspicuous than a black man who looks like he has a job."

"So you freeze to death in January to make the French happy?"

"I make them happy to get what I really want—a television or film role. It's just a matter of time before they make that mistake."

Our eyes met. "Where's your boyfriend tonight, Chloe?"

I took a deep breath. "What boyfriend?"

His eyes flickered. He lit a cigarette and sat back in his chair, peering at the teenagers in fluorescent vinyl and platform boots, heading for the discos.

"It's funny," he quietly observed. "Here we sit in a quarter of the city where only Arabs live, and the only people we see are French. Do you think that those white people are Arabs in disguise?"

I laughed again, and he grinned at me. "Even stranger is the fact that you never, ever see any blacks after dark. Not in any quarter of Paris."

"I guess the police have taken care of that."

"Yes," Emil agreed. "First we work, then we pay taxes, and then the police are paid with our taxes to break our woolly heads every time we venture out after sunset."

He shifted in his seat, uncrossing his long legs and shaking out his arms like an acrobat. "Let's go back to your place, Chloe. I'd like to see your work and, frankly, it's nearly midnight. There's a cop over there, and we're already pressing our luck."

I hesitated, looking into his eyes.

"Don't worry," he said. "I won't try to stay—unless, of course, you insist."

Emil seemed instantly at home in my jumbled-up studio. I sat stiffly at the table while he wandered among the canvases making soft, crooning noises. He paused a long time before the painting of *Seraphina*, then crossed the room and turned to stare at her again. I heard him laugh as he discovered my sketches of his face. Finally he whistled softly, shaking his head.

"I never imagined you'd be so good. And—" he paused, becoming uncharacteristically silent. I glanced up to find him looking not at the canvas, but at me. "And these paintings, all these black people and brown people— Chloe, you weren't abandoning your home when you came here. You were searching for it."

My pulse sped up even as I muttered, "I'm American, Emil. You said so yourself."

"Oh, no. I'm not talking about nationality." He threw back his head and raised his arms. "You're one of us! One of those black people who's been condemned to wander the earth just to find your *true* home."

A *true* home? Could such a place exist for me?

"That painting of the woman with her baby is incredible," Emil said as he strode toward the table. "But the most incredible thing is that she looks like y—"

He reached down to touch my cheek, and I cried out and flinched. For a long moment we remained fixed in that pose: my arms raised in a defensive gesture, his hand hovering in midair.

Pretending to ignore my reaction, he threw a long leg over the opposite chair. He went on talking, his face relaxed, his tone warm and friendly. Only his eyes revealed his immediate understanding.

"So," he said lightly. "How long have you been painting?"

"Forever," I answered, struggling to collect myself. "How long have you been acting?"

"My whole life, like all black people." He crossed his legs comfortably and began tapping a loose rhythm on the tabletop with his thumb and middle finger. "Five years ago I arrived in Paris, ready for my first starring role, but you know how it is . . . I wasn't blond enough. So I roamed around the streets, picked up as many unemployed blacks as possible, and formed the company." He paused for breath, his voice growing serious. "Actually, I hooked up with some old friends from home, and we've been working off and on until now."

"Why Paris?"

He shrugged. "Typical story: Descendants of slaves get fed up with the cane fields and decide to seek their fortune in the colonial mother country. My family moved to France when I was seven. To Marseilles. A very special town, Marseilles. You have to be an actor, there, to survive without getting your head smashed either by the police, the *pieds noirs*, or the Arabs."

"The *pieds noirs*?"

"Yes—the French who are still pissed off that they lost North Africa." He laughed. "I hate Marseilles even more than Paris. But at least there you have the sun and the sea."

"Where do you work when you aren't acting?"

"In the stockroom of the Galeries Lafayette."

"And where do you live?"

"In Aubervilliers."

"Alone?"

"That depends," he chuckled, his brilliant eyes glittering. "Now," he said, "let me ask *you* some questions."

"All right," I grudgingly agreed.

"Well, first of all, do I get the job? Look, baby, no one has put that many questions to me that fast since I got the stupid job in the store. It's not that I mind answering. It's just that, well—" he raised his shoulders "—part of my profession is the ability to improvise."

"You made all that up?" I asked, incredulous.

"I'm an actor, Chloe. Underneath my many faces is a very boring guy. Why don't we talk about you?"

"For example?"

"What happened with that boyfriend?"

I felt tears leap to my eyes, and he glanced away. "So, madame needs some cheering up?" he asked amiably. "I've got an idea. Les Xenos is taking the play on tour. We need some new sets, and I thought that maybe you could help."

"What did you have in mind?"

"Nothing too big: these things must be packed in our truck when we're traveling. Of course, we can't pay you much. But if you wanted to, you could come along and help us eat and drink up the profits."

"Where are you going?"

"The whole world lies before us," he answered, rising to his feet and lifting his arms. "Italy, Spain, Greece, perhaps Egypt. We only want to go where it's warm, of course. We're black people, after all."

I laughed again, feeling my sadness wash away like water. "Be serious for just sixty seconds, Emil!"

"If I must," he pouted. "We really are going on tour," he said in a normal voice. "We'll wait until the Cour des Rêves throws us out. Our success in Paris will mean larger audiences in the provinces."

"How long will you be away?"

"A few weeks. We all have jobs, and we don't want to lose them. But you're free to leave whenever you'd like, aren't you? That is, unless you couldn't live without that restaurant."

Christ! What an idea—to just abandon Paris and disappear into the sunset with a bunch of Caribbean actors! To escape the quest for a gallery! To be free of the likes of Anya and Jacques and the sorrow that was Lucien . . .

Emil observed me with a cool smile, squinting through a spiral of smoke like a celluloid lover. "Madame is tempted, I see."

"Temptation has led many a good woman down a bad path."

"The rest of France really isn't so bad, no matter what the Parisians think. Bring your brushes. Add some landscapes to your portraits."

Once again I felt his gaze tug at me, enticing me to go on a journey that I could barely even conceive. I tried to look away, but his eyes asked for trust—not for ownership, or devotion, or even love.

"There are thousands of artists in Paris," I said faintly. "Why me?"

"Paris has nothing to do with it."

"I don't know if I can give you what you want."

"I'm willing to wait," he murmured, "if you're willing to try."

The calm from deep within his solid frame seemed to reach out toward my desperate loneliness. I was awash in his amazing gentleness, coaxed like a wild animal to the outstretched promise of his caring. I rose to my feet, ignoring the pain that still swept up through my knees, and took a step toward him, teetering on the brink of trust.

He pulled me close and pressed my head against his heart while burying his face in my hair. *"Pitite mwen,"* he murmured, "my beautiful Chloe."

A shaft of light seemed to penetrate the darkness that had surrounded me since that night with Lucien. Emil's arms opened up a whole new world—a world that I had never known. His body moved sensuously against mine, but I felt him resisting his own growing desire. He seemed to be searching for something deeper than one night in my bed.

Suddenly he was on the move. He sprang to the door, pushing his arms into his jacket. "Stop by the theater this week and meet the others," he said without looking back.

I quickly followed him. "Why are you leaving?"

He glanced around at the canvases. "It's not time yet, Chloe. I've already told you: I'll leave until there's space for me to stay."

"But how are you getting home? It's too late for the *métro*."

"That's no problem," he said. "Don't you remember *Les Enfants du Paradis*? An actor's school begins after midnight." He opened the door. "And besides," he added, "my sister lives a few blocks from here in Barbès."

"Emil—" Something in my voice halted him. He gazed down at me and his whole face changed.

"Chloe, I have a feeling that somehow you're always attracted to the wrong man."

I didn't answer.

"And I don't have to tell you that I'm very attracted to you," he said. "Which means that if I stayed, I'd be the wrong man."

He kissed my cheeks gravely. "Let's give it a little time and see who I turn out to be."

Bounding swiftly down the steps, he turned and threw his arm up into the air. And I wished with all my heart that I knew the words to make him stay.

A tearful young woman pushed past me at the threshold of Anya's office a few days later.

"Oh, Chloe!" Anya looked up from her desk. "You actually showed up to give me a hand with these sketches!"

I sat down and picked up a drawing board and a box of colored pencils. "What's wrong with her?" I casually inquired.

"I fired her. She's spiking her veins, and I won't have that shit in my factory. And by the way, you look as if you haven't slept in a week."

"Thank you, Anya."

"I don't mean it as a compliment."

"You never mean anything as a compliment."

She had a new haircut, having let all the blond grow out, and now her hair was swept back behind her ears in a masculine wave, with soft red highlights playing over her temples. She looked hard, and serious, and successful.

"Quit the job at the restaurant and put in more hours with me," she commanded, meeting my gaze. "I can pay you much more now that I've got all these orders. I'd like to see more of you."

"You'd like me to *draw* more for you."

"It's true you're an excellent illustrator. So what do you get from that restaurant?"

"A little bit of money and a lot of privacy."

She went back to her sketches. "I don't get involved in your affairs anymore, Chloe. I just try to help you whenever I can."

I rolled my eyes, and she sighed. "I've really messed up our friendship, haven't I? I guess I never thought you'd be as independent as you are—I've wanted you to need me the way I needed you when we were in New York." She looked earnestly into my eyes. "And I should have known that you weren't really serious about Lucien. You certainly dealt with him the right way."

"Dealt with him?"

"Of course. You threw him out and kept right on with your life."

She turned back to her drawing. "I guess it's just another adventure for your gallery."

"Right. I get involved with men so I can paint portraits of them when they leave me."

She laughed her barbed-wire laugh, then slipped her pencil behind her ear. "It does seem strange not to have Lucien around anymore. In the past he'd continue to show up, even though he'd just broken up with—"

The phone rang, and she answered stridently with the mouthpiece tucked under her chin. Models flitted back and forth outside her office, and an occasional burst of raucous laughter erupted over the piped-in music. I thought of how thrilling it had all seemed just a few months before.

Anya hung up and grunted in irritation. "My new photographer. Great ideas but very opinionated. I don't know if it's going to work."

"What happened to Jules?"

"He joined the exodus to Milan. It's crazy: all the French fashion people are heading down to Italy and all the Italians are taking over up here. Even the guy on the phone. He's got a pretty successful studio near the Eiffel Tower, and he doesn't really want to take any orders from me."

"What's his name?" I asked.

"Alessandro Varese," she said. "Why?"

I lowered my eyes. A few days earlier I'd received an envelope from his studio containing an advertisement clipped neatly from a magazine. The ad featured a soft-focus shot of the models clustered around the Dionysian Giovanni, their hair forming swirling, undulating tendrils over their breasts, their eyes glowing and expressionless. The slogan, in Art Nouveau letters, read: "Seek the Divine . . ."

Stapled to the advertisement was a check for thirty-five hundred francs.

Anya was watching me carefully. "Now that Lucien's over, you really should get back together with that gallery owner."

"Right. I could beg him to sleep with me and pretend it has nothing to do with an exhibition."

"What were you pretending with Lucien?"

A roiling anger surged up in me. "If you really want to help me out, why don't you let me exhibit right here?"

Blinking back her surprise, she replied in a businesswoman's guarded tone. "No one would buy your paintings, no matter how good they are, if they thought your exhibition was an act of charity."

"But whoring myself with a gallery owner would make me marketable?"

"You're going to have sex with *someone*, Chloe. So it might as well be someone useful. After all, it only took Lucien ten minutes to hook up with that mindless blonde from—where *is* she from now? Oklahoma?"

The news of Lucien's new liaison was a stunning blow, though I knew that my lingering feelings for him were dangerous—even deadly. I tried to force myself to move on by purging everything in the studio that meant Lucien, including the spike-heeled boots and tight miniskirts and cone-capped bras. And I never went anywhere near the places we used to go. But, as usual, it was the letter I received from you, Michael, that forced me to begin the next chapter in my life.

February 15, 1971

Dear Chloe,

The police called from Chicago yesterday afternoon. My mother was killed in a car accident on the way home from a bar. I wanted to call you, but Grandma's been on the phone all night, contacting everybody in our family. The funeral's next Monday, here in Washington.

I don't know what to feel, really. She was my mother, even if I haven't lived with her for ten years. I can't really say I'll miss her, because she hasn't played a big role in my life. This probably means that I won't see my father again any time soon, although he never really lived with her anyway because of his job in Detroit.

Anyway, I guess that you and Grandma are my only real family now. Grandma's getting older, so I know I'd better get serious about school and try to make something of myself. I know she'd be proud if I ended up being as strong and independent as you, Chloe. I wish that I could see you. I hope that you're well. I love you.

Me

There was no time to pretend anymore. I needed to find a way to become the woman that you believed me to be.

The Cour des Rêves seemed deserted in the midafternoon, but the houselights were on and several black people occupied a table in the rear.

"I was looking for Emil—"

My declaration was met with a round of laughter as three of the men stood up, bowing in time to an imaginary fanfare.

"He's done it again!" One of them declared. "And this time she's not bad at all!"

"But she's from Martinique, no doubt," another said sarcastically.

"*Tu découds!* She rather has the air of a—"

"Stop being rude!" a woman said wryly. "Maybe she's from a film studio with a big bag of money for us!"

"Kiteye trankil!" I heard a familiar voice speaking in Creole. "It's Chloe! The artist!" Emil shouted.

And to my surprise, they all broke into a round of warm applause.

I was introduced to the group, who looked me over with casually evaluative expressions. It was clear that I was far from the first woman Emil had invited to meet the company—in fact, there was a quiet irony in many of their faces. But it was also clear that they believed him when he said that I was the right person to create the sets for their tour.

Soon I was making regular afternoon visits to the café-theater and spending my free evenings with the company. I sketched them while they rehearsed their lines or tried out new dialogue or stagings of the play. Emil was the driving force of the group, prodding them along with his vision, humor, and unquestioning dedication. The others listened to his ideas and criticism and seemed to give their best just to please him. At the same time, however, they were remarkably realistic about Les Xenos's meager chances for long-term success, and they sometimes offered him kind, but disbelieving faces.

And that's when he'd turn to me, citing my year in Paris as an example of a true commitment to a dream. They'd look at me wearily, thinking that no American could possibly understand what it really meant to be *Antillais* in France. Yet gradually their eyes registered a certain gentle respect for me. And soon they were including me in their discussions, their plans, their artistic decisions. Some even spontaneously addressed me in Creole.

"I'm sorry," I exclaimed with embarrassment when one of the actors described an entire scene to me in his native dialect.

"Oh my, Chloe." He laughed. "I keep forgetting—" he squinted at my features "—or is there a Caribbean branch somewhere in your tree?"

"You know what they say about the kinfolk in America," someone said with a snort. "First they were colored. Then they were Negroes. Now they're black. Sooner or later they'll remember they were African!"

"Leave her alone," Emil cut in. "Chloe's really a *soukougnane*."

"A what?" I asked.

"A night spirit. A sorceress," he explained. "You make magic with your brushes."

We all laughed. But when I assembled all the sketches I'd made of the members of Les Xenos, painting them in vibrant oils on one large canvas, I placed my own face in the rear.

Les Xenos took me in like a long-lost sibling who needed to be reacquainted with her origins. We'd share intense afternoons over backgammon boards—a particular passion of the members of the company.

"Sit down, Chloe!" one of the actors exclaimed while I hovered behind the players. "You can practice your Creole while you're learning about your ancestry!"

"That's right!" someone exclaimed. "Backgammon goes all the way back to Mother Africa!"

"And if you turn out to be a good player," another said slyly, "you can help me win some of my paycheck back from Emil!"

"You need to feed this woman some *roti*," Emil's sister Marie would complain when we'd invade a Vietnamese restaurant after the evening performance. "Chloe's already too thin! She needs to taste some good island cooking!"

"It's Mama's kitchen or nobody's!" Emil would answer with a grin, to the absolute approval of the others.

"Isabelle Mathurin is the best *cuisinière* ever born in Basse Terre!" someone remarked, "although you wouldn't know it by looking at her ragamuffin son!"

"All he needs," came the inevitable answer, "is a good woman to fatten him up and keep him off the streets at night!"

After sampling every dish on the menu and drinking copious amounts of beer, the party would move to an after-hours club in the immigrant fringes of the city. Africans, Arabs, and *Antillais* shared breathlessly small dance floors, moving sinuously to a flowing United Nations of rhythms. We'd dance to *zouk* and share saltfish and funghi, and sometimes, if the music was working just right, I'd even let myself drink too much rum. No one in Les Xenos ever made a serious pass at me, although everyone flirted like mad. Emil protected me like an older brother, fastidiously warning me away from *les tombeurs*.

Emil was the glowing center of our constellation. His heat left a vacuum in its wake. Women watched him with expressions of awestruck desire, and he clearly enjoyed their adulation. Many nights I watched from a darkened corner as he courted some tiny woman who filled up her skirt. If I felt any stirrings of jealousy, I swallowed hard and looked away, determined never to climb that cliff again. But Michael, when he welded hips with some girl whose clothes fit like aluminum foil, and when his eyes were locked on her face and his body was slick with sweat, and when the whole room was shouting in Creole in time to the booming bass, I ached to have him move with me that way.

One evening, as I was in my studio finishing the troupe's new sets,

Emil appeared at the door. Climbing over the canvas and scattered tubes of paint, he paused for a moment in front of the large portrait of Les Xenos.

"Although I knew we're destined to change the history of French theater, I never dreamed our faces would one day hang in the Louvre."

"No, Emil. This is for the lobby of the Théâtre des Xenos," I said, coming to stand beside him. "You can't play in these café-theaters forever. One day Les Xenos must have a home of their own."

Looking at the portrait, he nodded thoughtfully. "You're right. A theater for our people. In a quarter where they live." I saw his intelligent eyes weigh the idea and place it respectfully aside for further consideration. Then he turned to me.

"The tour's all planned, Chloe. We go to Strasbourg, Lille, and Orléans, then we move south for two full weeks on the Côte d'Azur. By the time we've finished we'll have infiltrated most of France with our strange and subversive ideas."

I laughed, and he leaned forward and wrapped his arms around my waist.

"Marie must return to Paris during the last week of the tour. We need someone who knows the production and can check everything before and after the show. Would you be willing to do it?"

"Where will you be?"

"On the Côte d'Azur, near Italy. We'll pay for your room and train fare. We'll be staying at pensions—very simple, of course, but you would eat with us and have plenty of time to paint."

"I don't know," I hedged, walking slowly across the room. I stared at the linen panel of swirling turquoise and mauve, my thoughts bounding between the paintings stacked in every corner and my wild fantasies of escape. Then I felt Emil's hands stroking my tense shoulders. "What is it?"

"Perhaps I should just accept the inevitable. I'll never find a gallery before my grant money runs out. The immigration police will never extend my visa. I can't afford to live in Paris without work, and when I go home I'll be thousands of dollars in debt."

"I foresee that you will have your gallery," he said mimicking a fortune-teller. "And I know this because I truly believe you are my . . . how do you Americans say it? My soul mate!"

I laughed shakily. "I'll really miss—" I paused and dropped my gaze "—Les Xenos. You all love each other so much. You're a family. And you have a home."

"If you want a home," he said slowly, "you'll always have one with me."

"And love?" I glanced up, and he snorted softly.

"You know it's not that simple. Love is more than just an emotion between two people. It's a way of living. Every gesture, every moment of human contact, every word must have some measure of love." He made a sweeping gesture. "All these faces you've painted, these lives you've captured— There's already great love here."

Reaching up, he ran his fingers along my chin. "You need to see something besides Paris. I want to show you the Mediterranean. I'd like to walk with you in the hills above Nice. I need to take you to Marseilles and introduce you to my mother. She'd worry a lot less about me if she got a look at you."

Once again I was struck by the deep repose that flowed beneath the frivolous faces he assumed and discarded at a moment's notice. This nexus of calm was the source of his strength and creativity, and it surged outward, enveloping the people he cared for.

"Emil," I said, "what do you see when you look at me?"

"Fear," he answered simply.

Suddenly I felt a deep, wrenching desire to be free of the woman who was Reginald Roman's wife and Lucien Laurent's lover. To see a new woman in the mirror. To be infected, in some small way, with this man's strength. And with his inner peace.

"Will you do something for me?"

"Anything, *mon amie*."

I crossed the room and returned with a pair of scissors. Placing them firmly in his hand, I sat at the table and resolutely pulled a towel around my shoulders.

"Cut it. All of it."

For one of the few times since we'd met, Emil was absolutely silent.

I felt him pause, then gingerly lift one of my locks and, after some hesitation, clip off the tip. He held the fuzzy curl up so that I could see it. I nodded. He paused again, then carefully clipped off another inch. He cleared his throat. I pulled the scissors from his hands and, grabbing up a handful of curls, hacked off a huge hank of hair close to my scalp.

"Coco sec?" he wondered softly.

"Yes," I answered. "Every bit of it."

Grunting, he removed the scissors from my fingers and brought the blades alongside my temples. I shut my eyes and heard the soft *crunch.*

After what seemed like a long time, he brought me a mirror and eased himself down on the chair across from me. I took a deep breath. Then I gazed at my new self. The face in the mirror was a cross of vulnerability and defiance. It was an African face: Nude. Ferocious. And free.

Emil again cleared his throat. "If I could paint, I'd . . ." His voice trailed off.

I felt a smile bloom from deep inside, working its way through my body to my lips. Troubled, he gathered up his jacket and walked quietly toward the door.

"Wait!" Quickly shaking off the towel, I followed. As he placed his hand on the handle I grasped his shoulders. "Don't go."

He looked down at me. The light caught his cheekbones and held. "Are you sure, Chloe?"

"No. But please don't go."

A brace of emotions crossed his face. Choosing one, he glanced around us and stood tall, solemnly addressing my paintings. "We who are about to love salute you."

"Just ignore them," I said.

"Mais non," he replied. "They're all part of you." With this he began to kiss me—first gently, his fingers caressing my face as if I were a child. He smoothed back the raw kinks of newly shorn hair, his lips drifting from my forehead to my temples, testing the soft flesh beneath my cheekbones and discovering the well at the base of my throat.

Then he brought his mouth to mine—our first true kiss—and I felt a swelling rush of desire mixed with a raw, vibrant vulnerability that sent my fingers groping blindly for anything that might protect me from giving in to my need.

Instantly he drew back, peering deep into my eyes. "What is it?" he asked, knowing without knowing.

A child answered from deep inside. "He hurt me, Emil."

"Oh, woman." Pulling my head down to his chest, he stroked my back until tears burst from my eyes. He held me gently, as if his answer would come not with words, but rather from the talking drumbeat of his heart.

And, Michael, I began to cry. I don't even know how long I cried. I can't tell you how long he held me there, in the nucleus of my studio, surrounded by the children of my brushes. I'm not even sure when the kisses that calmed and soothed me slowly began leading my body toward desire. I don't remember when his touch sealed away the aching void of my emptiness. I do remember that we undressed each other in a slow, roaring silence that became more urgent as we discovered yet more beauty to embrace.

I loosened his braid, watching the rough waves spring upward into a fuzzy black halo. And he grunted softly at the revelation that our nipples were the same shade of reddened ebony. It seemed ordained that my body should fit so perfectly into his palms, his hands moving as if he were molding me from his desire. And I knew that when his long legs slipped between mine we were graced with a kind of perfection that needed no words to guide it. We were meant to become lovers.

Emil responded to even the most minute sensation—the whisper of my lashes against his flesh, the different textures of hair on our bodies, the way that his fingertips elicited my laughter or tears, the moment to draw in or pull away. I heard him speaking Creole to me, the round tones weaving us together as we began working toward that destination. And as we shared the explosion, the hard angles of his face softened and he drew me close, his joy grafted on my sense of wonder.

I watched as dawn stole over his face, Michael. I watched the light come into the room as he brought his warmth into my life. I felt his presence transform my crowded studio from a prison into a temple. And my flesh knew a kind of deep repose with the certainty that he would never hurt me.

Michael, I knew from that very first night that Emil had come to heal me.

Aziza's baby was born two nights later in a clinic in Neuilly. The midwife came out to announce that a fat and protesting girl child had come into the world, and the new mother was fine.

I sat beside my friend as she slept, wrapping her long fingers in mine and watching her ebony features in the room's soft light. Her face emanated an enormous calm, as if all was right in her world, and I let some of that peace drift through her hand into mine.

She stirred, her doe eyes finding mine. "Did you see her?"

"She's beautiful."

"And big, isn't she?"

"Like a lamb."

"You'll be her godmother," she managed, drifting away for a moment.

"Yes," I replied.

Aziza squeezed my fingers, fighting off her sleepiness a few seconds more.

"I'm going to be all right," she said in a voice barely audible. "My baby and I are going to do just fine." Her eyes closed. I kissed her forehead, straightened the sheets, and walked softly to the door.

"Sister," she murmured as I crossed the threshold, "I'm going to name her Chloe."

I took a night train, sleeping badly in a cramped compartment with five other strangers. The train stopped and started intermittently throughout the journey, with shouting porters in deserted stations unloading the mail and other assorted wares. Cold and sore on my narrow bunk, I peered through the crack between the shade and the window and saw the names on the cement platforms in tiny villages that simply found themselves strewn along the route from Paris to Cannes. My only consolation was that my journey was taking me closer to Emil.

The dawn had just managed to seep in beneath the tattered shade when the conductor pounded on the door and woke up my headache. As we slithered into the station, I found my knapsack and tried to smooth my dank and wrinkled spirit.

"You look like you rode under the train!" Emil kissed my cheeks and hoisted my belongings to his shoulder.

"I feel like it, too."

He laughed heartily and took my hand. Slowly we navigated the palm-shaded Grand Promenade. The gracious hotels were just beginning to show signs of life as uniformed waiters hosed off the terraces and busily set the tables for breakfast. The smell of espresso blended invitingly with the promise of warm croissants, and I forgot my misery when I caught a glimpse of the calm, lavender sea.

"Jesus, Emil."

"I know; whenever I come back here I ask myself why I'm struggling to live in that rancid city full of unhappy people."

My simple room faced a quiet courtyard carpeted with orange poppies and a sliver of sea, visible just over the roof of the adjoining building. The narrow bed was covered with a faded flowered duvet and the one wicker chair was chipped and marked, as if it had stood sentinel in that room since the days of Cézanne.

"Welcome to my world," my companion remarked as he leaned casually against the window. "You know, woman, I've missed you."

"You've been too busy to even think of me."

"That's not true. Every night I get up on the stage and surround myself with you."

"And then you're thinking about the audience."

"No, Chloe. There's a part of me that always thinks about you. Even when you're far away."

"This sounds heavy," I said, keeping my voice light as I unpacked my small bag.

"No, it's not." He changed position, rearranging his long legs and folding his arms across his chest. "I know that both of us have dreams to fulfill." He made a restless gesture, then gently touched my knee. "But it was hard for me to leave you in Paris two weeks ago. It was hard for me to leave your room. Even harder to leave your bed."

A thyme-scented breeze with a hint of the sea filled the small chamber, and I was filled with an overwhelming urge to tell him I loved him. "So what are you feeling, now?" I whispered.

He sat beside me on the narrow bed.

"I've had many lovers," he answered pensively. "And I've learned that most women are attracted by what they see. But you—" he paused, carefully considering his words "—you're drawn to the man beneath the faces I wear."

He laughed easily and pressed his lips against my open palm. "I'm not used to anything so deep, Chloe. But making love with you was more than physical. It was almost a spiritual kinship. As if I can love you both as a woman and an artist."

He had said it: *Love!*

I felt my heart leap, and I grasped about for something light and humorous to say. "Well, I'm glad you haven't met any other artists lately."

"Chère sorcière," he replied softly, "there'll never be another woman like you."

When we entered the Town Theater, the first thing I saw was my sets, put into place and properly lighted. I had painted two curtainlike panels of steel blue clouds, swirling in indefinable whirlpools, but softened by cottonlike blots of gold like the sun breaking through a storm. This was the heavenly limbo in which the newly dead characters find themselves at the play's beginning. The panels were done on a very fine canvas that I found at the Marché Saint-Pierre, and when a small fan was placed behind them they billowed softly, gently, soothingly. In short, Michael, *beautiful*!

The crew was already testing the lights, so I went backstage and began checking to make sure that all the props were in their places. I helped the actors with their costumes and makeup. I wasn't a specialist, but I'd learned a trick or two from Anya's models.

Finally the audience arrived. The sound engineer put on a tape of the troupe's "theme" song—Art Blakey's recording of "A Night in Tunisia." The actors were in their places. I checked the set once more and turned on the fan to set the heavenly clouds billowing. The music changed, then faded away. The curtain swished open. Emil and Marcel strolled onto the stage.

Standing in the wings I watched Emil as he drew the audience into his world. I had seen the play many times, but now I caught my breath at the grace and fluidity of his gestures and the richly expressive voice that made me laugh during the day and made love to me at night. Before a crowd of strangers Emil's keen intelligence, strange beauty, and acute comic timing fused into a vibrant presence, and I couldn't take my eyes away.

Between acts I was busy with my list. The audience buzzed contentedly, while the actors dashed to the dressing room and the crew came backstage to roll up our canvas "heaven" and install the urban apartment.

When the final curtain fell, the house exploded into a roar of approval. The clapping went on and on, the bewildered actors standing stunned as the curtains opened, closed, and opened again. Someone reached for me and I found myself on the stage with the other actors, embarrassed by my scruffy pants and frayed list of props. When the curtain finally closed the last time, I turned to Emil: "You shouldn't have done that!"

"You're one of us," he declared, "and a part of me!"

That night the troupe invaded a local restaurant and ordered all the pasta that the cook could produce—along with a crate of wine. The merriment increased when several local residents asked to join the celebration and began trading tales about disasters they'd survived on their rare trips to the capital.

We slipped out into the frosty, fragrant night and strolled slowly along the promenade, Emil singing songs in his dialect and laughing at jokes I couldn't understand.

"I don't speak Creole," I reminded him when he asked why I didn't find him funny. "You've had too much to drink."

"You *can* understand. Just listen closely: You'll hear the French resonance and the African tonalities."

"But—"

"Listen with your *heart*, not your mind. It's in your blood, little sister. I felt it the first time we made love."

"Oh, Emil."

"Let's make a pact." He stopped walking and smiled drunkenly.

"You teach me English, and I'll teach you Creole. I know you can do it," he said to my shaking head. "You're not the same woman who wandered into the café-theater last fall. All that frustration, that fear, that . . . that *desperation* to succeed is finally fading away."

"Come on, Emil: You have dreams, too!"

He turned, his features etched to clarity by the street lamp. "You weren't so sure about your talent when you came here—"

"No," I admitted.

"And you thought that success was only possible in a gallery."

"Yes."

"And you never thought you'd love anybody."

"No."

"And now?"

"I guess . . . I guess I was wrong."

Emil smiled down at me, his eyes sparkling, and to my own surprise, I laughed.

"There it is!" he shouted. "She laughed! She actually laughed!"

"Oh, Emil—" I laughed again.

"She's laughing! And she doesn't have a gallery and she's lost her boyfriend and she's wandering around the Riviera with a bunch of pitiful black people who have an impossible dream of becoming famous actors!" He threw his arms around me, lifting me off the pavement. "She's alive! She's finally really and truly alive! She's learning how to love her life!"

He set me down gently, his arms still laced around my waist. "Now," he said with stunning honesty, "if only she'd let herself love me."

The following morning Emil coaxed me onto the train to make the short trip to his hometown, Marseilles. And to meet the Mathurin clan.

"Be prepared," he said as we approached the apartment building where his mother resided. "She's probably invited every living member of my family. And some of the dead ones, too."

"On a Saturday morning?"

"They'll all be celebrating the fact that I survived another winter in

Paris," he said wryly, looking up toward the balconies hung with billowing sheets. "And, of course, they'll be trying to convince me to stay."

We could smell the dirty rice and curried meat before exiting the elevator, and the sound of highly syncopated music would have led the blind to the flat. Emil opened the door with a shout and pushed me into a rollicking mass of laughter and limbs. Voices began bouncing like Ping-Pong balls, and the crowd surged forward in greeting.

"He did it—Maman, Emil really did it!"

"What? Dragged some poor woman off the street?"

"He probably convinced her they're married!"

"No woman would be with him for any other reason!"

"Unless he said he's a movie star!"

"No—he's still too shabby for that!"

Emil protested grandly, and I laughed with the others until I realized with a start that everyone was speaking—*and I was understanding*—Creole. He saw my bewilderment and threw up his hands, calling for an immediate silence. I peered into the sea of faces—some weathered and white-maned, others still swaddled in infant blankets—and marveled that I could feel so safe—so quickly—among so many strangers.

"All right, all right!" Emil announced, taking a gentlemanly pose behind me. "Marie's told you about this mysterious artist, and you've all wanted to ask for her blessing before she walks across the water back to America—"

His voice was drowned out by a good-natured roar, and it took him some minutes to reestablish the calm. "Brothers! Sisters! Please, help me to be serious for a moment!" Several people refused, so in my pitiful, elementary dialect I spontaneously introduced myself: "*Bonjour* to you all. I'm just learning to speak Creole, so please forgive my horrible accent!"

I was instantly buried in so many welcoming arms that Emil vanished from sight for some time. Numerous women identified themselves as siblings, and several men were presented as brothers-in-law, and I got an especially long hug from Isabelle Mathurin, a shorter, rounder version of her son.

"I've been waiting for him to bring someone home," she said, stroking my face. "But I never dared to hope she'd be as pretty as you!"

I blushed, thinking that "pretty" was rather an exaggeration for a thirty-four-year-old—especially when I looked at Emil's clan of smooth-skinned lanky men and lushly built women with bright, teasing eyes. Emil himself, surrounded by children, was jabbering in accents and tickling ribs and producing pocketfuls of candy. His gaze met mine above their heads, and for a moment I was astonished by the love in his eyes.

His mother's smile deepened. "You're good for him," she said in a contralto that carried clearly and distinctly above the roar. "When he went to Paris, he was like a leaf, flying in any direction the wind blew. Now he's making something of himself. He knows what he wants. He's working hard."

"I can't take any credit for that," I said. "Emil was a gifted actor when we first met."

She placed a firm hand on my arm. "I know my son. And I've never seen him like this before."

Together we looked in his direction.

"Great gifts can be a burden," she said softly. "He's had a difficult time finding someone who shares his passion." Smiling up at me with her son's brilliant eyes, she nodded slowly. "I'm very happy that he's finally falling in love!"

I blushed again, and she burst into the hearty Mathurin laugh. "You don't have to worry, Chloe. I won't spoil anything by insisting that he marry you before somebody else does!"

Emil came up behind me. "Don't listen to a word of it," he cautioned me. "She goes out on the street and asks perfect strangers to be her daughter-in-law."

"There'd be something wrong if I didn't think my own son was worth marrying!" Isabelle cried, throwing her arms around Emil. "And you can't blame me for giving her a few hints—"

"Mama 'Bella!" he teased, rocking her back and forth. "If I let you talk to Chloe too much longer, she'll run away in terror!"

They both looked at me with identical, love-filled eyes. And I swear that if he had dropped to his knee at that moment, I would have accepted his proposal just to add to their pleasure.

Later Emil and I were sitting on the balcony with his uncle Pierrot, sipping spiced rum punch and gazing out toward the shimmering harbor.

"What you need," the older man was saying, "is to buy yourself a house down here, in the South."

"A house?" Emil exclaimed. "Why, for God's sake?"

"So you'll have somewhere to go when you're not working. And so you'll spend more time with your family."

Emil gazed inside the apartment, where the younger people were dancing to the latest hit from Port-au-Prince. "I can't afford to buy a house. I'm scraping to keep things going in Paris."

"Paris! You need to start thinking about a wife and some babies!"

"A wife! I can't afford one of those, either!" Emil replied, avoiding my eyes.

"Just get a little place and let one of your cousins live in it when you're away."

"You know I hate Marseilles."

"I didn't say you should move into the apartment next door," his uncle said. "Look for something in Cannes or Nice." The uncle turned craftily to me. "It's beautiful here, isn't it, Chloe?"

As we were preparing to leave, I found one of Emil's young cousins clutching my hand. I knelt down and asked her name.

"I'm Celestine," she declared. "I'm five."

"You're a lovely little girl," I said, and she began to giggle.

"Are you going to marry Emil?"

"I—I don't know," I stammered, unsure whether a negative answer would please or crush the child.

"Can I come and live with you in Paris?" she asked.

"I'd rather live with you right here," I answered. "It's rainy and dirty in Paris. Here in the South, it's so warm and sunny. I love the flowers and the mountains and the sea."

The little girl nodded sagely, then threw her arms around my neck with a child's intuitive trust.

Emil stroked my shoulder. "The curtain rises in three hours, Chloe."

I rose with a reluctant sigh, unable to believe how hard it was for me to leave. As we sat on the train, the impossibly verdant hills rolling by, I thought about Paris. And about my painting. And, yes, I thought about Emil.

Emil had become my anchor, Michael. In the few months since I'd met him he'd completely changed my life. He listened when no one understood my despair, and always found the words to bring me back to hope. He'd found me a place with Les Xenos. Offered me his language, his music, his culture. He had even sprung the lock on the prison of Paris and made my art a part of his dream.

Emil had given me his family, Michael, and their deep, enveloping love.

And when we made love—I swear to you—no man had ever touched me that way.

His hand found mine as we stood on the stage that night while the audience stomped and cheered. Secretly I prayed that he would never let go.

My last day with the tour found us in Menton—the border town between France and Italy—a beautiful village built beneath red mountain cliffs overlooking the cerulean sea.

We awakened to a day perfumed by spring flowers and patchworked with fat, scuttling clouds. From the window of our tiny room, I could see people sunbathing, while others strolled up and down the beachfront promenade eating Italian ices.

"Why don't you stay with us a few more days?" Emil purred lazily from the bed.

"I've got work to do," I replied, watching an elderly woman wrestle an orange Chow down the sidewalk.

"You can paint here, Chloe."

I looked across at him, unable to avoid his perceptive eyes. "I know, Emil. I just keep hoping—"

"That you'll find a gallery," he said. He sat up and held out his arms. *"Viens ici, chère sorcière."*

I lay down beside him, and he held me close.

"I promise that everything will work out," he said. "I waited too long to find you to simply let you vanish."

"But Emil—"

"Shhhh," he whispered, bringing his lips to mine.

After lunch Les Xenos decided to try out some new dialogue, so I climbed a stone footpath that led up above the town, my watercolors in a backpack. The sea spread out in the distance like a cobalt carpet, and the air was spiced by shoals of dried lavender. Standing in a bank of deep, flowing grasses, I took a deep, deep breath. It was time to face the shipwreck of my year in Paris.

In three months the grant money would run out. The immigration police would be waiting at my door. Most galleries were reserved for months, even years in advance, and didn't want to exhibit work like mine, anyway. Yes, I'd completed more than fifty paintings, but with nowhere to show them and no means of selling them, soon a basement or garage would become their home. The cost alone of shipping them back to the States would be crippling, and, of course, I'd have to refund the grant award.

So my future was clear: New York or D.C., because I wouldn't need a car. A day job that would cover the rent. Then a waitressing job on evenings and weekends for the tips and free food. Four or five years to pay off my debts.

And worst of all, a life without Emil.

Where had I gone wrong?

Had it been so stupid to come to Paris with a dream of succeeding as an artist? Was I wrong to have rejected Anya's world? Should I have slept with Jacques for the sake of a gallery? Or sacrificed my art to the lie of Lucien?

Perhaps I should have painted statues and bridges, or portraits of well-groomed Parisians. I could have used those parties to find a wealthy lover, or become a fashion illustrator, or gone into advertising or even tried modeling—

And then I saw your face and heard your voice, Michael. The words of our vow echoed past in the warm, sea-salted winds:

I vow to be a strong black woman,
To become a success,
And never to let a man turn me away from my dreams . . .

I realized that it was strength, rather than weakness, that had brought me to that hill above the sea. I hadn't given in to temptations that would have made me no different from the others. I had painted my truth. I had lived my hope. And I had found love with a man who understood and respected my dream.

Yes, I could finally admit it. *I was in love with Emil.*

Paris had beaten me to my knees, Michael. But Paris had given me Emil.

That night the theater was packed. When the music started, there was a round of excited applause that worked on the actors like a charge of electricity. The play took off at a pace that surpassed anything I'd seen before, and ended so quickly that my head was spinning when Emil's hand found mine for the curtain call. The *sixth.*

He stared at me in disbelief as the crowd kept on cheering and crying for another look at the players. Then he swept me into his arms and turned me around with a deep, sensuous kiss. The entire troupe bounced joyously in and out of hugs and kisses, and we felt something like a collective ecstasy—as if nothing could stop us from reaching the sky.

The excited audience poured onto the stage like water from a broken main, and we were swept back toward the dressing rooms like leaves caught in a storm. The din was tremendous, and the crush of strange, perspiring faces would have been frightening if we, ourselves, had not been so full of joy.

Pushed and pressed and squeezed and embraced, it was with a kind of raw instinct that I *sensed* the single figure standing immobile before the rear exit, half in shadow, frozen in a pose so terrifyingly familiar that my breath caught in my throat.

I began to work my way through the milling crowd, muttering excuses and apologies while keeping my eyes fixed on that apparition. I forced my way across the stage until I rolled panting and ridiculous into a space of empty air, and nothing stood between the figure and me. Then I waited, in a stillness that wiped out all the noise and movement behind me.

For a moment longer than any moment in my life, there was nothing. Then: "You've cut your hair. It becomes you."

His hand reached for mine. It was cold. Strange, in the heat of all those people! We stood this way, hands linked, but he did not come out of the shadows.

"I needed to clean house," I said mechanically, still searching for the flecks in his golden eyes.

"Well, Chloe, so did I."

"You left Paris without telling anyone."

"I had destroyed everything. There was no reason to stay."

"No, Lucien. You destroyed everything so you'd have no reason to stay."

He hesitated, moving just a few inches toward me, and his face came into the light. Steeling myself, I looked into his eyes.

I can't describe what happened next, Michael, except to say that something clicked, and I gasped as a jigsaw of images leapt into place: Lucien in blue linen, leading a model into a bedroom on my very first night in Paris. His aqua reflection in the dashboard lights the evening he drove me home from Le Kansas. His huddled form in the bar on the rue Saint-Jacques. His mocking smile the first time he took me to Vincennes.

Suddenly I knew why his flat seemed so barren. I understood the reason for his long absences from Paris. The cause of his distaste for Anya and her *entourage*. And his vicious anger when I discovered his Great Truth. Suddenly it all made sense.

"You—you had already decided to leave Paris," I stammered in disbelief. "You'd already chosen this place. Paris meant nothing to you, and you *never*, from that first night at the restaurant, until that last night in my studio, had any intention of staying with me."

He stared at me blankly, his chest rising and falling.

"It was all a game," I continued. "A way of amusing yourself until you'd had enough. You even told me once that you were 'dreaming of your escape to the south of France—' "

"Wait, Chloe," he said, his voice echoing weirdly in the vacuum left by the departing crowd. "Just slow down and let me explain." A hush fell between us.

"Several years ago I started developing contacts in Brussels, London, and Milan. Things went well, so I decided to move my business here, where it's cheaper, more private, and—"

"Where no one knows anything about your past," I said.

He looked away. "By last summer everything was arranged. I planned to occasionally go to Paris to finish up some contracts, then close out my leases at the end of the year.

"Everything was fine—that is, until you appeared. You, Chloe, were the last thing I ever expected to find at one of Anya's parties: an intelligent, beautiful woman with real talent. A woman with an absolute commitment to her gift. And," he added darkly, "a commitment to her people.

"At first I told myself that I was wrong; that you really were mindlessly ambitious, like the others. But after the night of my father's funeral—and after you refused to sleep with me—I realized that you really were different. I hoped that perhaps, with you, I could have a better life. I thought we could leave Paris together. I thought that with you I might even become my—" he stumbled over the words "—my mother's child."

The hall was now very quiet, and my voice flattened out into the vaulted, empty space.

"No, Lucien," I said. "You only saw me through your father's eyes. Being with a black woman made you feel like a failure. Our relationship shut you out of Anya's privileged world. It gave you no power to succeed in French society. So like your mother, I paid with my flesh for your lies."

His voice tightened, and he stared into my face. "You left me no choice, Chloe. You wouldn't let go of your obsession with galleries, or that miserable, dirty studio, or your pathetic fantasies about Paris. You never gave us a chance to grow."

"To grow?" I repeated softly. "Well, Lucien, I've left Paris. I don't have a gallery. And I love the world I'm discovering outside of my miserable, dirty studio."

He stepped forward swiftly, and I flinched as his hands found my waist. I tried to pull away as his lips touched my forehead, and my terrified heart almost drowned out his next words: "Forgive me for what happened that last night. I drank too much. And those people made me feel so cheap—so filthy. If you'll give us a chance, I promise you with all my heart that nothing like that will ever happen again."

I stumbled backward, hardly breathing as he whispered, "You do know how much I love you, don't you, Chloe?"

A confused rumbling seemed to spring up from my core. Through my pounding anger and terrible fear, a small piercing voice screamed out: *He said he loves me! Lucien Laurent said that he loves me!*

I felt him reach for me again, drawing me slowly close, and my trembling hands grasped his encircling arms. Was it possible that after all the pain he really did care? Could Lucien Laurent really love me? Should I—

"Chloe! *Sa kaye?* I've been looking for you!"

I pushed Lucien away guiltily as Emil came striding across the stage toward us. He stopped by my side, took my hand gently, and stared down into Lucien's eyes. There was a long, tense moment as the men measured each other. Then Emil turned to me.

"Excuse me, but there's someone I want you to meet."

"That's all right. I was—" I steadied myself, looking into Lucien's face "—I was just saying good-bye."

"Good-bye?" Lucien smiled. "It will never truly be good-bye, Chloe."

I crossed the empty hall with Emil, swallowing my tears. It was all that I could do, Michael, not to look back at the figure I knew was waiting in the shadows.

Emil opened the dressing room door and presented me to a white-maned Frenchman leaning comfortably against the makeup table.

"Chloe, this is Constantine, the man most responsible for my being an actor."

Constantine smiled warmly. "That's not entirely true. Many years ago I was Emil's drama teacher. He was one of the most brilliant students I ever had. He was also one of the worst. I've never seen talent as wasted as his was in the classroom."

"Really, Constantine, I wasn't all that bad. I was only acting!" They laughed, and I managed to laugh with them.

"Constantine now runs the Centre des Études Artistiques in Aix-en-Provence," Emil explained to me. "They have music, dance, and arts classes for all ages. And," he added slowly, enunciating every word, "they've got a beautiful gallery."

The three of us had dinner in a small bistro near the sea. Emil and Constantine traded stories about their years in Marseilles while I struggled to put Lucien out of my mind. As we drank our last glasses of wine, the conversation grew serious.

"So how are things with the center?"

Constantine nodded slowly. "I'm very satisfied with the progress we've made. We moved into a larger building last year, and the class enrollment has almost doubled. I'd like to get Les Xenos to come and teach some classes in script development, staging, and perhaps dramatic reading. . . ."

Emil chuckled and turned to me. "Can you imagine what it was like when this guy started assigning homework?"

"And by the way," Constantine added, "it would be very nice if you could come too, Chloe. We rarely get anyone who does set design. I have some art students who'd love meeting you."

"Well, I'm not really a set designer," I said, feeling Emil's hand squeeze mine beneath the table. "I'm a trained artist. I work in all media, but I prefer acrylics and oils."

"Would you be interested in a teaching position? I'm looking for someone to run our art program."

"My visa's good for only three more months—"

"If you'd agree to stay at least one year I could certainly arrange something with Immigration." He smiled warmly. "I can't pay too much, but I'd schedule your classes to give you time for your own work, and you could use the center's facilities."

"Chloe has a great gift," Emil said to his teacher. "Her studio in Paris is packed with extraordinary paintings."

"Would you be interested in an exhibition?" Constantine asked me. "We like to show our professors' work to the community. Our exhibitions often draw gallery owners from across the region."

I stared wordlessly at Emil, whose eyes glimmered with pleasure. "There's only one problem," he said quietly. "Chloe would fall in love with Aix, and I'd never get her up to Paris again!"

We all laughed as Constantine took out his calendar. "I'll be in Paris next week, Chloe. Let's meet at your studio to discuss it further."

Late that night I wandered down the deserted promenade beside an exquisite man whom I loved, and who loved me. Our thoughts were softened by the lulling voice of the sea.

"Aix is just a few hours from Paris," Emil was saying as we passed in and out of the lamplight. "Don't think that you're going to get away from me."

"Losing you would be losing a part of myself," I said as he slipped his arm around my shoulder with a quiet chuckle.

"My mother's going to kill me for not dragging you to the altar."

"Being married wouldn't change the way I feel."

We stopped walking, and he peered into my face. "Could another man do that?"

Lucien's face crossed my mind, and I shook my head to clear it. "I promise you, Emil: I will never love anyone as much as I love you."

Michael, on that starry, starry night I truly believed that I would spend the rest of my life with Emil Mathurin. I was certain that nothing, and no one, could ever separate me from the man who had honored my strength, worked for my success, and perfectly understood my dreams.

And I was sure that since my dreams were finally coming true, yours couldn't be very far behind.

"So Emil led you back to our vow?"

"Yes, Michael. And our love was the most perfect time of my life."

"Like my twelve perfect years with Drew." You pulled in your breath and held it before continuing, and I knew that the next question would be painful for us both.

"How did we both walk away from men we love so deeply, Chloe?"

"Maybe they loved us so much that we were afraid to stay."

You laughed, but the sound was hollow with sadness. "You know, it was my idea. This philosophy that we could have lovers, as long as we truly loved each other. Drew took me at my word and never lied about his feelings. It was my desire to punish him that drove us apart."

Your fingers stole through your feathery hair. "Chloe, I know you still don't understand what happened with Drew. Let me explain exactly how Jonathan Bennett became my lover."

"I'm listening, Michael."

Four

As I pulled my car into a parking space that Monday morning, I found myself counting again. Counting the number of times Drew and I had had sex in the past two years. Counting the number of days—and then weeks—between those encounters. And counting the number of men I'd had before Drew—twenty-four—and always stopping short at the slightly uncomfortable realization that for fourteen years he had been my only lover.

My gaze crystallized on my reflection, thrown into focus by the sudden spray of autumn rain on the windshield. What happened to that strapping young woman who planned to travel the world and bed men from every nation? How did I fall into the trap of complete dependence on one man's love? If Drew really loved me, why did he still desire other women?

My thoughts drifted to you, Chloe, and the love you'd shared with Emil. He'd been a calm, stabilizing presence in your life—as Drew had been in mine. But Emil gave you his complete devotion—while I'd spent my entire married life watching Drew feast on the desire in other women's eyes.

Slamming the car door, I almost ran into Jonathan Bennett, who was hunched up in a light wool blazer against the downpour. I made room for him under my umbrella, and he looped his arm around my waist so that we could move more easily together.

"Jesus! Is this the end of summer or is it fall already?"

"This is England," I answered flatly. "It rains in England."

We reached my office, and he began shaking himself dry with exaggerated motions. I laughed and he grimaced, closing his eyes. "There's no place like home. There's no place like home—"

"You're not tap dancing hard enough."

"Maybe I'm trapped forever in Whitefolksland."

"There are worse places to be," I said, hanging up my raincoat.

"Your colleagues certainly think so. Would you believe I've been told at least ten times that I should enjoy teaching in a *real* learning environment, as opposed to the 'factories' that pretend to be universities in America?"

"Meaningless noise, Jonathan." I sat down at my desk and flicked my computer on.

"How can you stand these condescending people?"

Swiveling in my chair, I turned to the printer. "Do you teach at a black university in California?"

"No, but I teach in the black studies program at my university, so I'm educating whites about black people."

"Well, let's just say that I'm doing the same thing here in England."

"Black Americans need role models like you."

"White Europeans need black role models, too."

"Think of the lives you could influence."

I faced him, keeping my voice pleasantly neutral. "Many years ago I flayed myself with all that guilt about 'betraying my people' and 'marrying outside of the race.' But then I lived in Africa and traveled throughout Europe and discovered that there are black people everywhere who are struggling to make it."

He grunted. "Sure, Michael. But if you live in this isolation your whole life you end up not knowing what blackness is."

"I'm no less black because I live in England. In fact, I experience my blackness in a much more acute and challenging way because I'm so often alone."

"But, Michael," he said with a sudden protectiveness, "you shouldn't have to be alone."

"Do you think that I wasn't alone in America? My professors ignored me until a question on blacks came up. Then I became the spokeswoman for the entire race. Even back then I had to think white and talk white and write white. And the few available black men on campus ran marathons to get in bed with white—"

"You didn't date white men?"

"Only when the black men vanished."

"Then you were a model of assimilation."

"I was fighting to survive," I replied. "In fact, I'll never forget one subzero night when I got locked out of my apartment and a university security guard refused to believe I was a graduate assistant until I got a professor out of bed and on the phone. After opening the door the guard remarked that 'It's niggers like me that keep white people from getting into good schools.' And you know what? I didn't tell anyone for fear of being branded a troublemaker and losing my position!"

"I've been there, believe me," he agreed. He sat down at his desk, and the room was quiet for some time.

"Excuse me, Michael," he said suddenly. "I need to check a reference. Do you have a copy of Du Bois's *Souls*?"

Although I was far from certain that he was serious, I suddenly felt a very strong need to prove that I had whatever book Bennett might need. "There's a copy of it somewhere. Look on the top two shelves—that's where I keep the nonfiction."

He crossed the office and scanned the books dutifully, then shrugged with an exaggerated roll of his shoulders. "I don't see it. I'll go over to the library."

"No, it's there. I used it a few days ago." I stood up and joined him at the shelf. Some of the books were placed in front of others; I began to pull down the books in the front to reveal the back rows. Soon my arms were full.

"I see it," I announced. "It's there—behind that dictionary."

He reached up and pulled the book out carefully. He set it on the edge of a lower shelf. "Let me help you with those."

One by one he removed the books from my arms, placing them in careful stacks in the few empty spaces. Twice we laughed when it appeared that all the books might fall.

"Thanks, Michael," he said, reaching for the last book in my arms.

This was not the first time that I'd seen Bennett's beauty, but it was the first time that his beauty stopped me cold. The dark eyes, bearing shadows of unspoken emotions, were matched by flawless brown skin and a wide, sensuous mouth. His short hair formed gentle curls at the temples before sweeping back into tight, clipped waves.

We stood together, hands sharing the book, our faces slowly melting into smiles. We stared at each other for a full minute, while the voices on the Commons outside melted into a surging, swirling song.

What happened between us during that long moment? Sixty seconds can create an epic, Chloe. A whole lifetime can pass between a man and a woman in far less time. Lifelong resolutions can be made and broken in half that time. What was it that took sixty seconds to happen between Bennett and me? I wasn't sure when I finally looked away, struggling to find my balance and raising my brows with a sigh.

Bennett returned to his desk. "Playtime over, Michael. Let me get some work done."

I've never known you to be nostalgic for your youth, Chloe. But I'll confess that the disco days will always live on somewhere deep down in my heart. I can never resist going out to dance, even if the music is provided by a fireman's band. And that's what made me drag Drew to the faculty disco party.

The underground club was cavernous, its walls lined with floor-to-ceiling mirrors that reflected everything back fourfold. Entering from a darkened hallway, one could look down upon a spacious dance floor surrounded by tiered levels, where drinkers could sit and watch the dancers, as if in an arena. Bass notes pulsed from enormous speakers perched on the edges of the dance floor. Yep. It was my favorite kind of dance hall.

As I expected, there were few people at the tables and only two couples dancing listlessly to a number by that seventies Swedish group. In one corner some twenty people from the department huddled together, lifting their glasses in drunken unison and making a fair amount of noise. Drew and I exchanged glances, then moved slowly down the steps to join our colleagues. A warm cheer greeted us. Drew ordered a beer, and I asked the waitress for a glass of white wine; then we seated ourselves at the center of the group.

"I just love disco parties," Rupert Billings shouted, leering at me over his fifth or sixth gin and tonic.

"You love *any* party," I answered, watching the table's lava lamp cast a scarlet glow to his deeply bloodshot eyes.

"I'd love to dance with you," he gushed. "Always have wanted to dance with you. Drew! Would you let me dance with your wife?"

"Absolutely not," Drew answered.

"Do I get to say something about this?" I asked them both.

"Yes, of course," Drew replied in a loud voice.

I turned to Rupert. "Absolutely not!"

Our colleagues roared with laughter.

"I'll dance with you, Rupe," the wife of the medievalist called out. "But I'm not sure if you can stand up, much less keep the rhythm!"

"I don't know anything about rhythm," Rupert answered. "I'm only a white man!"

"Oh, pitch it, please!" Joshan, the one East Indian in the department, exclaimed. "I've never seen anyone with a worse sense of humor!"

"How long have they been here?" Drew inquired as politely as he could over the banging of the speakers.

"They arrived loaded," Joshan, a nondrinker, replied.

A new song began, and several members of our group moved down to the dance floor, laughing uproariously at some joke. Drew watched them, then turned to me. "Do you really want to stay?"

"I feel like dancing," I answered.

From some secret control panel colored lights began to illuminate the entire room, and a mirrored ball descended slowly from the rafters. Rupert had found a dance partner and was now relentlessly shaking his hips with his arms held high above his head. The flashing lights added a convulsive quality to his ludicrous behavior, but he didn't care in the least.

"Did we come here just to look at him?" Drew asked me in a low voice.

"All right, Drew. Go on home. I'll ask Ann and Eric to give me a ride."

He stood up without a word and reached for his coat. "I'll be up reading," he said as he kissed my cheek and headed for the exit.

"Let's dance," Ann said to me. We rose and clambered down the stairs to the dance floor while her husband settled back to watch.

The music was a balm. I closed my eyes and allowed myself to melt into the rhythm. I raised my arms and really began to relax, my supple body twisting and rocking with the pounding beat.

As a young woman I bathed in the rainbow colors of dance floors, my hips tracing out intricate patterns between the drumbeats while my shoulders worked out a rhythm in response. I danced with men who made love to me without touching me, their bodies acting out a pantomime of desire that was so real I would walk away throbbing.

Now the music slowed to a reggae so deep that it vibrated through the club. The few remaining couples cleared the floor, and Ann, shaking her head, deserted me. A lone man and woman danced nearby, each in a separate world. I knew that I should join the others; I knew they wouldn't understand why I was dancing alone. But I didn't give a shit what they thought. I closed my eyes, planted my feet on the floor, and started to wind my hips very slowly and deliberately to the rhythm.

Suddenly I sensed I was no longer alone. The man's frame as he leaned over me blacked out the flashing lights. I couldn't make out his face, for his features were obscured by the scarlet strobe behind him. The only thing I knew was that he was with me, there, inside the music.

He danced like I danced, and he danced well. He felt it, understood it, loved it as I did. He was meeting me move for move. His hips found the unexpressed rhythm inside the rhythm and, as I strained against it, so did he. I rolled my shoulders away, feeling the delicious pull of muscles all over my body. He did the same. He was uninvited, but terribly desired. He was unknown, but completely welcome.

Then I realized my partner was Jonathan Bennett.

I might have been concerned had I not felt so deeply alive at that moment. To find a partner—a *true* partner—was an indescribable pleasure. Smiling, I lifted my arms toward him, and he took my hands, never losing the rhythm. Without speaking we continued the dance, our bodies pressing out a slow series of thrusts and turns, our fingers locked, our foreheads beginning to glisten. Silence had fallen as every head turned to watch—but Bennett and I were too deeply engaged in the dance to care.

Standing on the edge of the dance floor, Kristin stared helplessly, stupidly, angrily at the scene. I dipped backward, as Bennett leaned forward. His hands found my waist as I took his shoulders and let my head fall back, almost touching the floor. I was laughing soundlessly. He was laughing, too. He swept me up close to his body, letting his hands slide down to my hips. He pulled me toward him, and as our bodies made contact sparks seemed to fly. The music pumped hard around us.

From the stands came a whistle, shrill and mocking, that pierced the music. I ignored it but was once again aware of our colleagues' observation, their judgment, their inability to understand. Looking hard into his face, I caught a glimpse of his measuring gaze. And then I knew: He was staging this scene, hoping the others would mistake the dance for a sexual familiarity that had nothing to do with the disco. *He was insinuating that we were lovers.*

Suddenly I was enraged: this was no longer simply a dance, a shared moment of sensuality within the boundaries of the dance floor. I turned to walk away and was amazed to feel him grasp me by the hips and spin me toward him, into his arms. "Stay!" he ordered in a low voice, his head next to mine. He pressed his body against me. "You're so beautiful. I want to make love to you!" He grasped one of my thighs between his legs, and rubbed his chest gently against my breasts.

I stopped dancing, standing stock-still in the middle of the floor. He had no choice but to do the same.

"I'm sorry," he said immediately.

"You bet you are," I replied, turning to leave. I was amazed to feel him grasp my fingers, pulling me toward him yet again.

"Michael, wait—" he said above the music. I jerked my hand away and in a moment was off the dance floor, bounding past Kristin up the stairs to the others. I was so angry that I could barely catch my breath, so I snatched up my glass of wine and took a long draft. A titter came from the direction of the women while several men applauded my arrival.

I glanced at the leering faces of my colleagues and knew that my dance with Jonathan Bennett would provoke inspired gossip for months to come. Kristin had joined him on the dance floor and they were doing a casual two-step, as if they were strangers. I flushed with frustrated rage.

Ann appeared beside me and touched my arm. "Do you want another glass of wine?"

"Actually, I think I'll just get a cab and—"

"Not quite yet."

I started and turned to look into Drew's eyes. He was standing beside me, his coat still draped over his arm.

"I thought you'd left."

"Not until I've danced with you," he said in a voice so low that no one else could hear. He put his coat over a chair and offered me his hand. Slipping his arm around my waist, I let him guide me back down the stairs. I heard no sound from our colleagues as we descended.

Drew was no dancer; in fact, he had seldom danced with me in all the years of our marriage. Now, despite the insistence of the beat, he gathered me up close and began to sway gently from side to side. There weren't many people on the dance floor, but the other couples were obliged to dance around us. Drew acted as if no one else were there—in fact, as if we were alone in the world.

"Why didn't you leave?" I asked him.

"Once you started dancing I couldn't."

"You saw what happened?"

He didn't answer but held me more tightly. Over his shoulder I saw Bennett and Kristin nearby.

"Why does he behave like such a bastard?" I asked.

"He wants you."

"What should I do?"

"Do you want him?"

I stopped moving; Drew pulled me close, lowering his head and rubbing his face into my hair. The angry frustration seemed to flow out of my body as I was enveloped by his scent. Once again we began to dance, but my breath quickened as my thigh brushed against the evidence of his arousal. His hands gently kneaded my back, then slid slowly down to pull my hips against his.

For a moment I was aware of the echoing silence from the tables above. Then I let myself drown in the pleasure of being desired by Drew—and knowing that the whole world saw it.

"Let's go, Mickey," he murmured.

We walked off the dance floor just as Bennett and Kristin stopped dancing. Moving quickly, Bennett approached Drew and held out his hand.

"It's good to see you, Professor!" he shouted.

Drew glanced at the outstretched hand and threw back his head, laughing as if greatly amused. He grasped Bennett's hand and shook it warmly, saying, "What a desperate man you are!"

Bennett froze. Aware that we were being watched from above, he quickly regained his composure. By this time, Drew and I were halfway up the stairs. Kristin came up behind Bennett and touched his back; he tore his eyes away and managed to smile at her. Drew and I were met with near silence as we wished the group a good night.

A rain-washed sun strained through the lead-paned windows of the lecture hall, filtering weakly over my shoulders as I addressed my students. I was standing, one leg out, my hands on my hips, in an attitude of barely attenuated fury. My voice rang out in a defiance of history, for each time I spoke on this subject I became, despite all my attempts at self-control, deeply angry.

"I am this color because of a white master's sexual relationship with one of his slaves. Imagine it! We African Americans are a rainbow race, created solely by the sexual activities of white people, who had the full rights of manhood and womanhood in the United States, with their black servants, who shared none of those privileges.

"The African American 'race' did not exist before the transatlantic slave trade. Listen, students, and consider carefully what I am saying. A new racial delineation was forged, quite literally, by slavery. Before the sixteen hundreds there were black Africans, white Europeans, and North Africans and Middle Easterners of various skin tones and hair textures. But African Americans, a people today legally classified as a 'race' in the United States, did not yet exist."

I paused. "Think about the enormity of that statement. There was enough sex occurring between white and black people to result in a whole new 'race' of people. And that sexual activity was, both by law and by social custom, expressly forbidden! While black people were being treated like animals by their masters and their masters' consorts, they were being impregnated at such a high rate that within a century a large percent of all blacks in America had white blood!"

Hands shot up. An intense debate began between two students about the propriety of sex between master and slave. The young man suggested that sexual attraction should know no bounds, either social or racial; the woman argued that in situations of such obvious social disparity, interracial sexual activity could never be truly consensual.

You wandered into my thoughts, Chloe, and I wished, as I've wished a thousand times, that you could have been there to add your wisdom to this debate. I wished you were at home in Nice so that I could talk to you about Drew. But you were somewhere between Luxembourg and Germany, opening several exhibitions of your work, and you wouldn't be home until the week before Christmas.

I refocused my attention on the class as the discussion turned to modern attitudes about interracial relationships. The debate became so intense that the entire class was startled by a voice that rang out from the back of the room.

"Excuse me, ladies and gentlemen."

All heads turned to find Jonathan Bennett standing inside the open doorway, his arms crossed casually over his chest. "I just happened by, and when I heard the subject of your discussion I couldn't tear myself away."

Several students laughed, mistaking his cool manner for humor, but I knew that Bennett wasn't trying to be amusing. He glanced across the room at me.

"First, I have to congratulate your students on their perceptive analysis of the tensions caused by interracial relationships. Second, I'd like to pose them a question." He paused thoughtfully.

"Considering the immense difficulties faced by members of minority groups in the United States and England, is it ever really possible for the partners in an interracial relationship to be truly equal?"

There was an uncomfortable pause. Then a young woman raised her hand.

"Women generally face more social challenges than men, yet we still manage to live with them!"

"Considering the divorce rate," a male student retorted, "that's obviously a myth."

Everyone laughed. Bennett took several steps into the classroom.

"How would you respond to the statement that even when white men and women understand the systematized oppression experienced by minority groups, it is nearly impossible for them to know the pain caused by the routine, almost daily acts of discrimination faced by their nonwhite partners?"

The class fell silent. Then, slowly, all eyes turned toward me. Bennett watched, glowing in silent pleasure as the entire room waited for an answer.

"This question," I said firmly, "will make an excellent topic to begin next week's session. Please give it some careful thought and prepare a short reaction paper on it over the weekend. I'll be looking forward to hearing your ideas."

My eyes met Bennett's. He nodded, as if acknowledging my mastery over the situation, then vanished.

I returned a set of papers and reviewed upcoming assignments, finally drawing the session to a close. Still talking with an animated group of students who followed me all the way to my office, I was prepared for neither of the things that greeted me when I arrived: Kristin Proctor and the box wrapped in gold.

Kristin was standing at my office door, intently reading the course descriptions posted on a bulletin board. I brushed by, assuming she was waiting for Bennett. When I entered the office, however, she followed.

"Can I help you, Kristin?" I dropped my load of books on the desk.

"I need to talk."

"That's what I'm here for," I responded evenly, wishing that I'd had a few minutes alone.

Kristin walked slowly into the room, glancing around as if she'd never been there before. She was wearing tights, a thigh-length sweater, and hiking boots. Meager fare for the late autumn weather.

"This has been bothering me since I had dinner at your house," she stated simply.

"What is it?"

"Your husband . . . well, he isn't proper with his students."

"What do you mean, 'isn't proper'?"

"I mean, he sleeps with his students."

"What students?"

"He slept with me two years ago, just before I graduated."

I stood by the desk, grasping a folder and staring at the younger woman. "Kristin, let me repeat what you've just told me. You said that Professor Northcross had sex with you two years ago, when you were an undergraduate student here."

"That's right."

Remaining calm, I looked deeply into her eyes. "What were the circumstances?"

"I was in his lecture. I came to him for some extra help, and he asked me out to dinner. Then we went to someone's apartment, and it happened."

I sat down slowly. "What you're suggesting is very serious. It could have very far-reaching consequences to my husband's career, as well as our marriage."

A flicker of emotion crossed Kristin's otherwise impassive face. "I'm not going to tell anybody else," she said. "But I thought you should know." She shook her hair clear of her eyes and turned on her heel, starting out of the office.

"Wait a minute," I ordered.

She looked back over her shoulder.

"Kristin," I said with utmost control, "I don't believe you."

"But it's true!" she insisted, turning defiantly to face me. "I can prove it. He has a scar on his hip. A red scar."

I paused, and then continued speaking softly. "Why did you decide to tell me this now?"

"Because of the way he acted at your house," she said. "He pretended to be so moral, so *real*. It made me sick!"

The door slammed on the word. I stared into space, my mind on fire. And then I spun around in anger, knocking something bright off the corner of the desk. I bent down, and my fingers closed around a small box, wrapped in gold.

I knew instantly that it was from Bennett. Turning it over, I weighed it in my hand, then pushed it into my pocket. I walked down the corridor to Drew's office. The light was on, the door slightly ajar. Drew was perched on the edge of his desk, looking intently at a letter. He lowered it when he heard me enter, then raised his brows at the sight of my face.

"An earthquake or tidal wave?"

"Quicksand." My voice was trembling as I walked over to him, and we stood face-to-face.

"Did you have sex with Kristin?"

"God, no!"

"But she says—"

"I've never lied to you about other women, so it doesn't matter what she says."

My shoulders fell. Drew reached up and touched my chin. I pulled away.

"This is Bennett's doing," he said. "Do you believe him over me?"

"Why should I," I said, moving miserably to the door, "when our marriage is so perfect?"

Later I wouldn't be able to remember clearly how I made it home. I stood in the kitchen, riveted by the thought that if Kristin's accusations were true, they were perfectly timed with another incident—an "indiscretion" that Drew himself described to me, with excruciating honesty, two years before.

He had been attending a five-day conference in Hull. He sat through the sessions without much interest; the days were long and the meetings tedious. He felt a strange restlessness that he could neither identify nor define.

On the last day he found himself in the hotel bar staring at a woman sitting several tables away. Of average height and build, she had raven black hair and the most translucently pale skin he had ever seen. Unable to tear his eyes away from her glowing face, he realized she was returning his gaze with unveiled interest. When he left the table, she rose and followed him into the corridor.

Before he even thought about what he was doing, Drew found himself in this woman's room. It was with a real sense of horror that Drew realized—much too late—that she had disrobed while in the bathroom and was standing before him naked. As she walked toward him, a distaste rose in his throat like bile, and the smell of expensive perfume and the sight of her floating black hair chafed against the image of a lean, powerful brown body bathed in scented oils.

By the time she reached for his pants, he grabbed her hand, denying her his manhood. His reaction was unmistakable.

"Get out," she spat, and with as much dignity as possible, he did.

Drew told me all about the woman that night, when he returned from Hull. Sitting beside me in the dark kitchen, he recounted the tale in a strangely subdued voice, as if he were talking about a different man.

"You've made it impossible, Michael. Every woman I've known in the past twelve years has seemed like some kind of freak: her body was too soft, or too short, or too pale. Her hair was bleached, or colored some absurd and unnatural shade. She had a nasal voice, or found it disgusting to sweat, or moved without your dancer's grace. Her nose was too sharp, her lips were too thin, her breasts too fleshy, her eyes too painted."

He reached for my hand and brushed my fingers across his lips.

"Those other women don't smell of sandalwood mixed with jasmine, or patchouli with a hint of lavender. They don't dance in the kitchen to the radio while making tabouli, or drink iced espresso with a shot of milk. They don't blow bubbles with fluorescent pink gum. They don't run along the cliffs in the rain, lift weights while watching alien movies, or make love to me while looking into my eyes. They don't speak French, love Degas and Miles, and Santorini, and Zimbabwe. They would never order vanilla ice cream with ginger preserves, or eat mussels by the sea with a dry white wine. They'd simply never be you."

He raised his eyes.

"I don't think I realized until I was with her how much a part of me you are. Or how little of Andrew would be left over if Michael ever went away."

"That didn't stop you from going to her room."

"I wasn't there for the sex," he replied sadly. "I think I was searching for my youth. . . ."

As I stood in the silent kitchen, thinking about Drew and the black-haired woman, the phone rang. I answered quickly, in the wild hope that you were calling, Chloe.

But Jonathan Bennett was on the line. "Listen: Kris told me what happened. Are you okay? I called the office and no one answered."

I paused, forcing my frustrated rage into a fistful of words: "You are full of shit."

It wasn't until I was peeling myself out of my clothes some hours later that I found the little box in my pocket. Out fell a single tiny earring, a gold scarab. When Drew got home that evening he found me sleeping, the light on the bedside table throwing back its muted gold reflection like a brand on my face.

At first I wasn't sure why I did it, Chloe. In fact, I only began to understand why I had sex with Jonathan Bennett when I had to make sense of it to Drew. Strange, isn't it? Perhaps his insistence that we always be honest with each other was really a way of forcing us to be honest with ourselves.

I waited a few moments after Kristin drove off before pressing the buzzer. An irritated voice replied: "Not your keys again!" Then the latch clicked, and I stepped into the hallway. The door to the flat was open; I heard the sound of naked feet walking toward the bedroom.

"The top of the fridge!" he called out, trying to temper his annoyance. When no one answered, he repeated his assertion more loudly. "They were on top of the fridge. Hurry up, or you'll be late for your tutorial—"

He broke off as I entered the bedroom. He took in my loose-fitting sweater, jeans, and the leather jacket I'd thrown over one shoulder. My eyes were hidden behind dark glasses.

"What a surprise," he said softly.

Wordlessly I removed the glasses, then let the jacket slide to the floor. Crossing my arms over my chest, I pulled my sweater over my head. I was wearing nothing underneath. Next I unzipped my jeans and pulled them down, pausing only to pull the condoms out of a pocket. Staring into his eyes, I stepped out of my black panties and stood tall before him.

For a moment Jonathan Bennett did not react. Then he pulled back the sheets, revealing his own body to me. I tossed the condoms on the edge of the bed. He looked at them, nodded, and waited.

Soon I was touching his full upper arms, stroking the muscles, pressing my lips silently against his childhood scars. My mouth roamed the ridges of his chest, sucking at his nipples. He watched, waiting to take his cue from me. I raised my head, looked at him calmly, and slid my hands down toward his thighs.

The sex was as if we had known each other for a long time—as if we'd shared an earlier life. His full mouth sought mine like my teenaged lovers, the boys who kissed me so softly and deeply that my whole body ached. The taste of his tongue and the scent of his hair transported me back to another world, another age, another time of my life.

I giggled as I resurfaced from a drowning wave of pleasure, and smiling into my eyes, he began to chuckle, too. Suddenly we were both laughing—laughing at the richness of the moment, the obstacles we'd created, and the fact that we'd desired each other from the moment we'd met.

Finally we lay together, wet, breathing slowly, his palm flat on the center of my stomach. I found myself smiling up at the ceiling.

"What are you thinking about?"

"A boy you remind me of."

"Did he do it to you real good?" The question rolled out in a low throttle.

I breathed in the thought, sighing. "Yes, he most certainly did."

"Your first time?"

"I was sixteen. He was a kid—fourteen, maybe. He had gigantic hands—athlete's hands. Green eyes and deep brown skin."

Bennett began to stroke my breast. "You were classmates?"

"God, no. They'd sent me down to my aunt Delia's in Georgia to get me out of the city and away from the boys." I laughed. "And there I was, rocking on the porch swing, bored to distraction. Gordon came strolling out of the sweltering dust like some kind of apparition. When he moved, I could see every muscle of his thighs through his jeans. And his voice was deep and rough and full of the South. Once those eyes hit mine, I thought I'd died and gone to heaven."

"So the two of you went sneaking off into the bushes?"

"No, he wasn't like that. He hung around, throwing a football and singing songs from the radio. He was still so bloody young." I rolled onto my belly, cradling the memory in my folded arms.

"Then one night they sent me to a movie with a nice boy from a nice family who went to my aunt Delia's church. He was nice, all right. We didn't have anything to say to each other after about three minutes. I was driving my aunt's car, so as soon as the movie was over I took him back to his nice house."

I laughed softly. "It was still early, so I just started driving. There was Gordon, walking down the road, all by himself. I picked him up. We looked at each other, and he pointed the way to a grove of pine trees." I stretched, reluctant to release the memory.

"You don't even want to know how I lost my innocence," Bennett said softly. "I was so obsessed with books that my father had taken to calling me a faggot. He got together with my uncles and found this girl and paid her something to take me up to her room. She made me drink a couple of malts, then gave me the short lesson on the facts of life."

He shifted restlessly. "That's the way it was. You had to be a man on their terms. Nobody wanted to hear anything about you climbing out of the barrel or making something out of yourself. You did what you were told. One step too fast or too far, and you were selling them out."

"They didn't want something better for you?"

"I was supposed to stay around to support them when they got old. My father was going back to the Delta to build his house and die. I certainly didn't need an education for that."

"And the rest of your family?"

"Two brothers in the pen, a sister on the corner, and another sister who—" his voice quavered "—who took off when she was seventeen and never came back."

"I'm truly sorry," I said softly, and he took a deep breath.

"You know, Michael, you're dangerous. It would be very easy to fall in love with you."

"Don't do that," I answered smoothly. "You might go all soft. And this game is only as good as its players."

His eyes narrowed. "Players?"

"Kristin, for example, was not a very good pick for your team."

He blinked quickly, but I went on speaking calmly, softly. "She described a scar on Drew's hip to me to prove they were lovers. But Drew didn't have that scar when she says they were together."

"So she got the dates wrong."

"No, she got them right. I checked the records. She was his student two years ago. Then she graduated."

"That doesn't mean they weren't seeing each other."

"She was in Australia, Jon." There was a tense silence. "Drew got that scar in a biking accident, with me, in Teneriffe last summer. Where did you see it? In the gym?"

"You're in my bed, accusing *me* of trying to wreck your marriage?"

"No," I answered. "This was sex. Nothing more."

"And I suppose you're going home now to tell Drew all about it?"

I stood up and began collecting my clothes. "I'll be honest with him. If I leave my husband, it won't be because of lies and deceit. And if I come here again, it will be because I enjoy the sex." I paused as I reached the door. "You don't have to use Kristin as bait anymore."

"Did you do it to hurt me?"

The inquisition began as soon as Drew entered our bedroom, only moments after I'd returned from Bennett's bed.

"How did you know, Drew?"

"I looked for you all morning. Finally I drove to his flat. You were just leaving."

"Excellent timing," I said dryly. "Like all the nights I've listened to the phone ring in empty hotel rooms."

"You didn't have sex with him?"

"I did."

"Why?"

"To take some control over my life."

"To take . . . *control*?" the word trailed off into an incredulous whisper. "Screwing Jonathan Bennett proves that your life is totally out of control."

"No. It means that my life is out of *your* control."

He reached around me and snatched up a book from the bed stand, hurling it against the wall. "Then damn you! Damn you both!"

His rage spent, I watched as he sank to the edge of our bed, breathing heavily. "He doesn't love you, Michael."

"And I don't love him," I responded quietly. "Hasn't that always been the rule, Drew? We could both have our little extravagances, as long as we were perfectly honest? And as long as we knew who we *really* loved—"

"Then you're doing this to punish me?"

"Punish you? For fifteen years I've stood by you while you wandered. For the last two years you've asked me to wait, and I don't even know what I'm waiting for. I've never stopped loving you, but I just can't play your game anymore."

"This is no game, Michael."

"Then tell me what's wrong, Drew!"

We stared at each other. Then something passed over his face and his voice changed. "Come to me," he commanded softly.

I hesitated, knowing all too well what would happen if I touched him. I tried to look away, but instead my gaze rose to the portrait that you, Chloe, painted of us before our wedding, Drew's arms wrapped protectively around my breasts. There he was, standing behind me, his head lowered and tilted against mine, and I was pressed safely against him.

Now he pulled me down beside him.

"None of this began with you, Michael," he said, his eyes also fixed on the painting. "I'm struggling to overcome something that happened to me long ago."

He lay back, wrapping me carefully into his arms. "There's something I want to tell you, Michael. Something I should have told you long ago."

His words began pouring out like bitter and ephemeral smoke in the darkness.

"When I was eight my mother took me to the market with her every day after school. My two brothers stayed with a neighbor; she claimed she couldn't get the shopping done with them underfoot.

"We lived in a small town, a village, really," Drew continued. "And we always shopped in the same stores, one after the other. Everyone knew us—knew my father was the schoolmaster, knew where we lived.

"Well, there was one shopkeeper—a butcher—who was different. I'd heard my father telling her to stay away from him, to keep me out of there. But she kept going into his place, and they always had these jokes together. I can remember her exploding with laughter at the things he'd say. I just stood around, looking at the chunks of animals, wondering why it took so long to buy a few sausages.

"What I didn't know, then, was about her drinking. She'd been in the house all day with the little ones, drinking whatever kind of alcohol she could find, and when she got to this bloke's shop, he always offered her a beer.

"One afternoon something happened. Maybe she'd been drinking too much all day, or perhaps he gave her something stronger. First they were laughing together, then all of a sudden she wasn't laughing anymore. I looked around and saw that she had slumped over on a bench next to the shop entrance. I ran to her, and he said she was all right. 'Just a bit too much of the good stuff,' he said. He told me to let her sleep for a while.

"Then he did something strange. Rather than calling my father, he locked the door of the shop and pulled down the shade. 'Now, your mum wouldn't want anybody to see her like this, would she?' I was standing next to her, terrified, shaking her and trying to wake her up."

Drew stopped speaking. A car passed outside, its radio blaring distorted female voices. He reached up and wiped his mouth, his eyes fixed on the ceiling.

"The butcher began to speak in a kind of falsetto, as if he were talking to a little dog. He offered me a treat if I would go into the back with him. He said I could see all the animals just as they looked when they came from the farms. I told him I didn't want to; I hated blood.

"He said that I would like the things he wanted to show me, that I should be a brave little boy, that my mother wanted me to go with him, and that's why she came into the shop. I didn't know what to make of that.

"Then he did it. He didn't want to reason with me anymore, so he just picked me up with those butcher's arms and slung me over his shoulder. I began to kick and scream, and he laughed. He laughed exactly the way he'd always laughed with her. I guess animals kicked and screamed, too, before he butchered them.

"He took me into a back room. It was cold, dimly lit, and the floor was slick with blood. It smelled like nothing I've smelled since. He put me down and I backed away, brushing up against the dripping carcasses hanging from hooks on the ceiling. In that singsong voice he said to me, 'You don't have to be afraid. I won't tell nobody you was here.'

"I ran a few steps, but everywhere I turned there were dripping lamb and beef and horse carcasses. I slipped on the bloody floor, screaming while he laughed. I was certain that he wanted to kill me like he'd killed those beasts. I finally lay on the bloody floor, holding myself in a tight, tight ball while he smacked me and fumbled with my clothes."

Drew stopped speaking, staring unblinking into his past. I lay beside him, almost afraid to breathe.

"Suddenly someone was standing in the door. It was someone who worked in the bank, I think. My mother had awakened and managed to open the shade. Some people in the street saw her and came to her aid. They heard my cries from the back room and saved me from being raped."

Drew's hands had tightened to fists, and I could feel his body shaking beside mine. I had a sudden image of his crouched and broken form as he'd wept in our study, hopeless and naked and alone. He continued to speak, his voice low.

"I wasn't punished, but the shame my father felt—and the fear that perhaps I had in some way brought this man's attentions upon myself—caused him to seek some means of sending me away. The town was too small, and his position as the schoolmaster required him to have an unblemished character. He discovered that a contest was being held for entrance into Gainsworthy. He drove me to Oxford for the test and saw that I was enrolled after I was admitted."

I lay stock-still, staring at my husband. "This is why you never went home?"

"My father didn't want to see me. And after I left, my mother just got worse."

Neither of us spoke. I reached for his hand, pulling it away from his eyes. His fingers were wet.

"I've lived with this for forty-five years," he murmured. "Forty-five years, and I still can't really understand it." His voice cracked. "Would you like to hear something ironic? Many years ago—" he stopped speaking, his voice fading to a rough whisper "—in fact, the first time that you and I ever made love, you asked me if I was fulfilling some fantasy about a master having sex with his slave. I thought you were mad. But then, the idea kept coming back, over the weeks, the months—"

"And now?" I asked, my face hidden in the shadows.

"Sometimes I think that—" He stopped. "That I ran all the way to Africa," he said in a hushed voice, "to escape my father's world."

Shaken, I climbed out of the bed and wandered to the window, longing for a cigarette. The naked tree branches bowed wildly, waltzing to December wind.

"And now I know why you chose me," I said. "My love was supposed to save you from becoming like them."

Silently I left the room. Wetting a towel with cool water, I began to wipe my streaming face. Drew appeared behind me, and I faced the reflection of our marriage.

"You've always been my equal, Michael."

"No," I answered. "I've always been your prize."

Chloe, your postcard from Berlin arrived on what felt like the grayest day of my life. I peered blindly at the script, barely recognizing the handwriting that had been my lifeline for so many years.

December 10, 1995

Guten Tag, *Michael!*

Berlin is in a turmoil of reconstruction, so museums are the quietest places for a soul seeking tranquillity. My exhibition is going well, but I'm looking forward to spending the holidays with you in Nice. How are things working out with Drew? Hang in there—we'll be together soon.

I love you.

I turned the card over to find a pair of Klimt lovers locked in an ardent embrace. Quite an ironic choice, since I'd told you nothing about Jonathan Bennett.

Later that day I wandered through a florist shop, searching for something fragrant and fresh to buoy my mood.

"Hullo, Professor Davies! What a pleasure to see you!"

The vigorous voice came from behind the irises, and I slipped your card into my coat pocket. Peeking over the top of the purple flowers, I found myself face-to-face with the round figure of Caryl Somerset, a former student whom I hadn't seen in several years.

"What a surprise!" We hugged and stepped back to admire each other.

Caryl had grown stouter since her graduation, but she seemed hale and far happier than she'd been in the past. Her college years had been a time of great turmoil as she sought out her sexual identity, and I had spent many hours listening to the young woman's misadventures as she experienced her first romances.

"Is Professor Northcross still the most debonair man in all England?" she asked, gently teasing.

The question caught me off guard, and I stammered something affirmative before changing the subject. "Are you working here, Caryl? I thought you'd be off teaching somewhere."

"Not a chance! I took a position in a local school and tried to get those ruffians to appreciate the Brontës, but after two weeks I knew it was a lost cause!"

"So you've become a florist?"

"I don't just work here: I *own* the shop!" she said proudly. "Bought it two years ago after my grandmother died. I'm not alone, either. Come on in the back and meet Bernie."

I followed Caryl through the flower shop to a tiny office ensconced between great glass coolers full of orchids and birds of paradise. Caryl threw open a door to reveal a lean, dark-haired girl who appeared to be no more than seventeen.

"Professor Davies, this is my partner, Bernadette Marin. Bernie's from France. She came over to help me set up the shop and never went back."

I greeted the young woman.

"Now I get to use my expensive university French." Caryl chuckled. "We're the only flower shop on this side of town, and we get loads of weddings, funerals, receptions, and the like. And you should see the cottage we found! We've got our own little paradise—sea view and all."

"So you're happy?"

Caryl and Bernadette exchanged glances. "Yes." Caryl nodded. "And now that you know where to find me, I hope you'll plan on having a meal with us. There's a nice little flat upstairs; we often run up for a nap or a snack, as you Americans say. I want to have time for a real conversation with you, Professor Davies."

We stopped at the door of the shop. Caryl bent down and lifted a bouquet of heather from a vase next to the cash register.

"Take this, Dr. Davies. I hope it cheers you."

"But I'm fine—" I choked back the lie at the look of quiet caring in her eyes.

Sitting in my car with the magenta blossoms on my lap, I once again read your card, Chloe. I wished that I could crawl into a warm, dry space, far away from my confusion. But I was still a long way from finding that place.

Passing by the study a few days later, I found myself swaying to Stella Chiweshe's lovely Mbira music as it poured past the open door. Drew had hidden himself away earlier that day, and now he seemed deeply preoccupied with a document that lay before him on his desk. He didn't look up as I came down the hall and stood at the door.

Moored to his leather chair, Drew set down his pen and silently studied the paper. His finger traced its raised seal while his eyes weighed its contents, his mouth unfolding into a smile of quiet contentment I hadn't seen in many years. A smile I'd rarely seen, in fact, since Africa.

I moved in the doorway, and Drew looked up, startled. His hand closed over the paper, and his expression leapt from vague guilt to sharp irritation.

"What can I do for you, Michael?"

"I was just enjoying the music," I answered defensively. "What are you reading?"

He hesitated. "An announcement about the conference in Ireland. I've been asked to give an address on the connections between African and British anticolonial texts."

"Surely," I said facetiously, "that will be more fascinating than spending the holidays with Chloe and me in Nice."

"I'm sorry, Michael, but they're expecting me."

"That's all right," I replied. "Being with you is like being with a stranger anyway."

I went into the kitchen and made myself a strong coffee. When I passed the study again, the document was gone.

"Are you still having sex with Kristin?"

"Are you still having sex with Drew?"

Ignoring Bennett's question, I kicked the sheets away and stared at my hands, stroking the interlaced leaves on my wedding ring. "Does she know about us?"

"She knows what I want her to know," he said slyly, bringing his lips to my throat.

I smiled despite myself. "You're shameless, Jon."

"Don't pretend you feel sorry for Kristin." He laughed. "I saw your face when I brought her to your house that night."

"I was pissed off because you were late to dinner!"

"You just don't like sharing the attention with other women," he replied, stretching so that the muscles on his chest rippled gently.

"You're used to making all the men want you, then walking away with Drew. I guess I messed up that little routine."

"Maybe I let you mess it up."

"I have to admit I do get tired of Kristin's frilly panties, candlelit dinners, and sickly sweet German wines."

He shuddered and leaned up on his elbow. "And then come the scented massage oils, banana-flavored condoms, and fully illustrated erotic manuals."

"You should stick to sex with women your own age."

"I'm trying," he said as he began to stroke my breasts. "But it's hard, Michael. Young women see sex as good, clean fun. Older women tangle it up with a whole set of complicated emotions. And I'm just no good at emotional vulnerability. That's a white man's luxury."

I groaned. "You wear the role of a black revolutionary like a Halloween costume."

He laughed. "You really believe that there's someone hiding beneath my big bad wolf? Someone who nuzzles and likes to eat ice cream?"

"I hope there's somebody beneath all your posturing."

Ignoring my comment, he glanced wistfully toward the sleet-coated window.

"I have a little Mission bungalow in San Diego with a veranda that looks out over the city. On clear days you can see the mighty Pacific. On hazy days you can see the illegals working their way up from Mexico."

"Sounds delightful."

"Gets lonely."

"I seriously doubt that."

"Even Darth Bennett knows the difference between sex and love."

"And this is?"

"Feels like love to me," he sang, his hand sliding down my belly.

I rolled onto my stomach. "Have you ever loved a white woman?"

"Sure. And tan and brown. And the occasional Asian. But white women are different. They're so obsessed with the "sweet forbidden" that it's hard to say no."

"I wasn't talking about sex, Jon."

"Neither was I." He paused, looking into my eyes. "My ex-wife is white."

"You were married to a wh—" I broke off in shocked silence.

He burst into laughter. "What's wrong, Michael? Do you think you're the only one who's crossed into the 'No-Zone'?"

I rolled over and snatched up my clothes. "You accuse *me* of abandoning black people when your own wife was white?"

"*Was* is the key, Michael. You see, I got over my infatuation with the enemy."

"Fuck you," I said as I pulled on my jeans.

Leaning back, he watched me dress. "You know, Michael, you're the only woman I've ever known who's more attracted to a man she despises than to the man she really loves."

"Don't worry," I replied, "I'm getting over *that*."

"Well, before you return to your *colorless* life with Drew, I've got a proposition for you. I've been invited to speak at a conference in Paris on minority literature next June. Let's coauthor the paper and present it together."

"Why the hell would I go to Paris with you?"

"First, so you can show off that excellent French. Second, so we could enjoy some *intellectual* mating. Third, I'm certain that some friends of mine will be there from the States, and—" he added with mock innocence "—I could reintroduce you to black people."

"You're an embarrassment to black men, Jonathan."

He laughed. "I won't tell anyone if you won't."

Late that night I lay awake, my heart a matted ball of sadness, guilt, and resentment. I thought of Jonathan Bennett's skin and hair, his smell and the insistence of his touch. I thought of the strange sense of knowing such intense pleasure with someone I disliked so deeply. Shifting in the bed, I felt Drew's hand on my face. He stroked the line of my jaw gently, his fingers coming to rest on my shoulder.

"You can't chase him away, can you?" He leaned up on one arm and, in a gesture remarkably like Bennett's, placed his hand flat on my stomach.

"Are you falling in love with him, Michael?"

I stared into the darkness, ashamed to admit to my husband that I truly despised my lover. Drew stroked my belly, then moved his hand into the soft thistles below. I forced myself to lie still, to hold my breath steady.

"Do you still want me?" he asked in a deep, hoarse whisper. "Tell me."

"I've never stopped wanting you, Drew."

"And does he please you more than I do?"

"No," I whispered.

"That's not enough," he answered, covering me.

"Drew—" my voice breaking.

"Say it, Michael!"

Caught up in the bittersweetness, I repeated the words he needed to hear. The words I had to say.

"I love you, Drew," I whispered, my face wet with tears.

Tendrils of your hair were blowing loose from beneath your chenille cap when I burst through the airport gate and flew into your arms, Chloe. Only five months since I'd seen you—yet every day had seemed like a year! We held each other until our arms ached, then leaned back, looked into each other's eyes, and began hugging all over again.

"Welcome home," you whispered, examining my face with those astute artist's eyes, then taking in my short hair with the glance of a lifelong friend. Finally you measured my thin frame and air of guarded weariness with your loving, maternal gaze.

"Well," you said with a wizened smile, "all things considered, you don't look *too* much worse for the wear."

"Don't get cute," I replied. "I've still got those Frankenstein shoes in a box somewhere!"

Soon we began the laborious ascent in the grinding, battered Deux Chevaux, up the pitched roads to your house, set high in the rocky, snow-dusted hills above Nice.

"And Drew?" you shouted above the roar of the engine.

"Gone to his conference in Ireland," I answered, glad that the noise hid the disappointment in my voice.

"That's all right! I wanted to spend some time alone with you, Little Sister."

The countryside had a soft, pink glow at this time of year, as if the muted blues of late autumn had blended with the reds of dusk and dawn. The leaves on low-growing grapevines patchworked the hills, dancing golden in the warm wind. A hint of the sea lingered on the breeze as shredded gray clouds drifted along the horizon.

Wandering through the sun-warmed house, I sensed that there was something missing. With the artists gone for the holidays, memories roamed like ghosts through the bright, vacant spaces. The daylight painted pastel patterns through the blue glass panels of the doors and windows, and the air was full of the tinkling of wind chimes from the garden. As I passed through the breezeway connecting the house to the kitchen I suddenly realized what seemed so strange: *There were no paintings*. No new works on the walls. No canvases placed in corners to dry. Nothing on the easels in the studio. No evidence of an artist's life. Anywhere.

I found you standing at the stove tasting a simmering vegetable soup. Your faded denim shirt and loose drawstring pants enunciated a new fraility about your shoulders and hips, as if the fleshier emotions had been worn away with time. I stared at you, and it seemed that the woman wrapped in old clothes and diffused December sunlight was but a blur of that strong, ambitious woman from my youth. What had happened to that Chloe? And what had happened to the passionate, joyful Michael? When had we grown so much older? Suddenly my eyes were brimming with tears.

Glancing over your shoulder, your brows came together. "Hey! What's the matter, baby?"

The love in your voice broke the flood I'd held to a trickle during the past months, and I sank into a chair and began weeping as if my world were ending. You were instantly by my side, gathering me up into your arms, and I submerged myself in the warmth of your skin and the scent of your hair as you rocked me like a child.

It was a long time before I trusted myself to speak. "I don't know where to start," I sobbed.

"Start with Drew," you murmured.

So taking a soul-deep breath, I grasped the edges of the table and pushed out the words I thought I'd never have the courage to say.

"Chloe, I'm going to leave him."

You watched in silence while I wiped my eyes. Then you rose to your feet and began to pace the kitchen, head down, arms folded across your chest. After a time you spoke.

"Are you doing this because of me?"

"You?" I repeated, confused.

"Well, you've always seen my life as some kind of sweeping adventure, full of romantic places and handsome lovers. And you believe that I'm a strong and independent artist who'd rather live alone than compromise her craft. And maybe, just maybe—" you raised your hands to stop me from arguing "—you believe that living alone, like me, will help you find your own focus and strength. But to leave someone who loves you as much as Drew means you'll spend the rest of your life proving, like me, that you don't need anyone."

"But, Chloe," I said, "you don't know what it's like to be bound so tightly to a man that you can't breathe."

You gave a single, taut laugh. "No. I always managed to lose them."

"I don't need Drew to survive!"

"That's true," you agreed. "But surviving isn't the same as living, Michael."

I sat in stubborn silence as you shook your head slowly. "When did you decide to stop loving him?"

"I still love him. But I need to grow."

"We're always growing—smarter, wiser, lonelier, older." You laughed. "But we're very rarely loved."

We stared at each other. Then, sighing deeply, you opened your arms.

I needed some time to think, so I put on my running clothes and took off through the crackling cold air and into the hills. As my legs found their rhythm, I pulled the fresh sweetness of the Mediterranean winter into my lungs, expelling the madness of the last few months. I ran and ran, surrendering myself to the sense of raw freedom that coursed through my body as my legs carried me across the warm, red earth.

You were in the kitchen when I returned, pensively drinking coffee by the crackling hearth. You raised your head when I came in, panting and shaking off the cold. I paused, wondering why you weren't in your studio.

"What's up, Chloe? You're not working?"

"My easel doesn't like me too much anymore," you said without emotion.

"Is that why this place is so naked?"

"I've got to sell what I've got while I can."

"What the hell is that supposed to mean?"

"It means that it's time for me to think about retirement."

"That's crazy. You can't retire from yourself!"

"And you can't walk away from Drew!" We stopped, staring at each other.

Long after midnight we lay on the studio floor with mugs of spiced wine on our laps, our legs propped up on stools and the doors thrown open to the cold night. The only light was provided by a solstice moon trailed by countless glittering stars.

"You ready to tell me the whole truth?" you asked into the night. A leaf blew in and glided gracefully toward your empty easel.

I took a resigned breath, knowing it was useless to try to fool you. "There's someone else, Chloe. A guest professor from the States."

"Big surprise," you replied sardonically. "There's nothing like warm, available flesh to lure us away from the men we love."

"I suppose you're comparing Drew to Emil," I answered. "But since you've always been so secretive about your breakup—"

"I can't change what happened fifteen years ago," you interrupted. "But maybe you can learn from my mistakes."

"First, you'd have to tell me the truth, Chloe!"

"Are *you* willing to tell the truth?"

"Of course!"

"Then let's take inventory," you said, smoothly changing the subject. "Your lover treats you with more respect than Drew?"

"No."

"He helps you feel strong?"

"No."

"You're the only woman he's sleeping with?"

"No."

"He's offered you a chance for true happiness?"

"No."

"He's kind to you when you're together?"

"No."

"You're in love with him?"

"No."

"Then why choose him to mess up your life?"

"Because he was holding the net when the only man I've ever loved forgot I'm alive."

"That wasn't a net, Michael. It was a hoop."

The breeze picked up, scattering more leaves across the balcony to rest near our feet. You sipped your wine, then laughed ironically.

"So it all comes down to sex?"

"Being with him takes me home, Chloe. Home to the life I'd almost forgotten. He's sensuous. Intelligent. And," I hesitated, "he's black."

"Ahhh," you said softly. "We can add a little bit of guilt to all that good sex."

"I didn't choose him because he's black!"

"Would you be sleeping with him if he were *white*?"

A tense silence separated us for what seemed like a long, long time. Then I heard your voice in the darkness.

"You think you can win this little game with your Homecoming king? After everything you've just admitted, how do you think he *really* feels about *you*?"

Your question addressed the one truth I'd deliberately refused to see: *Jonathan Bennett could not possibly be in love with me.*

Before I could respond, however, I watched in dismay as you ended the discussion by climbing to your feet and crossing the studio to close the balcony doors. When you looked down at me, your expression was dark.

"You're not serious about your lover, but you're planning to leave the man you love. In the twenty-five years I've known you, I've never seen you do anything so stupid."

Christmas morning dawned bright and cold, with echoes of tolling church bells rolling up from the city below. I ran as hard and fast as I could, the clouds of my breath blending with the vision of the blue-gray sea. Following a winding road higher and higher into the hills, I welcomed the pain in my calves and my air-torn lungs. When I returned to the house, sweat-soaked and exhausted, the Deux Chevaux was gone.

A note in the kitchen informed me that you'd gone into town, so I turned on a steaming shower and stepped inside, wishing that I could stay in the scalding spray forever.

After a while I heard the car lumbering up the drive. Bounding down the stairs into the kitchen, I was unprepared for the scene that I discovered. There, in the driveway, stood a tall figure whose dark head was bent close to yours. With a startled cry I stumbled forward. You both looked up at the same instant.

"Look what arrived with *Père Noel*!" you announced.

"Merry Christmas, my love," said Drew.

"Explain it to me," I ordered in a clipped voice when we were alone.

"I thought I'd surprise you."

"Drew Northcross missing a conference to spend Christmas with his wife? That *is* a surprise."

"I'd hoped you'd be glad to see me." He opened his small suitcase.

"Three days ago you refused to come to France."

"I apologize," he said calmly, unpacking his belongings.

"You need to apologize for some other things."

"So do you," he said curtly. "You're part of this, too."

"I don't care if I never see Jonathan Bennett again," I said emphatically.

Drew took a long, slow look at me. We'd both lost weight in the last few weeks, and our faces were gaunt in the dim light.

"Touch me, Michael," he said very gently. "We need each other so badly."

"Sex isn't always the solution, Drew."

"It's Christmas," he murmured. "Can't we be together today?"

I slowly backed away and leaned against the door.

"Why are you doing this?" he cried, his voice shrill.

"It's strange, isn't it? For fifteen years I've been afraid I'd get a call from a conference, or some woman's flat, or a hotel, and you'd tell me—with your characteristic honesty—that you didn't love me anymore. And now, suddenly, I've lost that fear. I feel liberated. I don't even know how to live without my terror of losing you."

"You'll never lose me, Michael."

"That's just the point, Drew. I don't really care anymore."

Our Christmas dinner began like a glacier. We ate in a strained semblance of congeniality; I was glowering under a polite smile while Drew chatted with you, Chloe. The conversation flittered around safe subjects like food and film and wine, and suddenly Drew asked if you had any cigarettes hidden away someplace.

"Sure." You tossed a blue packet to him from a kitchen cupboard.

"Don't start again, Drew!" I cried out in irritation.

"It's only a little Christmas celebration," he said.

"But you haven't smoked in nearly ten years!"

"Then one French cigarette in the south of France on Christmas day won't send me into instant cardiac arrest—"

I reached across the table and grabbed his forearm as he brought the cigarette to his lips. "Even if I leave you it doesn't mean that I don't care about you!"

He froze. "You're leaving me?" he asked softly.

"I—I don't know."

"So I was going to get one of those phone calls you were always so worried about? Perhaps from Jonathan Bennett's bedroom?"

He stood and left the room with as much dignity as possible. A few seconds later we heard the bedroom door open and close.

"Go to him," you said.

"I didn't mean to—"

"Go to him!"

Drew was standing by the open window. I touched his arm, and he glanced wearily at me. "I came here to try and work something out."

"You mean, to regain control."

"I don't know how else to make you listen. Will you listen, Michael?"

I didn't answer, and he turned to face me. His eyes reflected the glow from the stove as he reached into his pocket and handed me a small package. I removed the paper carefully, and opened a ring case to discover a delicate circlet of intricately woven leaves in fine red gold.

"It's exquisite. It reminds me of—" I searched my memory "—Greece. Yes, Milos. Our room had a border of leaves painted around the ceiling."

"Yes, Michael. That's it. Put it on with your wedding ring."

I slipped it on and held my hand up to the cool moonlight. The new ring fit perfectly with my wedding ring, the new band of golden leaves clasping the old.

Drew's eyes were barely visible in the dim light. He stood waiting, open and vulnerable to whatever I might say or do. And for a moment, I wondered, too.

It was useless to pretend that I didn't love him. And absurd to imagine my life without him. He had touched every part of my flesh and had known the darkest shadows of my spirit. He had been at turns my father, brother, lover, and friend, and even though he had lately seemed a stranger, I'd never truly be Michael without him.

I walked into his arms. He gazed down at me questioningly, then held me tighter. Without speaking I began to open his shirt, running my hands over his chest and shoulders. Still he waited, expressionless but for his glittering eyes.

I kissed him until he murmured, "What are you doing to me, woman?"

My answer was to lead him to the edge of the bed and to push him down, slowly, until he was sitting. Then, with all the patience in the world, I began to remove my own clothing. I didn't even feel the cold.

I stepped up close to him, drawing his face against my breasts. Gently he stroked my back, his hands moving from my shoulders to my thighs. I leaned toward him, softening under the growing insistence of his touch, feeling my heart quicken as his hands brought me home.

For Drew was my true home. Suddenly I closed my eyes, aching to find myself with the beautiful man who'd led me up the stairs to his jumbled flat so many years before. I longed to rediscover the vanished essence of our young, hopeful love—the love that could span any distance, heal any wound, give new life.

I lay beside him and he called to me, his voice almost as unsure as the voice that tested my name the first time we made love. Taking him deep inside of me, I resigned myself to the fact that I would love Drew until the end of our time on earth. I gave myself to him wholly and completely, and as we came rolling and struggling and surging toward perfect joy, I knew that I would never be at peace without him, no matter how desperately I tried.

At first light he held me, the covers pulled up high against the cold. "So will you come with me?" he murmured.

I stirred sleepily. "Where?"

"To Ireland, of course."

My thoughts cleared. "You said you'd canceled!"

He paused. "I'm on the schedule to speak tomorrow."

"So," I said, tears filling my eyes, "you just flew in to fuck me and fly out!"

"Come with me, Michael—"

"Stay with me, Drew."

We lay in silence. He didn't dare touch me, and I didn't trust my voice. As the sun rose he stood up and began packing. I threw my legs over the side of the bed and began casting about for my running clothes, keeping my head lowered to hide my tears.

Drew closed his leather bag and walked to the closet, removing his suit bag. Turning, he faced me with a closed expression.

"I've asked you to come."

"If you leave now, then you've made your choice."

"Do I hear a threat?"

"I have to keep on living, no matter what you do."

He stared at me in exasperation. "My taxi will be here in fifteen minutes, and I'd like to have a coffee before I go."

I listened to his feet on the stairs and felt like howling in rage and defeat. Pulling on my tights, my bra, and a sweatshirt, I thrust my feet into my running shoes and shoved my arms into my jacket. I bounded down the stairs on my tiptoes and exited the house, ignoring Drew's back in the kitchen.

Outside the sun was already up, pouring forth over the hills and casting long yellow fingers over the bony branches of emaciated trees. I threw myself into the run, striding with such vigor that my cold muscles sent waves of pain through my system. My feet slammed the asphalt, and I pulled myself forward with my pumping arms, leaning into the race against my rage with all the power of my body. A voice sang darkly in my head, its disjointed melody bounding like a wild horse through my helpless frustration. Hurtling blindly toward the sun, following the road as it wound downward into the city, I was passed only once, by one car—a taxi, with a dark-haired passenger wearing dark glasses who stared straight ahead, never glancing back, enveloping me in a swirl of dust.

On I ran and on, into the old town, up passageways with narrow alleys and tall, elegant houses looking out at one another with windows holding back their histories. Still I ran, searching with each step for the woman in the white dress, the woman who would find after many years that love is not enough when she can no longer deny her need to be free.

A clock struck in the darkness and I stopped speaking, shocked at the swift passage of time. You stood and stretched, then began to massage my back with strong, loving fingers.

"I tried to reason with you, Little Sister."

"It was the first real argument we've ever had. Twenty-five years, and there we stood, shouting at each other in your garden on New Year's Day."

"My heart broke when you drove away, determined to abandon your home."

"And my heart broke when I looked back and waved, and you wouldn't meet my eyes."

"You were going to leave Drew, just as I'd left Emil. And I was terrified that your life would end up as empty as mine."

"Why did you leave Emil? He adored you, Chloe."

"That," you said quietly, "is the real reason why I brought you here, tonight."

Five

"*J'avais raison, n'est ce pas?"*

"Yes, Emil. You were right."

"And I'm always right."

"Well—"

"Repeat after me, Chloe: *Yes, Emil. You're always right.*"

And he was, Michael. It had all worked out. Just the way he'd promised.

Emil's former teacher Constantine hired me to run the art program at the Centre des Études Artistiques, and I moved to Aix-en-Provence in the early summer of 1971. I mounted my first exhibition there, in the center's gallery, soon after my arrival. Thirty-three of my forty-two paintings on display were sold on the opening night. It was a record for the gallery, and released me from all my debts in America. I was finally free to begin a new life.

And, *mon dieu,* what a life it was!

After the muted tones of Paris, living in Aix-en-Provence was like walking into a van Gogh. My apartment looked out over a cobblestone-lined ramble in a maze of poppies and plane trees. The sun shone fearlessly through fat, clumsy clouds and the thyme-scented sirocco blew hot during starry nights. Foods tasted of saffron from nearby Spain, and cigar-smoking pensioners played *boules* all day in dusty, beech-shaded courtyards.

My work at the center was wonderful. Rough-kneed little kids burst in every morning and we painted, threw simple vases, and made scrapbooks. I enjoyed their unbounded energy, and they enjoyed my French, often chortling hysterically at my American accent.

All afternoon I painted in an enormous, sun-drenched loft that echoed with strains of piano music from the dance studio below. Evenings marked the arrival of the older students, including many immigrants from North Africa, Italy, and Spain. Slowly I moved away from my self-isolation to a real pleasure in working alongside others. I forgot about the gray rains of Paris and the long winter of my life in America. For the first time in my life I was deeply happy.

I didn't have to make up any stories for you about those years in Aix, Michael. You were there with me, studying French at the university every summer. And each time you arrived from the United States I found a more beautiful, articulate young woman.

Your adolescent curves vanished, replaced by the lean, athletic body that would remain yours in the years to come. You began braiding your hair in cornrows that were replaced by intricate plaits in the style of African women. And your hip urban schoolgirl talk became the poised expressiveness of a confident intellectual.

That third summer you had a passionate romance with a towering student from Tunisia, a sand-toned man with deep-set carob eyes, who begged you not to return to America.

"Hamid says he loves me," you solemnly stated as you packed your bags for the return flight to Boston. "He says we could get married and go to live with his family in Carthage."

"What would you do there?" I asked innocently.

"Whatever I want. They're rich. His father has servants—"

"And at least three wives—"

"And a summer house by the sea—"

"And a harem of beautiful women—"

"I could travel and write and just be in love."

"You could change your name to Scheherazade," I replied.

You laughed and turned to me with a deep sigh. "You know, if I became Mrs. Hamid Abdallah I'd probably never go to graduate school. Hamid doesn't want his wife to have a career."

"What *does* he want?"

"At least ten sons."

"And what do you want, Michael?"

"I'm not sure," you said helplessly.

"Do you love him?" I asked gently.

Your hands flew to your hips and one leg came out defiantly. "Hamid is fine, and he ain't too bad between the sheets. But I'll never love any man enough to let him stop me from—"

"I know," I intoned dryly.

You lifted your chin at the sarcasm in my voice. "You've proved that it's possible, Chloe. You have the perfect life: a great career in a beautiful place and a fabulous man who absolutely adores you!"

"I've got a sassy little sister keeping her eye on me, too."

You crossed the room to hug me. "Isn't that what sisters are for?"

You returned to America and went on with your studies. And I went on with my life—painting, and teaching, and loving Emil.

"Salut, sorcière!" he'd shout as he burst into my apartment, arriving just before dawn on the night train from Paris. He'd begin pulling off his clothes as he strode through the flat, calling my name softly as he climbed naked into my warm and waiting bed.

"What spells have you been conjuring while I was away?" he'd whisper as he gently explored my body, and I'd murmur, "Whatever it takes to bring you back, baby. . . ."

Some things aren't meant to be painted, Michael. But I wish I could have captured on canvas the sea-foamed coves where we'd hide from the world, thinking up plots for Les Xenos. We'd spend hours planning nomadic tours through the capitals of Africa and the islands of the Caribbean. Or dreaming about our shipwreck on a beach of crystal water fringed by trees swept low by their fruit-laden boughs. Sometimes, lulled by the soft voice of the waves, we'd even joke about—as they say in French—"making *un petit bébé. . . .*"

"I want her to have your beauty, talent, and intelligence, Chloe."

"And what will she get from you?"

"My ears, of course."

"Your *ears*?"

"Between us she'll learn three languages, and she'll need a good ear to master several more!"

"And if she's a boy?"

"He'll need my sly sense of humor and my ability to pass virtually unperceived at night."

"And what will he inherit from me, Emil?"

"Everything that *really* matters, *mon amour . . .*"

You can well imagine the nights we'd sweat alongside West Indians and Africans in Marseilles's pumping *boîtes de nuit.* Or the excursions we'd make to San Remo or Monte Carlo, or the tiny fishing villages with open-air restaurants serving grilled salmon and pastis by the sea.

But no words can describe the times we made slow love, in my room full of canvases, to the deep-throated warbling of doves. Once, as we labored in silent passion, I looked into his eyes and felt myself fall away so that we were one body, one spirit, one life. My pulse was his heartbeat, his flesh was my own, and I thought: I want our child to be born to the song of the doves. . . .

Isabelle Mathurin considered me her daughter and expected me in Marseilles, even without her son, for her incredible Sunday dinners. My arrival was always greeted with cries of pleasure and the wry comment: *"Emil fe mwne ron!*—I'm ashamed of Emil!—Why hasn't he married you yet?"

His sisters would suck their teeth and calmly shake their heads, touching my shoulders in sympathy as they passed the table.

"Maybe he'd propose if you got another boyfriend," his uncle suggested with a sly Mathurin grin.

"No, no!" Isabelle cried from the kitchen as she pulled a pot of steaming rice from the stove. "Chloe already has another love—her art!"

"Mon dieu!" a sister cried. "You want Chloe to stop her painting?"

"Certainement pas!" Isabelle replied, coming to the doorway to smile into my eyes. "She wouldn't be Chloe anymore if she couldn't paint," she said sagely.

"Then he'll never get married," someone predicted.

Isabelle went on looking at me with her patient, reassuring gaze. "One day," she answered simply. "I'm sure of it."

In many ways Emil and I were married, Michael. Did we need rings and papers to prove it?

"You're truly happy here," he remarked one evening as we sat on my small balcony, observing the townspeople returning from vespers.

"It's a kind of refuge," I admitted, remembering the bruising scenes I'd witnessed in Paris.

He cracked the shell of a pistachio. "Do you ever miss the city?"

"I miss you, Emil. Not Paris."

He turned thoughtfully to the sunset, breathing in the swooning perfume of night-blooming jasmine.

"No matter where you go, *chère sorcière,* I'll always be with you."

Yes, Aix-en-Provence was everything he promised me, Michael. I thought the spell would last forever. Who would have imagined that an evening spent among friends would provide the elements to tear our love apart?

It was the weekend of Anya's show, and I'd made that rare trip back to the capital to be fitted with my "special outfit." Anya knew that without her guidance I was likely to turn up in paint-splattered jeans, and she couldn't allow that. So I let her transform me into an ambassador, a person in the audience who proved that her dresses really looked good on real people. Well, just for one afternoon, anyway.

It was the only way to preserve the remnants of our friendship.

I'd passed the morning at FAB, standing on a podium and being pinned into a flowing sueded silk kimono with giant burnt-orange poppies on a sandy background. Anya, now brunette, with her hair twisted into an elaborate knot of tiny beaded braids, was busy comparing her collection to the latest trends exhibited by her competitors.

Two or three models wandered in and out, their faces empty and their bodies sexless. The phone rang incessantly, and Anya indicated with a flick of her wrist that Ramon, her harried assistant, should answer.

"Are you still seeing your actor?" she fired at me from across the room.

"Every Tuesday night on Channel Three." Les Xenos was appearing in a half-hour television program largely written by Emil.

"You know I'm not talking about his television show."

"Well, I am," I said brightly. "And I think he's great!"

"So do I!" one of her assistants called from the next table. "*La France des Xenos* is the funniest show on television!"

Two or three other people agreed, and Anya addressed her congregation.

"You all have to be contented with the screen. But Chloe has been having an affair with Emil for centuries!" she cried in mock outrage. "She should make him *buy* her a gallery!"

Anya didn't have private conversations anymore.

When the fitting was finished, I reluctantly followed her into her office, which had been enlarged to accommodate her burgeoning archives. She placed her elbows on her new Plexiglas desk and scanned me with the mocking arrogance of the Parisians.

"So you're still enjoying life in the provinces?"

"Better than I enjoyed life in Paris."

She leaned forward craftily. "How *do* you manage without Emil?"

"He flies down every few weeks. The television show has given Les Xenos a fixed schedule. Of course, they're busy renovating an old theater near Barbès to use as a base when they're not on tour."

"Why don't you just get married? You've been with him almost four years now!"

"Marriage wouldn't make me love him more," I said.

"But you could become a French citizen, move back to Paris, and finally earn what you're worth."

"I've had seven exhibitions since I moved to Aix," I said patiently, "and not one of them was in Paris. Now tell me, Anya: What interest could I possibly have in moving back here?"

She sized me up quickly, pursing her lips at my henna-reddened curls and Nigerian batik dress.

"Do you ever see Lucien?"

"In my nightmares."

"What's your little friend Michael doing these days?"

"Applying to doctoral programs. It looks like she's going to be a scholar."

"Well, what are you doing this evening?"

"Dining with Aziza and baby Chloe."

"Aziza's business is doing quite well. She really looks terrific."

Strangely, then, we didn't seem to have anything more to say to each other. We fumbled around, telling stupid stories and trying to remain polite while her assistant dashed in and out of the room.

As I approached the English bookstore, I was annoyed to see a crowd in front of the door. I had come to buy a book on West African sculpture as a birthday gift for Emil and had no time for babbling tourists. Putting on my bitch armor, I shouldered my way through the gaggle of overweight, gym-shoe-wearing sightseers and slipped into the store.

I was met by an eerie silence. In my rush I had failed to notice the signs for the poetry reading that had evidently attracted half of Paris. I stepped forward in irritation.

". . . and I say, beware that the spirit,
so long ignored, yet unforgotten,
rises in each of us, fully armed,
and . . ."

The voice was rich and resonant, calm even in a room steaming with bodies. I took two more steps, straining to see the speaker over the heads of the listeners.

". . . brings the season to truth.
For we must become that

which life intended,
regardless of the fear
it rouses in the oppressor."

The poem ended, and there was a moment of magical silence, the stillness of rapture, the transition from inward searching to outward voice.

The poet began to speak again, this time addressing the crowd.

"It's getting late, and some of you have been standing for some time, so I'll do just one more short selection. Thank you for coming, and for making my first visit to Paris such a success. Oh! And one more thing: Please buy lots of books—any books, not necessarily *my* books—so that we'll get invited back here again soon."

The room laughed and then the stillness fell again as we waited for him to begin.

"This poem is called 'The Battle.'

"Joshua joined to see the other side.
He didn't care much for the prayers
or the smoke of burning bushes,
And he really had seen enough desert
without the forty years.
Tents were fine against the sand, but
he wanted to bathe in a basin tiled
with papyrus designs, and
he'd heard many tales of
honeyed breads and
sweet Jericho wine.
Lifting his horn, he thought the
wind that filled his lungs was strange,
but there was no time for wonder:
His men were waiting.
Joshua fought in the guise of a saint
but a leader must first be a man."

Again the poem ended with a thoughtful pause, and then the room burst into energetic applause. The crowd began milling about.

Greetings were called out, and hands reached obediently toward the bookshelves.

I moved forward slowly, my curiosity growing with every step. The poet was seated at the back of the room, still hidden by a large group of admirers.

"What do you think?" someone said softly, and I heard a muffled reply. I glanced at two white women just as one said something indistinct and the other laughed with a trace of lewdness. Their giggles ceased when they met my eyes, and then I was certain: The poet was black.

A bone-brittle blonde was leaning over the armchair, her head raised so that her hair fell in a grassy curtain over the shoulders of a heavily built man. He was the color of stained cherry wood, with thickly lashed, ebony eyes. His full lips were dark, partially hidden by a neat mustache, and his head was completely bald.

When he glanced up from the autograph he was signing, I saw the intelligence in his gaze—and the strength that could easily intimidate—but both were carefully disguised by an open and self-deprecating smile. He stroked his hairless scalp as he answered questions and signed books, and I was surprised by the air of outward simplicity that seemed to contradict his shrewd intelligence.

I extended my hand when the crowd thinned. "I enjoyed your reading, although I only caught the end."

He looked me over quickly. "Thank you, sister."

"Are you enjoying Paris?"

"Frankly, there's nothing here I can't find in the States."

"Then why are you here?"

He laughed. "To show them something they can't find in France!"

I raised one eyebrow and turned away. "I'm sure the French are very grateful."

The art tomes were upstairs, so I negotiated the steep staircase, leaving the noise and humidity below.

Soon I was digging through the African art, finding many more books than I expected. I sat cross-legged on the floor and began to read when someone touched my back. I whipped around. The poet was standing behind me, leaning awkwardly against a shelf loaded with books.

"Excuse me," he said. "I think I was just a bit rude downstairs."

"Forget it."

"I want to apologize. I'm just a little tired of everybody thinking that Paris is some kind of paradise for black people."

"I don't think that," I replied. "I don't even live here."

"Oh." He paused. "I didn't get your name."

"Chloe."

"Perfect."

"*Perfect?* I didn't pick it out of a book."

His eyes flashed in anger controlled so quickly that I wasn't sure I'd seen it. Then he spoke again. "There's nothing wrong with naming yourself. Slaves did it all the time when they became free."

"I've never been a slave," I answered, "and I think it dishonors them to compare our lives to their struggle for survival."

Again something passed through his gaze. "You'll have to speak for yourself on that one," he responded. "I'd say that I've earned my name many times over."

"Good for you," I said, looking down at my book.

There was a pause. Then his voice returned. "Good god, woman, I haven't been froze like this since Detroit."

We stared at each other until slowly, very slowly, we both smiled.

"Can we start this thing again?" he asked. He held out his hand. "I'm Malik Emmanuel. I've been in Paris for two months. I'm a veteran-slash-student-slash-poet. I'd like to know your name."

"Chloe. I'm an artist. I'm here for the weekend."

"No last name?"

"Not since I shook my former husband loose."

"Oh," he said again, raising his eyebrows and rubbing his head. "Well, what kind of art do you do? Where do you live?"

"I teach in Aix-en-Provence. And I work in all kinds of media," I answered.

"Could we have coffee? A beer? A glass of wine?"

"Sorry. I've already got plans—"

"That's all right," he said quickly. "It happens that I've got another reading this afternoon, and I'll be in Orléans tomorrow."

"Then take it easy," I said pleasantly.

He nodded briskly. "You too, sister."

He turned to leave, and it was only then that I saw that he was so huge above the waist because he walked with a crutch. One of his legs ended at the knee.

I sat until the dull thud of his crutch on the narrow steps faded. Slowly I stood up and, taking Emil's gift, thought that I'd probably never see the poet again.

But life just doesn't work that way, does it?

"Why would Marcel even try to do this?" I asked as Emil led me later that day toward the entrance of the Maubert Mutualité. The auditorium, located just blocks from the Sorbonne, had long been a site of social protest; some of the most influential leaders of the American civil rights movement had spoken there.

"He says that the poet in his heart wants to be free."

"But he's an actor, Emil. He's never written a poem in his life!"

"He's been my friend for thirty years, Chloe. It's my duty to applaud while he makes a fool of himself!"

According to the flyers posted outside, the program that afternoon would "unite French dissident writers with the new generation of American protest." But I didn't feel like protesting. I was angry that Emil would waste any of our all-too-brief time together on something as juvenile as this. And on his *birthday*!

Soon we were pressed into a standing-room crowd of several hundred listeners who occasionally reacted to the speakers by giving the black-power salute (apparently they hadn't heard that it wasn't really intended for white French kids) or crying out, *"Dis la verité, mon frère!* Tell the truth, my brother!"

I glanced up at Emil to complain, but my anger faded at the imprint of his long hair tucked into his trademark black beret. He'd had his ear pierced since we last met, and now his gleaming eyes refracted the gold of a stubborn little stud. Restless and excited, his fingertips caressed the back of my neck to remind me that he'd be all mine later that evening. And frankly, all I wanted was to be with him, touch him, talk and laugh and make love with him.

Bored, I let my eyes rove the crowd of young people, coming to rest on the unexpected vision of a skeletal blonde assisting a broad-shouldered amputee to the stage. Emil was watching them, too, and after a moment he remarked in a stage whisper: "It's so generous of these black poets to give jobs to poor, lost white women."

Malik read different poems from the selections I'd heard at the bookstore that morning. The auditorium fell silent as his melodious voice wafted out over the auditorium, and Emil shifted impatiently, anxious for an audience of his own. At the end of Malik's selections the blonde handed him his crutch, and he began the slow process of leaving the dais.

"À bas la guerre en l'Indochine!" Emil cried, and suddenly there was a tumult as the entire crowd took up the refrain: *Down with the war in Vietnam!* Emil threw back his head and shouted *"J'adore les dissidents!"* but his voice was drowned out by the tempest of protesting youth as Malik again struggled to take a bow.

"C'est splendide!" Emil remarked. "As much protest as anyone can stand in one day!"

"That's right," I said. "And I've had enough. I'll wait for you outside."

I squeezed out of the auditorium as the roaring applause greeted the next speaker. Malik was standing alone by the door, and I approached him casually.

"I enjoyed your reading," I said while extending my hand. "My name's Chloe."

He looked up, stunned. For a moment he said nothing, then, grasping my fingers hard, he answered, "I'm glad to hear that, Chloe. It's good to meet a sister from home."

Emil appeared behind me. "I guess that makes me your brother, since we all started out in Mother Africa."

The men appraised each other. Malik introduced himself, squinted at Emil, and raised his hand, one finger extended. "I know you from somewhere, don't I?"

"For some of us Paris is just one big neighborhood," the actor said coolly.

"Emil is the director of a theater company called Les Xenos," I explained. "You might have caught them on TV."

"That's it! Whoa! I'm impressed. Now I've met two together black people in Paris in one day."

Emil blinked in surprise. "You've already met Chloe?"

"I had the good fortune to speak with her this morning in a bookstore."

Emil swung around to face me. "Why didn't you tell me?" he asked in French.

"There's nothing to tell. I didn't even know he'd be here."

"Hold on!" Malik said. "What's all the French about?"

Always the actor, Emil blanketed his irritation with an easy laugh. "We were discussing dinner this evening."

"It's Emil's birthday," I added. "We're going to a friend's place. Why don't you join us?"

"Yes," Emil said, regarding me curiously. "Aziza is a wonderful cook. And she's so beautiful you won't believe it." He grinned broadly and slipped his arm around my waist. "I'd marry her if I weren't so madly in love with this woman."

"I'm tempted," the poet said, reaching for his crutch. "But it's been a heavy day." As if on cue, the blonde appeared from another door, carrying a small suitcase. She approached us swiftly, without a smile.

"This is Hannah, my business manager," Malik explained. She flicked her head in our direction. "Are you ready?" she asked with an accent I found hard to place.

He swung his crutch beneath his muscular shoulder. "I hope we meet again sometime," he said.

The door closed behind him, and Emil peered at me, one eyebrow raised. "Now, what's this? You're looking for a new love?"

"What—just because I spoke to Malik? It was *your* idea to come here, not mine!"

He looked into my eyes and decided something. "Why don't you see if you can catch them! We'll take a taxi to Aziza's!"

"Why, Emil?"

"Because I'd like to get to know our *brother*," he replied dryly.

Baby Chloe was just shy of three and talked in passionate French about everything she could see. Her head was a curly thatch of goldenrod curls, and she peered out at the world through enormous gray eyes. She was madly in love with her "uncle" Emil and never let him out of her sight.

Malik was finding it painfully difficult to take his eyes off the willowy frame of baby Chloe's mother. Aziza moved through the flat like a dancer, her graceful arms clicking with wooden bracelets and her shaved head an exquisite sculpture. Beside her, Hannah had become a faded wraith, her blond hair lackluster and her face a sullen mask.

"I take it you're a model?" Malik asked.

"Not anymore." She laughed. "After my daughter was born I created Femme d'Afrique, a line of cosmetics for African women. I market it through my brothers in Senegal. They keep quite a bit of the profit," she added, "but it stops them from interfering with my life."

Of course, Emil was in marvelous form, and took over with wild mistranslations between English, French, Wolof, and Creole. Hannah was German and had a textbook French that served her well in conventional situations, but that evening she was as lost in our conversations as Malik.

But none of that seemed to matter to the poet, who sat with his eyes fixed first on Aziza, then on her daughter, then on the panoramic views from the penthouse windows. From this summit the city was a circuit board of twinkling lights, with glowing necklaces around the Arc de Triomphe and Notre Dame.

The apartment itself was a joyful chaos. Before baby Chloe's birth, the vast spaces held little more than pillows and rugs. Over time, crayon and watercolor portraits of the sun, clouds, flowers, and the Tour Eiffel had taken over. Grass mats and graceful plants competed with the toys to turn the rooms into an obstacle course. A hand-carved rocking camel emerged from a pile of wooden blocks stacked in the shape of the Great Pyramid. Dolls in kinte-cloth dresses with braided tresses peopled every corner, each one named after one of Aziza's siblings.

As the evening lengthened I noticed Malik peering at me in a kind of disbelief whenever a French word exited my mouth. Irritated, I finally asked him if something was wrong.

"It's crazy to hear a sister speaking another language so eloquently."

"You should hear her Creole," Emil teased.

"A pe té la pen," I responded smoothly, and he laughed.

"Was French difficult to learn?" Malik asked me.

"Well, I needed a marriage, a divorce, and a very unloving lover before I found this excellent teacher," I replied, nodding toward Emil.

"Long live pillow talk!" Aziza purred. Emil leaned over to kiss me, and Malik looked away quickly.

Aziza turned to Hannah. "Why don't you give Malik some French lessons?" she asked, her eyes twinkling.

"I believe that one should only teach one's native language," she answered stiffly.

"The truth is that Hannah believes the entire world should speak German," Malik remarked dryly.

"I believe we should all learn Latin," Emil replied. "Everyone who spoke it is dead, so there'd be nothing to fight about."

"Exactly what kind of theater company is Les Xenos?" Malik asked Emil.

"It's the theater of bad conscience. We help our audiences understand the true nature of their colonial guilt."

"Sounds depressing," Hannah remarked.

Emil brayed in amusement. "You want the truth to tap dance and sing?"

Malik turned to Emil. "You know, brother, I respect your use of the arts as a means of political protest, but don't you think it would be more effective if you took your message directly to the government?"

"Didn't I meet you at a poetry reading?" Emil replied.

"Yes, I'm a poet. But my real mission is far more concrete. I came down from Germany to check out the programs at the Sorbonne. I'm finishing a doctorate in political science."

"So," Emil said lightly, "those little letters behind your name will help you change the world?"

"My university degree will give me access to the leaders who do."

"And my theater gives me access to the people who choose those leaders," Emil responded. "I will never trust a government until I can trust the people who select that government."

"Same ends, different means," Malik asserted dryly.

"I disagree." Emil laughed. "Very few governments really represent the most vulnerable in society. By aspiring to power, you are already losing touch with the powerless and needy."

"I'll never forget where I came from," Malik replied, "because I'm going back. It would be impossible for me to live here, exiled from the struggles of my people."

"That struggle is shared by many people," I suggested, "and I think that there are many ways of helping them."

"I didn't survive 'Nam just to hide out in somebody else's country," Malik said vehemently. "I've earned the right to live well in my own nation."

"I'd say you were born with the right to live well anywhere in the world," Emil answered, becoming deeply serious. "Nationalism can only serve to divide us, when ultimately we're seeking the same goals."

Malik looked at Emil with carefully tempered anger, then smiled as if indulging our hopeless naivete.

Deliberately ignoring him, I turned to Emil. "Happy birthday, baby." I handed him his gift, and he leaned over and kissed me full on the lips, eliciting applause from Aziza.

"You should have bought him a *ring*, not a book," she teased.

"The book is beautiful," Emil answered. "But Chloe knows what I *really* want." They all laughed at the innuendo, but I did, indeed, know that Emil dreamed of our having a child. "Thank you for the gift," he whispered, his lips brushing my ear. "I can't wait to open it."

Aziza turned to Malik and placed a hand on his arm. "You're sitting beside two remarkable people, you know. Aside from the fact that they've managed to stay in love for years, Emil is the first black television star in France, and Chloe's going to be the first major black artist on the continent."

Malik shifted uncomfortably, plastering his face with a smile. "I had no idea that I'd landed in a hotbed of black excellence," he said ironically. "I suppose I should thank you all for putting up with Hannah and me."

"Oh, no." Emil laughed. "We heard some excellent poetry this afternoon, and tonight I've learned a great deal about my brothers in America."

The German woman rose wordlessly, and Aziza went to call a taxi. Emil slipped his arm around my waist as Hannah assisted Malik into his coat.

"I'll be watching you on television," he said to Emil in a tone that was almost a warning. "And I'll get down to Aix to see your work one day soon," he promised me, looking directly into my eyes.

When the door closed behind them, Emil emitted a sigh. "I've never seen any people wear their race as uncomfortably as black Americans."

"Well," I replied with a laugh, "I've never seen an actor having such a hard time acting friendly."

Aziza put her hands on her hips. "Now tell me, both of you: Where exactly *did* you find them?"

It was an exhibition in Florence the following spring that became the cornerstone of my international career. The owner of the gallery bought five of my best pieces, including *Seraphina*, for his permanent collection. Bookings immediately appeared for four more shows—London, Strasbourg, Munich, and Geneva. Within a few months I was catapulted from my place as a popular local artist to—as the Arts and Leisure column of the *International Park Tribune* suggested—the "leader of a new school of postmodern portraitists." Realistically, my unexpected success meant that I cleaned out most of the paintings I'd completed since arriving in France—and had commissions for many more. Suddenly there was a great deal of money to play with, and after four years of teaching I wanted more time to paint.

One weekend Emil flew down from Paris, and we decided to explore his beloved hills above Nice. The afternoon was brilliantly clear, the air scented with spring wildflowers, and we could see the calm Mediterranean sunning herself along the beaches below. Walking up an overgrown driveway shaded by towering poplars, we rounded a crest and came upon the house.

It was a small abandoned villa in a forest of blooming magnolias. The two-story structure was constructed in the elegant Italianate style of the early twenties. Light poured into the high-ceilinged chambers through graceful rows of double-paneled windows, and faded hand-painted frescoes of grapevines still traced out the baseboards and doors. We wandered from room to room, past the marble baths and echoing stone-floored kitchen. By the time we'd explored the entire property, I was breathless with excitement.

"Do you think it's for sale, Emil?"

He looked thoughtful. "I'll call my uncle and see what he can find out. But, Chloe—do you really want to leave Aix to live up here alone?"

"No. I'd turn it into an atelier. A retreat where artists pay tuition to live and work. I'd have more time to paint, and," I added shyly, "there'd be plenty of space for a baby."

Emil nodded. "That last part sounds very enticing." Then he laughed. "We'll call it the *Atelier Exilée*."

"I don't think anyone will pay to stay at the Studio for Exiles, Emil. What about the *Colonie des Artistes*?"

"I'm not so crazy about colonies. All the artists would be escapees from the Foreign Legion or something—"

"Look! There's something painted over the door." We climbed up on the stone banister to decipher the faded letters.

"Maison Azur," I read. "Like the *Côte d'Azur*."

"No," he said quietly. "The poets used to believe that the 'Azur' was a state of spiritual and artistic wholeness. A kind of creative perfection."

"Then we'll call it the *Atelier Azur*."

We soon learned that the owner was a Corsican who had settled in the Riviera during the last war. He had died only a few months before—almost penniless, intestate, and without heirs—and the property was slated soon to go up for public auction. With Constantine's help I found a bank willing to extend me a mortgage, and I acquired the house from the local government for an absurdly low price. Within a matter of days the *Atelier Azur*—my private studio—was born.

I used my savings to convert the downstairs into six bedrooms, then removed the nonessential walls from the upstairs to create a bright, open workspace. There were three large baths with claw-footed tubs, four toilets, and each room had a pewabic-tiled wood-burning stove, though most of the house had been outfitted with central heating.

The enormous kitchen was attached to the main house by a stained-glass breezeway. Roaming the regional flea markets, Emil and I came across a massive wooden table—cast off from a defunct monastery—and eight nail-studded leather armchairs. The kitchen became the communal living area.

There was a panoramic sea view from the upstairs windows, while the downstairs rooms faced a garden of overgrown lilac, dogwood, and magnolia bushes. A bank of wild herbs sent sage and thyme-perfumed breezes wandering through the house, and fields of wildflowers poured over the once-cultivated yard, changing hue as the seasons progressed. The winding drive lined with swaying poplars tied the property to the main road.

After studying a number of books on the technique of frescoing I painted the exterior of the house a muted rust tone, carefully restoring the ornamental borders of painted vines that lined the upstairs windows beneath the roof. I replaced the tiled floors in the upstairs studio so that the splattered paint could be easily cleaned. I found an elderly carpenter who had worked on the house decades before and he was delighted to craft new shutters for the tall windows, and to fashion a hand-carved banister for the staircase. I had never even dreamed of owning a house before. And now, just past my thirty-ninth birthday, I had a castle.

Four artists came to live and work at the atelier in its first year. I was a teacher in the morning, giving them formal lessons in technique and style. Then I became a kind of mentor, working alongside the artists as we each pursued our own projects. The whole house was up at sunrise for an early walk, run, hour of yoga, or meditation, and we went to bed late, after fireside discussions in the warm, crackling kitchen.

A live-in Italian housekeeper named Amelia cooked, shopped, and helped with the cleaning. The perfumes of her pestos and marinaras and baking sourdoughs filled the house long after we'd gone to bed. A family of parakeets in a wicker cage appeared, singing ethereal symphonies from dawn till dusk. I inherited a golden retriever puppy named Gustave and tamed two tiger cats, Mignon and Minou, who chased each other in dizzying patterns through the kitchen and garden.

I easily withdrew from the world beneath those hills. I began a life that would vary little for the next few years: from September to May I worked very hard, venturing from the atelier only to buy painter's supplies or to take my daily walks in the rolling countryside. In the summers I closed the house down and traveled across Europe, exhibiting in galleries and attending openings of my work. It was the perfect balance between near seclusion and complete public accessibility.

The television program was such a success that Emil could afford to fly down from Paris quite often. I'd pick him up from the airport in my Deux Chevaux and we'd chug our way up the steep, winding roads to the Atelier Azur. He'd stay two or three days, sometimes a week, spending quiet afternoons writing scenes for Les Xenos, other times insisting that we make pilgrimages to the sites of his boyhood adventures.

But our nights were for different kinds of adventures. The conversations in the kitchen sometimes went on until dawn, but Emil and I would excuse ourselves and climb the stairs to my rooms at the rear of the house. We'd throw the windows open to the secret chants of the wild grasses. As we lay on my low bed, it seemed we could step out onto banks of stars, and even the moon leaned close, cool and clear in the hot blowing darkness.

"Every time I come here I find a different woman," he said to me one night. "Each painting brings out a different part of you."

"But every part of me loves you," I answered.

"Still, sometimes I'm afraid," he admitted to the darkness, "that if I stay away too long, I might come back to a stranger."

Michael, it was only at that moment that I really understood why he so badly wanted us to have a baby. He believed that a child would moor us together with the strongest of bonds. Deeply moved, I tried to put into words what my heart answered.

"No matter who you see on the outside, you'll always live inside of me."

He took a deep breath, as if resigning himself to be satisfied with as much as I would give.

"Don't ever vanish, *chère sorcière,*" he whispered.

As we made love that night I secretly prayed that nothing would ever happen to make me disappear.

The clock struck again, but you were still gazing at me with alert, watchful eyes.

"Michael, I need for you to listen carefully to everything I'm about to say. And if you can, try not to judge me until I've told you everything. After all this time—all these long years of silence it's— Promise me. . . ."

You nodded solemnly. I sat down beside you, gathered my thoughts, and began.

"This is the story of how I drove away the only man I've ever really loved."

I think it was Emil's simplicity, or the depth of unquestioning love we shared, that made me fall into the waiting caverns of my own dark past. Looking back, I know now that it was just a matter of time before the truth finally fought its way to the surface of my life. In reality, I'd been living the lie much, much longer than anyone would have believed possible.

That afternoon we were hiking in the hills above the house. The whole world was blinding yellow, as if the sun had painted each blade of grass, each leaf, each vine and bloom a rich, golden shade of late autumn. The afternoon breezes were deep and honey slow, and my gauze skirt danced and turned around my knees.

I was enraptured with the plays of light and shadow in the shreds of clouds as Emil described his recent adventures in Paris. The city, with its eternal gray dampness and incessant roar of traffic, seemed like another universe, and listening to the grass, I had to struggle to keep even a part of my attention focused on his words. I felt myself drifting between a dream of woven grasses, the lulling sound of his voice, and the insistent drilling of the locusts.

Suddenly he pulled me close and we tumbled into the grass. Gently he rolled on top of me, slipping one arm protectively beneath my head. His lips touched my ear, my mouth, my neck, and his other hand moved teasingly beneath my skirt.

Startled, I looked up into his eyes. We often wrestled playfully when we made love. There was no meanness in his gaze, but at that moment something ugly rose up in me, and wordlessly I shoved him away.

"Not so fast, my beauty!" He pinned me to the earth again, mimicking a cinematic Sinbad. Kissing me deeply, he began to stroke my breasts.

I pushed him again, but he was so close that he couldn't see the mounting fear in my eyes. I tried to move, but, locked beneath him, I was blinded by the sun and my cries were muted by the whipping grasses. I kicked at his legs and he moved sensuously against me, his hands pulling my hips against his swollen body. Beneath my back the earth was hard and rocky, and the scream of the locusts seemed to explode inside my skull.

For a moment the sun vanished, and I plunged backward into a strange darkness, surfacing only as I willed every cell in my body toward freedom. My nails became claws, and I ripped into his flesh, hearing him cry out as my teeth closed on his lips. He threw himself back, rolling away from me with a bloody hand on his mouth. Three scarlet seams traced a perfect line from his ear to his throat, and I saw a trace of blood beneath his open shirt. I scrambled up to a rock a few feet away and faced him, still panting from exertion.

"Why?" he whispered, the question lost on the dry wind. I heard a bird cry mournfully in the distance, its song half swallowed by the calm, methodical barking of a dog.

"I won't let you do that to me," I said in a high, reedy voice.

"Do what?" he stammered. "You know that I would never hurt you!"

Sweat poured into my eyes, and I pressed my fists across my temples, only then discovering that I was grasping a sharp stone. Emil saw it, too.

His body unfolded, and he looked directly into my eyes, ignoring the blood that was already drying into a dark necklace on his chest.

"Tell me, Chloe."

He ventured a few steps closer, standing warily in that sun-painted apse. Reaching carefully forward, he took my chin and raised my face toward him.

"After five years, don't you trust me enough to tell me?"

"Trust you?" I asked, staring at his swollen mouth. "What good would it do?"

"It's the only way that I can help."

"There are some things that must never be spoken." I shuddered, pulling my face away.

"What things?" He moved closer, and I smelled the warm scent of bloody sweat.

"I can't," I repeated, hearing my voice grow childlike, with a high-pitched, whining quality.

"I need to know—"

"You won't understand! I've never told anyone—"

"No," he said. "No, that's not true at all." He shook his head, his insight growing as the words poured out.

"You've been telling everyone for years. Telling it in your painting. In all those portraits of women—those women who are struggling to survive. But I think—" he paused "—that nobody's ever really listened."

He pulled me close, his arms a protective cage. Looking far away into the distance, he said softly, "Chloe, I want you to tell me now, with words."

I wanted to weep, but there were no tears anywhere in my body. In a voice as elusive as the whispering grass I gave him my damaged soul.

"Somebody—somebody did that to me when I was a child."

There was an icy, stunned silence. He stopped breathing, his muscles tense as wire. I waited as if he were my executioner. My savior.

At last he spoke. "How old were you?"

"Five."

Again there was nothing. After an infinity I heard him ask, "Who was he?"

"My brother."

His hands tightened on my back. I welcomed the pain.

"Did your parents know?"

"I didn't tell."

"But did they know?"

The question was strange, inconceivable, and yet so intuitively right. A sudden hot gust ripped the leaves from a branch overhead and swept them into golden scraps at our feet. I pushed away from him and grasped at the adolescent trunk of a nearby sapling, lunging forward into the grass. My stomach heaved violently, and I could do nothing but remain crouched on the ground, retching thin spit from my shivering frame.

Emil's voice came calling from somewhere far, far away. I felt his hands on my shoulders and back, steadying me, trying to calm me. Disembodied, emptied of the truth that had formed my being for over thirty years, I felt strangely void. I seemed to drip like fouled water into the earth. Very slowly I settled on the ground, pulling myself into a tight ball in the blowing grass. Dropping beside me, Emil looked deeply into my eyes.

"What about your husband? Did he know?"

I shook my head.

"And Lucien?"

I looked away, and Emil touched my face. "Did he—did he do something like that, too?"

I stared back into that night, five years before, when Lucien had become my brother. Emil's fingers moved gently over my shoulders as if searching for invisible scars.

"Chloe," he whispered, "how can I help you if you don't tell me?"

The tears finally exploded from my eyes and I heard myself scream. "Because I *did* tell! I told my mother—"

"And she didn't protect you?"

"Protect me?" I screamed. "She said it was *my fault*!"

I retched again, choking on the bitter syrup that shot up from my belly, and he held me close. Everything faded to gray, and I gratefully swam into a cloud so thick and opaque that I later wondered if I'd passed out. When I could open my eyes, I found Emil holding me, kissing me, stroking the wild hair from my face. He was singing something low and sweet in Creole.

"Now I see," he said softly. "This is why you're alone. Why you have no family and no home. Why you stay here, in these hills." I closed my eyes, mute.

"And this is why," he added very softly, "you don't completely trust me, even though you know how much I love you."

I didn't move, my face buried against his chest.

Emil pulled me closer. "It's not your fault, Chloe. It isn't, it wasn't, your fault. You've done what you had to do to survive."

He was still whispering, his torn lips in my hair. We remained that way for a long, long time. We were almost invisible in the dancing grasses until I heard him repeating, "It's all right, Chloe. Rest a while. Just rest."

And feeling at least five centuries younger, I did.

Until my life began to unravel.

Not my painting. Not the atelier. Not my relationships with my students.

The worst thing that could possibly happen. After that day in the wild grasses, I began to lose Emil.

It was simple enough: the drawer was open, and after thirty-four years of silence, the voices of my past snatched control of my life. I rose before dawn, walked for miles and miles alone through the hills, reliving scenes that, despite the decades of trying to forget, still resurfaced with a terrifying clarity. After walking in the autumn wind and rains to the point of exhaustion, I would manage to shove everything back into a corner of my mind and return to the house to speak, paint, work with the others.

On the surface I was still the teacher and the critic. Beneath the surface I was pandemonium. My hair came out in handfuls. Alone in my room, I braced the window wide open and wept silently, painfully, but without the relief that comes after despair. I found I could eat nothing. I could think of nothing else. And one night I bled a strange dark blood that I now know was our unborn child.

Clogged with a thick, congealing guilt, I sometimes lay awake at night, unable to breathe. During the daylight hours it took all my strength to continue talking, laughing, interacting. In the silence of my room I sat in front of the mirror and stared into hollow eyes.

I was close to breaking.

None of this made any sense to me, for I had learned many, many years before to separate that secret girl from the woman who faced the world. I taught myself that it was useless to dwell on what happened when I was a child. As far as I was concerned, until Emil pried it out of me, I'd been free of my brother's control.

But I wasn't free anymore. The images of my shattered childhood crowded in, and I was overwhelmed with a bestial rage. Glasses broke in my hands. Dishes slipped though my fingers to shatter on the stone floor. I burned bread. I painted huge black canvases slashed with scalded scarlet strokes. I pounded clay with my fists until it streamed through my fingers. I ran deep into the woods, hurling vicious insults at my mother, my father, my brother, Regi, Lucien, and Emil. Yes, even Emil.

It was simple enough; nine weeks after the day of the warm winds, and after hours of strained silences and sudden outbursts of anger over ridiculous things, Emil came down from Paris and forced me to speak not of the unspeakable, but of how I was going to survive it.

It was near Christmas, and my tenants had made a trip into town to do some shopping. Amelia had begun roasting a chicken early that morning, and the kitchen basked in the safe scents of rosemary and white wine. I opened two bottles of beer and dug out a pack of English cigarettes left behind by a visitor.

Striking a theatrically nonchalant pose, I leaned back on one of the chairs at the massive oak table and blew a long stream of acrid smoke toward the cold afternoon sun. Emil sat across from me in an uncharacteristic silence, his expression calm and nonthreatening.

"The group has decided to do a tour in Africa. We're leaving in three weeks and we won't be back until May. I want you to come with us."

"I can't just take off for six months."

"Yes, you can." He paused, framing his words carefully. "You and I need to be alone together. Away from everything familiar. These six months will give us the chance to build a new life. It will give you time to heal—"

"I'm fine." My fingers moved involuntarily to the swollen ridges beneath my eyes. He moved restlessly in his chair, watching as I drained off a good portion of the beer.

"Chloe," he said quietly, "when are you going to let me touch you again?"

"What difference does it make? There'll be plenty of women in Africa."

"I'm worried about you."

"Sounds like you're more worried about sex."

"That's not fair—"

"Sex rarely is," I shot back.

He moved closer to me. "I've been thinking about this for days. You can't go on living with this without talking about it."

"You coerced the truth out of me, and now you're punishing me for it."

He remained calm and full of resolve. "We need to get some help."

"No!" The bottle smacked the table. "I won't discuss my private life with strangers."

"You don't have to live this way—"

"I've never lived any other way."

"You need to overcome what happened in your past."

"I've never let my past influence my life."

"Your past has never stopped influencing your life."

"Then it's who I am, Emil. I'll survive."

"I don't know, however, if *we* will."

"Before my confession you never worried about *'we.'* "

"Before your confession I didn't think I had to."

"And now?"

"Now," he surmised with hideous honesty, "I'm watching us die."

I leaned toward him, lowering my voice despite the fact that we were alone.

"I've never made you any promises."

"I've never asked for any," he answered. "But I thought—" he hesitated as if suddenly realizing that the idea was laughable "—I thought that now that Les Xenos is doing so well, we might find a way to share our lives."

"Your home is in Paris. Mine is in Nice. Mission impossible."

I watched him warily, enjoying the reckless sense of power my anger gave me. Lucien's face suddenly flashed through my mind, and for a fleeting instant I wondered if Emil would ever become angry enough to hit me.

"Chloe," he was saying with lowered eyes, "I want to give you a child."

"I'm not ready," I answered automatically.

"I want you to be the mother of my baby," he continued in the same level tone.

"I can't do that."

"I want to create a new life with you."

I heard the word *create*, and for a moment I was silenced. Could it be that having a child was truly an act of creation? Something similar to working on a painting?

"Listen to me," he said gently. "We need to grow, Chloe. We need to take the risk of making something good and unique—something that will bind us together for the rest of our lives."

"It's too . . . too dangerous," I replied, feeling the words slip uncontrollably to my lips. "Things can happen to children. Terrible things. And I just can't—" I looked into his imploring eyes "—I just won't take that risk."

"If anything happened I'd be there with you."

"The only thing that's ever protected me is my art, Emil. Even when I was a child—" I grasped the neck of the bottle in my fist, unable to meet his gaze. "There are things I want to accomplish. Just like you. But I can't do them if I tear my life apart, or leave my home, or suddenly decide to—to have a baby."

"There's nothing sudden about this," he answered, a glimmer of anger entering his voice for the first time. "We've been together for years, yet you're still treating our relationship like a game of chance instead of something to plan and work for."

"Don't tell me about planning and working!" I exploded. "While you were performing on street corners and roaming through flea markets, I was suffocating in an office, dreaming that one day I might get my chance to paint!"

"I've never had the chance to work in an office," he said quietly. "I've never been to a university. I grew up in three rooms with eight other people, in the country that enslaved my grandparents. I've had my share of troubles, Chloe. But I refuse to live in anger. Pain is not the source of my inspiration."

"This is who I am," I repeated.

"No, Chloe. It's who you choose to be."

He pushed his untouched beer aside and leaned forward, bringing his face close to mine.

"Don't give in to this," he pleaded.

"Give in?" I countered. "I'm completely in control—"

"You're not just lying to me, Chloe. You're lying to yourself!"

"I'll be just fine, Emil."

"You've got to try to find another way, or someday your heart will die."

"My heart doesn't matter," I said, "as long as I can paint."

Desperation crept into his hauntingly bright eyes.

"Marry me, Chloe."

The words shocked me into silence. He placed his hand on my arm and I realized he was trembling.

"I love you so much," he said. "You love me, too. Even more than you can admit to yourself." His face was open, his eyes filled with sadness. "It's been nearly six years since our first night together. I knew even then that there was someone—your former husband, perhaps a lover from your past—who taught you never to trust. But I thought that with time you'd understand that you could be happy with me."

His words reached some shadowed place inside of me, and my anger collapsed into a ringing, and all-too-familiar sense of defeat.

"I'll always love you," I began, my own voice shaking. "You understand me in ways that I can't begin to describe. You've been my anchor when I couldn't even see the shore."

I lifted my hands and showed him my paint-stained fingers. "But I can't tear down these walls, Emil. I can't dismantle my life. I won't risk falling apart, or becoming obsessed with my past."

"Make it a commitment to our future."

"Our future?" The words sounded strangely foreign, even in French.

"Chloe," he said, "six years ago I told you I'd leave until the day that there was a place for me to stay. Please, please don't send me away."

I took a deep breath.

"I won't marry you, Emil. And I can't have your child."

The look in his eyes almost destroyed me, Michael. Because

beyond the unfathomable hurt I saw the aching, worshiping, selfless core of his love. Only one other time in my entire life have I seen a man look at a woman with so much love in his eyes. That, Little Sister, was many years later when you first brought Drew to meet me.

"Chloe," Emil whispered, the sound flowing like blood, "Chloe, I love you."

"I love you, too," I answered, my heart imprisoned by the strength of my fear.

He didn't say another word. Neither did I. And that night the sex was incredibly intense and already impersonal because we both knew we were saying good-bye.

There was an agonizing silence before your voice splintered the night.

"How could you do this, Chloe? How could you keep these things from me for all this time?"

Dawn had entered our quiet chamber. Hesitant light poured down over my shoulders, and I moved vaguely toward my empty easel, as if it could protect me from your fury.

"For twenty-five years I've loved you and trusted you more than anyone in the world. You know things about me my own grandmother never knew. And you've held me together whenever my life fell apart. Now, after all this time, you bring me here and prove that I've never really known you—"

"I didn't do it to hurt you—"

"So that makes everything all right? I'm supposed to ignore the fact that you were my idol? Forget that your life gave meaning to my dreams? Christ, Chloe: I even asked your permission to marry Drew!"

"None of that's been changed by what I've just told you—"

"The hell it hasn't! You're a fucking stranger!"

Your despair flooded the studio. I pulled in my shoulders and looked back at the blank canvas.

"That's not the complete truth. And tonight, Michael, we absolutely have to tell the truth. You've always known that a real woman lives behind the image of Chloe Emmanuel. A woman who can make mistakes, show weakness, and know failure. You've known that this woman

exists, even if you failed to acknowledge her. And you even admitted it, Michael, at my wedding. Don't you remember?"

You stared at me in silence, then lowered your eyes.

"Let me finish, Michael. That's all I ask of you now."

Malik walked back into my life on a Saturday. I remember the day well because it had been raining since dawn, and I had received a letter from you, Michael.

Standing in the kitchen, I turned to let the lamplight illuminate the onionskin paper with your bold, confident writing. One paragraph arrested my attention and called me back to your words again and again.

> *It's scary, Chloe. The longer I study, the fewer black men I see. Sometimes I wonder whether all these casual relationships can really replace true love. But I haven't met a man who really cares about me. I wish I had someone in my life like Emil. . . .*

I heard Malik's voice before I saw him; he had found his way to the end of the drive and mounted the hill to arrive at the house, soaked and exhausted. I threw open the door to a dark figure huddled against the leaf-strewn, late-autumn rainfall.

He had aged.

His hair had grown in and now formed a dark, soft shadow against his sun-reddened skin. His beard was thicker, too, and he'd acquired a pair of gray-lensed glasses. His enormous arms were invisible beneath a heavy wool sweater and a leather jacket in the style that French men often wear. He filled the doorway, his eyes taking measure of the fragrant oven, the exposed beams and stone floors, and coming to rest on me.

"I'm sure glad I made that climb," he said.

Malik was now wearing a prosthesis, and his crutch had been replaced by a cane. Sitting heavily at the monk's table, he dropped his cane and loaded knapsack as he pulled off his woolen cap.

"Bonjour, madame."

"Did I hear French?" I remarked, coming forward to take his jacket. I hung it on a hook near the wood-burning stove.

"Absolument," he answered. We looked at each other, and suddenly we were both laughing.

"How did you find me?" I asked.

"Aziza, of course. We have dinner together whenever I'm in Paris."

"*When* you're in Paris?"

"Oh, yeah. I moved to Aix six months ago. It turned out that no one at the Sorbonne was interested in directing my dissertation."

"You've been in Aix for six months? Why haven't you called me?"

"No phone," he answered evasively. He looked at me to see if I believed him, then glanced around the kitchen, nodding his approval.

"Nice place."

"Emil helped me buy it and renovate it."

"I see. Where is the celebrated Monsieur Mathurin?"

"Aziza didn't tell you? He's in Africa with Les Xenos."

"Too bad," Malik replied, avoiding my eyes. "I would have enjoyed seeing him."

"I'd enjoy seeing him, too."

I saw Malik regarding me more carefully, his eyes taking in the scarf tied loosely around my head and my paint-stained clothes. My slightly haggard look. It was apparent that I hadn't seen a man for quite a while.

"You're looking good," he lied. On another day I might have reacted flippantly. But that day, immersed in the lonely rains, his words were like a balm.

To my surprise, Malik seemed comfortable with the other artists. Throughout our evening meal he entertained us with vivid stories of the military, referring to his lost leg as his "wild youth." They all studied him, clearly fascinated with his corsair's face and chiseled body.

The talk continued and Malik turned to me. "I saw a pretty cheap *pension* down in the city."

"You can stay here tonight."

I gave him a small, unused room at the rear of the house. It was heated only by a wood-burning stove, so I went in to prepare the bed and make the fire. The stove was beginning to glow when I sensed him standing in the doorway, his body creating a massive shadow against the light from the hall.

"It will be very warm in here in a few minutes," I said. "I'll get you a lamp."

As I walked past him, he caught my arm. "I don't need any more light," he said, raising his cane toward the carroty glow from the side panels of the stove. "This is just fine. I'm so tired I could fall out right now."

I made a move to walk away, and he tightened his grip on my arm. I winced and he said, "I'm sorry, but I can't move as fast as I'd like." He pulled me carefully around to face him. Our faces aligned, he bent forward and kissed me very carefully. His lips were full and soft against mine.

I looked directly into his eyes. "Just because Emil's not here doesn't mean that—"

"I only wanted to thank you."

We stood there a few moments, and I waited for something to happen—for my heart to leap, or my pulse to speed up, or to experience a sudden lightness of being. But there was nothing.

The next morning he ate breakfast with the others while I went for a long walk. When I came into the kitchen, wringing wet and cold, I was met with an awed silence: Malik was reading his poetry. I listened, strangely moved by the sight of this black man surrounded by rapt listeners in clothes nearly as paint-splattered as my own.

"Somewhere a man dreams a woman.
He knows her by the paper edges curling away the foliage of his youth;
He needs her as the stream needs its rocks to create its song,
And he wants her as all men seek the Self.
She is deaf, and dumb, and blind to his love,
Which seems but a broken urn from a mythic place,
The fractal memory of her lost childhood.
But the moment waits, poised in the amber of certainty,
When his dream will breathe life."

Bound by his resonant voice, his aura of solemnity and his seeming intuition, we all waited, suspended, as if he were a seer. At last one person applauded, and we all burst into laughter.

"The Atelier Azur needs a writer-in-residence," someone said jovially. "Why don't you invite him to stay, Chloe?"

I smiled automatically, peeling off my wet jacket and gym pants.

"The poet is welcome as long as he pays his rent like everyone else!"

Malik's crafty eyes met mine. "I could *sing* for my supper," he said, to the general approval of the group.

"Ah!" I answered with a little mocking bow, "if only music paid for fuel and grub."

"Oh, there's government subsidies for that!" he exclaimed, and everyone laughed once more. I resented his staging this discussion in front of the group rather than speaking to me in private. He knew it, too.

"Well," I said coolly, "please excuse me. I need to get to work."

As I mounted the winding staircase to the second-floor studio, I heard his voice begin again with the words: "This is a poem about an evening I spent with a woman who very much deserved to be loved."

Later that day I came upstairs to discover him in the studio. I stood in the doorway for a moment, irritated that he had entered my private realm without my permission. Often, when the other artists weren't present, I carried on conversations with an imaginary Emil while I worked. Malik's presence in the room felt like a violation of far more than my art.

"What's happened to Hannah?" I asked dryly.

"She went back to Frankfurt. France was too French for her."

"You must miss her."

"Hannah," he said without looking up, "was a necessary inconvenience."

"I see," I said. "And your studies?"

"I've got a thesis committee together," he replied nonchalantly, while staring at a canvas. "And they expect me to go off and bring them something extraordinary in a year or so."

"What exactly are you writing about?" I began shuffling some tubes of paint in a cabinet.

"The means by which the French war in Indochina became the Vietnam War in America."

"Do you think the Americans are ready for that?"

"It has to be done," he said. "The war's already been over for a couple of years, and I want to be one of the first scholars to write on it."

"Shouldn't you be in the States?"

"I'll get there," he promised with a hint of bitterness in his voice. I looked across the room at him, and he added, "No one has ever looked at the war from the perspective of the people who started it. Being in France will give my writing an unusual resonance—especially as a black man."

I went back to my tubes, listening as he moved slowly around the high-ceilinged studio. The light from the tall windows was almost painfully white, despite the autumn rain, and he squinted as he leaned down on his cane to take in the view of the ocean in the distance.

"Chloe, I might as well tell you why I've really come. I need a place to stay while I write my dissertation."

"This is no boardinghouse."

"I need a retreat. If you'd let me be your tenant, I'd be very happy in the room I slept in last night. All I need is a bed and a desk."

"You're miles from a library."

"I'll go over to the university once in a while and bring back as many books as possible. I'll be no trouble to you."

"Why don't you go up to Paris?" I asked. "That would make much more sense."

"Paris costs so much more. And," he added, "my body hates that climate. I nearly died of arthritis in Germany. I hope that being near the ocean will give me a chance to get myself back in order. I just—" he paused "—I just need time."

"I don't know you very well, Malik."

"Do you know any of your tenants?"

"They pay to live and study here."

"Money isn't really the issue, is it?" He pushed his sleeves up his powerful arms and waited until I put down my brush. "I can make this simple: I was born Marcus Freeman in Black Bottom, the toughest little corner of Detroit. I never knew my mother. Her sister brought me up with her seven kids. A teacher picked me out of the bunch when I was eleven and got me into the ROTC. Uncle Sam let me study through my master's. Then I had to pay my dues. I'd like to paint you a more colorful picture, but to tell you the truth, next to my adventures in 'Nam, my childhood fades to a pale shade of gray."

"How long do you plan to be here, Malik?"

"I intend to finish in a year."

"A year? You certainly don't lack confidence." I smiled to humor him, but his voice went brittle.

"The only thing I lack," he said, "is twenty inches of my body. But even that doesn't matter. I see it like this: The lower half of my leg got blown off by a land mine, and I crawled through a swamp filled with dead women and children to keep from joining them. Do you think that these French people can do anything to stop me?" He paused, gripping his cane tightly.

"Chloe, I haven't stopped thinking about you since the day we met. I want to know you better. And if I can't be more, I'd like to be your friend."

Wearily I looked down the long, empty passageway to my bedroom.

"Just your friend," he repeated, his deep voice sending vibrations through the wooden frame of my easel to the tips of my fingers. I suddenly wanted more than anything in the world to gather up my brushes and be absolutely alone.

"Let's give it a try," he said.

"Give what a try?" I asked.

"Friendship," he said.

"That never works—"

"Then what does?"

"I don't know," I said with sadness.

"All right, then. Let's give 'I don't know' a try."

Malik moved into the atelier a few days after his unannounced visit, with little more than a few suitcases and twelve boxes of books. His portable typewriter could be heard tap dancing its way through the days and into the nights. He read voraciously, worked tirelessly, and only emerged from his room for an evening meal and a bit of banter with the others. He paid his rent on time, relied on Amelia to get into town, and was maddeningly polite with me.

Our first winter passed so swiftly that I often forgot he was there.

We were alike in some ways—both intensely focused on our work and both solitary by nature. And I was busier than I'd ever dreamed. The legend of the mysterious artist who signed her name as *chloe* on the bottom of paintings was growing like an avalanche. I'd been commissioned to create works for several important buildings, and I was being interviewed fairly regularly by art reviews and journals. The only drawback was the long, dark nights, when Emil's absence was an aching wound that never seemed to heal.

I sent you photos of my work, Michael, and you sent me copies of the papers you were writing on black literature and culture. I let you go on thinking that Emil was part of my life. Maybe I needed to go on thinking that, too. Anyway, I never saw it as more of a secret than any of the other secrets I'd kept from you.

"Chloe—" I heard Malik's voice before he came up the stairs to the studio one Sunday evening when the other artists had gone out.

"You're not writing?" I asked, slipping into my pocket a photograph of Emil I'd come across in a pile of sketches.

"Actually, I've just completed the manuscript of my next book of poetry. I was wondering if you'd have a look at it."

"I'd be honored," I said. I took the bundle of neatly typed papers to my room and stretched out on the bed. He'd called the volume *Azur*.

The first poem, "Celestine," was dedicated to his "Muse."

I have wept only twice since I became a man:
Once, when waking on a pallet I learned
That my leg was gone
And I would never be whole again,
And once when my soul stepped out
Onto a ledge of stars outside my window.
That night I thought that anything is possible
In a world such as this,
Where legs are not needed to reach the heavens
And god is not needed to feel whole.

That night I wept for joy
For I was a cripple no longer

And no longer would I ever
Fear freedom.

I lay awake for a long time. The following morning I went to his room. Knocking gently on his door, I found him reading in bed.

His prosthesis was placed next to the mattress; his cane was lying on the floor. He was covered only by a sheet, and I could see the clear imprint of his whole leg, and the other, which ended just below the knee. He was propped up on pillows, one arm behind his head, but he pulled himself to a sitting position when I entered.

"I wanted to tell you how much I enjoyed your work," I said very quietly.

He didn't smile and didn't answer. For a moment I stood self-consciously by the door, then I turned to go.

"Chloe, wait," he rumbled, clearing his throat nervously. "I'm sorry. I'm just so moved because you came to me, here—" The words stopped.

"It's okay, Malik." Again I put my hand on the door.

"Don't go," he whispered.

Our eyes met and again there was a silence. "I always walk in the mornings," I said needlessly.

"Walk . . . yes, that's right," he mumbled. I made it out into the hall and firmly shut the door behind me. I heard him talking to himself in a low voice. "Shit," he whispered. "Nice job, brickhead!"

Malik had already lived at the atelier for five months by the time the artists moved out and the summer season really began. I'd been invited to attend several regional art festivals, and I had canvases in seven galleries between San Remo and Bordeaux. Leaving Malik alone in the house, I traveled extensively, crisscrossing the area to attend openings, meet art dealers, and interview artists for the atelier. When I returned I found everything perfectly intact and Malik at his desk, diligently working on page after page, chapter after chapter.

Then Emil called from Marseilles, having just returned from his tour of the Congo, Liberia, and the Côte d'Ivoire, and he invited me to his mother's house for lunch. In the months since I'd refused to marry him, I'd tried to convince myself that we'd find a way to be together. Every morning as I strode through the hills, and every night as I lay sleepless with the stars, I prayed that he'd return to my life. And when he met me outside his mother's door, I knew that I was lost. Emil was my true home.

He'd lost weight in Africa. His hair was neatly plaited into a swirl of tightly woven braids, enunciating his Sphinx-like face. He stood tall and graceful, one leg folded back casually against the wall, baiting my approach with his deep, slanted eyes. In a fleet movement I was gathered into his warmth, breathing his skin and hair, and the sad ragged bird inside me beat a crazy retreat from the rickety months of barely surviving his absence. He said "Chloe" very softly, and I admitted to myself what I was fighting to deny—that a life without Emil was a life without myself.

After enveloping me in a gigantic hug, Isabelle Mathurin set in with a vigorous, finger-in-the-face denunciation of a son who was stupid enough to take off to Africa and leave the woman he loves in a secluded house in the mountains. Emil respectfully absorbed the tongue-lashing, then apologized to her, and to me, and led me out onto the balcony as she vanished with a shaking head into her peppery kitchen.

He stood with his back against the railing and looked into my eyes. "Is my mother right, Chloe? Was I stupid to leave?"

"Not if it was a good trip."

"It was wonderful beyond description," he said, "but you should have been with me."

"I'm sure you weren't lonely."

"I wasn't often alone," he responded casually, "but lonely and alone are two different things." Instinctively he reached out to embrace me, then paused, instead crossing his arms awkwardly over his chest.

"The trip gave me lots of time to think," he explained. "I realized that it's probably impossible for us to work things out when we're living so far apart. So I've decided—" he moved restlessly, as if he found the words very difficult—"well, I'd be willing to move down here if you'd like."

"Move here?" I echoed. "But what about Les Xenos?"

"They'd have to accept it."

"But you're their leader—"

"And you're my life," he answered with such utter sincerity that for a moment I couldn't answer.

I looked down. "What—what would you expect in return?"

"We wouldn't have to live together," he said quietly. "At least, not right away. But I'd need to know that you love me, Chloe. And that you really want to be with me."

I let my eyes follow a seagull as it drifted out over his mother's balcony toward the blue-white harbor of Marseilles.

"And then?" I murmured.

"That depends on you."

Michael, at that moment I wanted more than anything on earth to walk into his arms and return to the all-encompassing safety of his love. But it was already too late; we'd lost our innocence on that windy day.

"You were born to be a great actor, Emil. And I have to be a painter. You need to be in Paris, and I need to keep the reins on my life."

"But we also need each other."

Isabelle appeared in the doorway with two glasses of lemonade. She looked intuitively from one to the other of us, handed us the drinks, and went back inside.

I took a sip of the tart liquid and rubbed the sweating glass against my cheek.

"Do you remember Malik?" I asked the question offhandedly, deliberately avoiding his eyes. "He came by a few months ago—"

"And," Emil snorted, "I suppose you're already living with him."

"He's a tenant, not my lover," I answered defensively.

"Then he'll be a lover who's nothing more than a tenant."

"I'm not sleeping with him."

"That," Emil said bitterly, "is only a question of time."

"Are you saying that I can't have a man in my house without having him in my bed?"

"Let's be honest," Emil replied. "Sex is the only reason you let men into your house. You certainly don't let them into your life."

"You're the best part of my life."

"No, Chloe. I'm nothing more than your fantasy life." He rubbed his palms hard against the balcony rail. "All the way though Africa I kept wondering what I should have said. What I could have done. And after a while I realized that once I knew the truth it was already too late."

My jaw tightened, and I took a step back, unwilling to go any closer to that windy afternoon in the hills. But now Emil raised his head.

"You won't try to heal yourself because your pain inspires you to paint. But until you're healed you'll never be able to give and receive true love. You're condemning yourself to a lifetime of loneliness for a crime you didn't commit."

"You don't understand what I feel."

"You won't let me understand."

"I can control it."

"No, Chloe. Your past is in control of you. And until you're able to be honest about it, you'll continue to be a victim."

I didn't know what to say, Michael. He stepped forward and reached up to caress my face.

"Together you and I were able to create. Don't let him turn your house into a prison. This man does not live for joy, Chloe. He's creating a world from his anger. And you can't build anything with hate."

I grasped his hand, rooting it against my cheek.

"I don't want him, Emil."

"I know that, Chloe."

"I need you so much."

"I know that, too," he replied. "But as long as he doesn't pry into your past, you'll let him keep you warm at night." He pulled away, his face expressionless.

"You can't just leave me like this—" I began.

"Oh, didn't I tell you? Les Xenos finally got a film contract," he answered, looking away. "We'll be filming *L'Enfer Blanc* this fall. I'm expected in Paris to sign the papers tomorrow."

"But you said—"

"By the way," he interrupted in a voice I'd heard a hundred times on-stage. "I brought something back for you." He stepped past me into the house and returned with a box. Inside lay a hand-carved backgammon board of inlaid ebony and mother-of pearl.

"Consider this a welcome gift for Malik," he said coolly. "I'm sure he'll enjoy playing with you."

There was nothing left, Michael.

Except, of course, to remain unloved.

August arrived, and France closed down. The beaches overflowed with tourists, and we felt the heat of long, cloudless days without the relief of the sea breezes. Nothing moved in the hills, and the upper level of the house became a furnace.

I temporarily moved into one of the empty downstairs bedrooms. Now I was much closer to Malik at night, and he used this fact to talk to me for long hours, between the bedrooms, with our doors open to encourage the occasional breezes that found their way through the rustling trees and bloom-laden bushes and into the house.

In the velvety darkness of the night we lay sweating as he described his life in the long-lost America of our youth; the summers he'd spent working in car factories, and his time as a minister in a storefront church. He recounted in a low, thoughtful voice tales of growing up with seven cousins—none of whom escaped poverty.

Listening to our bodies as we moved restlessly on the sticky sheets, I tried not to picture his powerful chest and huge thighs as he conjured up the Motown summers of melting asphalt and girls skipping double Dutch, the elevator rides in Hudson's on Woodward Avenue, and a mythic place called Belle Isle, where everybody worked hard at losing their virginity.

It was one such night, in the midst of the relentless, merciless heat, that he asked from his chamber, "Chloe, do you ever think about me?"

"Sometimes," I answered, after only the briefest of pauses. His voice came again, testing out its own boldness in the security of the darkness.

"As a man?"

"Sure."

"The difference in our ages doesn't matter?"

"No."

"And my leg?"

"That either."

He was silent for so long I thought he'd fallen asleep.

"What are you wearing?" His voice had dropped a full octave.

"In this heat?" My laughter cracked strangely.

"Me, either." There was no sound for another minute. "Woman, I'm imagining you."

"You see me every day."

"I'm imagining you with me in this bed."

"And what do you imagine?" I asked, caught somewhere between the game and the truth of his desire. And mine.

"I imagine you touching me while I kiss you everywhere."

"Imaginations can get you in troub—" Now I stumbled, realizing it was too late. He already knew what I was feeling. He spoke softly.

"Oh, its all right, baby. I know very well how to accept things that I can't change."

Suddenly I felt my breathing speeding up and my nipples tingling. Struggling with myself, I mentally shifted into low gear, trying to reason it away. I rolled over again, kicking the damp, twisted sheet away from my ankles.

"Chloe, I'm thirty-four and I haven't had sex in—"

"Don't tell me."

"Why not? We're friends, aren't we?"

"I don't sleep with my friends," I called out firmly.

"Then let's suspend the friendship, at least for tonight."

"Malik!"

"We can go back to being friends in the morning."

"It's too hot to have sex."

"Detroit men know how to make love when it's very hot *and* very cold."

I laughed, despite myself.

"Don't tell me you don't want to, Chloe."

"Why shouldn't I tell you?"

"It would be a lie."

"How do you know?"

He didn't answer, and I rolled over again and lazily put my feet up against the wall. "Malik? I don't hear anything," I called.

"That's because I'm tired of shouting," he said from the doorway. I started, glancing up to see him leaning on his cane, huge and firm and glistening in the shadows. The muscles of his arms and neck, hard and sinewy from supporting his lower body, stood out against his satiny flesh. He looked down at me with an intensity that made his missing leg irrelevant—or rather, made it a part of his unbelievable beauty.

"May I come in?" he asked, never taking his eyes off of my bare legs.

I sat up slowly and held out my arm. He reached forward and touched my fingers.

There were no words after that.

For he came to my bed and lowered himself, pushing his back against the wall and letting his cane drop as if he would never need it again. And he took me into his arms, wrapping our wet flesh so close that the sweat actually seemed cool and sweet.

We kissed, and his mouth took mine, forcing my thoughts of Emil away. I straddled Malik and he pushed inside me. I rode him deeply at first, then faster as his hands found and guided my hips. He never released my mouth: his tongue held and sucked mine, and we gasped our shared pleasure as the heat welded our bodies together.

Later we lay in silence, and he stroked my belly. His eyes were serious, calm, concerned about something that I couldn't grasp, for my thoughts were loose and free, like fireflies. I touched his massive shoulders, my hands moving forward to his muscular chest and hardened nipples. Gently he kissed me, his lips finding my face, neck, and swelling breasts. This time he rose over me and came gently inside, and it was slower and longer and more complete.

"Chloe, when are you going to marry me?"

"No weddings," I murmured, near sleep.

"I know I'm not Emil," he said quietly, "but I could make you happy."

I didn't bother to tell him that it was useless to even try. How could I explain that my mind, spirit, and deepest feelings were always focused on one thing—how to find my way back to myself?

"I'm going to make you fall in love with me," he remarked when I returned from my morning walk a few weeks later.

"Maybe," I agreed, peeling off my sweaty shorts and T-shirt.

"And I've got to get you while I can," he said, restlessly pushing a stone across the backgammon board, "because I never know when someone else might show up again and steal you away."

I stopped undressing and eyed him cautiously. "There's nobody else, Malik."

"There's always Emil." Malik laughed softly when I lowered my eyes. "A long time ago I realized it was pointless to lie to myself about anything," he said. "I know you love this man. I don't know why you're not with him. But I've never met a woman who could be so present and yet so unreachable at the same time." He gave a half chuckle. "I know you don't want to hear it. But please don't be angry with me for trying."

And I couldn't be angry with him, Michael. His presence soothed a part of me that had never stopped aching since that fateful, windy day. He was courteous to the artists and helpful to Amelia, and proved to me again and again that he was a skilled and patient lover.

At the beginning of September, Malik came to my room and sat down heavily on the bed.

"I have a problem." He held out two papers. "One of the professors on my committee is on leave in the United States. He'll be back in late October, just before the semester starts. But look at this."

He handed me the other document, which bore the seal of the French Immigration Authority. I read it quickly. He was being informed that he had exhausted the amount of time allowed by the government to complete his studies. He would have to leave the country within fourteen days.

"I'm sure you can renew your student visa."

"I don't have a student visa. I'm here by special arrangement with Uncle Sam, and now they've decided my time is up."

"Do you want me to call someone for you?"

"I've tried. There's only one thing that will work." He looked into my eyes. "Will you marry me?"

"So you can stay in France?"

"I have to finish this doctorate."

"Then you plan to leave?"

He paused. "I've always told you—"

"—that your place is in America," I cut in.

"You want me to say that I love you enough to stay here forever, when I know you don't love me."

"And you want me to agree to marry you, when we both know you're going to leave."

"Give me this chance, Chloe," he said with dignity. "I have to go back and make things better for our people. Without this degree I'm nothing."

He had taken my shoulders in his hands, his voice hopeful. Now he waited for my reply.

"I don't believe in marriage," I said, "and I've already played and lost the green-card game."

His face fell, and he began to turn away.

"Wait!" I said, seeing the defeat in his eyes. I hesitated, then took a deep breath. "I'll marry you, Malik, but only if you understand that this is my life, and no man—"

"Stop!" He placed a finger on my lips. "If we get married, you'd be giving me my future. Why in the hell would I want to steal yours?"

Malik and I were married in the town hall a few days later. I only told Aziza, but the news sizzled across my landscape like a lit fuse. Anya canceled her vacation in Martinique to fly to Nice and arrange a reception, and I saw a quiet glass of champagne turn into a heady bacchanal.

Anya transformed the terrace of my favorite seaside bistro into an elegant garden restaurant by draping it with garlands of gardenias and paper lanterns that swayed with warm orange light. A small orchestra played traditional *bal musette*, and the guests rose from the long wooden tables to dance across the stone courtyard under the velvety night sky.

Almost everyone I knew in France showed up, including some of my former students from Aix. Many of the agents, gallery owners, and customers I'd dealt with over the previous five years also appeared. Aziza flew down with baby Chloe, who was wearing a tiny version of her own oyster-silk Anya original. And Anya was clad in one of her signature pieces, a flowing silk caftan that whispered around her in a heavily perfumed breeze.

There were some surprises: Lucien—whom I hadn't seen in six years—appeared with a raven-haired Basque on his arm. When I saw his linen suit in the doorway, I glared at Anya, who shrugged. "Relax, Chloe. No wedding party would be complete without a few broken-hearted lovers!"

My greatest shock, however, came with the arrival of a twenty-four-year-old woman in a splendid white dress who walked through the sea of guests with regal, Egyptian bearing. I leapt up from the head table as *you* entered into the garden, Michael, Kore earrings flickering in the warm light.

We held each other so long that everyone began laughing, and, of course, my tears left mascara smeared all over my face. So we withdrew to the rear, and, removed from the chaos, I finally found the courage to meet your piercing gaze.

"How'd you get here, Michael?"

"Anya called, and I took the next flight." You smiled, but there was anger and confusion in your gaze.

"Chloe," you said, taking me by the arms as if I were your child, "who the hell is this Malik? And what have you done with Emil?"

"Emil and I are over. It's already been months and . . ." My voice began to tremble, and I paused to collect myself.

"Months? Why didn't you tell me?"

"I thought I'd—he'd—come back, but . . ." I gave up, unable to raise my eyes.

"You don't love Malik," you whispered, "and you've always promised never to let any man—"

"You know I don't believe in love," I rasped, challenging you to disagree. You stared at me incredulously, and I straightened my back, trying to sound convincing. "Love is only one reason to be with someone, Michael."

"But this doesn't make any sense. Emil loves you—"

"He's gone, Michael."

"Then you're doing this to hurt him?"

"No!" You continued to stare at me until I wavered. "I don't really know, Michael."

For a long moment neither one of us spoke. Then, taking a deep, disappointed breath, you opened your arms to me.

Malik rose graciously when we walked up. "So I'm finally meeting the mythic Michael," he said, bringing your hand to his lips. "Chloe's words and pictures certainly don't do you justice."

"No, they don't," you replied under your breath. You turned to me, and I was shocked to see tears on your face. Before I could react, however, Anya waltzed up with a gallery owner from Paris.

As the night progressed the festivities grew in intensity until some of the guests were dancing wildly and singing boisterously along with the musicians. Suddenly Anya swept to the stage, waving the musicians to a stop.

"Attention, tout le monde," she began in a loud voice. "It's getting late, and I've got something to say before you're all too drunk to understand!"

There was a round of loud laughter followed by enthusiastic applause. Anya arranged her flowing caftan around her hips so that her silhouette was enhanced by the breeze.

"I met this woman, whom you today know as Chloe Emmanuel, when she was a sweet, virginal teenager with pigtails and pimples. That's the truth!" she asserted to the party's delight. When the noise abated, she shook her head slowly.

"I was with her when she met her first husband, Reginald Roman—" She snapped her head toward Malik and added in an undertone, "Believe me, *mon beau*: he was a handsome devil, like you!"

More laughter. Now she looked out into the guests. "I was also with Chloe the night she met another of her loves, who shall go unnamed." There was a gentle ripple among the listeners. "We all made a similar mistake, thinking that Chloe would be easy to get and easier to keep."

Her expression grew cunning, even as her smile deepened. "Be forewarned, Malik: Chloe Stevens Roman Emmanuel often claims to have no interest in men and yet—she's had more of them in love with her than any woman deserves in a lifetime. Maybe," Anya concluded as she whipped around to face me, "it's time I took some *art* lessons from you!"

The guests exploded, many of the women cheering for me.

"I knew Chloe some years ago," I heard a sandy voice say, "and I have to admit that she's the only woman who has ever *really* known me." Lucien stepped to the front of the crowd, gently swirling his glass. His eyes flickered up to mine. "Chloe knew what she wanted when she came here. The only problem was that the rest of us wanted her for ourselves." He turned his head slowly toward Anya. "None of us understood just how strong Chloe really is," he added obliquely.

"The truly sad thing is that I learned much too late to respect exactly those things that drew me to her. Now," he conceded as he slowly raised a toast to Malik, "the pleasure is all yours."

"And what a pleasure it is, my friends!" Malik shouted suggestively as the garden again burst into laughter. "In fact," he added when the guests calmed down, "I can't wait for y'all to go home!"

Now the men roared out their approval. Aziza stood up and swept to the center of the garden, clapping her hands for calm.

"I, too, have something to say." She rose to her full, regal height and waited for absolute silence.

"Chloe once convinced me to live when I considered giving up. She opened her arms and gave me her strength when she, herself, was in a strange land living virtually among strangers. I believe," Aziza said as her eyes swept the crowd, "that all of us could tell a similar story about how Chloe changed our lives."

She turned to me. "I thank you for your strength, your loyalty, and kindness, and I wish you both great joy in this union."

There was more applause and Malik raised his glass as you, Michael, stepped boldly to the front and stood like a pillar of radiance in the night. Addressing the crowd in perfect French, your deep, lovely voice caught them and held them in silence.

"Friends," you began, "I'm honored to be able to share in this celebration tonight. Chloe has been a friend, sister—almost a mother to me—since I really *was* a child. And like a child, I've always believed she was absolute perfection."

The warm wind played with the soft tresses of your hair.

"Over the years Chloe's given me a home. She's helped to pay for my education. She's talked me through countless emergencies in the middle of the night. She's listened to me, counseled and guided me. And yet—" you paused, your young voice growing strangely hoarse "—and yet there are parts of Chloe I can't begin to understand."

You turned as if confused, and looked straight into my eyes. When you spoke, your words were meant for me alone. "Maybe," you said softly, "it's time I simply let you be a woman."

You raised your glass through your tears. "I love you, Chloe."

There was a confused silence, fueled by the strange toast. Malik quickly rose to his feet, his glass held high.

"First of all, I want to thank all of you for coming to our little celebration. I'm just meeting many of you, yet I feel as if I'm surrounded by friends."

There were a few cheers. He again lifted his hand.

"Secondly, I have to thank those of you who've loved Chloe and been a part of her life for so long." He looked squarely at you, Michael. "I promise you that I will be a good husband to her. She won't have any reason to regret bearing my name."

He turned to me. "Finally, let me offer a toast to my new wife, who has won us all with her gifted hands, her generous heart, her stubborn head, and—" he growled softly "—that luscious, sexy body."

Now the party exploded in a kind of relief, and the dancing went on until the sky grew light.

So I became Chloe Emmanuel, and have signed my paintings with this surname ever since. Malik lived up to his promise to be a good and faithful partner for the time we shared, although sometimes it was hard to live with him because he fought so hard against the path I'd chosen.

"If you're black, you can't be happy here!" he'd shout in frustration whenever he read about some evidence of French racism.

"Right. There's no Klan and no Nazis in America," I'd reply, and he'd roll his eyes impatiently.

"We're organized to fight in the States, and here nobody does anything!"

"There are demonstrations against racism all the time, Malik. If I remember correctly, the day we met you spoke at one."

"But we're so isolated here in Nice. Don't you want to be around other black people?"

"Nice is full of Africans. Don't they qualify as 'black'?"

"I don't see them fighting the racism here."

"Then get angry with them, not me."

"Be real, Chloe: Seven years of exile is long enough!"

"Do you think that I could live like this in the States? Do you think my work would get the kind of recognition it receives throughout Europe?"

"The only recognition you need is from your own people!"

"How can I expect it from others when I don't even get it from you?"

"You're an excellent artist," he scoffed. "But you need to be at home!"

"Slave traders made America your home, Malik. I'll make the decision about mine!"

Our arguments turned in circles, with Malik growing more adamant in his belief that African Americans should contribute to the freedom struggle by living only in the States.

"You can't do anything for your people by hiding out here."

"I guess I need a man like you to tell me how to live."

"That equal-rights bullshit is for white women, Chloe."

"Then my individuality is bullshit, too."

"This has nothing to do with your individuality!"

"But it has everything to do with the reasons why I paint!"

"Then why do you paint?" he asked sarcastically.

"Painting is my voice, Malik. If I can't paint in America, then I'll have no voice in America."

I knew that he was trying to convince me to return with him, and he knew that he could never offer me a life like the one I had built in France. So the arguments provided him with a foundation for the inevitable: losing the woman he'd chosen because he loved his principles more than his woman.

He delivered the completed manuscript of his dissertation to the university on November 1. The professor sent a brief note to acknowledge its receipt. Then we heard nothing from him until May. Not that Malik didn't try. The professor's assistant screened his phone calls, and Malik's letters were answered with polite cards saying that the evaluation committee hadn't had the time to read it. All he could do was wait.

Malik's hopes very quickly withered into bitterness, honed by his unstated certainty that the university's silence was a form of racism. He spent hours at my side while I painted, talking about blacks and whites and the histories of empires and slavery and European colonies. As the weeks went by, he talked about black men and white women, and white men and black women, and self-hate and the need for black liberation.

He then talked to me about the betrayals in his life: the loss of his parents, the failures of his cousins. He told me of doomed love affairs and incompetent teachers and especially railed against the doctors who amputated his badly maimed leg.

I responded by trying to draw him in closer to the routine of the atelier. I insisted that he take his meals in the kitchen with the other artists and me. I deliberately coaxed him into our conversations, often asking him to read his poetry at the close of the evening. I even asked him to accompany me on short walks into the nearby hills, where we'd eat bread and cheese while he talked about his future.

"Sometimes I wonder why I had to meet you here and now," he remarked one day as we started back to the atelier. "Under different circumstances, you and I could have changed the world."

"What do you mean?" I asked, kicking a stone out of the way of his cane.

"In the States we'd be unique. But here," he said bitterly, "well, nobody even knows I'm alive."

"Sometimes it's necessary to spend some time in a safe and quiet place, Malik. A place to grow. To heal. To find your strength—"

"I've been 'healing' for almost five years, Chloe! Now it's time for me to do something with my life!"

I stopped walking, and he halted a few steps ahead, turning back impatiently. "The problem with you," he said gruffly "is that you don't know what it's like to lose everything. You have no idea what it feels like to be truly helpless. Or completely alone. I wonder," he added, "what you'd do if you couldn't paint anymore?"

Stung, I struggled to remain calm. "You don't know me very well, Malik."

"I know that this place is not reality," he said, gesturing toward the gently swaying trees.

"Why does it make you so angry when I try to help you?"

"Don't you understand? I've needed help every day of my life since that fucking war! I don't want anybody 'helping' me anymore!"

He walked away brusquely and I stayed behind, listening to the wind and thinking about the loneliness of living with a stranger.

"Why are you painting pictures of white people?" he asked one day as I varnished a portrait of a Moroccan girl, her pale face bearing the turquoise tattoos of her village.

"This is part of a series on exiled children," I explained as I carefully placed the painting against the wall to dry. "They'll hang in the entrance of the International Children's Fund building in Geneva."

"There are plenty of black kids right here in Nice," he insisted.

"And plenty of other kids throughout the world who live in the same inexcusable misery."

"Let one of *their* artists paint pictures of them!"

I turned around slowly, seeing the need for an argument in his eyes.

"Nobody owns my brushes, Malik. Not even you."

When we finally got a call from the university, the trees were already in their summer wear and the tourists were beginning to arrive. Malik prepared himself for the interview by hiding his desperate hope behind a mask of sardonic indifference. I drove him to Aix and waited in the student lounge while he met the professor.

When he came to find me, I saw with a glance that things had not gone well. He went directly to the car, easing himself inside without a word.

I drove out of the city without speaking. As soon as we reached a country road, he asked me to stop and he climbed out with great difficulty and stumbled into the bushes. When he returned a few minutes later I could see that he'd been weeping. I held him awkwardly, our bodies jammed into the small compartment, for a long time.

"Tell me."

"The bastards haven't even read it," he managed, his voice raspy. "He said he'll be in Corsica all summer and the others—" his voice shook "—the others will read it when he's finished. These assholes could go on jerking me around like this for years."

"That won't happen."

"It could. And Uncle Sam won't pay for this forever."

"Money is no problem. The atelier pays for itself, and I'm making plenty of—"

"I didn't marry you for your money!" he shouted. "Leave me some sense of pride!"

"This has nothing to do with pride. You're too close now to—"

"You don't have to tell me that!" He turned his anger on me. "I have no intention of letting any of these white men stop me. But I hate—" he clenched his teeth "—my powerlessness."

I didn't speak. We drove back to the house in silence, and he refused my help in getting out of the car. He closeted himself in his room for the rest of the evening and into the night. When I saw him again at lunch the following day, his face had gained a steeliness that never left it, even after he left me.

Sometimes he hurt me when we made love, his body becoming heavy and unyielding with a violent kind of need. I'd whisper, "Ease up, baby," and he'd adjust his weight, or his stroke, with a mechanical distance, as if shifting into another gear. Sex became a mere release, losing its tenderness, and I complied out of a sense of pity, or duty, or wonder that this man could have been so easily broken.

"Do you need anything?" I asked him one day as he sat in the garden, staring out toward the sea.

"Are you kidding?" He pulled himself to his feet and leaned toward me, balancing his weight on his cane. "Why don't we start with you learning to love me?"

His eyes were bright, filled with pain.

"If I didn't love you, Malik, you wouldn't be here," I answered in a measured tone.

"We need to get out of this place!" he thundered, glancing toward the house.

"I don't need to go anywhere," I countered.

"You're hiding from something, aren't you?"

"No," I said too quickly.

He stared at me perceptively, as if really seeing me for the first time in a long while. A flurry of questions passed across his eyes, but he grunted and looked at his legs. "I'm sorry for the sadness I've brought into your house, Chloe. But this life is just too empty for me," he said in a strangely subdued voice. "I need people. I need my people. I need to be part of something bigger than this."

He paused, then looked prophetically into my eyes. "There'll come a time when this house is too empty for you, too. I wonder," he added quietly, "what'll happen to you then, woman? When there's nothing left, where will you go?"

One day I brought home a magazine with a cover story on Les Xenos. The article traced the company from its roots in the café-theaters of Paris to its growing international renown throughout the Caribbean and Africa. To my surprise, the article mentioned my contribution as set designer on some of their early productions.

When I came home from my morning walk the following day, I found Malik sitting before the open article. He was in one of his most malicious moods.

"Been daydreaming about your glorious past, Chloe?"

"What are you talking about?"

"Those days before you got trapped in this prison with your crippled husband."

"I can walk out of here any time," I replied, "and your feeling sorry for yourself isn't enough to make me stay."

"So you're on your way back to your *actor*?" he snarled, pointing to Emil's face on the cover.

I sat in the middle of Malik's dusty books and responded quietly.

"First of all, Emil quite obviously has his own life," I explained. "He's not hovering in the shadows, wasting away over me. Secondly, I don't even know if he would take me back after the way I left him. And third of all, my life with Emil has nothing to do with you, Malik. Don't waste your time—or mine—thinking that you took me from him."

I stood up and left him sitting at his desk, his eyes filled with impotent rage.

Later that day he found me working alone in the studio, and he sat down heavily on an empty crate.

"If you love him so much, why are you with me?" he asked sullenly.

"I'm not the woman he deserves," I responded without turning my head.

"You won't join the struggle, and you won't leave this fucked-up place," he accused. "When *do* you actually ever give?"

"I'm giving you your future, remember? Now, remind me what you're giving *me*."

The summer passed, and one cool Tuesday morning I went into his office and found him staring at the thinning trees, his face empty and sad.

"I would never have dreamed that Malik Emmanuel would give up so easily," I said.

He looked up at me. "I'm sick of being reminded that whites will confer 'manhood' on us black savages at their own time and pace."

"It's not that simple," I said briskly, lighting a fire in the wood-burning stove. "After all, your professor does this to French students, female students, Algerian students, older students, married students—"

"Why?"

"Because he can."

"Then this is only a game?"

"Yes, but giving up lets him win it." Turning on my heel, I exited the room.

Malik didn't appear for the rest of the day. But when I went to get him for dinner I found him studying his manuscript. He nodded at me, and for the first time in many days, he smiled.

Shortly after the New Year the professor's secretary summoned him to a meeting. We again drove to Aix, and ten minutes after he went into the professor's office he walked right by me, his face drained of color.

I called out, and he turned mechanically, blinked twice, and held out his arms. "It's done."

"He likes it?"

"He says—he says it's the most impressive research he's ever read. My defense is scheduled for March seventh."

"Your birthday?"

He looked down at me. "It really *will* be my birthday. . . ."

The Sunday before his oral examination I took some food to his room. When I entered, I noticed that he already had his suit laid out, his shirt and tie and socks and underwear folded neatly nearby.

"Hungry?" I asked politely, seeing that he was lost in a stack of articles.

He took off his reading glasses and placed them on the open text, leaning back to rub his eyes. "What time is it?" he asked absently. It was already dark outside.

I placed the food on his desk and began rubbing his shoulders. He sighed. "I guess we need to talk."

Pushing his chair away from the desk, he turned to face me. "Chloe, you only married me because I plan to leave."

"You asked me to marry you so you could stay. Now you're asking me if I married you because I want you to go?"

"I know. It doesn't make sense." He closed his fatigued eyes. "There's something I didn't tell you, Chloe. When I met with the professor, he asked if I'd consider staying and becoming a lecturer at the university."

"Would you be happy if you stayed?"

"With you? Yes. Here in France? Never."

He leaned forward and rubbed his hands up and down my thighs. "Come back to the States with me, Chloe."

"I can't," I answered.

"Then I'll go my way and you'll . . ." His voice trailed off. "It's wrong, woman. You're a black American. You don't belong here."

"There are many ways of being black, Malik."

His jaw tightened. "I don't have any choice. I lost more than my leg in 'Nam: I lost my youth, my health, my manhood. My manhood is the only thing I can get back. But I can't do that here. I need to be in the States, where I can make a difference." He paused. "You should be there beside me."

"You've got worthy dreams, Malik," I said gently. "But I've got dreams of my own."

His eyes narrowed. "You're still not over him, are you?"

"Over him? Malik, you should know by now that Emil will always be part of me."

He left in the late spring, his books shipped ahead in sturdy boxes and his poetry manuscripts sealed into plastic tubes. He had two interviews for government positions in D.C., and a telephone number for someone Aziza knew at the United Nations. He'd bought himself a well-designed prosthesis that allowed him to walk almost effortlessly, without even a cane. He had, in a sense, not only recovered the part of himself he'd lost in the war; he was also on the way to becoming the man he saw in his dreams.

In my studio, pinned to the back of my easel, I found his good-bye:

CHLOE

A cadence, a chord of life's dissonance;
A refuge from abandoned battlements
Where war once seemed an ease;
You brought me home and healed me,
Taught me and concealed me from my own demons,
So there was nothing left but to succeed.
It hurts so much to go my way,
To break the knot that kept me safe
And clean and cool and unafraid that

I leap

So I won't stay.

Forgive me for taking everything,
Leaving nothing
But memory.

Malik left me in 1979, just a year before you came to England, Michael. Maybe his departure and your arrival meant that I exchanged one kind of love for another. Or maybe it simply proved that no one ever really comes to stay.

Malik's departure signaled the end of the peace I'd worked so hard to create. It was the epilogue in the long and tragic comedy of my love for Emil. And without the dream of Emil, the rooms of my house, just as Malik once predicted, soon seemed too large and too empty, even for a hermit like me.

And so, Michael, began my vagabond days. Galleries, colleges, and ateliers throughout Europe were graced with my presence. Museums vied for my works; academies invited me to teach. Men of many colors, from many corners of the world, added their portraits to my private collection. I was careful never to slow down long enough to take measure of my life.

Over the years the media bore witness to Emil's growing success. There were photographs of his opening nights at the Théâtre des Xenos, and shots of the parties following the premieres of his films. Often he was accompanied by an actress or popular singer—always lovely and talented women. Once a fashion magazine did a spread on a loft in Montmartre that he shared with a striking attorney from Guadeloupe. Then there was a long episode with a dancer from his television show. He won a César, was nominated for an Oscar, and penned a best-selling memoir about his impoverished childhood.

Aziza tried hard to bring us back together, but I couldn't face the truth in his keen, judging eyes. Until I was able to reveal the secrets of my past, Emil and I had no future.

Michael, I looked across the studio and found you staring at the paint-stained floor. I had no idea how to cross the gulf that my confession created between us. Before I could try, however, you began to speak.

six

Things ended badly between us in Nice, Chloe.

You were standing in your naked, frost-glazed garden as my taxi pulled away just after New Year's Day. We had argued almost violently about my decision to leave Drew. It was the first real fight we'd ever had. I looked back and saw your solitary figure hunched up against the cold, but when I pressed my fingers against the car window you turned away.

You were deeply opposed to my resolution to live alone, and your disappointment rested on my shoulders with all the weight of our life-long bond. But remember, Chloe—you had never explained how you'd lost Emil. I didn't know the truth about your childhood. I had no way of understanding why you wanted me to stay with Drew.

So I turned my stubborn attention to Levant Hill and focused on what I'd have to do in the coming days.

Caryl didn't seem very surprised at my call, nor was she the least bit hesitant to rent the small flat above the florist shop to her favorite professor. I instantly fell in love with the parlor's exposed brick walls and tile-crowned, wood-burning stove. The bedroom was flanked by a small, shelved chamber that would readily serve as a study. The tall windows overlooked bustling cobblestone streets, and the bath and kitchen gleamed with polished brass fixtures.

Drew returned from Ireland to find me moving out of our home. He said nothing, standing stunned on the landing as I carried out my belongings, and only once asking—mordantly—if he might help. I handed him the address and telephone number of the new flat and drove off, much as his taxi had driven off the week before.

The first weeks, however, were a minefield. The winter darkness fell early, and after Caryl and Bernadette closed up for the night, the smell from the shop below became funereal. I dialed your number until my fingers ached, but there was no answer at the Atelier Azur. So I threw open the windows and stared out into the night, praying for the strength to combat my addiction to Drew.

In the ensuing days our paths often crossed in hallways or on the university commons. Sometimes we stopped and talked casually about bills, phone calls, or even each other's health. He looked through me as we spoke, his hurt even more obvious in his steely resolve to appear unmoved. To a casual observer we might have seemed mere acquaintances. Never in our life together had Drew been more an Englishman.

But then the inevitable arrived with a toy gondola. "So, how was the break?" Bennett asked, placing his little wooden gift on my desk.

"Renewing. And yours?"

"Beautiful. Except that the Venetians don't serve deep-dish pizza, and the person who told me that Spanish is practically the same as Italian was a liar."

He chattered noisily as he unpacked his leather briefcase, unable to mask his low-frequency exhilaration. He had hardly looked at me when he came into the office, but if the others had heard, then surely he knew, too.

"Did Drew go with you on vacation? Where was it now—to Nice?"

"Yes, and I'm sure that Kristin enjoyed Italy."

"She's obsessed with the idea that I'm seeing someone else."

"But she has no idea who?"

"I don't think she'd appreciate the fact that her false accusations against the husband brought the wife careening to my bed."

I stood up, preparing to leave. "You can assure her that your mattress is free."

"Why?" He reached for me, wrapping his arms around my waist. "I've heard that the inevitable has finally taken place. It's time to discuss our future."

I pushed him away. "We don't have a future. I didn't leave Drew to demean myself with you."

"Being with a black man wouldn't demean you, Michael."

"If you had any pride you'd keep your mindless, self-serving, sex-centered bullshit completely separate from the lives of black people."

"Bravo!" He applauded. "What a finely crafted speech from someone who knows nothing about those lives!"

I blinked back tears of outrage. He at once read my emotions. "Oh, I've gone too far," he sneered. "The delicate bloom of your pride has been blemished." Shaking his head, he picked up his briefcase. "I'd like to continue this lesson," he said, "but I've got younger students than you to teach."

I stood trembling in the room that had once been my refuge. The young voices from the commons below seemed to echo back the sickening exchanges those walls had witnessed since Bennett's arrival, and I saw myself standing there, stupid with frustration.

"I'm done with this shit!" I blurted, pushing my belongings roughly into my knapsack and marching down the corridor to the office of the department chairman. His secretary sat outside his door, going through student records.

"I've got a problem, and you're going to fix it for me. My hours are the same as my office partner, and it's impossible to get any work done. Move him somewhere else for the duration of the term."

"But Professor Davies—"

"Just *do* it." Our eyes met. The secretary raised her brows but didn't finish her sentence. When I arrived the following day, most of Jonathan Bennett's belongings had miraculously disappeared.

I might have floundered after that incident, Chloe, but I spent a restless night thinking of your fight to survive during your first lonely year in Paris. Watching the sunrise through the window of my freedom, I vowed that Bennett would never send me whimpering back to Drew.

So I held on to my routine: teaching, writing, running—and pretended not to miss my old life. Or you.

That Tuesday morning had a bold brightness that offered a long and challenging run. I gazed in the bathroom mirror, inspecting the dark circles under my eyes, then pulled on my tights and a lightly insulated jacket and clattered down the stairs of the florist's shop.

I chose a road that led to farmlands where cars were rare and my only companions were curious cows and sheep. The air was painfully rich, filling my lungs with a mad perfume of wet earth and dung. Even the asphalt had a sweet odor of morning sun and a hint of wild heather, and my heart swelled with pleasure as I paced my steps against a song that played over and over again in my head. The only sound was my feet hitting the pavement to the rhythm of my breathing.

A car rumbled up from behind me, and I moved closer to the road's shoulder. Slowing down, I felt the driver's stare as he adjusted his speed to stay even with me. I peered into the vehicle, seeing reddened eyes and an unshaven face, then made myself look up ahead.

He drove closer, and a surge of panic sent my heart slamming against my ribs. Unconsciously I'd begun to run too fast, though I knew that I needed to reserve my energy in case I'd have to outrun this man—or fight him. I hardened my expression to hide my fear and, still running, forced myself to look once again into the car. The driver's face twisted into a leer.

The car swayed, and once again I increased my speed, my fear overcoming my reasoning. The horn blew loudly, and I threw up my middle finger, screaming "Asshole!" at the top of my lungs. Suddenly the driver twisted the steering wheel hard while speeding up, showering me with a spray of gravel and exhaust. My ankle came down hard on the edge of a rock, and I lost my balance, pitching forward two or three steps to land on my hands and knees. I rolled sideways off the asphalt and into the wild heather that bearded the road. The car shot away, and I was alone.

I sat on the ground, my palms and knees ripped raw. I waited for my fear to subside, then I began to work my limbs slowly and carefully, testing them for sprains or broken bones.

Painfully I got to my feet. My wrists hurt, but not badly enough to suggest a fracture; my hands and knees were skinned and felt as if they were on fire, but there was little blood and no open wound. I raised each foot and lowered it, then slowly turned back toward the town.

I began a slow and limping jog, punctuated by little barks and cries. My pace mounted, and the pain curiously helped to assuage my anger. I closed my hands into fists, but the perspiration made them burn even more, so I opened them to the scalding morning air.

Just as I approached my running pace I felt a veil fall over my face and my breathing came up short, as if I were running at a very high altitude. For an instant I expected to fall again, and desperately I tried to pull my legs and arms up short. I struggled to maintain a balance between my flying body and floating head and the sudden wave of nausea that sent me scrambling into the bushes. I heaved up the remains of my dinner and the toast I'd eaten for breakfast, and stayed crouched in the dirt, my body quaking, my mind choked with an echoing fear. Nothing like this had ever happened in my many years of running.

At last, panting with disgust, I managed to find my feet and start out again, despite the cramps from deep inside my gut. My mouth tasted of old paper, and my skin was covered with a thick, cold sweat. Unsure whether to walk or run, I decided that I needed to get home as quickly as possible, so I continued my limping jog.

It seemed to take hours for me to round the last bend in the road. The florist shop was already open; Caryl and Bernadette always arrived early to sort out the shipment of flowers and freshen the window display. To my mixed relief and chagrin, they were standing near the door as I approached. Bernadette looked up and cried out, and I found myself wrapped in Caryl's strong arms. They brought me into the store and helped me sit down.

Bernadette made herbal tea and wouldn't let me speak until Caryl had washed my hands and knees with warm water. I discovered that I could hardly describe what happened—not because of my fear of the car—but because of the vertigo afterward.

"You're too far from the university, Professor. These farm people aren't used to seeing women out alone in the dawn. You must try to run on campus from now on!"

"I know, I know." Slowly I got up. "I'm almost afraid to look into a mirror."

"I'd shower first, if I were you," Caryl answered tartly, her hands on her hips.

"Well, I'd better get going. I'm giving an exam at two this afternoon."

As I reached the door Caryl's voice followed me. "Are you sleeping enough? You seem so tired lately."

"Maybe my age is catching up with me," I admitted, without looking back.

I mounted the stairs slowly and, following instructions, managed to shower without looking at my reflection. I then sat on the bed, trying to organize my thoughts about the rest of the day. The next thing I heard was a familiar voice calling my name.

"Hullo, Professor! Wake up!"

I struggled against the strangest, deepest sleep I'd ever known, coming out of black water as if taking my last breath.

Caryl stood over me, peering into my face. "Professor! Don't you have to go to campus?"

My horror sliced through the clouds of exhaustion as I realized I had fallen asleep. "Oh, shit! It's after one—I'll never make it now!"

"Yes, you will. I'll drive you over if you can get yourself into some clothes."

Only then did I realize that I was still naked. I hadn't even managed to put on my underwear before falling asleep. I looked up at Caryl and saw my fear reflected back in the young woman's eyes.

"Come on," she said. "You can fix yourself up in the car." She left the bedroom and headed downstairs for her keys.

Gratefully I scrambled into a blouse and a pair of pants. I found a blazer and snatched up my backpack, hoping that everything I needed was already inside. As I descended the steps, I felt another wave of nausea, but it subsided in the fresh air.

Caryl drove amazingly fast, but with a calm that bespoke years of practice. I opened the window and let the wind bathe my face.

I survived the exam by staring out of the window at the gently swaying branches. I held my body tight, trying hard not to move even a muscle. When the test was over, I staggered across campus to the infirmary.

Late that afternoon I sat crouched on a bench, trying to wrestle down my continuing nausea. Jonathan Bennett, passing by, stopped to observe me, then walked closer, Kristin following silently.

"Michael?"

I looked up with hollow eyes.

"What's wrong?"

The concern in his voice made me laugh sarcastically. I tried to rise, but clasped my heaving stomach and sank back heavily to my seat.

"Can I take you somewhere?"

My forehead moistened. "Home. You can take me home."

He immediately turned to the younger woman. "I'm going to see that Professor Davies gets in safely. Please take these books and put them in my mailbox at the department office."

"Jon—" she began, but was frozen by his expression. "Naturally, Professor Bennett," she snapped, tossing her hair over her shoulder.

Bennett was already leaning over me. He took my arm and helped me stand, at once noticing my torn hands. "What the hell happened to you? Did Drew—"

"Fell during my run," I muttered, allowing him to place his arm around my waist. Then, ignoring the curious stares of the onlookers, we began a hobbling dance across the commons. Twice I was hit by such extreme vertigo that I gripped his arm to keep from fainting. He peered at me with open apprehension: Never had he seen me so vulnerable.

Once in his car he watched me buckle myself in and immediately roll down the window. He put the car into gear and began driving, noting that I white-knuckled the door handle at every curve.

"Have you seen a doctor?"

I nodded, eyes clutching the horizon.

"Did he give you something?"

"Yes, *she* did." I sucked in enough air to continue. "It's the flu and an ear infection. Nausea and vertigo. And I feel like absolute shit, all right? Hope you don't catch it."

"That's for damned sure!"

I was climbing out of the car at Caryl's when the dizziness hit me again. For a moment there was blackness, and when I resurfaced Bennett was holding me, his face close enough for me to breathe in his warm cologne. Strangely, it cleared my head. His eyes were dark with concern.

"What is this?" he repeated, his voice soft and tense.

"Just get me upstairs," I begged.

We made it up the sixteen steps by walking extraordinarily slowly, his arms supporting my waist, with frequent stops for my dizziness. At the top I fumbled for the keys and pushed them into his hand. The rooms were sickly sweet and I gagged, making a crooked run to the bathroom and barely managing to close the door before throwing up another stomach full of bitter liquid.

I heard him go into the kitchen, fill the teapot, and light the stove. When I came out, he had a cup of mint tea for me, and he guided me to the sofa.

"Nice place," he said, his tone grudgingly approving.

Too sick to care, I throttled, "Good night, Bennett."

"Let me stay and help you."

A dull timpani began throbbing deep in my chest, but I dredged up a smile, determined not to offer him the slightest reason to linger. "No, thanks."

He stood waiting for something, but my head was too thick to work it out. Then he broke the silence with a confession.

"The one thing I don't get is how willing you are to trust."

"Trust? Who?"

"Everything and everyone." His eyes traveled the length of my body. "It's fascinated me since the night we met. And it's not just in the way you teach, or talk to our colleagues. It's not that you expected Drew to accept our relationship. It's not even the fact—" he glanced around the room "—that you actually left him."

"I don't understand." I began breathing deeply against my returning queasiness.

"No, I don't suppose you would," he remarked, shifting his weight to the other foot. "You know, I've never felt completely safe in my entire life—not one day, not even for one moment. I've never been in a place where I could count on anyone or anything. And I look at you, here with these tea-and-crumpets people, and I don't understand how you do it."

I peered at him through my bottomless fatigue, realizing that this was perhaps the most honest statement I'd ever heard him make.

"Jonathan, I trust them because someone taught me how to trust." An image of you, Chloe, filled my mind, and for a moment the pounding in my chest subsided.

"You trusted Drew," he shot back, "even when you knew he was lying."

"Maybe I trusted the idea of Drew," I conceded softly.

He laughed, opening and closing his hands. "I know that being with you would make me a better man. But you've already figured out that it would have the inverse effect on you."

"You're only as good as you choose to be," I murmured weakly.

"Oh my," he said with a grin, "now, that sounded *exactly* like Mrs. Andrew Northcross."

He walked to the door and glanced back, studying me carefully.

"I got the program for the conference in Paris," he said. "We're on it. Shall I write them to take you off?"

"No. I'll just pretend you're not there."

He smiled. "Call me if you need anything," he said, finally descending the stairs.

Soon after his departure I heard Caryl's voice. She stepped into the parlor, accidently kicking over the knapsack I'd abandoned in the center of the floor.

"I'm so clumsy!" she complained as she began replacing its scattered contents. She picked up a small bottle. "Do you need to take your medicine?"

"It's not medicine. It's vitamins."

"Vitamins?" She glanced down at the label and exploded. "Oh, Michael!" she cried, addressing me by my first name for the first time. "This is jolly wonderful news! And you don't have to worry about anything. Bernie and I will take good care of you. I've even had a course in midwifery."

I looked up at her, and, despite my rollicking stomach, we both burst into giddy laughter. She wrapped her arms around me and held me tight, but I was secretly sad that neither you, Chloe, nor Drew should be the first to find out that I was going to be a mother.

I've never needed to talk to you as much as I did during those days, Chloe, but you were nowhere to be found. The phone still rang unanswered in Nice, and I couldn't remember whether you'd told me of any plans to travel after the New Year. Something vaguely disconcerting about your "retirement," or your easel not "liking you much anymore" lingered in my memories of our time together. I was frightened and lonely, and I didn't know where to find you. But Drew's surprise arrival at the atelier, and the events that followed, had eclipsed everything else. In short, I didn't know where the hell you were.

So when the phone shattered the lonely silence one evening, I quickly snatched up the receiver.

"Michael?"

"Oh, Drew!"

The pause was palpable. "You seem pleased."

"I am," I admitted, surprised by my flush of pleasure at hearing his voice.

"Can I see you this evening?"

Drew mounted the stairs slowly and stopped in the entrance, his head nearly touching the top of the door frame.

"Welcome, Mr. Rochester," I teased, walking forward. He held out his arms and embraced me, then handed me a single red rose. "I wanted white, but something told me to get this one. I didn't realize you were living above a florist," he apologized. "I suppose you've had enough of flowers."

"Oh, no," I lied, my stomach muscles tensing. "I love the smell."

We sat at the small kitchen table, arms touching and legs interlaced. Drew spoke in a subdued voice, swirling the milk in his coffee.

"I've had plenty of time to ruminate about my life in the past few weeks." He lifted his eyes to mine. "After twenty-five years in Levant Hill it now seems pointless to leave. But it's hard to resign myself to this sameness for the rest of my days."

"Then what do you want?"

"A future," he answered simply. "I can't survive on my past achievements. Yet during the past two years I've been strangled by the certainty that there's nothing left to accomplish."

"And—what about our life here?"

"There's no challenge in houses, cars, and dinner parties."

"So you want to leave Levant Hill?"

"Would you come with me?"

Go with him? Where? Was he suggesting that I simply walk away from the life I'd worked so hard to build—a life that was even more important to protect now that I was having a baby? I turned away, sinking into a vacuum of solitude, despite—or because of—his honesty.

"Talk to me," he urged, aware of our swelling distance.

I leaned against the sink. Should I tell him about the baby? Of course! It was the right thing to do. But a grudging voice inside of me said that admitting I was pregnant would only make our separation more complicated and painful. He'd insist that I come back home, and I needed more time alone.

"There's something different about you," he said, interrupting my silence with clairvoyant eyes. "A kind of quiet. An inner calm. I don't think I've ever seen you like—" His voice broke off, then he cleared his throat. "Please, Michael. Let me be with you tonight."

Soon I found myself resting in his arms, my head against his heart, feeling my fatigue give way to a rich, unhurried desire. Borne high on the thought that this man had touched the core of my being to create a new life, I opened like a night-blooming flower, all depth and heat and sensation. Drew's face reflected his surprise at the way my body melted, flowed, poured around his. Moments after the loving, we slipped into a sweet slumber, our bodies still entangled.

The next morning I found him in the kitchen, washing dishes. He dried his hands.

"I know that expression," he remarked. "You want me to go."

I looked at the floor, deeply confused by my desire to tell him about the child and my need to remain clear, focused, and free.

Mistaking my silence for rejection, he inhaled deeply. "It makes sense, really. You know, Michael, I've never really understood why you settled for me. You're so beautiful. So strong. Intellectually brilliant and braver than anyone I've ever known."

"Then why," I asked, "have you always needed other women?"

He gave a mean, self-deprecating laugh. "Other women? There aren't any other women."

"But what about the hotel rooms? The conferences? All those rumors—"

"—were what you wanted—no—*needed* to believe."

I stared at him in disbelief. "You're telling me that you've never cheated?"

"Cheated?" he said sarcastically. "Weren't you the one who insisted on having your freedom, as long as we were honest with each other?"

"But you've always denied that you were seeing other women!"

"And I was being honest. I have never been with another woman. Never. Not since the day you walked into my lecture, sixteen years ago."

"Then why," I cried, "have you played this game with me?"

He blinked back sudden tears. "What would you expect of a man whose mother brokered him to a pederast in exchange for alcohol? A man whose father sent him into exile before he was ten years old? A man who spent his youth lost and alone on another continent?"

He coughed to free his voice, gone rough and deep. "Sixteen years ago you walked into my life, and I knew even then that you were strong enough to walk right out again. I almost let you get on that plane, because although I loved you more than anything on earth, I didn't know how to make you love me."

"I don't understand!" I shouted.

He stepped forward, struggling to lower his voice. "That's the nature of our game, Michael. No matter how much you loved me, you needed to believe that I wanted other women."

He was right, Chloe, though I had never admitted it to anyone. Even myself. Wordlessly I stared up at him. He wavered a moment, then brushed past me and started for the door.

"Wait, Drew!"

He paused at the threshold, his face turned away. "Wait? For what? Can't you see that losing you is destroying me?"

I came down the hall behind him, but he had already clattered down the stairs.

"There's something I need to tell you," I cried, my voice strident. "Something that could change everything. Something that could give us a future!"

The door closed, and I ran back into the kitchen. From the window I watched him move blindly through the rain-swept dawn, hurtling with the force of a comet, its destination unknown.

You know, Chloe, the terrible calm of the next few weeks reminded me of the summer storms that formed in the Chesapeake Bay and hurled themselves across Annapolis and Baltimore, pounding Washington so hard that the dome of the Capitol disappeared behind walls of steaming rain. Some summer Sundays, picnicking with my grandmother and cousins on the beach, we'd watch as the bruising sun was smothered by purple clouds that came boiling across the horizon to send hot pellets of sand dancing around us as we ran screaming for the shelter of the sweltering car.

A Friday afternoon found me trapped in the musty office of Rupert Billings. Five of us had come together to discuss the following year's schedule, including invitations to potential guest professors. Feeling especially tired from a restless night, I stared at my watch to signal my impatience with their circumlocution.

"I'm thinking that we should look for a Comparatist," Robert Herrington offered. "We haven't had a really good comp lit course for a while."

"What I'd like is a Hemingway scholar," Eric Davison said. "With the Hemingway centenary just three years away, perhaps we could mount a symposium."

"What about someone from the Caribbean?" Robert queried. "Post-Colonial lit is the going thing in the States right now, isn't it, Michael?"

I heard my name and pulled myself out of a daze. I'd nearly fallen asleep, for the closed air in the office was like a narcotic.

"Sorry, Robert. What was that?"

Robert cleared his throat. "We're thinking about bringing in a Post-Colonialist for next year."

"Oh," was all I managed in the thick air of competing colognes, cigarette smoke, and hot tea.

"There's a woman in Connecticut writing some interesting things on the West Indies. Perhaps she could replace Drew," Rupert continued, nodding at me. "What do you think about that?"

I was certain I'd misunderstood him, so I didn't respond. Robert looked at me, and so did the others. Realizing that they were waiting, I ventured a response.

"Why replace Drew?"

"Because we normally take into account the need for one visiting professor, not two."

Still I sat stupidly, unable to comprehend the logic behind their reasoning.

"Clearly we need to replace Jonathan Bennett," Robert said evenly. "But Drew's absence might continue for several years, and that will create a rather sizable void."

"What do you mean, *absence*?" I stammered, my eyes widening.

"Don't tell us you don't know!" Rupert interrupted curtly. "Honestly, Michael. The two of you really ought to stop the theatrics!"

"Know *what*?" I almost shouted.

"Drew's going back to Zimbabwe," Eric said gently.

Shocked, I lowered my face into my hands for a brief moment, discovering too late that I was rolling into an uncontrollable dizziness.

How stupid! I thought as the room began to dance and their voices melted together and despite all my efforts I slipped forward, feeling myself float the long distance from the chair to the wooden floor below.

I awakened to a circle of faces and laughed out loud at the thought that they looked like weird petals on a human daisy. Someone spoke to me and I laughed again, deciding that they looked more like a group of cows standing in a circle. My third thought was that it was truly a crappy coincidence that to help me someone had managed to find Jonathan Bennett and not Drew.

"Don't move her," a voice ordered. "The doctor's coming!"

"I don't need a doctor," a voice said from far away.

"Michael, you could be hurt. Stay where you are!" I thought that might have been Bennett, but his mouth was strangely dislocated from his voice, as if I were watching a poorly dubbed foreign film.

"This floor is cold," I complained, trying to sit up. The dizziness immediately returned, and I giggled. "Oh, shiiiiit!"

"She's light-headed," someone commented.

"You all have disgusting noses." I laughed. "Come on, help me up!"

"Don't move her! It's too dangerous," Rupert again declared. I watched the secretary's eyes darting from face to face as if to register every line of dialogue for future repetition.

The doctor entered and pushed through the group. Kneeling beside Bennett, she reached into her bag, pulling out a stethoscope.

"Can you tell me what happened, Professor?"

"I fainted. It's the first time it's happened, and otherwise I feel fine."

"Nausea?" she asked, gently pressing the stethoscope against my chest.

"Past it," I answered crisply.

She held my wrist while the room waited, then nodded, and with Bennett's help I was hoisted back into the chair.

"Home again, jiggity-jig!" I declared with mock brightness. The doctor put her stethoscope into her bag. "Come over for a complete examination if you feel any pain tonight, Professor Davies. And ask someone to drive you home."

She left and the crowd closed in again.

"Do you need anything?" Eric asked gently.

"Didn't you hear the doctor? I'm not sick, for Christ's sake. I'm pregnant!"

The hush in the room was palpable. I felt like a Cheshire cat, taking in the astonishment and horror on each face. The last face I encountered was Jonathan Bennett's.

"How far are you?" It was the secretary who broke the silence.

"I'm due in early autumn," I answered. "But now is neither the time nor the place to plan the baby shower. I appreciate your interest and support, but I'd appreciate some fresh air even more. After all, it's your designer colognes that caused this little drama."

"Well, pregnancy certainly hasn't softened her tongue," Rupert commented.

"I'll drive you," Bennett offered.

"I'll drive myself," I asserted firmly. "So please excuse me. I'd like to go home now."

I managed to get to my feet, and, although somewhat shaky, I walked with dignity out into the corridor. Of course Bennett followed. He stopped me by the stairs.

"Whose is it?" he asked through clenched teeth.

I wheeled around. "You must be joking!"

"Then I'm the fool," he said very softly. "The whole point of our little romance was to get Drew to agree to a baby."

"I didn't plan this pregnancy, and Drew doesn't—well, *didn't*—even know about it, though I'm sure someone is telling him this very moment."

"Well, congratulations, Michael. You're in complete control, now."

I looked into his face and spoke slowly and clearly despite the tears that threatened to flood my eyes.

"Jonathan, I've left my husband and my home. I'm going to have a baby, and I've just learned that the father is preparing to move to Africa. Now, what kind of *control* do I have?"

"Africa?" he echoed. His expression clouded, and he looked away.

"I'm going up to my office to collect my things. Then I'll drive myself home," I said. "And if I don't make it, it will only prove that I'm telling the truth: I have even less control than I think."

Moments later I locked my office and began the weary trek to my car. As I descended the hall, I heard familiar voices, and I paused behind Drew's open door.

"So what is it, Bennett?"

"Well, Professor, the day of reckoning has come."

"I don't have the slightest idea what you're talking about."

"I wanted to be the one to tell you, and now I see that I'll at least have that pleasure."

There was an impatient silence. Bennett lowered his voice.

"You have quite a lovely wife, Professor—steady, smart, and sexy. No *Kama Sutra* beside the bed, maybe, but good, deep, dependable stuff."

"The hell with—" Drew began, but Bennett continued speaking.

"But it's tough when you're surrounded by young flesh, isn't it? Eager and willing and lawless flesh. New flesh every class, every term, year in and year out. It's a constant struggle."

"I don't have time for this crap."

"All right, friend—I know I'd better move a little faster if I'm going to keep up with the two of you."

"What do you bloody want?"

"I really thought that taking Michael from you would scramble up your little board game. You'd have to confront all the times you tested other flesh—oh, I haven't been deaf to department lore—and she'd have to admit to herself that this perfect English life was nothing but theater, so to speak. But look, Drew: The script got thrown in the trash this afternoon. Your wife didn't know about your defection, and the news knocked her out. Literally."

Drew reacted quickly. "What do you mean?"

"Michael passed out in a committee meeting when she heard that you're taking off to Africa."

"Passed out?" Drew echoed.

"Not to worry," Bennett said in a mock British accent. "It's to be expected, really."

"Where is she?"

"Gone, of course. Michael has a dead-on sense of the dramatic. She delivers her lines and exits, stage center."

"Excuse me," Drew said with extreme politeness.

"No, wait!" Bennett said, laughing. "You haven't even heard the punch line."

"What the fuck do you want to tell me?" Drew asked impatiently.

"Stay cool now," Bennett said. "You're going to need it in your new role, *Daddy*."

I heard the sounds of a chair shoved hard to the side as Drew moved quickly toward the door. Bennett began to laugh, and I moved away as fast as I could, not wanting them to find me listening. Just as I reached the stairway, I heard Bennett's voice echoing down the corridor.

"I don't care what she says! You'll never be sure if it's yours . . . or *mine*!"

I mounted the stairs one at a time, leaning forward to balance the weight of my brimming backpack with my keen despair. I was pregnant. I'd left my home. I detested my lover. My closest friend had vanished. My husband was abandoning England for Africa. My mind raced with his echoing words: *These past two years I've been strangled by the certainty that there's nothing left to accomplish*. . . . I should have heard his good-bye when he announced that *there's no challenge in houses, cars, and dinner parties*. . . . And, of course, there was that final confession: *You needed to believe that I wanted other women, Michael. That's the nature of our game*. . . .

For the first time in my life, I was truly alone.

Finally reaching the top stair and fumbling for my keys, I began to wonder how I would survive in the months to come. How I'd manage to raise a baby without a partner. How I'd face the end of my marriage and the loss of the man I loved. How I'd stand the loneliness of Levant Hill. A terrible desolation washed over me and I dropped my backpack in the doorway, breathing heavily and listening to the wintry silence.

Minutes passed. Darkness was quickly falling, and I stumbled through the flat to the kitchen, the room swirling again.

I collapsed into a chair, feeling as taut as a water balloon. I could barely kick the shoes off my throbbing feet. The bloating in my hands had turned my rings into shackles, so I tugged at the ivy leaves I'd worn for fourteen years, and the matching band in red gold that Drew had given me the night the baby was conceived. They made a musical sound as they popped off my finger, bounced across the tabletop, and rolled far out of reach beneath the table.

Lowering myself to my knees to retrieve them, I saw in the toaster the reflection of a weathered face smeared with lipstick and mascara. I felt old and ugly and completely alone, and suddenly I lowered my head to the floor and began to sob in abject despair.

I don't know how long I lay there, the weird refrains of my weeping echoing through the flat. But suddenly there was a movement in the shadows and I looked up to find Drew standing in the doorway.

"What is this?" he asked, his chest rising and falling in a carefully controlled rage.

Immobile, I covered my face with shaking hands.

He went into the bathroom. There was a long silence, then I heard him running a bath. He came back to the kitchen, knelt beside me, and began to wipe my blackened eyes. "Come on, Michael. You've got to get up."

I started to rise, groping about blindly to find my balance. I almost fell. He placed his hands under my arms and lifted me carefully. Like a foal, I staggered on uncertain legs, and he practically carried me into the bathroom.

"Are you all right?" he asked as I grasped the edge of the tub. I nodded, but he lingered by the door.

As I undressed I felt his eyes land on my swollen legs, then leap to my thickened, ringless fingers. My breasts were heavier, too, and he saw that my nipples were larger and darker than before. But his gaze froze on my rounded belly, the skin taut and navel extended.

"Be careful, Mickey," he whispered, moving quickly forward to help me into the water. I submerged myself slowly, pulling my legs to my chin and lowering my face to my knees.

He sat down beside me, his rage abated.

"I had the good fortune to learn about your pregnancy from Jonathan Bennett."

"And I had the pleasure of learning about your departure from our colleagues."

"He believes the child might be his."

"What difference does it make?" I rasped. "You won't be here anyway."

Throwing a folded towel on the floor, he lowered himself beside me. Slowly he began washing my legs with long, gentle strokes.

"Why didn't you tell me, Michael?"

"You've never wanted to be a father. A child would have interfered with your freedom to travel and write. Taken you away from your conferences and your women. Interrupted your Great Professor's Life." Angrily I pulled away from him and sat up.

My breasts formed small islands in the bathwater. Our eyes met, and he blinked to hide the flood of desire in his eyes. Placing his hands on my shoulders, he gently guided me back into the bath. His gaze lingered on my belly, and I knew he was wondering if I could feel the baby move.

"Is Bennett right?" he asked in a small voice.

"*You* are the father of this child," I said, "and I really don't care whether you believe me or not."

"When did you intend to tell me?"

"I tried to tell you four weeks ago."

"You've forgotten what I look like since then?"

"You didn't want to see me."

"I still had a right to know."

"What right is that?"

"You said it's my child."

"The child is in *my* body."

I climbed stubbornly to my feet and carefully stepped out of the tub. He followed me into the bedroom.

"Can you manage, living here alone?"

"You don't have to worry about this baby."

"And if I *want* to worry about it?"

"You can worry in Africa."

"I would never have taken the position if I'd known about your pregnancy."

"Did you forget what *I* look like? This job in Zimbabwe didn't just happen."

"No, I received the offer before Christmas."

"*Before* I moved out?"

"After you began your affair with Bennett."

"So this is my punishment?"

"Didn't you sleep with Bennett to punish me?"

"I slept with him to try to salvage some part of myself."

"Well, let's just say I'm leaving England for the same reason."

"That's not fair, Drew."

"What's unfair? You chose another man, then left our marriage so that you could 'experiment' with your identity. I've accepted a position at another university so that I can make something out of the last years of my career. The only unfair aspect of this is your notion that I'm supposed to sit in the house and wait for you let me know when—and if—you're ever coming back."

"I waited in that same house for you."

"I wasn't sleeping with another woman!"

"You weren't sleeping with me!"

"Oh, for god's sake, Michael!" he cried loudly. He stared at me, then swallowed back his anger. "I'm scheduled to leave in six weeks, at the end of the term. You can move back into the house. There's no point in it standing empty. Besides, you'd be closer to campus, and there'd be people nearby to help you—"

"I have Caryl and Bernadette. I'll be fine right here."

There was a long, angry silence.

"I never knew you wanted a baby," he said, his chest rising and falling.

"We made this child on Christmas, just before you rode away in that taxi." I pulled the sheets up around my shoulders. "Drew," I said so quietly that my voice was almost a memory, "didn't you see me running behind you? How could you leave me that way?"

"Why did you give yourself to him?"

"You know the answer. It's the same for you, I suppose, with all those women at your conferences."

"What do you mean?"

"It's the simplicity of it. The beautiful simplicity." I managed to smile. "Bennett's pretending to be in love with me so he can convince himself there's something good left inside of him. I feel manipulated by him and ignored by you, so I've got an excuse to go searching for a new life. And you—" I stopped speaking, looking directly into his eyes "—you, Drew, have played the ultimate game, pretending to be the hurt and betrayed husband, when what you really want is your freedom."

He looked at me vacantly, unable to speak.

"The funniest thing of all," I continued, "is *this*!" I rubbed my belly slowly. "Our nasty little triangle is finished. There's a new person in the game. This baby is the wild card." I laughed darkly, my voice rolling out in a rich, ironic chuckle that ended with tears again bursting from my eyes.

"It's a new game, isn't it? I think I'll call it *Blackgammon*. Bennett will go back to America, and you'll go back to Africa—both of you wanting to destroy the other by turning out to be the father of this baby. And as far as I'm concerned, this child is *mine*. I'll care for it and raise it and neither one of you will have a damned thing to do with it. After all," I added, forcing as much triumph as possible into the words, "I'm the queen—the most powerful player on the board. The two kings can't do anything without me."

Drew's harsh breathing was the only sound in the room. He moved abruptly to the door.

"One last thing," I said. "For fifteen years I've survived this isolation just to be with you. Now I'll survive it for my child. I'm stronger than either one of you realizes." Reaching over to the bedside table, I flicked off the light. He went on standing in darkness until after I was asleep.

And so I came to Paris, Chloe.

I had no idea that you were here, only a few blocks from my hotel, in your darkened, memory-drenched studio. I hadn't talked to you for so long that I'd almost learned to live without your voice, though some nights I thought my heart would break from missing you.

I'd tried to put a brave face on my heartache, defying the mocking smiles of our colleagues by attiring myself in bright swirling dresses and elegant, loose linen trousers. I avoided Jonathan Bennett and never saw Drew, who had withdrawn from university life to prepare for his departure to Africa.

I actually began to look forward to coming to Paris. It had been years since I'd attended a conference. Those conferences—packed with bloated, parroting, self-congratulatory academics babbling their meaningless jargon while ogling every available female—were my worst vision of hell. The fact that Drew's superstud reputation was gleaned from his secret conference activities didn't exactly raise them in my esteem.

But when Jonathan Bennett met me in the hotel lobby on the evening of my arrival, I soon realized that my views needed updating. First of all, the place was swarming with people of color, and among them, lots of Americans. Perhaps, I admitted to myself, Bennett was right: My little corner of England really was a desert island. Second, there was a real camaraderie in the air—

"Lalo! Lalo Figueredo!" I called as a classmate of mine from graduate school, a Puerto Rican who hated living in Boston, strolled through the lobby. He looked in our direction, then leaned forward, squinting. "*Quién es? No es possible!* Is it you, Michael? Michael Davies?"

We hugged for a long while, Bennett's head cocked impatiently.

"What are you doing here? And look at you—*both* of you," Lalo cried, leaning back to take me in. "You're as beautiful as the last time I saw you—no, even *more* beautiful—and that was ten, no, maybe twelve years ago!"

"Seventeen, Lalo, seventeen."

"You were leaving for England. Don't tell me you actually stayed!"

We dined together at a sidewalk bistro, the men shouting greetings to acquaintances over the roar of the other guests, the scurrying waiters, and the evening traffic. After a huge salad, a bottle of good French water, and five or six trips to the ladies' room, I began to feel the fatigue of the day, and Jonathan, predictably, suggested that he accompany me to the hotel.

I stopped at the door to my room. "I'll see you tomorrow morning."

"Hold on—could I have just a few minutes? Only talk, I promise."

Reluctantly admitting him, I sank down to the bed and kicked off my shoes. He sat on the bed beside me.

"Michael," he began, "I want you to know that I really do love you—"

"Not tonight, Jon!"

"And I really tried to make you love me."

"It was sex, and love enters not into that landscape."

"Then why are you here?"

"I thought I came for a conference!"

"No. You wanted to finish us on neutral territory, where no one would hear the blows."

My left hand moved protectively to my stomach. "You need to leave, Jonathan."

"Not yet, baby." His face strangely tense, he dropped to his knees beside the bed. Reaching forward, he gently grasped my right hand. "If you come to America with me, I'll raise this child as my own."

Blinking in anger, I opened my mouth to reply. He placed a finger on my lips.

"No, listen, please! Just hear me out." He stared earnestly into my face.

"Last fall I asked you to spend a year teaching at my university. Now things have changed. Drew's going off on his little safari, so I can give you and the baby a real life in California."

"You're asking me to live with you?"

"I'm asking you to marry me."

"I'm al-rea-dy mar-ried."

"Confront reality, Michael: Your husband is leaving you."

Stung, I retaliated. "I'm not a ball that you and Drew can kick at each other!"

"Hang on, baby—I just asked you to think about it." He rolled back to his heels and stood tall, his eyes cool and flinty. "I'm offering you a brave new world. With glorious people in—"

The knocking startled us both, his eyes shooting to the door as if Drew might break in. I pushed myself to my swollen feet and lumbered across the room. "Who is it?"

The voice that answered made my hand freeze on the door handle.

I jerked the door open, afraid that I might be dreaming. You stood before me in black, Chloe, your hair chopped into uneven swaths of gray, your face worn and hardened. Wordlessly you gathered me into your arms and held me against your unexpectedly brittle frame. For the first time in many weeks my defiance ebbed, instantly vanquished by the jasmine scent of your skin. We stood, filled with unspoken need, in silence.

After a few moments Bennett cleared his throat. "Everything okay?" he began, slipping into pseudo-gallantry while examining you carefully.

Your head snapped up in hostile recognition. "Absolutely," you asserted, fixing him with your fierce, slightly feverish gaze.

Unnerved, he moved toward the corridor. "Well, ah, call me if you need anything," he stammered. "And don't forget, Michael—we're on at eleven tomorrow."

In the moments that followed we examined each other. You took in my face, stumpy legs, and my great ballooning belly. I noted your faded clothing, your air of rough impatience, and wounded, penetrating eyes.

"My god." You sighed. "You're so very beautiful, Little Mother."

Your simple words were like water in the Sahara of my soul. I flushed, submerged in embarrassed pride. "I—I couldn't find you to tell you, Chloe."

"I've been in hibernation," you responded. "I spoke to Drew. He told me everything."

Before I could answer, you reached up and with unexpected gentleness smoothed the hair back from my face. "I know it's late, Michael. But we need to talk."

We were silent as our taxi skirted the Seine. The grand boulevards near the Opéra were practically deserted, but the streets became congested as we drove north into the immigrant quarters. We mounted a hill beside a park I'd never visited and came to a stop in front of a tall building crowned with wide skylights. I recognized it immediately from the sketches you'd sent me twenty-five years before.

I stopped to catch my breath at the top of the winding stairs while you unlocked a badly battered door. A rush of oil and mineral spirits and aging wood wafted out. You preceded me into a womblike room.

The lights were low, and the shadowy, dank studio was cluttered with canvases, tubes, and brushes. There was almost no furniture, but through a low arch I could see a mattress strewn with restless sheets. A few scattered articles of clothing and a torn plastic bag of apples were the only real signs of human life.

I lowered myself gingerly onto a rickety wooden chair, but you remained standing before a broken easel. There was a large canvas on the easel, but the canvas was blank. I realized that all the canvases in the room were blank. That was the moment I became afraid.

"How long have you been here, Chloe?"

"Six months. Although sometimes it seems much longer."

"*Six months?* I called Nice, but when no one answered I thought you were traveling, or teaching or exhibiting somewhere—"

You burst into sharp laughter. "No, Michael. That's done. Finished. I'm not burdened with my gift anymore." Twisting in a slow circle, you raised your arms to indicate the naked, yawning room. "These last six months have witnessed the demise of Chloe Emmanuel."

"What the hell are you talking about?"

"I'm talking about our vow, Michael. And about keeping a new promise I've made in the last few days."

"I don't understand."

You took a deep breath and gently grasped my shoulders.

"We swore we'd never let a man turn us away from our dreams. And I kept that promise. I didn't allow anyone—not Lucien, or Malik, or even Emil—stop me from becoming a successful artist. I made it, Michael. And it didn't matter that all my relationships failed, or that I never had a child, or that I've lived alone for so many years."

You smiled bitterly. "The only problem is that I can't paint anymore. Ironic, isn't it? I had nothing but my art, and now even that's gone. I've sacrificed everything just to end up here, where I began."

"You can start over again, Chloe—"

"Believe me," you said with a glance toward your easel, "I've tried. But one thing keeps coming to the surface: If I'm going to climb out of this empty, hopeless life, I can't tell any more lies."

"Lies? About what?"

"About everything." I watched in wonder as you returned to the table and stood before me. "There's a dark night ahead, Little Sister. But if you'll take this trip with me, we may find a light at the end of the tunnel."

You sat down, grasped my hand, and looked into my eyes. *"My name is Chloe. My life was destroyed when I was five years old."*

"How could you do this, Chloe? How could you keep these things from me for all this time?"

Dawn had found its way into the studio, and the sounds of early traffic bleated up from the street below. Faint, new light threw its mantle over your shoulders, and the sight of you staring into your empty easel enraged me.

"For twenty-five years I've loved and trusted you more than anyone in the world," I cried. "You know things about me my own grandmother never knew. And you've held me together whenever my life fell apart. Now, after all this time, you bring me here and prove that I've never really known you—"

"I didn't do it to hurt you—"

"So that makes everything all right? I'm supposed to ignore the fact that you were my idol? Forget that your life gave meaning to my dreams? Christ, Chloe: I even asked your permission before I married Drew!"

"None of that's been changed by what I've just told you—"

"The hell it hasn't!" I screamed. "You're a fucking stranger!"

My fury filled the studio, and you looked away, your despairing gaze again coming to rest on the blank canvas.

"That's not the complete truth," you replied quietly. "And tonight, Michael, we absolutely have to tell the truth.

"You've always known that a real woman lives behind the image of Chloe Emmanuel. A woman who can make mistakes, show weakness, and know failure. You've known that this woman exists, even if you didn't want to acknowledge her. And you even admitted it, Michael, at my wedding. Don't you remember?"

I stared at you, breathing hard, until my anger slowly drained away.

My eyes dropped to the splattered floor, and you continued speaking, your voice tight and low.

"Let me finish, Michael. That's all I ask of you now."

Numb, I listened as you told me about the man you married without love, and how you fought to maintain control over your gift against his constant criticism. I began to understand that your fear of needing Emil had driven you into the arms of a man who would never be his equal. And I saw, with hideous clarity, that my own search for self-determination was leading me to do something dangerously similar—I had abandoned Drew because of Jonathan Bennett.

When your tale of Malik ended, I didn't raise my eyes. Instead, I began to tell you how I left my own home, and my own love, and how I, too, had ended up stranded on an island called Strength. An island in a sea of loneliness.

The morning sun was flushing out the darkest corners of the studio when I laid the frayed ends of my own story beside yours, at the foot of your empty easel.

"There's only one thing I don't understand, Chloe. I've trusted you more than anyone in my life. Why couldn't you have trusted me?"

"I was afraid that if you knew the truth I might lose your love. And without your love, Michael, I could never have become that strong, independent woman we dreamed up in Washington."

"But I'll always love you."

"Don't you understand?" you said quietly. "That's very hard to believe *if you've never loved yourself.*"

The words echoed sadly around the dusty room. "Michael, you've got to accept the fact that there will always be parts of me that you'll never know. Parts of Drew you haven't even begun to understand. You're going to spend your whole life trying to understand *yourself.* That's the nature of life's journey, Little Sister."

I looked up to find the white canvas staring back at me. As I looked at your broken figure something inside of me shattered. I finally understood your desperate desire to save me.

Rising shakily to my feet, I slowly crossed the room until I was standing beside you. "I'm so very sorry."

You smiled, raising your tear-filled eyes to mine. "It's not your fault. I've never let you see me any other way."

"But, Chloe," I admitted, "I've never really wanted to." Reaching up, I carefully took off one of the Kore earrings you gave me on that dusty day in Washington so many years ago. I pushed it into your palm and closed your fingers over it with my own.

Suddenly we were in each other's arms. We stood before your easel, holding each other as if we could shut out the rest of the world. We wept until our tears drifted into tentative smiles that slowly bloomed into lilting, liberating laughter. Still smiling, you raised the earring and it caught the sun, sending flashes of radiant light throughout the somber studio.

Finally you took my shoulders in your hands.

"Little Sister, there's one last thing I've got to say to you. For twenty-five years you and I have based our lives on that vow we made back in Washington. It was a good vow. Now, I think it's time for something different—"

"Different?" I repeated. "Why?"

"Because we've grown up," you explained. "That vow was for women who didn't believe that anyone would ever really love them. And neither one of us can live that way anymore, Michael. We simply have too much to lose."

"So what are you saying?"

"Lucien showed up here the other day. He's bought a place by the sea, and he's asked me to live there with him."

"You can't go back to him!"

"I won't," you said emphatically. "Living with Lucien would make a mockery of my life. But his visit did make me face something very, very important, Michael: I don't want to spend the rest of my life alone."

"Then what will you do?"

"Last year the owner of a very important gallery in New York came to visit. He's offered his gallery for a retrospective of my entire career."

"That's wonderful," I began, but you shook your head.

"It's taken twenty-five years for an American art dealer to think that the climate in the States is liberal enough to handle me. Twenty-five years for my work to be recognized in my own country. And the funny thing is that I'm not even sure I'm American anymore."

"What difference does that make? You've exhibited all over the world."

"The difference is that they want me to stay."

"Stay?" I gasped.

"I could do a lot in New York. Teach. Travel. Open doors for other black artists—"

"Is that what you want?" I asked, unable to hide my dismay.

"What I want, Michael, is a chance for happiness."

"But what would I do without you?"

"That's easy: Be the mother that you and I never had."

"The baby won't know you."

"That matters much less than the baby not knowing its father."

"I don't need Drew to raise my child."

"We're not talking about *you*."

You stood beside me, staring into my eyes as you had so many times over the years. Now, however, there was an intensity in your gaze that I had never seen before.

"Michael, you and Drew have both lost your way. This baby can help you find each other again."

"I've never pretended not to love him. He's chosen a new life without me."

"I know how deeply Drew loves you," you said, placing your hands on my belly. "Doesn't your child deserve his love?"

"Love isn't always enough," I answered defiantly.

You reached up and held my face between your hands as my angry heart wrestled with my wounded pride. "Love *is* enough," you whispered. "Because when everything else is finished, only love remains."

You extended your hand. I pressed my own palm against yours in trust, feeling the reassuring warmth of your touch.

"Repeat after me, Michael," you said in a clear, strong voice:

"I vow to honor those who love me,
And cast off those who don't;

To love myself completely,
And to allow myself to be loved."

The distant clock struck nine times. You stretched and straightened your shoulders. "You're on in two hours, Little Sister. Come on: We'd better get you back to your hotel."

Together we crossed the room. We stopped at the battered wooden door, and you paused, glancing over your shoulder as if you were bidding farewell to your past.

Jonathan Bennett and I sat on the dais, waiting for our turn to address a group of some eighty scholars. Some were scribbling notes as if eager to refute the claims of the speakers. Others stared impassively, or coolly, or with open hostility. I recognized no one.

I vow to honor those who love me, and cast off those who don't. . . . Wrestling with my heavy eyelids, I looked at Bennett, who was absently sketching little pyramids on the edge of his paper, his face expressionless. My legs were beginning to ache, and I fidgeted with the conference program, causing several annoyed people to look my way.

. . . to love myself completely, and allow myself to be loved . . . Suddenly something stirred, touching me deep inside in a warm, tickling ripple. I jumped and grabbed my belly, both startled and confused. Jonathan looked hard at me, my bewildered expression reflected in his eyes. He leaned over. "What is it?"

"I—I don't know."

"Are you in pain?"

I was about to answer when it began again. Even as my fingers groped my stomach to find the source of the stirring, I understood what it was. I turned to him with an expression of wordless ecstasy, and he reached over, placing his own hand on my body in time to feel the baby move.

At that moment a round of polite applause signaled the end of the speaker's presentation, and the session moderator rose to introduce us. I heard my name and felt Bennett take my arm.

"We're on, Michael," he said gently. Gathering my scattered thoughts, I stood and let him guide me, floating, to the podium.

Fortunately we had planned for him to speak first. Standing beside him, I let my mind venture inside of my body to the tiny creature who had chosen that moment to introduce itself to its mother. Bennett's voice screened me as I listened intently to the quickening life, and as he spoke I felt a sudden, immense joy frothing up from my toes through my veins to my belly, then outward to the tips of my fingers and my tingling scalp. I began to smile, and the smile widened to a grin, and then the grin sent tears pouring out of my eyes. *To love myself completely!*

Finally he stepped aside, and then I was speaking, my voice lilting like a wide-winged bird, soaring out over the heads of the dour listeners. Looking up from the text that I had honed to perfection, I let my imagination fuel the written words while envisioning the child in my growing womb.

I didn't even notice that the listeners began leaning forward in their chairs, as if caught up in the net of my private passion. Something in my voice captivated them, as I had captivated thousands of students over the years. This was, however, a spell woven from the most extraordinary moment of my life—experiencing the first movements of my child. *And to allow myself to be loved!*

When the applause began, it was a trickle that increased in volume until it was thunder, and I looked out in wonder, still completely unmoved by my surroundings.

Jonathan offered me his arm and escorted me back to our seats. "Everything okay?"

I looked at him blindly.

"Do you want to lie down?"

"No. I feel like—" I paused "—I feel like eating ice cream."

He smiled. "Is it possible you're pregnant?"

We found a table in the hotel restaurant that looked out onto the boulevard. Bennett sat down beside me and perused the menu.

"Can't read a word." He shrugged. "Please order me a coffee and a sandwich. I'm going to run upstairs and get rid of this briefcase."

I'd been alone for only a few seconds when someone addressed me.

"Excuse me," a man said. "We were in your session this morning, and we just wanted to congratulate you on your excellent work."

I glanced up at a couple who could have passed for my parents. Middle-aged and overweight, they were easily identifiable as Americans by their matching polo shirts and white gym shoes.

"Thanks. I'm glad you enjoyed it."

"I'm Bill Jackson and this is my wife, Marian. We're from Michigan."

"That's nice," I said. "Won't you join me?"

"This is our first trip to Paris," Marian announced as she squeezed into the metal chair. "We didn't know what to expect. You hear such bad things about the French!"

"I keep telling her we're safer here than in some parts of Mississippi," Bill laughed. "We noticed you're teaching in England, but we thought we detected an American accent."

"I'm from Boston— Well, actually, I grew up in Chicago and Washington."

"Three distinct cultures in one childhood! Well, we're Michigan born, raised, and schooled. Taught there all my life, except for a couple of sabbatical leaves at other colleges."

"I wouldn't want to live anywhere else," Marian added.

The waiter arrived and took our order.

"You presented your paper with Jonathan Bennett. Is he a colleague of yours?" Bill asked casually.

"He's a guest at our university."

"I worked with him some time back when I was on leave in North Carolina. Is his wife here?"

"I believe Jon's divorced, but I don't know any of the details," I explained as the Jacksons exchanged ironic glances.

At that moment another black man approached the table, and Bill excused himself.

"That's David King," Marian explained. "They'll be presenting their paper this afternoon."

She leaned closer to me. "We were surprised to see that Jonathan Bennett is teaching in England—and at your university."

"Why?"

"Years ago Jon had some kind of vendetta against a professor there. An Englishman. Something about a conference."

"That's crazy," I said lightly, holding my voice steady against the sudden pounding of my heart.

"His wife was so concerned about it." Marian knotted up her brows and lowered her voice. "Dierdre was a white girl, you know, but very nice. He gave her such a hard time with the ladies!"

"Well," I said dryly, "I can't imagine that."

"At the end of that year we moved back to Michigan and never heard from the Bennetts again. Over the years we've wondered where they ended up."

"Jon never mentioned that he taught in North Carolina."

"That's no surprise," she sneered. "He lost his job and had to leave."

I glanced up in time to see Bennett at the entrance of the restaurant, chatting with someone. He looked in our direction, and his smile faded.

Bill returned just as he approached the table. "Bill Jackson! Marian! I haven't seen you in ages," he said, extending his hand. "How the hell are you?"

"Alive and kicking, despite those Michigan winters," Bill answered, while Marian made friendly noises. The waiter arrived with our food, and I realized I'd lost my appetite.

"Excuse me, everybody," I said, leaving a handful of francs on the table. "I think I need a nap. It was nice meeting you both. I hope you enjoy Paris."

Bennett smiled warmly. "Let me walk you up, Michael."

He followed me into my room, and went on the offensive the moment the door closed.

"Whatever they told you was bullshit."

I sank to the bed and looked into his cool, enraged eyes.

"I thought that you met Drew for the first time at that party last September."

"Correct," Bennett answered. "But I made it clear I'd seen him at a conference some years ago. Think about it."

I searched my impressions of that distant evening, so many lifetimes ago. Yes, Bennett had mentioned something about a conference—a Soyinka conference.

"So what happened at that conference?"

"I questioned Drew's view on something, and all the white people in the room jumped to his defense. When I argued with him, the moderator ended the session. They literally formed a human barrier around him, like I was an animal."

"So you inflated that incident into something like Racist Whites Silence Black Scholar. You made it your defining moment."

"It wasn't my imagination. A few months later Drew caused me to lose my job."

"Lose your—?"

"After seven years of kissing those redneck motherfuckers' asses, swallowing their crap and ignoring their racist remarks, my career got thrown into the trash because of an evaluation he wrote, supposedly assessing my 'scholarly potential.' "

"What do you mean?"

"They sent him several articles I'd published and solicited his 'expert opinion' on the 'quality' of my scholarship. And he found me unsatisfactory."

"Why would anyone ask Drew to comment on your work?"

"They claimed they were protecting themselves from a discrimination lawsuit. They said that if an American reviewed my materials unfavorably, I'd certainly accuse them of racism. But by asking an Englishman to do it, particularly one who had devoted his career to helping whites understand and respect black cultures"—he grunted bitterly "—there could be no accusations of racism."

"But surely your name wasn't on the articles. Only a blind evaluation could have protected them from litigation."

"So they made a very quiet phone call," Bennett said.

"But why would Drew do this?"

"Maybe he was taking out the competition. Or maybe I really pissed him off at that conference."

"Then you *did* come to England because of him," I whispered. "And that's why you set out to seduce me."

"Until the night of that goddamn party I didn't even know you existed. And how could I have guessed when you came walking across that room that you were his wife? I wanted you from the first moment

I saw you, and it had nothing to do with Andrew Northcross." He paused. "I never meant to hurt you, Michael."

"But Drew is part of me, Jon."

Bennett looked over at me, the cool white light transforming his face into a haggard mask. "That's right. Michael Davies and Andrew Northcross make it appear that everything's fine. We can all get along together. We can share ideas and respect each other's cultures. We can overcome the decades of oppression. We can intermarry. We can have biracial children. We can—"

His voice broke and he fell silent, overcome with emotion. I felt tears rise to my own eyes as the words of our new vow echoed in my head: *Honor those who love me, and cast off those who don't . . .*

We sat in silence while he mastered himself. I wiped my face on my sleeve, and he cocked his head, his smile mocking.

"Come now, Michael. You must love living the myth."

"I don't love the myth," I answered, "I love the *man*."

His hands tightened into fists, and he came toward me, trembling, the stony muscles of his rage enclosing my fluttering heart. Beneath the fortress of his hatred I saw fading traces of a beaten and terrified child. Then, as quickly as he could, Bennett slammed the gangway shut. I felt him pull away and he walked with slumped shoulders to the door.

Despite my fear and disgust I heard myself ask: "What's going to happen to you, Jon?"

He blinked slowly, full of cool contempt. "I'll survive," he answered. "I always have."

"Let me take your bag," a voice said over the roar of humanity, and without turning my head I knew that he had come. He took me in his arms and hugged me gently, careful not to press my stomach.

"How was it?"

"Enlightening."

"Your paper was well received?"

"Very."

"And your escort?"

"Fired."

Automatically we moved toward the exit.

"Did you get out into the city?"

"For one evening."

"You're not sick?" he asked quickly.

"No."

"And the weather?"

"*Please,* Drew!"

Lowering myself carefully into the Volvo, I pulled the strap up high over my belly, feeling a deep sense of relief as he climbed in beside me. I reached over and covered his hand on the steering wheel. "Thanks for coming."

"Caryl wanted to, but I—" he suddenly stammered "—well, it was the least I could do."

As we gained the main highway, he again asked how I felt.

"Enormous. Bloated. Constipated. And happy as hell." Suddenly tears filled my eyes. I stared at the passing cars until Drew touched my hand.

"What happened in Paris, Michael?"

"What do you mean?"

"Even when you're tired you love to talk."

I sighed. "Take me somewhere quiet, and I'll tell you."

He turned off the highway and drove down a narrow road for several minutes. A village emerged from behind rolling hills of heather.

It was early afternoon and the darkened pub was virtually empty. A sullen waitress led us to a table, tossing the menus down and retreating to her romance novel. I eased myself into a chair and slid carefully forward as Drew watched, amused.

I caught his expression and smiled. "You know, it's as if every moment of my life is amplified. I can't take perfumes. And I'm completely nocturnal, so I'm sleepy all day. My hair is growing like wildfire and—" I touched my blouse "—look at these balloons! I never know what I'll discover when I look in the mirror."

"None of that sounds like a complaint."

"I've never felt anything as—" The baby moved and I held my stomach, looking down quickly.

"Michael," he said suddenly, "I could postpone my appointment until the New Year."

"Do you think it'll be easier if you leave six months later? It'll be harder on the baby. And," I added, "on me."

The waitress returned. We ordered, then again faced each other.

"Listen," I said, measuring my words carefully. "Jonathan Bennett claims he lost a position in North Carolina some years ago because of a negative evaluation you wrote."

"An evaluation?" Drew shook his head in wonder. "I've written countless evaluations over the years. But Jonathan Bennett entered your life the same evening he entered mine. I had no reason to cause him any intentional harm."

"He asked me to marry him."

Drew's eyes filled with rage. "Whatever you decide," he said, struggling to contain his emotions, "please don't make him the father of our child."

I quickly reached across the table. "That will never happen."

His eyes searched mine with an urgency that made my breath catch in my throat. For the first time, I understood how much the being in my womb meant to him.

He leaned forward, grasping my arms. "Come with me to Zimbabwe, Michael! We could have a new life. And—" he paused, dropping his eyes "—and we'd have a family."

The word echoed strangely in my mind—a *family*—as if it had never occurred to me that such a thing could really exist.

He continued speaking before I could respond. "You can raise the baby in Levant Hill without a father. Or we can bring the child up together in Africa. Think about it: You grew up without your parents, and I grew up alone at school. You and I have this chance to spend our lives together. To make something that will last—"

"Only a few days ago you were prepared to leave me—and the baby—here in England."

He closed his eyes for a long moment, and when he opened them again I knew that he had come to a border. And that he'd decided to risk crossing it.

"Please listen, Michael," he began, choosing his words carefully.

"Thirty-five years ago, when I first lived in Zimbabwe, I worked for a time deep in the bush. There were few medical facilities for the poor. Medicines were scarce, and physicians even scarcer. Most of the sick or injured simply died.

"Then I met a woman who had just come from the capital, where she'd trained as a doctor. She chose to go into this remote region specifically to treat women and children. Sometimes, when she was faced with a really difficult case, she called on me to help."

"Why haven't you told me this before?"

"Do you want to know the truth?" he asked. Reluctantly I nodded.

"The first night we made love, you asked me whether you were my first black lover. Before I could respond you decided that the answer was obvious because I'd lived in Africa."

He stopped speaking for a moment. "Do you remember that conversation, Michael?"

Again I nodded.

"Your comment seemed incredibly callous to me, because you assumed that I went to Africa in search of sex with women of color. Your culture had taught you that all white men exploit black women. And that included me."

I lowered my eyes, and he continued speaking, his voice low.

"That mentality has made it very difficult for us, because you've never really believed that I could truly love you."

"That's true," I admitted. "I've always felt guilty for being with a white man."

"That doctor who went out into the bush was black. She was not my lover. We were never lovers. I don't even think that she found me attractive. But I admired her deeply. And I tried to earn her admiration."

"Then why didn't you tell me about her?"

"Because I couldn't bear to have you make fun of her, or what she did to help people. After that conversation our first night together, I didn't think you'd understand."

I fell silent for a time. "Was I really so shallow?"

"No. You were the product of your world, as I was the product of mine. And I loved you then, even though we disagreed about many things."

"Where is she now?" I asked quietly.

"She died. And it was after her death that I decided to return to England." He exhaled slowly. "For many years I thought about her and what she'd given to others. Like her, I tried to use my position to bring about meaningful change. I searched for someone who shared her qualities. And then one autumn afternoon I looked up and found you staring back at me with your angry, beautiful eyes."

He smiled sadly. "I've loved you with all my heart since the day we met. What else would make a man pretend to arrive by chance at the same table, the same hour, on the same day of the week for nearly a year? What else would make him desperate enough to almost lose you before he begged you to stay?"

"Then it wasn't all a game?"

"No, Michael. I enjoyed being with you without sex. Some of the most meaningful relationships in my life were with women who weren't my lovers."

"And after our marriage?"

"My deepest joy as we've traveled this world was seeing the world through your eyes. And every page I've written, every lecture I've given reflects your voice, your ideas, your strength. Despite everything—all the endless, destructive contests—I love you even more today."

In a voice as soft and strident as on that distant afternoon, so very many years ago, he asked me for my heart.

"Please don't leave me, Michael."

I didn't know how to answer, Chloe. Then I thought of you, and the new vow we'd taken only hours before: *To love myself completely, and to allow myself to be loved . . .*

I looked across at him. There was so much yet hidden beneath the slowly graying hair—so many experiences, so many thoughts and emotions that even fifteen years had not uncovered. Even if I left that table, walked out of that restaurant, and never saw him again, he would be as much a part of me as my own skin and hair. My thoughts. My dreams.

He straightened his back and looked hard into my eyes. "When are you coming home?"

"We've given up our home, Drew."

He reached for my hands. "So we'll make a new one."

Was there shame in need? Was there weakness in admitting that having found it so difficult to leave, I had no idea how to return? Could I frame in words my sense that the victory of independence was senseless when drained of love? What was it you said, Chloe*? When everything else is finished, only love remains.*

"If it's a girl," I said, "I want to call her Chloe."

"And a boy?"

"I like Andrew. Andrew Michael."

He held my hands tighter. A current passed between us.

The baby moved, stretching its limbs in a long and lazy movement that sent my belly gently rippling. I leaned forward and pressed Drew's hands against my flesh.

"Andrew Dalton Northcross, say hello to our child."

REBIRTH

I wasn't looking for sanctuary anymore, Michael. You see, with all the lies, the shame, and deceit swept away, there was nothing left to run from, Little Sister.

So that morning, only hours after your departure, I threw open the balcony doors and let the sun illuminate the darkest corners of the room. I let it bring warmth to my canvas. I let it strip away the clinging shadows of my past.

Standing in the open doorway with Paris sweeping out below me, I finally faced my brother. I thought about his voice, his madness, the deep cruelty of his touch. And I remembered my mother, wasting away from the unspeakable burden of our shame. I thought of Reginald, who had no intention of loving me, and Lucien, who had nearly drowned in his own self-hatred. I even turned my mind to Malik, who had never really tried to know me.

As I stood before the canvas, I thought once more about the scenes that studio had witnessed. My life in Paris began when Anya turned the key in the rusting lock. In that room Aziza first sought out my friendship. The studio had witnessed the beginning and end of my hundred days with Lucien. My hope of succeeding in Paris died there with Jacques's angry departure, and my real life as an artist began here, with Emil's love.

Michael, I finally understood that my heart had never left that room, despite my many years of wandering. And it was like the first time, Little Sister, when a woman's voice from somewhere deep within guided my hands toward creation. First I touched the canvas, my fingers testing its texture, judging its willingness to bear witness to my deepest emotions. Then I opened the tube of onyx paint and watched it pour richly onto my palette. Taking a heavy brush in my trembling left hand, I dipped the tip into the pigment and brought the brush to the virgin plain.

Swiftly and deftly, my face took shape, staring out from the canvas with a mixture of deferent hopefulness and wisdom. She had once called herself "Seraphina," but the years had sculpted her into someone new. Shaded by solitude, the eyes reflected the lessons learned from loneliness. Deepened by the weight of caring for others, the ridges of the brows, the sweep of the nose, and the line of the jaw were set in firm strokes of pride.

Yet something else was emerging from the canvas: a simple, vibrant strength, unencumbered by guilt and fear. In the stark honesty of black on white, perhaps a new Chloe was being born.

I bathed slowly and dressed myself in aqua. Then I pinned our Kore, the fat little figure representing fertility, to my breast. After standing tall in the mirror, I walked through the battered door, down the echoing stairwell, and out into the sunlight.

Placards announced *"Une Démo des Immigrés"*—a demonstration for foreigners' rights—to begin at four at the intersection just across from the Théâtre des Xenos. A spectrum of skin tones, like a living loom of culture and color, already packed the sun-washed boulevard. There were blacks in the crowd, towering Senegalese in turquoise robes, and graceful women in kinte head cloths. Palestinians in checkered scarves chanted defiantly beside Rastas in gold, green, and red. Swarthy Tunisians and tousle-haired Algerians linked arms with light-eyed Macedonians. A contingent of Asians bearing the flag of Vietnam took their place beside students with posters calling for an independent Corsica. There were more whites than I would have believed possible.

I made my way along the necklace of riot-ready police officers whose steel-shielded vans barricaded both ends of the street. Perched in overhead windows and thick branches of trees, hungry camera lenses prepared to record every second of the scene.

Carefully I pushed through the mass of people as a black woman mounted a scaffold and began to speak. Her voice, enriched by bold traces of her island homeland, rolled out deep and full over a makeshift sound system, and the crowd shimmered in response.

"We are united in our quest for equality," she cried to the waiting faces. "We are determined at last to be free!"

The doors of the Théâtre des Xenos were open, just as I knew they would be. Aware that such demonstrations often erupted in violence, Emil would be prepared to offer his theater as a shelter for his people. And certainly he'd be there, somewhere deep inside.

The house was black, the stage was illuminated by a single arc of white. Slowly I descended the wide aisle, enveloped by the hush of the empty theater. There was no sound from the street, no sign of a technician or janitor or errant actor. I couldn't even hear my own feet on the thick carpet. Reaching the edge of the orchestra pit, I twisted around to look up into the distant projection booth.

Nothing but the single hot orb etching a wide sphere in the center of the stage. I threw my legs over the low barrier separating the audience from the musicians and took the few steps to the rim of the stage. Chairs were strewn haphazardly inside the space, and I mounted one, carefully stepping up to the wide wooden plain.

Tentatively I approached the circle of light, feeling weightless and formless in the echoing silence. Drawing closer, I strained to hear something, anything, from the swelling crowd outside. Finally I stood at the severe white border, daring myself to step inside into the light. I hesitated. Took a deep breath. Entered the blinding sphere.

"What do you want, Chloe?"

Emil's voice reverberated through the theater, seeming to come from everywhere at once. I strained through the burning light to determine the provenience of the sound, but the acoustics made it impossible. Uncertain where to look, I stood there awkwardly, stripped naked by the hot, interrogating glare.

"I—I've come to—" My faltering voice echoed weirdly over the rows of empty seats. "I've come to apologize."

"Apologize?" The word was rendered in a flat tone of disbelief. "For what?"

"For everything I did that hurt you."

I braced myself for a reply. But there was nothing. I waited, suspended in hopefulness. But there was no response. The seconds became a minute, and the minutes began to swell, even as I dropped my burning eyes. I looked from left to right, searching for a way to leave the stage with dignity. The chair was still there in the orchestra pit, so I stepped toward it.

"Wait." He came out of the wings and walked slowly across the stage to stand beside me, just outside of the light. He was dressed in overalls, like in the early days, and he was wearing his old black beret. He examined me, the spotlight burnishing his perceptive brown eyes to an all-knowing gold.

"Why now, Chloe?" he asked quietly. "Why, after all this time?"

"Because—" I met his gaze "—because I'm determined to be free."

He stepped up close, moving into the blazing light so that he, too, became a contrasting silhouette of sharp color and shadow. He looked down at me for an immeasurable moment, then spun around to face the empty, cavernous room.

"Mesdames et Monsieurs," he began with a deep, mocking bow, "welcome to the premiere performance of 'Chloe's Great Apology'!" He held out his arm, presenting me in his most resonant voice to a cheering, imaginary audience.

"After a failed marriage, countless lovers, and many lost years, our lonely heroine has reappeared to win over our long-suffering, deeply devoted hero." He gave a mocking laugh. "In this inspiring drama, Chloe imagines that Emil has done nothing but count the days since she replaced him with a man she didn't love. Chloe hopes Emil will forget that he was willing to give up his dreams to preserve their relationship. She expects him to ignore the fact that she sent him away rather than face the truth about herself."

Taking a step forward, he raised his hands in a sardonic gesture. "Chloe actually expects Emil to get down on his knees and beg her to stay."

"You're wrong—" I blurted, my voice reverberating through the empty theater.

"Then what is it?" he snapped, whipping around to confront me. "Run out of lovers, Chloe? Bored with your travels? Or just getting nostalgic for a past we never had—"

"*You* are the past I never had," I said, "and I've mourned it every single day."

"Not badly enough," he retorted.

"I couldn't come back to you until I was able to change."

"And now that's miraculously happened, after . . . how long has it been, Chloe?"

"A lifetime," I said.

"So this is some kind of 'rebirth'? A kind of 'immaculate reconception'?"

"I'm not a different woman," I answered. "I'm a *whole* woman."

"If that's the case," he replied coldly, "you don't need me any more now than you did then."

"You would never have succeeded if you'd left Paris."

"So," he replied sarcastically, "throwing our love away was an act of kindness! You're actually a saint who sacrificed her heart to a far greater cause—"

"No, Emil. I'm a fool who built my whole life on the belief that I wasn't worthy of love. I left you because I was afraid to love you. Afraid of the honesty you deserved from me."

"Don't you think I know that?" he cried. "Did you really think I expected our life to be easy?" He straightened his back and seemed to tower above me.

"My parents cut cane in the blazing sun before moving to a place where my mother cleaned public toilets. I lifted boxes in the basement of a store, then earned small change on street corners before founding

Les Xenos. We acted for years earning less than nothing, and never knowing when the police, or the public, would revolt against our message. But we stood together, Chloe. We didn't give in to our fears.

"If only you had trusted me, even enough to share your true thoughts and feelings, we might have survived your past. We might have saved—" his voice fell "—our love."

"I didn't have the strength, Emil."

"You had the strength," he countered, his chest rising and falling. "But you loved your pain more than you ever loved me."

"Forgive me," I whispered dully, closing my brimming eyes.

He looked away. "You can rest assured that I forgave you long ago."

"Then is it too late?" I asked his restless shadow.

His words snapped back. "Too late for what?"

"Is there—is there any love left to save?"

There was a long pause from the blackness. "I don't know you anymore."

I managed a trembling smile. "Neither do I."

His shadow shifted tensely. "What do you want from me, Chloe?"

"I only want you to believe me."

"To believe . . . *you*?"

He made an impatient gesture and turned quickly away. I grasped his arm, and he wheeled around, his features eclipsed by the spotlight.

"What is it, Chloe?"

"Once I believed—" I began, then faltered. I searched inside myself for the words, and finding none, focused my thoughts, Michael, on you.

"Once I believed that loneliness was strength. But if you want me to stay, Emil, I promise you that I will never, ever go away."

Silence. And then, silence upon silence. Emil's silence was the greatest emptiness I have ever known. I stood there, my body drenched in the blazing light, and tried to conjure up the young man who came to my table that distant night, his beauty powerful enough to snatch my breath away. I remembered his voice when he urged me to live my life in joy, not pain. And I knew his touch, sensual and lingering, as we stared at the stars from my hillside chamber.

Yet as I waited, I finally understood that the years had changed him, too. The young Emil Mathurin was nothing more than a memory, and his love for me, the love I had used and discarded for the sake of my art, was gone. The man who stood in the shadows had no desire to open his life to a woman who had given him so little in return. He had lived a full life and fulfilled his dreams. And he had done it all with love.

"I know we can't go back," I pleaded. "But we could have a future."

"It's too late, Chloe," he replied.

Defeated, I moved out of the light and walked to the front of the stage. I was about to step down into the orchestra pit when I looked back.

He stood rooted on the edge of darkness, his face taut with emotion. He was breathing deeply, and his eyes sought mine as if searching for someone he had known in another life. Yet still he did not speak.

"Whatever happens," I said, "I will always love you."

I stepped down and crossed the orchestra pit, my eyes now accustomed to the darkness. The center aisle fell open like the road to my promised land, and I mounted it, the small squares of light from the lobby doors beckoning me forward.

Outside, the milling crowd had swollen to a focused mass. I could make out the tense shoulders of the policemen. The speaker's voice, distorted by feedback, vibrated through the empty lobby. I took another step, preparing to rejoin the world, when something made me look up over my shoulder.

A fugitive shaft of sunlight riveted my painting of Les Xenos. I studied the group of young men and women captured in attitudes of mutual trust. Emil was in the center, the others standing around him. In the back stood Chloe. It was, until that very day, the only portrait of myself that I'd ever painted. It was the only record of the woman I used to be.

I emerged from the theater just as the speaker cried, *"À nous la liberté!"* The mass of protestors picked up the chant, and I plunged into the raised fists of their insistent desire. Pushing gently, firmly, I melted into the sweating faces and excited voices. I surrendered my pain, determined to leave the years of solitude behind me. Little children on their parents' shoulders shouted *"Vive la liberté, à mort la haine!"*

Hips broad and soft pressed against my own, as lips drawn away from broken and perfect teeth joined the cries of determined hope. A dark-robed man grabbed my hands and pulled me even deeper into the sea.

"Long live freedom; death to hatred!" Their words began pouring out of me. I released my sadness and breathed in their hope, becoming one with the ever-swelling tide. Up ahead were more struggles to survive, more challenges glowing in our flushed and fervent faces. Pressed so closely together, our angry flesh so battered and so strong, it seemed as if the rush to victory would never subside.

"Chloe!"

From deep within the rolling masses came the voice. I twisted around, recognizing no one. The crowd shifted, swaying back and forth to the rhythm of the chanting voices: *"Pas de justice, pas de paix—"*

"Chloe!"

"C'est le temps pour la liberté!"

"Chloe!"

Surrounded by impassioned faces, I felt his hands on my shoulders, my arms, then my waist before I could manage to find his troubled and joyful eyes. Eyes that were filled with hope. Eyes that were bright with love.

"Ma chère sorcière," he said as he gathered me into his arms. "Don't ever leave me. Do you understand, Chloe? Don't ever, ever go!"

The people shouted on as we held each other close, their cries surrounding us and smothering us and bearing us aloft toward tomorrow.

Celebrated Artist and Actor Wed

AFD—New York. *Chloe Emmanuel, 58, the artist whose self-portrait was recently purchased by the National Gallery in Washington for the highest price ever paid for an African American work of art, has married the celebrated French-Caribbean actor Emil Mathurin, 55. The wedding, held at Emmanuel's private atelier in the south of France, was attended by numerous celebrities, including her former husband Malik Emmanuel, who serves as director of the Rockman Research Institute for Political Affairs, and the internationally acclaimed fashion designer Anya*

Beauchamps. Many of the original members of Mr. Mathurin's historic Les Xenos theater company were also in attendance.

The maid of honor was the author and scholar of African American literature Michael Davies. Her husband, writer and noted professor of African literature Andrew Northcross, served as best man. The guests were entertained by the popular singer Chloe Aziza, whose mother, the former supermodel Aziza, owns the cosmetic giant Femme d'Afrique.

Ms. Emmanuel's work will soon be featured in a retrospective at the prestigious Humes Gallery in New York. Mr. Mathurin, writer and star of some twenty films and a popular social-commentator on race issues in France, owns and operates his own theater in Paris. This is the third marriage for Emmanuel and the first for Mathurin. The couple will reside in Paris and in Nice.

"Was I really that huge?"

"I'd say that *gigantic* is a better description."

"All you can see is Emil's grin and my big belly." You laughed, staring at the wedding photograph. I glanced over your shoulder at the assembly of people arranged on the front steps of the house. Anya was in full view, while Drew stood protectively behind you, Michael, with his hands resting gently on your shoulders. Emil and I were wearing matching hand-painted robes that Aziza brought us from Senegal. And Isabelle Mathurin was seated between us, her face bright with satisfaction.

"It was a perfect day," you said, "except that I couldn't dance very well."

"If we'd had the wedding two weeks later, C.C. could have danced with you."

"No, Chloe. My little girl was determined to be born in Africa," you said with a smile.

At that moment Chloe "Chipo"—whose Zimbabwean name meant "gift," trotted wildly toward the kitchen behind a streaking calico kitten, calling "Wait, Minou! Wait!" Emil followed, his arms outstretched to protect the bouncing toddler from the heavy beams of the oak table.

"Your turn, Drew," you intoned as the screen door closed behind the trio. "Uncle Emil is starting to look tired."

"I'll give him a couple more laps," Drew replied from the backgammon board at the other end of the table. "That way the baby might be ready for her nap. And," he added with a sigh, "I might figure out how to beat him at this game."

"You'll never get it," you teased as he tried to calculate his next move. "Backgammon is a game of skill *and* chance, Drew."

"That's why I feel so much safer with chess."

You laughed and shared a private smile with me.

In the two years since my wedding and birth of your child, you've grown much calmer, Michael. You've gained an air of deep contentment, as if places in your spirit that you never even recognized as empty have finally been filled. And with this contentment I sense a new, focused strength. A willingness to trust that your life has true meaning. And a radiant happiness with your beautiful daughter. And, of course, with Drew.

Emil returned a few minutes later with the squirming two-year-old in his arms. We got Chloe Chipo into her high chair and gave her a bowl of applesauce. Drew sat down beside her and began coaxing her along with a spoon.

"Chloe makes me walk five miles a day," Emil remarked as the baby drummed her feet against the footrest. "But I think we're going to have to double that to keep up with this little marathoner."

"She's just taking after her mother," Drew said, his eyes moving appreciatively over your long legs.

"C.C. learned how to run before she could walk," you explained. "There are at least fifteen kids in the faculty compound, and she loves trying to keep up with them."

"I'll bet that's why she started talking so soon," I observed.

"She gets her love of conversation from her father," you replied, baiting him with your eyes.

"Oh, come on, Michael," Drew replied in pretended outrage. "I waited nearly a year for you to stop talking long enough to let me propose to you."

"Just a year?" Emil echoed in astonishment. "It took me twenty-five years to get this woman to the altar!"

"Well," you asked both men politely, "weren't Chloe and I worth waiting for?"

Drew and Emil exchanged sly glances. "That," Emil answered craftily, "depends on whether you two will let us drive down to Monte Carlo tonight."

"What do you think, Michael?" I asked, winking at her with a grin.

"Well, we could let them go, as long as they promise to be back by eleven."

We all laughed. Then Drew looked over at me. "Where's your next exhibition, Chloe?"

"Paris, of all places. After my show in New York, it seems that the Parisians can't get enough of me." I laughed wryly. "The opening's in December, just in time for the premiere of Les Xenos's newest film."

"It's called *The Thirty-nine Thieves*," Emil chimed in.

"Thirty-nine? I seem to remember something about Ali Baba and the Forty Thieves," Drew commented.

"Actually, the film's about a group of Frenchmen who plan to poison the water on a tiny Caribbean island so that they can buy it from the government at a very low price and then turn it into an exclusive resort. The inhabitants discover the plan and think up all kinds of ways to scare them away."

"You can imagine it," I said. "Colorful snakes and singing hordes of mosquitoes and exotic rashes in sensitive areas of the body. This is Emil's idea of revenge on all the tourists who visit his birthplace."

"So you're planning a big premiere?" Drew asked, managing to get a spoonful of applesauce into the baby's mouth.

"Very," I answered. "Emil will make the rounds of all the interview shows."

"We were hoping you'd spend Christmas with us in Harare," you said.

"Maybe in February, when things calm down a bit," I said, looking at Emil. "Right, baby?"

"I've been thinking of a way to get us all together," Emil replied as he joined us at the table with a coffee. "It's time we collaborated on a project. And last night at dinner I came up with an idea."

He reached over to stroke C.C.'s rough curls, and the giggling baby held out her sticky fingers.

"We'll assemble a collection of folktales from Africa, the Caribbean, and North America. We'll adapt them specifically for children. Then we'll recruit some adventurous young people from all three regions to perform them. As I see it, we could take the show all over the world. We'd find a thousand ways to see one another more often."

"Michael and I gladly will be your talent scouts in Zimbabwe," Drew said, smiling in your direction.

"And you'll have no problem finding actors from the Antilles in France," you replied.

"I'll design the production," I added. "And the rest will be up to you, Emil."

"We'll call it *The World According to Blacks*," Emil teased.

"That works for me," you said, wiping the baby's hands.

"How about *Roots*?" Drew asked innocently. "It has a certain *je ne sais quoi*!"

"I like *Emil's Fables*," I said.

"Or *Les Xenos's Fairy Tales*?" you offered.

"Well—" Emil's dancing eyes fell on the open game. "We could call it *Blackgammon*."

"No!" The scream went up in unison, and when our eyes met there was a round of heartfelt laughter.

"Under the circumstances," Emil said, "we could work on the title tomorrow."